THE
BLOOD
OF
ANGELS

stephen gregory

the blood of angels	stephen gregory
source photography	pamela dawn
cover design & layout	larry friedman

Borealis is an imprint of White Wolf Publishing.

Printed in Canada

White Wolf Publishing
780 Park North Boulevard
Suite 100
Clarkston, GA 30021

BOREALIS

WHITE WOLF
PUBLISHING

PART ONE
toadstone

1

Harry Clewe had had a terrible migraine. It felt as though someone had hit him on the head with a very heavy, very hard object. At last it was over. Utterly drained, he went to bed and fell asleep straight away.

When he woke up, he was cold. But his headache had gone. It was dawn, and his bedroom was just light enough for him to make out the shape of his jacket hanging on the door. There was no sound of traffic on the road outside. The branches rattled in the fir plantation and sent a spatter of rain against the window.

Harry shivered in the narrow bed. Something stirred on his belly, something cupped in the palm of his waking hand: a warm live thing which shifted slowly and rearranged its limbs more comfortably there. He looked down to see what it was.

It was a toad.

The toad was round and fat, as soft and dry as a boxing glove. Its long tongue flicked out, over and over again, to caress the skin of Harry's palm. He smiled to himself and lay very still in the lightening room, holding the toad on his belly.

That summer, in the late 1960s, Harry Clewe was working in a hotel garden in Beddgelert, a village in Snowdonia. The manager had hired him to repair a dry-stone wall which had collapsed because the roots of a rhododendron had forced it apart. Harry was singularly unsuited to the work. Twenty-five years old and nearly six foot tall, he was thin and fragile, with a hollow, hairless chest. He was a stone underweight after a year as a volunteer teacher in Sudan; well-meaning, altruistic, he'd gone there at a time when it was more fashionable to travel overland to Istanbul and Katmandu. But he'd been ill. His freckled skin was an easy target for the desert sun; his red hair seemed to attract it.

His pale eyes had flinched from the dazzling whiteness of sand. A stomach infection drained him, and he'd grown thinner and thinner. Sudan had been difficult for him.

But he was doing his best in the garden. He demolished the rest of the wall by climbing onto the terrace above it and making a few well-placed incisions with a spade, so that the great mass of boulders came crashing down. That was the easy part. It then took two weeks of strenuous work with a pick axe to cut the rhododendron roots from the boulders. And in that garden, which rose steeply behind the hotel in a series of terraced lawns until it petered into the oak woods at the top, the only suitable place for the burning and disposal of the debris was high on the hillside, on a plateau among the trees. Harry was bruised and worn out by the repeated journeys he made from the bottom of the garden to the top, with armfuls of slimy rhododendron roots.

Each time he reached the plateau and threw down his load, he lay in the bracken and rested for a few minutes, to enjoy the view over the roof of the hotel.

Two rivers joined in the middle of the village, after their tumbling descent from the foothills of Snowdon. Then, a single, broader river set off toward the sea at Porthmadog, slowly at first through flat fields soiled by gray sheep, before accelerating spectacularly under the Glaslyn bridge and gathering momentum for another more leisurely stretch toward the coast. High above the hotel roof, Harry looked down on the village, its cottages and gift shops, the car park full of tourists' cars and caravans, across to the green sides of Hebog where tiny figures in orange and blue waterproofs moved toward the summit. A few people were walking along the riverbank to stand at Gelert's grave and read the questionable legend. There were jackdaws in the trees at the top of the garden, clucking like chickens among the branches. Ravens croaked and somersaulted overhead. The sky above the village was quick with swifts, brittle and black like splinters of coal. Harry sat and watched, trying to get his breath back for another armful of rhododendron roots.

One morning there came a shout from the hotel. There was a telephone call for Harry Clewe. He stumbled down the path, started to kick the soil from his wellington boots before going into the hotel, but the manager hurried him inside. Wiping his glasses on his shirt, Harry pressed the telephone to his ear.

It was his mother. There'd been a terrible accident. Lizzie, Harry's twelve-year-old sister, had been thrown from a horse onto a piece of farm machinery. She was in hospital in Shrewsbury with internal injuries and the possibility of permanent spinal damage.

Harry put the telephone down. He loved his little sister very much. He envied her, too, for her self-assurance and poise; he himself had none. Lizzie wore her red hair like a bright, dancing flame; Harry's gingery mop seemed to quench his face. He was for ever peering shortsightedly into the distance and being punched on the bridge of the nose: that was what it felt like. After a year of muddling incompetence as a probationary schoolteacher in Oswestry, after a bruising, debilitating year in Sudan, he'd come for a bit of peace and blessed relief in Wales.

He still had the headaches: he'd had them since his teens, when his eyesight suddenly deteriorated. They started with a spark in his right eye, which he would try to rub away with his fingers... more sparks, until there was an arc of light, shimmering like an angel in the top right-hand corner of his vision. And when the angel disappeared, his head was racked with migraine. There was a pounding, relentless pain. Lying in a darkened room, he would listen to the demolition of his faculties, a cacophony in his skull as though someone had recorded and overlaid the noises of abattoir, discotheque and iron foundry into one anarchical clamor. He could only ease the pain by vomiting, before falling into a nightmarish sleep.

In Wales, in lovely Wales, he still had the migraine sometimes, but never so often nor as badly as in Oswestry or Sudan. He was already a bit better for making his escape. Now he thought of little Lizzie, how quick and bright and funny she was... and he hoped so hard she'd recover from her accident that tears sprang into his eyes.

Harry quickly explained to the hotel manager what had happened. The repairs to the garden wall were straight away abandoned. In five minutes, Harry was hurriedly washing in his rented cottage only a mile or two from Beddgelert: and when he'd thrown some clean shirts into a suitcase, he was driving his battered, red sports car as fast as he could along the snaking valley road toward Betws-y-Coed. From there it would be less than two hours to Shrewsbury.

The car was one of three things Harry Clewe had picked up from his year in Sudan. The other two, salmonella poisoning and hepatitis, had gone. But he still had the car. He was Wabenzi.

Wabenzi! That was the sneering name for the wealthy Sudanese who cruised the streets of Khartoum in their Mercedes-Benz. And not just in Khartoum... Although he'd found the country so mystifying and distressing, although he was ill, Harry had stayed for another month after his contract was completed, traveling hundreds of miles west and south of the capital. The poor were as poor as only the sub-Saharan poor could be. Many of the people had nothing: no clothes, no food, no fuel, no shelter. But even in the most desperate of desperate villages, he saw the Wabenzi, who'd somehow managed to accumulate enough cash to buy the most precious symbol of power and influence: the car with the three-pointed star.

Now he, Harry Clewe, was Wabenzi... although he'd gone to Sudan to teach on a meager local salary in a girls' school in the northern desert. There'd been nothing to spend his money on. He'd lived in a schoolhouse with five of the Sudanese teachers, sharing their company, their beans and rice, their lamplight. So, at the end of his contract, when he'd called into the shabby, stifling, chaotic office of the ministry of education in Khartoum to negotiate his exit visa and his air ticket home, he'd been handed a money order for his entire year's salary. Puzzled, embarrassed, guilty, he'd stumbled out of the office. He'd clutched the slip of paper in his fist and wandered blindly in the blinding sunlight.

At home again with his parents in the affluent suburbs of Shrewsbury, restored to health by his mother, Harry had bought the Mercedes-Benz at an auction. A convertible sportscar, it was uncommonly cheap for a model that would normally have cost a great deal of money. Harry got it for exactly the amount he'd brought back from Sudan. The car had been driven hard and treated badly all over Europe; the man who was trying to sell it at the auction had picked it up in Marseilles, where it had stood in sun and sand for months without moving. There was no hood. The white leather seats were cracked and burst. The red bodywork was crazed by years of Mediterranean sunshine. The passenger door, heavily dented in some accident, was jammed permanently shut. The bonnet flapped; the catch didn't engage properly. The windscreen had a huge starburst of cracks, like a bullet hole, in the top right-hand corner. When the car came snorting into the ring, the air was blue with smoke. Worst of all, as far as its auction prospects were concerned, it had left-hand drive. Nobody bid at all.

But Harry, on impulse, approached the owner outside the auction and the deal was struck. The car burned oil, lost water, guzzled petrol. It might seize up at any moment. But it had a few months' tax and the tires weren't quite bald. Harry drove it triumphantly away. Wabenzi!

Now, impatient to see his sister in hospital, he was forced to crawl up the narrow, steep Nantgwynant valley behind a groaning bus. The peaks of Snowdon loomed raw and cold in a shroud of mist, and Harry tugged a scarf around his throat to keep warm in the convertible. As the road widened at the crest of the pass, as he accelerated past the bus, he saw a figure sitting and waiting in the distance. He concentrated on driving, shot by the bus and tucked in front of it, still accelerating as hard as he could. The figure was about half a mile ahead, conspicuous in a blue anorak against the gray and green of the hills. It seemed tiny, a little child, motionless until Harry's car came hurtling nearer, when it raised one hand and a hopeful thumb. Harry did an unusual thing, for someone who thought himself quite a careful and considerate driver: he braked with all his might as he came level with the tiny blue figure, so that the car slithered to a halt in the gravel and dust of the roadside. In his mirror he saw a bank of flashing headlights as the bus pulled out and went by.

The child stood up and ran to Harry's door, before realizing that the passenger seat was on the other side; running around the long, low bonnet, struggling with the dented door, leaping nimbly over and landing with a crash on the cracked white leather. Harry floored the accelerator. The tires scrabbled for a grip in the gravel as the car surged forward and howled in pursuit of the bus again. The air whirled with oil smoke.

Harry's passenger wasn't a child. She was a girl, about twenty years old.

"Shit! What a car!" she yelled above the bellowing exhaust. "Are you going to Capel Curig?"

"Of course!" he answered. Capel Curig was the next village. There was nowhere else he could have been going to.

"Drop me off at the youth hostel, will you?" And she added, as though she was longing to tell somebody, even a complete stranger, "I'm meeting a friend there."

Harry slowed down, for two reasons. Firstly, he'd caught up with the bus. It would be senseless to go past it again, only to stop a few miles on. So he eased off the accelerator. Secondly, he wanted to look at his passenger.

She was indeed very small, like a child. She was wearing a pair of tennis shoes, scuffed and dusty from the roadside; faded denim bell-bottom jeans, mended at the knees with colorful patches; a tie-dyed red and purple T-shirt; the blue anorak.

"Going hill-walking?" Harry asked, to make the girl look at him.

She frowned, pursing her pale lips. She was blonde and very pretty, the kind of perfectly obvious prettiness that makes an instant impression but might not last many years. Blowing in the open car, her hair was bronze with sunshine, completely natural and none too clean. Her brows and lashes were almost black. Her pupils had a circle of dark blue around them, giving her pale gull's eyes an extraordinarily piercing quality. Her face and throat were very brown; a big spot was blooming in the crevice of her right nostril. She frowned at first, surprised to find a carroty, bespectacled man at the wheel of a snorting, red sports car.

But then she grinned. And Harry Clewe's stomach turned over.

He felt such a sudden, incapacitating rush of feeling for this grubby, childlike girl that he thought he'd have to stop the car in case he fainted. It winded him. He had no recollection of why he was driving so fast through Snowdonia toward Shrewsbury. The image he'd had of a rearing horse and lashing hooves and the figure of his sister falling and falling and lying still... the image dissolved and was gone. Only there was this girl, with her gray eyes, her neglected blond hair and golden throat. Nothing else.

In another minute, long enough for Harry to have surged so close to the bus that the bonnet of his car nearly touched its exhaust pipes, they were in Capel Curig. There was time to find out that the girl wasn't going hill-walking, that she worked as a waitress in a restaurant in Beddgelert... and then she was springing from the car again, moving across the road with hardly a glance at the traffic, as children do. She disappeared through the front door of the youth hostel.

Harry drove on. For the next hour and a half he traveled very fast, without concentrating as hard as he should have done, arriving in Shrewsbury before he'd remembered why he was going there.

2

A week later, as Harry Clewe returned to his cottage near Snowdon, he'd made up his mind to visit the girl in her restaurant.

There'd been emotional scenes in Shrewsbury when it was revealed that Lizzie hadn't sustained any permanent injuries from her fall. She had to stay in hospital, to recover more from the emergency surgery, which had taken place as the doctors investigated the possibility of damage to her kidneys, than from the accident itself. She was horribly bruised, her ribs were cracked and her spleen was injured, but there was no damage to her spine. The horse had fled into the market-place of the next village, where it was captured once it had kicked over a couple of vegetable stalls and a few tables outside the pub. Harry didn't find out what would become of the animal. Certainly the little girl wouldn't ride it or any other horse for many months. But she was intact.

Harry remained at the family house for a week and visited Lizzie every afternoon. As soon as it was established that she would recover fully, he set off to Wales. It was a brilliant day toward the end of August. He enjoyed the drive, in spite of the congestion of caravans and coaches through Llangollen and into the Welsh hills. He knew the road well and had confidence in the car's ability to go safely past a line of vehicles when other drivers would have waited. Wabenzi! The car looked rough, but it fairly flew. He surged to the back of a queue of caravans and saloon cars, chose his moment and went bellowing past with a haze of oil smoke erupting from his exhaust. Sometimes he provoked a flash of headlamps from an oncoming vehicle, a gesture from its driver. But Harry tucked in in plenty of time. As he'd seen in Sudan, the power of the Wabenzi was arrogant and apparently limitless.

He slowed down in Capel Curig with the realization that he could be in Beddgelert in less than a quarter of an hour. He'd been thinking about the girl all week. Once, he'd begun to tell Lizzie about her, blurting the story of his violent maneuver into the loose gravel as he'd stopped for the hitchhiker. But he'd let the story tail away. As the family arranged itself around the hospital bed, he'd remained largely silent among the blooms of carnations and irises, ducking his head behind rows and rows of get-well cards. Lizzie held court, funny and beautiful in spite of the bruising she'd had, her glittering face and flaming hair quite vivid on the snowy, plumped-up pillows. Harry loved her very much; he envied her cheek, her gumption. He envied her talent, for she'd already been recognized as a musician with an exciting future, embracing her cello with her thin arms, straddling it with her thin legs, shining at all kinds of concerts. For a wild moment, he'd wished he could have brought the honey-blonde hitchhiker to Shrewsbury and showed her to his sister.... Perhaps one day he would. It was a mad idea he kept to himself.

From time to time he'd answered a question about his new life in Wales. Then his parents would shake their heads and sigh, bewildered that, after ten years at public school, with a university degree and a teaching certificate, their son should have quit the career for which he'd trained in order to wrestle the roots of a rhododendron in a hotel garden.

"Still star-gazing, my lad?" his father would say, as always. "Still got your head in the stars instead of getting down to an honest day's work?"

And his mother would tinkle with laughter and put in, as always, "Harry's been seeing stars all his life! The whole world shook the night he was born!" before launching into an elaborate description of Harry's birth in a London underground station on the worst night of the Blitz....

Lizzie had smiled at him and winked, so that Harry felt his heart rise into his throat and the tears tingle in his eyes, overcome with gratitude for the little girl who understood him and loved him despite his puzzling idiosyncrasies. The conversation passed on. Harry had withheld his account of the hitchhiker, although a picture of her face and throat and her slim brown hands remained locked in a deeper layer of his concentration, like fishes in a frozen pond.

Now, as he came closer to Beddgelert that afternoon, the ice melted around those slim brown fishes. He slowed down. His stomach ached as he thought of seeing the girl again. He was frightened. He tried to think of an excuse for driving straight through Beddgelert and onward to his cottage. But he stopped in the village and parked his car in the cover of a great, dark yew tree.

Above the entrance to the restaurant there was a big, clumsily colorful painting. It portrayed the death of Gelert, the faithful hound of Prince Llewelyn, after which the village was named. According to the legend, the prince had returned home from a hunting expedition, having left his baby son in Gelert's care, to find a startling scene awaiting him. The inside of his lodge was in chaos, the furniture upturned; he was greeted by his dog, whose jaws were running with blood. The child was nowhere to be seen. The prince jumped to the conclusion that Gelert had killed the baby boy. The painting showed Llewelyn, with an owlish expression on his black-bearded face, plunging a sword into the dog's side... although the baby was alive and well and peering at his father from behind an overturned table. Gelert had saved the child's life by fighting and slaying an enormous wolf which had come into the prince's lodge; the dead wolf lay partly hidden under a pile of bloodspattered curtains.

Harry cocked his head this way and that, squinting at the picture to delay going inside the restaurant. The blood was good. At last, he pushed the door open, hoping and hoping that the girl wouldn't be there.

She was there. As Harry opened the door, she was carrying a tray of tea and milk and sugar and cups and saucers and scones and jam and butter toward a table in the window. The door caught the corner of the tray.

She fought to control it, wide-eyed with astonishment and alarm. For a moment, there was the faintest smile of recognition on her mouth as she glanced at the man who'd pushed the door open. Then, with a squeal of pain as the hot water splashed her hands, she dropped everything. The tray smashed to the floor. Women and children sprang away from the splinters with little gasps of surprise. A man began an adolescent cheer, cutting it short when his wife barked his name. The girl stood still, as though immobilized under the weight of broken crockery. Her hands fluttered to her lips. Harry thought she was going to cry.

There was a sickening silence for a second or two... until she started to laugh. She shuddered with laughter, leaning forward to support herself by taking hold of the lapels of Harry's jacket. Her shoulders shook with silent sobs. Her eyes welled with tears, blurring the dark-blue rings of her pupils.

Harry found his hands going to her waist. He looked down at the debris, and the shards of a saucer exploded noisily as he shifted his feet when the girl leaned more heavily on him. She wasn't laughing any more. That had passed as quickly as a charge of electricity through her body. She went limp. And just then, a burly, black-bearded man emerged from the kitchen at the back of the restaurant and strode among the tables toward the scene of the accident. He looked very like Prince Llewelyn on the painting outside: enraged, incredulous, vengeful.

Harry reacted with uncharacteristic firmness and spontaneity. He moved his hands to the girl's left arm, gripped her hard, heard himself say, "Come on!" with unusual authority, and manhandled her through the open door. Over the fragments of crockery, the powdered snow of sugar and the steaming tea, avoiding the clots of butter and a great scab of jam on the floor, together they stepped smartly into the sunshine. Harry heard his voice again — "Let's go! Quickly!" — and then they were running, his hand clenched around her wrist, along the crowded pavement. Before they'd gathered exactly what had happened and what they were doing, Harry and the girl had bounced onto the cracked leather seats of the battered red sports car.

It was a dream... their flight among the tourists in the street, Harry's hurried reversing from the shade of the yew tree, the thrill of a howling acceleration and the perfume of burning oil as the car sprang out of the village. Hardly a minute after Harry had pushed open the restaurant door, he and the girl were surging along a sunlit mountain road.

"Where are we going?" she shouted.

She looked even younger and smaller than she had when he'd first met her. Her eyes were red with tears. She'd had her blond hair cut shorter at the neck, and now it blew around her ears like a boy's hair. The spot in the corner of her nose had grown bigger, and she'd dabbed some sort of masking ointment on it which only made it more obvious. In her working clothes, she could have been a schoolgirl of twelve or thirteen: tennis shoes and white ankle socks, a pleated blue skirt, a white cotton blouse, as though she was ready for a netball match against a visiting school team. Her arms and legs were very brown. In the pocket of her blouse there was a notebook and a pen, the orders for tea and cakes which her customers were still waiting for.

"Come and see my cottage!" he shouted. "It's in Rhyd-ddu, the next village. You can have a wash and I'll make you a cup of tea."

At the mention of tea she gave a little jump in her seat. Her hands flew to her mouth and fluttered there. But she was smiling. The hysteria had passed.

"What's your name?" she asked, as they stopped outside a row of terraced cottages. She tried to open the passenger door, gave up and got out by standing on the seat and slithering her legs across the boot. She stood in the road and appraised the car as Harry felt for his house keys.

"What a monster!" she said. "It looks bloody clapped-out, but it seems to go all right."

"Harry Clewe," he replied. "Let's go inside."

She disappeared into the bathroom, which was downstairs, while Harry switched on the kettle in the kitchen. Tiptoeing to the bathroom door, he squeezed his eyes shut and pictured what he could hear her doing: clack of toilet seat, rustle of clothes, trickle and fizz, rattle of toilet roll, rustle of clothes, toilet flushing. He held his breath until his chest hurt, moistening his lips with the tip of his tongue. When he heard her coming out, he dodged back to the kitchen. She'd rinsed her face. She looked ordinary and somewhat older, with her eyes clean and the cream washed off the spot on her nose.

"Don't make tea for me," she said, although at that moment Harry, his hands trembling, was pouring boiling water into the teapot. "I just want a little sit-down and a think."

"We can sit in the garden," he said. He opened the back door from the kitchen and let the girl out. He followed her, with a cup of tea he didn't really want.

Outside it was very hot. Behind the cottages that lined the road through the village, there were secluded little gardens down to a stream at the bottom. Harry's garden was overgrown. The cottage had stood empty since the spring, until he'd moved into it in July. Nobody had bothered with the garden, although the landlord had let the cottage for the occasional weekend. To the left and right, the hedges were neatly trimmed and the lawns were cut. In Harry's garden there was a winding slate path which was almost hidden by a dense tangle of bracken, rhododendron and fuchsia. There was no lawn, only beds of wild grass which filled all the spaces between heather and fern. But it was full of life and color. A flurry of chaffinches fled from the bushes as Harry and the girl sat on a tumbledown rockery. The stream gurgled at the end of the garden, under a cover of oak and ash which grew tall by the waterside and made the garden completely private.

The girl arranged her skirt over her knees and stretched her legs out straight, twitching her toes in her tennis shoes. The sun lit every tiny golden hair on her shins. She clasped her hands and laid them in her lap, very brown and still, like sleeping voles snuggled together. She closed her eyes and tipped her face toward the sun. In this way, quite unconsciously, she became a part of the luxuriant garden... for the heads of the bracken did the same and so did the fuchsia, unfolding in the humming heat.

Harry sipped his tea. He felt giddy as he watched the girl. Her upturned throat fluttered. The hairs on her forearms flared with light, pinpricks of gold on her honey-brown skin. He put his cup down quickly, and it clattered in its saucer. At this, the girl turned toward him, her eyes still closed, before opening them and smiling a brilliant, sun-flushed smile.

"What did you say your name was?" she asked.

Harry told her, spelling it for her. She repeated his name three times, and Harry was thrilled to hear her say it. Just as he was going to ask her the same question, she closed her eyes tightly and firmly and turned her face to the sun again. He gulped and said nothing.

Without opening her eyes, the girl leaned forward and untied the laces of her tennis shoes. She slipped her shoes off and took off her socks too. Her toes wriggled, as neat as a row of acorns. Her feet and ankles were very white, and the skin was ribbed by the tight shoes and socks she'd been wearing. She rubbed them until the skin was smooth again. Then she straightened up, hitching her skirt so that the sun was on her thighs, and leaned back to let the sunlight fall on her face. She basked like this, without speaking, without opening her eyes, as though Harry wasn't there. But she smiled, because she knew he was looking at her.

Harry looked. At her feet and forearms. At her upturned face. At her throat and her smooth brown thighs. His mouth went very dry.

She reminded him of a lizard that had lived in the yard of his house in Sudan, in the cool shade beneath the sweating clay water pot. Even when it was still, the lizard looked as though it was charged with electricity. It seemed to hum with energy, with heat, with power. There was an electric blue stripe down its back, from the top of its head to the tip of its tail. He was used to seeing it there, sipping with its long gray tongue at the droplets of water which dripped from the pot. But one day, a shrike had flown into the yard and taken the lizard away, impaling it on the spikes of a thorn bush with the rest of its larder, the sun-baked remains of frogs and snakes and scorpions.

The girl opened her eyes and grinned at Harry. His stomach turned over.

"Thank you for rescuing me, Harry Clewe," she said. "You saved me from that awful man. Actually he's my uncle. I'll have to go back soon. I'm not just an employee who can clear off and bugger the job. He'll be in the restaurant until six and then at home with my aunt this evening."

"Do you live with your uncle and aunt?" Harry asked her.

"Not exactly," she answered. "They let me use their caravan. It's in their front garden, so I'm always in and out of the house, for baths and things. I'm bound to see them both this evening."

"Stay here with me." The words sped out of Harry's mouth; he had no control over them. The girl ignored them, as though they were simply a noise in the garden, like the tumble of the stream or the flutter of finches in the overhanging ash tree. She snapped her eyes shut again and lifted her face to the sun... as still as the lizard, before the shrike came.

"I've been in lots of trouble with my uncle already this summer," she said, "so I'm due for a real bollocking this time. He gets at me for being slow in the restaurant, for chatting with the customers. And he seems to think that, because he's my uncle, he's been appointed as the guardian of my morals. He keeps nosing around the caravan if I have anyone in there."

She flicked at her leg, where an ant was crawling. Harry had seen it there. As the girl was talking, he'd watched its progress from her foot to her knee, to the pale, soft skin on the inside of her left thigh. She let the ant run onto her thumbnail and then she blew it softly into the bracken.

"'All I want is another few minutes in your nice jungly garden," she said. "It's better like this than all tidy. I've only met you twice, Harry Clewe, but I reckon it suits you, this garden. I can't imagine you wanting to get dirty with weeding and digging. You're a bit of a toff, aren't you? With that wreck of a bloody great car, as well."

Harry said nothing. He remembered suddenly that he'd have to go back to work the next morning, after his week in Shrewsbury. The job of rebuilding the garden wall at the hotel was barely half finished. All he'd done so far was to make matters worse by bringing down more roots and rubble.

"Since it doesn't look as though you're going to ask me," the girl said, frowning in the way she'd frowned when she'd first appraised him at the wheel of a red Mercedes-Benz sports car, "my name's Sarah. I only come back to Beddgelert in the holidays, I'm studying zoology at London University. But it's so bloody expensive down there that I have to work nearly all the summer vacation. This summer, for my wicked uncle."

"The painting outside the restaurant, of Llewelyn and Gelert," Harry blurted, "is that supposed to be...?"

The girl laughed, her hands flying from her thighs to her mouth. "Did you recognize him?" she said. "I painted it in London and brought it back with me as a present, something to liven up the front of the restaurant. I think my uncle's the only person in the village who hasn't seen the likeness."

"Yes, I recognized him," Harry said. "That's why I wanted to rescue you so quickly. Your uncle had the same murderous expression on his face when he emerged from the kitchen. You wouldn't have stood a chance... he'd have run you through with a cake knife."

So saying, he feinted at her with an imaginary weapon. She flinched. He touched her side for a moment. There was a sensation in his stomach of caving in, as though some vital organ had been punctured. She jumped up, so close to him that he could have ducked his head forward and pressed his lips to her thigh.

"I think it's time for me to get going," she said. "Sooner or later I've got to face the wrathful prince." She bent down to pick up her shoes and socks. She paused there, crouching, and then she knelt quickly to the ground. "Hey, now look at this!" she whispered excitedly. "Come and have a look, Harry!"

Harry knelt beside the girl. There was a toad on the path. It had moved through the dense undergrowth of bracken, on its way from the stream to the tumbledown rockery where it lived, running like a mouse, then stopping, pushing aside the blades of wild grasses and treading down the elastic fronds of heather. Now it was still on the path... so still that it was hard to imagine it had ever moved. But the jewel-like eyes trembled, golden green with glistening black pupils, blinking smoothly and silently as though the lids were oiled with a secret mucus. To Harry's surprise, the girl picked the toad up. She sat on the rockery, cupping the creature in both her hands.

"This is quite a find," she said softly. "Not just any old toad. Look, Harry! Look at the little yellow line down the middle of its head and its back. You've got a natterjack in your garden. A natterjack! It's only the second one I've ever seen. How marvelous!"

Harry bent closer, so that the girl's hair swung against his cheek. The toad was about three inches long, wrinkled and pimply and brown like an old leather glove, with a narrow yellow line down its back. It hardly moved, only stretching out its tiny fingers, perfectly formed like the fingers of a human fetus, to stroke the girl's wrist. The eyes alone relieved its prehistoric ugliness, for they were very beautiful.

"Here, Harry! Hold it!" the girl said, offering the toad to him. She laughed when he writhed away from it. "No, maybe you'd better not. Look at these glands here, these bumps on the sides of its head... they've got a poison inside them which comes out through the skin to frighten dogs or rats, or people, I suppose, who try to pick the toad up. It can burn your hands, like acid. It's completely relaxed with me, because it can tell I'm not going to hurt it or drop it. Maybe you'd better not touch it. But isn't it lovely? *Bufo calamita*, the natterjack toad."

The eyes were golden, as big as marbles, brilliantly yellow with elliptical black pupils. The toad blinked slowly. Apart from the eyes, it was repulsive; for Harry, it was revolting to see how the girl caressed the toad with her little brown fingers, dipping her face so close to it that the same golden hair she'd swung on his cheek now swung on the creature's pimples and wrinkles and blotches. At last she put it down. It sat for a moment like a clod of earth on the slate patch, and then it disappeared into the long grass. The girl rubbed her hands together, wiped them on her pleated blue skirt, sat on the rockery and put on her socks and shoes.

"What luck!" she said, standing up again. Her face was vivid with excitement. "It's always lucky to find a toad.

'The foule toade has a faire stone in his head,' so the legend says. But a natterjack! That's something else! And all thanks to you, Harry Clewe! You rescue me in your fiery red chariot, carry me back to your lovely garden and show me the natterjack toad! Will you let me come another time? I'd love to try and find it again. My tutors will be very impressed when I tell them about it, when I go back to university."

They went through the cottage, climbed into the car, and Harry drove the girl very slowly down to Beddgelert. He wanted her beside him as long as possible. When they reached the village, she wriggled her legs over the car door, slid across the boot and ran toward the restaurant. She'd said she might see him again, if only to rummage for a pimply, poisonous toad in the overgrown garden. That was good enough for Harry Clewe.

He drove back to his cottage, left hand on the steering wheel, right hand on the warm, white leather where she'd been sitting.

3

For the next few mornings, Harry Clewe worked in the hotel garden.

The wall refused to take shape. Somehow, there seemed to be less stone available in his pile of rubble than there'd been when he'd brought it all crashing down. He'd finally removed the remains of the rhododendron bush; there was a great twisted mass of it at the top of the garden. He'd arranged the biggest stones into the soft earth and packed them tightly with more soil, placing the boulders on top of one another until there was none left. The result was unimpressive. Where there had once been a bulging face of stone and rhododendron roots some eight feet high retaining the terrace above, now there was Harry's wall: it came up to his waist. Behind that, there was an ugly scree of earth and smaller stones.

Burning the roots and branches of the rhododendron was an easier and more enjoyable task. He stuffed a bundle of old newspapers into the core of the heap, and, as soon as he lit the paper, aromatic smoke began to drift between the layers of leaves and twigs; there was the whistle and pop of warming wood. The leaves smoldered before exploding into an ill-tempered flame. Bubbles of oil sprang up and hissed with steam. The branches turned black, too thick and damp to burn quickly, but soon they were running with fire, shuddering with heat. The woodland was filled with crackling and smoke. The jackdaws moved to the trees of the next-door garden, continuing their clucking conversation. Ashes rose like moths, with the same jerky, aimless flight, settled on the ground and on Harry's clothes in a monochrome confetti.

Shifting from time to time to keep out of the smoke as it changed direction with the wind, he picked up a newspaper and began to read. February 1966; it was six months out of date. He crushed the paper and jammed it into the flames, where the pages erupted into a ball of brilliant yellow, like a giant chrysanthemum.

He stayed at the top of the garden all morning. Anxious about the flames spreading to the woodland, which was very dry after a hot summer, he raked away the leaves until there was a fire break about six feet wide, dropped his rake, unzipped his trousers and urinated into the bare soil. A haze of pungent steam rose into the air. He was filthy. There were ashes and leaves in his ginger hair. The sweat had dried on his face, with all the dust of the bonfire, and his glasses were filmed with dirt. There was dried blood around the nails of his right hand from a gash on his thumb, clotted with soil from his efforts with the wall. When he ran his tongue across his lips, he could taste the smoke and sweat and the ammoniac tang of urine. At one o'clock he left the hotel and walked through the village, to see Sarah.

Very carefully, he pushed open the restaurant door. Apart from a family in one corner, the place was empty. Harry sat down near the window. Sarah appeared. She must have heard the door open and close. When she saw Harry, she frowned at first, worked her face into a smile and walked to his table.

"Well, Harry Clewe," she said, "you managed to come in a bit more quietly this time, didn't you?" She looked him up and down. "What on earth have you been doing, you dirty boy? I've a good mind to call the manager and have you thrown out!"

"I just thought I'd let you get me a cup of tea before I go home and get cleaned up," he said. "I've been gardening at the hotel. I work there every morning."

The girl raised her eyebrows so high that they disappeared into her hair. She was wearing the same clothes as the last time he'd seen her.

"Gardening? I was wrong, then," she said. "You're a bit hard to figure out, aren't you? The car, the cottage... and gardening! You don't seem to fit into any of them. What are you doing here?"

Before Harry could reply, before he'd decided whether the girl was asking him what he was doing in Wales or what he was doing in the restaurant, more customers came in and she had to see what they wanted. She was too busy to talk to Harry, although she smiled dazzlingly when she put a cup of tea on his table. Two young men, sitting by the window, looked her up and down and winked at one another; they whispered together and then laughed very noisily, feigning solemnity when Sarah went to take their order. One of them said something which Harry didn't catch, but Sarah giggled and blushed and slapped the man on the top of his head with her notebook. Harry felt a surge of jealousy, swallowing it with a gulp of tea.

The manager appeared, big, burly and bearded, red-faced from the heat of the kitchen, and looked around to see that all was well in the restaurant. He stared at Harry, pursing his lips as he recognized the gingery hair and the glasses, frowning as he saw the dirt on Harry's boots and trousers. Sarah pushed past him, going into the kitchen with the young men's order, and the manager disappeared too.

Harry finished his tea and went to the counter to pay. He wasn't going to say anything about her coming to his garden. But, taking his money, she leaned toward him and whispered, "It's my half-day, Harry. I'd love to see your little jungle again and have another look at the natterjack. Can I? I should get out in twenty minutes or so."

Something fine and powerful swelled in Harry's chest. His throat ached. Unable to speak, he grinned and nodded and walked out of the restaurant.

But, an hour later, there was still no sign of her. Harry sat in his car with a copy of the *Caernarfon & Denbigh Herald* and read it from end to end. Then he reread it: the personal columns, the parish notices, the classified advertisements. He got out of the car, dropped the newspaper into a bin so that a swarm of wasps rose from a matted heap of banana skins; then, with nothing else to do, he opened the car boot, took out the oil and water he always kept there, opened the bonnet and topped up the levels. The engine was black, the whole compartment was sooted with oil smoke. Wondering how much longer the Wabenzi power would be with him, he slammed down the bonnet and the boot, wiped his hands on his shirt and went back to the restaurant.

Every table was taken. The windows were steamed up. Harry's glasses blurred as soon as he stepped inside, so he took them off and smeared them on his trousers as he stepped carefully over outstretched legs, over handbags and cameras, toward the counter. It was very noisy and suffo-catingly hot, smelling of vinegar and cigarette smoke. Be-fore he'd put his glasses back on, the manager loomed in front of him.

"Can I help you, sir?" he said. "We're a bit full up at the moment."

Harry fitted his glasses onto his face. When he licked his lips, he could still taste the smoke of the bonfire.

"Can I have a word with Sarah, please?" he said. "I know she's very busy. Just for half a minute?"

"I'll give her a shout," the man said. "But she's stopping here for the rest of the day. She's not running off this time. Hang on a minute and I'll get her." He turned to the kitchen, adding over his shoulder, "Stay there, stand still, and don't bloody break anything while you're waiting."

Harry stood still and broke nothing. The customers ig-nored him, in spite of his dirty clothes and boots and his oily hands; they were all too busy with their children and chips and their postcards to notice the red-headed gardener who leaned on the counter. He looked forward to escaping the restaurant. A tremor of electricity went through him at the simple idea of the sunshine outside and a rapid accel-eration from the village... to sit in the bird-bright tangle of the garden for ten minutes while the bath was running, to soak away the sweat and the smoke and the urine while the wren and the dunnock moved secretly in the bracken and the blackbird sang in the ash tree; while the toad was feeling with its fingers in the cool undergrowth, blinking its huge, golden eyes from a crevice in the rockery....

The toad! Harry had never heard of the natterjack before. He didn't know that toads were supposed to be lucky, until the girl had said something about the toadstone.... Neither he nor the garden could be the same again, now that the girl had been there.

She came out of the kitchen. Her hair was lank, her face was red and shiny.

"Hello again, Harry," she said. She took a pink tissue from the sleeve of her blouse and dabbed her nose. "I'm going to be stuck here all afternoon, I'm afraid, now that we're so busy. No escape this time! You met my uncle?"

Harry told her what the man had said, that he'd been recognized as a breaker of crockery and a kidnapper of waitresses. As Sarah put away her tissue, pushing the paper into her sleeve, he saw the soft whiteness under her arm.

"What about tomorrow?" he said. "Can I pick you up tomorrow?"

She frowned, so that Harry wished he hadn't asked her.

"I'm going climbing with a friend tomorrow," she said. "On the cliffs at Tremadog. I suppose you could come if you like. I don't think Patrick will mind. You'd better say one way or the other, because I've got to get back to work now." She turned to a man who was waiting to pay, who was brandishing his bill and a pound note, whose wife and children were at the door and ready to go outside.

"I'll come," Harry said. "Where shall I meet you?"

"Outside the restaurant at two. All right? See you then." Too busy to look at Harry, taking the customer's money, checking the bill, giving the change, she whirled back into the kitchen.

Harry drove slowly out of Beddgelert, into the open, high countryside to Rhyd-ddu, the next village, where he was renting a cottage for a few pounds a week. He'd negotiated the use of a corrugated-iron shed in a nearby farmyard, so that he could park the topless car under cover; and now he left it there, walked to his front door and let himself in. It was a little stone-built cottage in a terrace of half a dozen other cottages: two up and two down, with a tiny bathroom and kitchen more recently added to the back of it. Pausing to switch on the immersion heater, he continued through the back door and into the garden. In half an hour the water would be lukewarm, good enough for a bath on a summer's afternoon.

He sat on the stones of the rockery, closed his eyes and leaned back, tipping his face to the sun. After a minute, keeping his eyes closed, he bent down, took off his boots and peeled off his damp, hot socks. All the time, he had in his mind a picture of the girl, Sarah, who'd done the same thing in the same place; it helped him to focus the picture, repeating her actions as exactly as possible. It was the best he could do, since the girl herself hadn't come to the garden that afternoon. He squeezed his eyes shut, rubbed the ribbings on his feet and ankles that his boots had made, leaned back again and hitched up his trousers to have the sun on his shins.... As he did all this, he could see the girl sitting on the rockery, with the sun on her throat and her arms and her little white toes. He even felt the ant on his foot, the same ant that had walked on Sarah's foot, on her calf and her knee and the soft shadow on the inside of her thigh. It was tickling the hair on his instep; but he left it there instead of flicking it off, because it might be the same ant he'd seen on Sarah's leg. The ant was the tiniest, most exquisite detail that made the picture perfect.

Harry felt giddy. The sun was heavy on his mop of ginger hair. He reeled, swaying on the loose boulders of the rockery, with the heat on his head and the vividness with which he'd conjured the presence of the girl. At last he could no longer bear the prickling on his foot. He blinked his eyes open and looked down to see what the ant was doing.

It wasn't an ant; it was the natterjack toad. It had stopped on the path, confronted by a strange object near the entrance to its crevice in the rocks. The object, Harry's foot, was long, bony and white, soiled and sweaty. It was warm, with a strong animal scent. So the natterjack paused to inspect it, instead of maneuvering past. It reached its fingers into the springy red hair on Harry's instep and gently pulled. And Harry, confronted by such warty, prehistoric ugliness after his vision of the golden girl, cried out and instinctively flipped the toad away with a sudden straightening of his leg, feeling it horribly soft on his bare foot, like a wrinkled, deflated party balloon. He saw the toad rowing its arms and legs in the long grass, struggling on its back, unable to right itself, and he knelt down and lowered his face to examine it, as Sarah had done. He put his face so close to the toad that he could almost have touched it with his nose or slipped out his tongue and licked the soft, white skin on its belly.

Then, overcoming his squeamishness with an enormous effort, he picked up the toad... as Sarah had done. To be like her, simply to touch and hold something that she had touched and held, he picked up the toad. It squirmed in his hands. It could feel that he loathed it, and it reacted as the girl had said it would. It began to swell, puffing itself up, so that, having been so flaccid and dull, the skin tightened and gleamed like the leather of a boxing glove. Inflating in Harry's hands, as he knelt and watched the remarkable transformation, it brewed the poison in the glands on the sides of its head. An acrid fluid oozed to the surface of its skin, until Harry's hands were stinging as though he'd torn up a tall green nettle. He bundled the toad into the bracken. Straight away, tiny white blebs stood up on his palms and fingers. Seeing that the toad had deflated, scurried and vanished, mouselike, into a hole in the rockery, he picked up his boots and socks and went inside. His hands were itching furiously. His picture of Sarah had entirely gone.

He dropped the boots and socks, flung off his shirt and trousers and pants in the kitchen, put down his glasses and went into the bathroom. For a minute, he stared at his face in the mirror. It was a nice face, a face that women found oddly appealing, a smooth, freckled face with clear eyes, a head of thick, red curls: a nice face but a puzzled face, which looked as though it had been punched a few times and was half expecting a few more punches. Even the toad had stung him, the toad that the girl had been so thrilled to find, that she'd nuzzled and stroked, that she'd described as lovely and wonderful. When Harry Clewe had picked it up, it had stung him. So the eyes in the mirror were apprehensive.

Harry reached for both the washbasin taps and gripped, intending to bathe his tingling hands. A powerful electric shock surged through his body. As his fingers clenched in spasm and couldn't let go, as his right knee jerked sharply upward and cracked against the underside of the washbasin, the face in the mirror opened its mouth and let out a stream of incoherent, jabbering yells. The eyes bulged. After what seemed like minutes, but was probably no more than five seconds, Harry wrenched his hands from the taps. Still shouting, he hobbled out of the bathroom and flung himself onto the living-room sofa.

He lay there, mewing. He was stark naked, bruised and dirty. His arms tingled with electricity, from his fingers to his shoulders. They were numb, although he could clench and unclench his fists. His right kneecap was hurting terribly from its violent impact on the basin. As the feeling returned to his fingers, he massaged his forehead and his neck, trying to rub the tension out of them. He looked down at his body and explored all the bruises on it: the gash on his thumb, his throbbing kneecap and the tingles and aches in his arms. Worst of all, when he squeezed his eyes shut, he saw sparks. "Please, no!" he whimpered. "Oh, God, please, no... not now!" He rubbed and rubbed with his fingers to try and make the sparks go away, hoping they'd been caused by the electric shock and would soon disappear. Oh, God, he thought, anything but the migraine, please, anything but that!

Enraged by the prospect of the kind of headache he'd dreaded since puberty, he ground his teeth together and stopped mewing, determined to tackle the problem in his bathroom. He strode into the kitchen, stepped into his wellington boots and went into the bathroom again. He had the vague idea that the rubber boots would protect him from electric shocks.

He touched the taps with his fingertips. There was a tingle of current. Gingerly, he gripped one of the taps. There was a surging of energy, even in the soles of his boots. His fingers curled, his right knee jerked, but there was no bruising impact with the sink. He breathed out and relaxed. His fingers unclenched. His face in the shaving mirror looked uncomfortable.

Nevertheless, Harry decided to run the bath. Somehow or other, he must get clean. Handling the taps with a dry towel, he let the bath fill to a depth of three or four inches and then he stepped in. The water hardly covered the instep of his wellington boots. Squatting on his haunches, he found that, if he dipped both his hands in the water at the same time, he received an unpleasant electric shock, despite the rubber boots, right through his arms and chest and into the back of his neck. He had to wash himself single-handedly. It was the most strenuous and least successful bath he'd ever taken. Deciding not to risk kneeling forward and submerging his head, he managed to rub some wet soap into his hair and rinse most of it out again with splashes of gray water.

It was worse than Sudan. There, he'd quickly grown accustomed to bathing from a tin bucket he carried from the Nile. It was simply a matter of practice. Perhaps he would adjust to the electrified bathwater, find better and less painful ways of using it. When at last Harry emerged from the bathroom and dried himself, his towel was streaked with the soap and dirt that had remained on his body. After dressing in clean clothes, he returned to the garden with a basin of clean water, where he sat on the rockery, took off his boots and washed his feet. The blebs on his fingers had stopped itching. When he squeezed his eyes shut, he was enormously relieved to find that the dancing sparks had gone.

The natterjack watched from within its cave. It solemnly blinked, licked its lips with a long, gray tongue and rubbed its little hands together.

4

Harry was sitting on the wall outside Sarah's uncle's restaurant at two o'clock the following afternoon.

Unlike the previous few days of brilliant sunshine, the sky was overcast. He'd spent the morning high up in the hotel garden, hiding from the manager, doing nothing to justify his wage. Getting out of bed, he'd found that his right kneecap was swollen and puffy and the joint was painfully stiff. In the garden, it hurt him when he attempted the climb to the bonfire with more rubbish to be burned. So he sat down and reached for the pile of out-of-date newspapers. Instead of repeating the journey, he made sure that the fire maintained a trembling plume of smoke through the branches of the trees, and he read. He wanted to keep as clean as possible; there would be no opportunity, between finishing in the garden and meeting Sarah, to go back to the cottage and have a wash; even if he could, it would be another hazardous and tiresome experience in the electrified bathroom. He sat with the newspapers, so preoccupied with the prospect of seeing the girl again that the pages flickered meaninglessly before his eyes like the faded frames of a silent film. The morning passed in a pall of smoke from the bonfire, in the cryptic conversation of jackdaws.

Sarah came out of the restaurant. She was wearing the same purple tie-dyed T-shirt she'd been wearing when he'd first met her, a pair of sheer red slacks, and a neckerchief knotted at her throat, red with white polka dots. Seeing Harry on the other side of the road, she smiled a seraphic smile which made his heart thud and his mouth go suddenly dry. But she didn't cross over. Instead, she skipped into the restaurant car park, where she started to rap on the rear window of a battered blue van. Harry stayed where he was and watched her.

The back door of the van opened. Sarah jumped inside and the door slammed shut. The springs creaked. There were shadowy movements behind the windows, then silence and stillness for a minute or two.

She was rather flushed when she stepped out again, and the spotted neckerchief was gone. She beckoned to Harry to cross the road. He did so, in such a daze that he was barely aware of a car which braked hard to avoid him. The driver shouted an unlovely word, and the car accelerated away.

"Hello, Harry," she said. Like a child, she leaned upward and brushed his cheek with her lips, flicking her hair on his face. His hands went to her waist, but she spun away to the door of the van. "Come and meet Patrick," she said. "I think he's capable of receiving visitors."

Harry peered inside. The van was so spectacularly untidy that at first he couldn't see anyone. There was bedding strewn about; blankets, pillows and sleeping bags. The air was stale with dirty clothes, pungent with the fumes of patchouli and marijuana. Ropes, belts and harnesses were tangled together; hammers and picks and all manner of aluminum clips and brackets dangled from the roof. A loaf of bread and a jar of marmalade lay in the rumpled clothes. A voice said, "Good afternoon," before Harry made out the man who was sprawling there.

"I'm Harry Clewe," Harry said, spelling his name, offering his hand.

The man ignored the hand, waving it away with the bread knife he was holding. "I know," he replied. "I'm Patrick. Sarah told me about your scene in the restaurant, how you rescued her from the ogre. Rock-climbing should be pretty easy for you, compared with that."

"I've never tried it before," Harry said. "But I'll have a go. My knee's a bit buggered at the moment."

This provoked an arpeggio of laughter from Sarah. The man snorted. Harry couldn't tell whether they were amused by his eagerness to mention his injury before the climbing began or by the awkwardness of his expression. He'd never been able to swear properly; there was something in his face and the cadence of his voice that made even the mildest oath sound wrong.

Patrick untangled himself from his ropes and blankets and sprang, barefoot, into the car park. Like Sarah, he was wearing slacks and a T-shirt, and Harry noticed, with a swooping in his stomach, that the man had the spotted red neckerchief around his throat. He and Sarah looked as lithe as a pair of otters, while Harry felt slight and shabby in the cheap tennis shoes, old flannels and tennis shirt he'd been used to wearing in Sudan.

Patrick cleared a space in the back of the van and Harry climbed in, wincing at the pain in his knee. Patrick and Sarah got in the front, slamming the doors so loudly that a pair of pigeons clattered from a nearby sweet-chestnut tree. The man started the van and maneuvered it into the road, making a great play of fumbling for Sarah's thigh instead of the gear stick. Laughing together, they continued their horseplay until the van was humming rapidly out of the village.

They drove for a quarter of an hour along the Glaslyn pass, in the direction of Porthmadog. Patrick, intrigued that a schoolteacher should be working as a hotel gardener, asked Harry to explain his presence in Wales. He laughed at Harry's account of his year in Sudan, how he'd gone as a volunteer to one of the poorest countries in the world and bought a Mercedes-Benz with the proceeds. That was all there was time for. Harry had a closer look at Patrick, with a rising sense of anxiety at this familiarity with Sarah. In his thirties, Patrick had a tangle of blond hair, curly and long at his ears and the back of his neck, and a bristly, blond beard. He twinkled in the driving mirror, a puckish, self-confident bantam, speaking with the rising lilt of a Birmingham accent. Harry was inclined to like him, despite his earlier gesture with the marmalade smeared knife and the way his hands wandered toward Sarah's right thigh.

They drew up in a lay-by opposite Tremadog cliffs. Harry rolled out of the van when Sarah ran round to open the back door, and then she pointed with a naked brown arm at the wall of sheer rock which rose from the woodland. There were climbers everywhere: they strolled along the road, with coils of rope hung over their shoulders, with jangling aluminum paraphernalia clipped to their belts; high above the trees, knots of them stood talking, gesturing expansively to explain the problems they'd encountered before achieving the clifftop; and silently, painstakingly, tiny figures on the cliff-face crept like insects on the wrinkled bark of a tree. They swung on their ropes like spiders; they stepped delicately on tiptoe and felt with their fingertips.

Patrick and Sarah unraveled the ropes from the van, preparing the equipment. To make up for his uselessness, Harry started to talk; he heard himself talking very quickly, too quickly, fidgeting his fingers in his pockets, adjusting and readjusting the glasses on his face because he was nervous about trying to climb the high, steep rock. Quite a lot of the local Welsh people, he said, liked to claim that the towns of Porthmadog and Tremadog had something to do with the great man Madog ap Llewelyn, who'd led a rebellion against the English and sacked Caernarfon castle in 1294... but in fact the towns were named after an Englishman called William Madocks, who'd built the harbors for the exporting of slate in the nineteenth century.

Patrick glanced up and said, "Is that so?" Then he bent to the ropes again.

Sarah said, "Shut up and relax, Harry. We'll be ready soon. You know, if you relax you might actually enjoy it." And, seeing from his expression that he'd been hurt and was expecting to be hurt again quite soon, she stroked his face with her grubby brown hand.

They crossed the road and went into the woodland at the base of the cliffs. There was a wreckage of huge boulders, overgrown with brambles, nettles, garlic and dock. A blackbird fled noisily as Patrick, still barefooted, led the way through the rocks and stopped in a cool, green glade. Looking upward, shielding his eyes from the sun which was beginning to break through a layer of gray cloud, Harry saw the dappled branches move slowly in the breeze; then the slabs of rock towered to the sky. Against the shifting clouds, the cliff seemed to move as well, bulging and beetling, so that Harry blinked and looked down again.

Again he was superfluous, as Patrick and Sarah rearranged the climbing equipment. Patrick would go up first, followed by Sarah. The man was helping her into the harness, making her ready to climb once he'd reached the top and secured his lines. Trailing a length of rope, Patrick began his ascent. He wiped his hands on his slacks, smeared his feet in the grass to clean off some mud, and moved easily up the rockface.

Harry was impressed. On the very tips of his toes and fingers, the man seemed to dance on the cliff. Quickly and gracefully, he moved higher and higher. Sarah was watching him, so that she might know the route.

Glancing from her upturned throat to the climber again, Harry said, "He certainly seems to know what he's doing, doesn't he? How on earth does he do it barefoot? How can he grip the rock like that?"

"Patrick's one of the best," she answered, without looking at Harry. "He's climbed all over the Himalayas and the Andes. At the moment he's instructing at the center in Capel Curig, the place you gave me a lift to. A couple of months ago he was climbing in Yosemite, in California, and that's where he started this barefoot thing. He's adopted it as a sort of personal trademark this summer. He hasn't worn any shoes for weeks, not just for climbing, but even around the town and in the pub. He's a bloody show-off. Anyway, this is a dead easy route, for beginners. Patrick can run up and down this bit of cliff all day without breaking a sweat."

They both stared upward, following the trailing rope. The man had disappeared.

"Looks like it's my turn soon," she said. "You stay here, Harry. Patrick will come down when I've finished and fix you up with the gear. Wish me luck! You're not the only one who's nervous, you know. This is only my second go at it — I'm a beginner, too!"

She tugged at the rope. There was an answering tug and a cry from above. She applied herself to the rock.

There was no sound in the woodland apart from the rub and knock of Sarah's feet on the cliff wall. The birds were silent. Rays of sunlight fell through the branches in columns of golden dust. The girl grunted, stretching for handholds and footholds, and Harry could see the spreading, darkening stains of sweat under her arms and in the small of her back. Her fingers burrowed for a grip in the folded rock. She splayed her legs apart, scrabbling with her toes. In this way, Sarah negotiated the cliff-face. When she was as high as the highest trees, the sunlight struck her, so that her hair shone like a helmet. And then she was gone, as the lizard in Harry's Sudanese garden had gone, leaving a dull, gray space on the rock.

For a quarter of an hour, Harry waited for Patrick to come down and help him begin his climb. The woodland came to life as he sat quietly on a boulder. He watched a flock of long-tailed tits, black and white and pearly gray, swinging their flyweight bodies like gymnasts. They disappeared when a jay beat through the trees, cocking a zany head, shouting an ugly shout, raising its tail to squirt a branch with a bright yellow mute. Harry moved to a spot where a sunbeam landed, and he wondered how long he'd be waiting at the foot of the cliff. He would have been happy to sit all afternoon, alone with the nuthatch and wren... except for the thought of Patrick with the girl in the long grass at the top of the cliff. He imagined, with giddying dismay, how the rock-climber's fingers might be stroking the small of her back or teasing her nipples inside the purple T-shirt.

Just then, with a crashing of undergrowth, Patrick and Sarah ran toward him through the woodland. The man came first, with the rope coiled over his shoulder. Harry's eyes flickered past him to the girl. She'd taken off her T-shirt and was carrying it in her hand. Her breasts shone whitely against the deeper tan of her arms and neck, rising and falling as she ran; there were smears of sweat on her stomach and the waistband of her slacks. She wore the spotted red neckerchief, knotted at her throat.

"Harry!" she called out. "I made it, Harry! I made it to the top!"

Before he could stand up, she launched herself at him and wrapped her arms around his neck. Her breasts lifted and tautened as she pressed herself to him. His hands flew to her waist and, for a second, he held her close. But she whirled away again, toward Patrick, her face as vivid as it had been when she'd found the natterjack toad in Harry's garden.

"Tell Harry how clever I am, Patrick!" she cried. "Go on, tell him!"

The man looked up from his aluminum clips, and he smiled so that his eyes disappeared in deep, dark wrinkles.

"You're a very wonderful person, Sarah," he said dryly. "You could be a good climber if you do everything I tell you to do. Good concentration, strong fingers, good ratio of strength to weight — what more can I say?"

"My turn, is it?" Harry interrupted. "Can I have a go?"

He was exhilarated by Sarah's success, as thrilled as she was. When he stroked his face with his fingertips, he could smell her body. He could feel the weight of her breasts on him, and the slither of her arms on his neck. Charged with her energy, he stepped into the harness which Patrick had prepared and let the man arrange it round his thighs and groin. The rope slipped through a flimsy clip which would support him if he fell from the cliff-face.

"It doesn't look very strong, this thing!" he said, with a grimacing smile in case Sarah was looking at him.

She wasn't. Patrick explained in his nasal Black Country voice that the clip, called a carabiner, was plenty strong enough for Harry's inconsiderable weight. Harry listened carefully, but he was watching the girl. She sat on a boulder, in the full beam of the sun. Shirtless, she leaned back and basked in the column of light. She glanced at Harry, smiling lazily, as though the heat made it too great an effort; then she closed her eyes and turned her face like a bloom toward the sun while her hands came up and untied the neckerchief. Her breasts tightened and lifted; at the same time, something tightened and lifted in the pit of Harry's stomach. She held out the neckerchief, her eyes still closed, so that Harry could stretch across and take it from her fingers. He tied it around his own throat. Patrick finished fixing the harness and rope. He snorted when he looked up to see that Harry was wearing the neckerchief.

"Let's go then," he said. "But first, Harry Clewe, a few words of simple advice. You've got two hands and two feet, right? Well, try not to use any other parts of your body against the rock, not even your knees. You shouldn't have to, with your reach. It's a straightforward route, for your first climb. And very important: always maintain three points of contact with the rock. In other words, just move one hand or one foot at a time. Got it?"

"Got it," Harry said.

"I'll keep the rope nice and tight," Patrick went on. "Just relax. You never know, you might enjoy it."

Once more, Patrick made the climb. He seemed almost to run up the cliff, bouncing from hold to hold until he was level with the branches where the long-tailed tits had been. Then he vanished. The rope trailed down to the clip on Harry's belt; Harry had already forgotten what the clip was called. Sarah was silent, as still as a statue, as though she were petrified by the sunlight. Harry waited nervously. Stroking his mouth, again he caught the lingering scent of the girl's body; but now that it was time for him to attempt the

climb, he felt her energy draining from him. To try and rekindle it, he fingered the spotted red neckerchief she'd
handed him. There was a cry and the rope tugged. Harry
applied himself to the cliff.

The rock was very cold. That was the first, disconcerting
impression. But the climbing seemed easy enough. After a
series of scrambles he found himself on top of a big boulder,
about fifteen feet above the ground... no, it was more than
that. When he glanced down at Sarah's upturned face, he was
surprised and somewhat alarmed at the height he'd achieved
so quickly. She was a long way down. But the rope was comfortably taut, running from his belt and humming in front of
his face. He climbed for another minute and stopped to rest
with his toes on a ledge about an inch wide, with his hands
around a bulging outcrop. A quick look over his shoulder
brought the unnerving realization that he was level with the
treetops, exposed on a slab of featureless rock. He could see
the road and Patrick's horrid van. Hands on hips, pointing, a
number of people were staring up at the cliffs. There was a
flashing of teeth in their anonymous faces, followed a second
later by a chorus of ragged laughter. Were they laughing at
him? Why? He glanced down at his feet in their flimsy, inappropriate shoes, and between them into the swaying branches
of the trees. Christ! He forced himself to stare at the stone in
front of him. His eyes followed the rope upward until it disappeared over the protruding crag. Was Patrick up there? Or
had he tied the rope to a boulder and abandoned him? The
bastard was probably down in the woodland with Sarah,
squeezing her nipples with his rock-horny fingers....

The rope twitched. Patrick's voice came pealing to him.
"You all right, Harry? Keep going! You're doing fine!"

Harry took a deep breath and started to move again.
When he groped for the next handhold, he felt nothing but
smooth, cold stone.

"That's it, Harry! That's the next hold!" Apparently, the
invisible Patrick could see the climber from his vantage

point at the top of the cliff. "Pull yourself up with that hold!" he was shouting.

Realizing that Patrick must be referring to a hairline crack hardly big enough for his fingernails to fit into, Harry heaved himself higher and dug the toes of his left foot into a tiny vertical crevice. There was nothing to hold on to. The rock face was completely bald. He embraced it with his whole body, his chest and thighs and knees, and sucked himself to the cliff.

"Try not to use your knees!" Patrick's singsong Black Country accent rang in the cool, still air. "Just your fingers and toes, please, Harry!"

At this, a runnel of sweat broke from Harry's forehead and trickled across his glasses. He couldn't move at all. His left foot was taking all his weight, wedged into a crack, while his right foot scrabbled vainly for somewhere to go. Both hands, about level with his face, were stretched out to their respective scratches in the rock. Then his left leg started to quiver, imperceptibly at first, then more and more, until his knee was jumping up and down and knocking itself against the stone. This spurred him into making another move, anything to relieve the pressure on his toes before they leaped from the crevice.

The rope tightened suddenly and lugged him upward. There was a sensation of delicious relief in his left leg and his fingers found a good hold; but he realized, through the sweat-smeared lenses of his glasses, that he wasn't really climbing; he'd been lifted bodily over the last six feet. When he glanced down again, the view made his head swim. Another hoot of laughter came to him from the antlike figures on the gray strip of road. The rope went completely slack, dangling in front of his face. He gripped the rock and wedged his right knee into an adjacent slit. And there he remained, his left leg hanging uselessly like a puppet's, with all his weight bearing on the bruises of the kneecap he'd banged on the bathroom washbasin. The sweat dripped down his chin.

"No knees, please!" The voice came calmly from above.

"Oh, bugger off!" Harry yelped.

He heard Patrick laughing. Straining every muscle, he tried to raise himself on his fingertips, just enough to dislodge his knee from the excruciating pressure. Both his hands slipped from the rock.

He fell backward. A space yawned between him and the cliff. With a hoarse cry, he jabbed his fingers forward, failing to touch anything but the empty air. His knee slipped out of the rock: he lost all contact with solid matter.

Nothing to hold... Nothing to touch...

He fell and fell, spinning through the emptiness toward the trees and the boulders below. The cliff was a blur of grays and browns. Then his knees struck hard. The side of his face banged an outcropping fist of stone. His glasses were smashed off. There was an impact like a punch in the solar plexus, rattling him to the very base of his spine, and the rope went tight.

And there he was, suspended in midair, helpless and disoriented, knocking and knocking on the cliff wall. Still much higher than the top of the tallest trees, he clutched uselessly at the space around him until the knocking slowly stopped and he scratched for a grip on the rock. His feet found a ledge, big enough for both of them, and at least he could lean a little and try to recover some shred of his wits. He was trembling uncontrollably, with his eyes squeezed shut. The blood pounded in his head, and his chest heaved. Voices came to him from above and below, Patrick's and Sarah's and laughter from the people on the road who'd seen him fall from the cliff. He ignored them all. Let them all piss off, he thought. Just let me grip and grip this rock and never let go. No one — not even Sarah whom he wanted with every bruised and traumatized nerve in his being and whom he'd wanted from the moment she'd jumped into his car — could persuade him ever to risk a movement from the safety he'd achieved. He put his lips to the stone and planted a long, long, trembling kiss. "Don't leave me, don't leave me," he whispered. "Just let me hold you like this and kiss you, please, oh please, oh..."

A miracle happened. He felt a hand on his shoulder. He raised his forehead from the gray wall and opened his eyes. It was Patrick.

"Oh dear, oh dear," the man said. "Calm down. We'll get you down in a minute."

Even without his glasses, Harry could see that Patrick was grinning. The man went on, apparently standing quite comfortably on another ledge, "You fell a few feet, that's all. Banged your face, by the look of things. Bleeding a bit, just a graze. Don't worry," he said, still with his hand on Harry's shoulder. "No one feels good about falling, even a short distance. I've done it myself, so I know it's not nice. You got a bit gripped, that's all."

Harry remained still, unable to move at all. Staring owlishly at Patrick, he felt himself forming a spastic smile. It hurt his face. He was glad his glasses had gone; content with his scrutiny of the rock in front of him, he didn't want to look at Patrick or anyone else. Meanwhile, Patrick had started shouting to someone on the top of the cliff.

"There's a mate of mine up there," he explained to Harry. "Another instructor. He's going to ease you down on the rope while I climb down with you. Right? The only thing, my friend Harry, is that you'll have to let go a little bit or you won't be able to move at all, will you?" Then there was a sharper edge on his voice. His accent was suddenly stronger. "End of sympathy now, Harry, or we'll be here all bloody day. Come on, we're climbing down."

He took Harry off the rock. Another minute's gentle persuasion, and then he lost patience. Ignoring the whimpers and pleas, Patrick prised Harry's hands from the rock and kicked hard with his own bare, callused feet so that Harry was knocked clear of the cliff. Harry squealed, dangling in midair again. He flailed his arms, scraping his fingers on the rock for any microscopic crack that might secure him; but Patrick kept barging him off with the flat of his hand and shoving him into empty space. For Harry, it was a nightmare of pain and sweat and cold, gray stone. He was suspended in the sunlight like a heifer in an abattoir. His knees and elbows cracked on protruding rock. Gradually, he began to relax a little as he realized the rope was safe and was lowering him into the shade of the woodland. The descent continued, and Harry even attempted a few moves to help. But Patrick's patience was gone. He tugged and cuffed at Harry to maintain their momentum, until they fell together into the sun-sweet glade from where the climb had begun.

Sarah hadn't moved at all from her basking boulder. She was a golden blur, as still as the lizard. Harry dropped into a bed of long grass and started to wipe the sweat from his face, using the piece of shirt he tugged out of the waistband of his trousers. There was blood as well. His cheek was raw and puffy from its impact with the cliff. He leaned back and closed his eyes, opening and shutting his mouth like a goldfish to ease the pain in his jaw. With a skid and a rattle, the rope and its assorted clips dropped into the woodland, landing in nearby nettles. Patrick retrieved it and neatly coiled it, checking every inch for any damage that might have been caused by Harry's fall. Nobody spoke.

The heaving in Harry's chest calmed down, and so did the banging of blood at the base of his neck. The overwhelming relief he'd experienced to find himself on the ground again and relatively unharmed now gave way to a wave of shame at his failure — and the way he'd failed. Sarah had succeeded, slowly and deliberately, in her ascent of the rock. Harry had been terrified: gripped, to use Patrick's word. He'd panicked. No wonder the shouts of laughter had reached him from the roadside; no wonder they were pointing at him. And Patrick had manhandled him from the ledge, after the bone-wrenching, bowel-churning shock of the fall. Harry kept his eyes shut. He felt safer, less exposed, in the thudding gloom of his own head.

"Your glasses," Sarah said.

He blinked at her. For a sickening moment, he saw sparks in the top right-hand corner of his vision.

"Here they are," she said, holding his glasses toward him. "When they fell off, I saw them come down and land in the nettles. One of the lenses is broken."

His knee hurt as he stood up from the grass. Indeed, his whole body was bruised from its repeated impact against the cliff. With blood on his face and shirt, with sweat in his hair, with the expression in his eyes somehow altered by the absence of his glasses, he limped toward her. She didn't move to meet him. She simply held out the glasses at the end of her slim, brown, naked arm.

"Thank you, Sarah," he said. The right lens had a starburst crack in its top right-hand corner, like a tiny bullet hole. Unable to resist it, even in his demoralized condition, he put the glasses on and attempted a joke. "Making a spectacle of myself!"

"Yes," she said, without a flicker of a smile.

"Let's go, Sarah," Patrick said. "I've got all the gear sorted out."

She got up and wriggled into her T-shirt, turning to follow Patrick through the woodland. Harry picked his way behind her, finding it hard to make out the path through the crazed lens. A cluster of sparks was dancing in front of him. Stumbling, he fell heavily and sat down, too weary and dispirited to get up again. Sarah had heard him fall. She stepped toward him, as though to help, but Patrick said sharply, "Come on, Sarah, leave him!" so she turned from Harry and followed the man out of the trees to the gravel of the roadside.

In no time, they were in the van again. Patrick had stopped to talk to someone while Sarah unlocked the doors. There was a volley of laughter from the people Patrick was talking to. Harry offered to take the rope from his shoulder, to put it in the van, but Patrick waved him away with the same lazy gesture he'd made with the marmalade-smeared knife. Harry climbed into the back, arranging his awkward, angular limbs on the rumpled bedding.

Sarah got into the passenger seat. She quickly spun round and asked in a clipped, matter-of-fact voice which he hadn't heard before, "Are you all right, Harry Clewe?" Then she turned away before he could answer, because Patrick was getting into the van. So Harry said nothing.

Patrick drove slowly to Beddgelert. Through his spangled glasses, through the shimmering sparks, Harry saw a flock of lapwings tumbling in the sky, a blurring of black and white wings like a conjurer's card trick. He heard the lunatic cackle of a woodpecker. He hugged his knees, ducked his head and squeezed his eyes shut.

The Mercedes-Benz was parked nearby, where Patrick stopped the van. The car looked ridiculous. Harry had thought it was grand: fine, big and powerful... worth having. It wasn't. It was a heap of clapped-out swank. Now, in front of Patrick and Sarah, after his humiliation on the cliff, he felt foolish as he sat at the wheel and turned the ignition key. The engine churned and churned and wouldn't fire. Patrick crowed with laughter. Sarah grimaced with the embarrassment she felt for Harry Clewe. Harry tried again and again, until, with a loud bang and a snort of filthy black smoke, the car started. Grinning, shaking his head, Patrick turned away and disappeared into the back of the van.

"Will I see you again?" Harry asked the girl.

He had to ask her, although he ground his teeth with shame. He had to. He couldn't not have asked her, although it exposed him to the worst and biggest humiliation of the afternoon. Like the hound, Gelert, in the picture the girl had painted, he offered himself up and waited for the killing thrust.

"Will I, Sarah?" he repeated, over the snort and splutter of the car's engine. "Will I see you at all?"

She wouldn't look at him. She picked at a blister on her little brown paw. "I don't think so," she said at last. "I'm sorry. You're a nice man, Harry. I like you. But I'll be with Patrick when I'm not working in the restaurant. Then back to London. I'm going back to university quite soon."

Picking her blisters, she climbed into the van with Patrick and the doors slammed shut. Harry drove out of the village.

In the cottage, he threw off all his clothes, tossed down the broken glasses and walked naked into the bathroom. His face in the mirror was a mess; the skin had been burned from his left cheek, and there was dried blood and dirt in the raked-over flesh. He studied his reflection through an arc of sparks which would soon eclipse his vision. He knew exactly what the immediate future held. The angel had come for him. Soon, the pounding, poleaxing headache would begin. Then he would retch until his chest felt as though it had been torn inside out. At last he would sleep, completely drained, his head aching as though he'd been slugged with something very hard and very heavy. Resigned to all of this, dreading the pain he knew was coming, he looked at himself in the bathroom mirror.

No wonder the girl didn't want him. His face was a palimpsest: imprinted, smudged, imprinted, smudged, with nothing brave or original of its own. No trace of heroism. With dismay, he remembered the touch of the girl on his fingers, the sweat on her flanks and her belly, how hot and smooth she'd been... Automatically, he reached for the taps of the washbasin.

The electricity flooded his body. It lit the blackest corners of his mind with a sizzling magnesium flare. It ground his teeth together. It rolled his eyeballs backward until he could see into the dazzling, floodlit hole in his head. His right knee jerked up and cracked on the bottom of the washbasin. Gibbering, wailing, chattering like a chimpanzee, he wrenched his hands from the taps and fled into the garden.

He collapsed on the tumbledown rockery. Everything that was Harry Clewe, inside and outside, was bruised. No part of him, concrete or abstract, had survived the day intact. Naked, mewing, wringing his hands, chewing his lips, he sat on the rockery and shook his head to try and shift the sparks.

Then he felt something gently tugging the hair on his instep.

A toad. It had emerged from its cave into the sunshine of the late afternoon. The long tongue flicked out and caressed the silken skin on his ankle. Its eyes were open, fixed in a golden stare.

Harry leaned forward with his arms on his knees and looked at the toad between his feet. It was the natterjack that the girl had found, that she'd handled and stroked. It wasn't swollen; there was no threat, no poison triggered in the glands of its head. But, remembering how it had nettled him before, Harry was loath to touch the toad with his bare hands.

He found that he wasn't quite naked after all. He was still wearing the spotted red neckerchief that the girl had given him. He unknotted it from his throat and took it off. Spreading it in his hands, he dropped it loosely over the toad's pimpled body and picked it up with the creature wrapped inside. He carried it with him, back into the cottage.

There, he pressed the toad to his forehead and tried to soothe the pain that was blooming in his skull.

5

So, Harry Clewe wasn't at all surprised to find a toad in the palm of his hand when he woke up. He felt at his cheek which had struck the rock when he'd fallen from the cliff. The graze had hardened into a scab. The swelling had gone down.

It was dawn, the beginning of September. Harry was cold. As the room became lighter and lighter, he lay in his narrow bed with the blankets pulled up to his chin and cupped the natterjack toad on his belly. It was warm there, like a little hot-water bottle. Thankful that his migraine was over, he stared at the ceiling and let the shreds of sleep drift away.

For a week, he didn't see Sarah. But he had his landlord come in, to investigate the problem with the electricity.

Touching the taps in the clammy, dingy little bathroom, holding his hands in the running water, the man agreed there was a tingle. That was as far as he would go: a tingle. He smiled when Harry described the shocks he'd had. He smiled when Harry rolled up his trouser leg to show him the bruises on his kneecap. The man was sympathetic but disbelieving. Looking with interest at the scabs and bruising on Harry's face and the starburst crack on his glasses, he must have thought that the Englishman was simply accident-prone. Harry went on to describe his efforts in the bath. The man guffawed at the idea of wearing wellington boots in three inches of lukewarm water. It was clearly impossible to make him appreciate the seriousness of the situation. All he could feel was a tingle.

But at least he explained the reason for the shocks: rats.

Previous tenants had complained of hearing rats in the roof of the cottage and in the floor space of the living-room ceiling. The landlord suggested that the rats had been gnawing at the wiring. He promised to call in the pest control to put down some poison, and he would check the wiring himself when he had a free weekend. He said all this with a smile trembling on his lips; he was looking forward to telling his wife about the carroty, bewildered Englishman who was renting the cottage, who wore wellington boots in the bath. Meanwhile, he pointed out the switch which governed the separate electricity supply to the kitchen and bathroom, the lean-to extension to the back of the cottage... yes, there was a switch beside the bathroom door, and the landlord recommended that, for the time being, until the wiring was fixed, Harry could heat the water in the immersion and then always turn off the power just before he got into the bath. No more tingles, with or without his boots on.

Harry had heard the rats in the roof. Lying in bed, he'd listened to the plodding of feet and the slither of tails inside the ceiling. He could follow their runs from one side of the roof space to another, hear the animals sniffing into the corners of the dusty darkness. He hated the rats, shuddering at the thought of them so close to his head, only separated from him by a sheet of plasterboard. He hated them more and more, now that he knew they were responsible for the shocks he'd had in the bathroom.

At least the switch by the bathroom door made it safe to touch the taps and the water. Browsing in a reference book in Caernarfon library, he'd been horrified to learn that a leakage of ordinary domestic current could be fatal to someone immersed to the neck in the bath when the charge passed through the water.

"Fibrillation: the uncontrollable, irregular twitching of the muscular wall of the heart, interfering with normal rhythmical contractions..." This could kill. Even the youngest and fittest, stunned into unconsciousness, might drown in the bath. So much for the tingle.

While he was in the library, Harry decided to investigate the natterjack toad as well. He'd carried it with him, wrapped in the spotted red neckerchief, tucked inside his shirt. In a quiet corner of the reference library, he took out the bundled neckerchief and spread it on the table. The toad began a groveling exploration of the books that Harry had stacked up.

It was undoubtedly a natterjack, *Bufo calamita* as Sarah had said. The distinctive yellow line ran from its forehead and down the middle of its back. It was about three inches long from its snout to the nub of its body; twice as long when it stretched out its long hind legs. The dull brown skin was pimpled and wrinkled and blotched as though the toad was in the last stages of a horrible disease; but the books said this was camouflage, so that the creature would look like a clod of earth. Apparently, the natterjack could even change color to match its surroundings, like a chameleon. Harry picked it up and turned it round when it reached the edge of the table. He could see the bumps, the parotid glands on the sides of its head, containing the stinging poison; but the toad hadn't stung him since the first time he'd handled it in the garden, even when he held it to his belly. Not very agile, toads had developed another means of defense, the book said, the ability to swell themselves up to be half as big again, by inflating their lungs. But the natterjack was more mobile than the common toad: it was nicknamed the "running toad" because of its scurrying, mouselike movements.

There were some splendid photographs of toads copulating. This always happened in the water, an element which transformed the toad from a cumbersome oaf into a graceful, balletic swimmer. In the sexual embrace, "in amplexus" as the book called it, the male sat on the female's back and clasped his forearms around her. The water buoyed them up and gave them the necessary freedom of movement to carry out their mating. Locked together, they swam dreamily around their pool, the male kicking away the advances of other interested males if they came too close. And then the female ejected her eggs just as he released his seminal fluid: strictly speaking, the act was not copulation, since the toad had no copulatory organ. Finally, the male would distribute the eggs with more movements of his hind legs, three or four thousand eggs in threads of jelly up to six feet long.

It was the expression on their faces that fascinated Harry. The female was frowning like a duchess, with the male's fingers entwined around her throat; the male creased his mouth in the widest of smiles, as though he was having more fun that he thought he was going to. To Harry, there was something perfectly idyllic in the idea of making love in the water, floating weightlessly on its silken cushion. He'd never tried it.

And he found the story the girl had mentioned in his garden: the legend that "the foule toad has a faire stone in his heade".... According to superstition, it was a stroke of the greatest luck to find a toad, and most unlucky to kill one: Deep in its pimpled, poisonous head, there was a jewel, the toadstone, which gave power over women and horses and was effective against snakebites and ratbites. The application of a living toad to the back of the neck would staunch nosebleeds and soothe headaches. The toadstone was magic.

Now, in a quiet corner of Caernarfon library, Harry Clewe smiled, took off his broken glasses, picked up the natterjack and pressed its belly to his forehead. It was cool and dry and as soft as velvet. It felt good. It felt wonderful. The power of the toadstone filled him with strength and peace.

Closing his eyes, he sat like that for a long time, until the lady librarian came to his table and screamed very loudly. Then he bundled the toad into his shirt, picked up his glasses and ran outside.

From that day onward, he carried the toad with him all the time, folded in the spotted red neckerchief. It was important to him. He'd been bruised and wounded. The toad made him feel safe.

6

Harry had had the headaches since he was seven. The first time he'd seen the cluster of dancing sparks, he'd told his mother that an angel had come for him. It was an angel he dreaded, one that brought him pain and wretchedness. His eyesight deteriorated as the headaches became more frequent and more crippling. He grew into a gawky, freckle-faced, red-haired teenager. Odd, introverted, nice-looking in a bewildered sort of way, he bumbled good-naturedly through public school and emerged from university with a gentleman's degree in English literature.

Schoolteaching was hard for him. His pupils liked him, for he was gentle and kind; for the same reasons, they took advantage of him. When he fled from the disorder of his classroom, he found comfort in the arms of the headmistress, a big, handsome, forty-year-old woman who took him aside, at first, to try and help him through his probationary year; and then, seeing that her encouragement and professional advice were making no difference to Harry's performance as a teacher, she took him to her bed. She would settle on top of him like a great, white, broody goose. With her eyes squeezed shut, she would rock and rock, shouting his name through tightly clenched teeth, until at last she would shudder and collapse, smothering him with her heavy, hot breasts. Eventually the school governors found out and objected. Harry had to go. To save her own job, the headmistress wrote a good enough reference to ensure his acceptance as a volunteer with the Sudanese ministry of education, and he left.

Sudan was hard for him, too.

He was posted to a girls' school in the deserts of the northern province. His head seemed to blaze with heat. His skin was dried by the baking sunlight, so that his knuckles split and bled. His pale eyes were dazzled by a glaring emptiness of sand and sky. He tried his best in the classroom, where sixty girls shared twenty desks, twenty books and twenty pens. Aged between fifteen and nineteen, the girls were lovelier than anything Harry had ever seen: impossibly slim, with perfect white teeth and gleaming, velvet-black skin. They made life a misery for him, giggling and hooting and chattering from the start of each lesson to the end. They cheated in the most blatant, outrageous ways when he tried to set tests, concealing notes in the folds of their dresses, whispering and signaling and even shouting in the overcrowded room to get the answers from their friends.

Lovely, sleek, inaccessible girls... Some of them were in love with Harry Clewe, the tall, white-skinned, flame-headed, foreign teacher whose lessons were so noisy. They would run round behind him, to reach up and touch his hair; they'd never seen anything like it before.

When the school was closed by strikes, Harry traveled on the Nile steamer. With no alternative, he drank water straight from the river, a gazpacho of feces, mud and globules of diesel oil. Coming ashore at riverside villages, his stomach in cramp and his head ablaze, all he wanted was to squat in the shade of a palm tree and void his gut in a torrent of brown liquid. But what happened? Children crowded round him, grabbing his hands, touching his face, jumping to stroke his hair. They laughed and sang, they loaded his arms with oranges and grapefruit and smooth golden pebbles from the riverbank. Why? They led an old man to him, a blind man who gripped his shoulders and stared blankly into his eyes before leaning forward and planting a kiss on Harry's forehead. Why? The children clapped, the women burst into tears. Why? In Port Sudan, ghastly beyond imagination, there were teenage soldiers goose-stepping on the Red Sea beaches, their boots all split, their uniforms too small, their rifles burst and broken. Swedish sailors from the supertankers bought boys in the marketplace and fucked them in shuttered hotel rooms.

Why was it all so ugly? Why were so many things smashed and discarded which could have been mended and used? Why was the desert strewn with bones?

Sudan was hard for Harry Clewe. The angel followed him there. Whole days slipped by as he lay on his rope bed, closeted from the sun, his senses obliterated by migraine. Then he spent evenings by the river, awakened to exhilarating sleeplessness by an infusion of tea and marijuana. The long, cool nights were a blessed relief for him, when, having driven off the pariah dogs by flinging handfuls of sand at them, he would sit by the Nile with a torch and a book of star maps and lose himself in study of the brilliant constellations. The stars were his asylum. So the months passed until the end of his contract. Released from school and the torture of teaching, he traveled on trucks to the barren lands in the west and south of the country before reporting to the ministry of education in Khartoum, returning at last to Wales with a dose of salmonella poisoning, a hepatitis hangover and a Mercedes-Benz.

And now, the natterjack toad. He carried it with him all the time, bundled in the spotted red neckerchief. The girl, Sarah, had found it in his garden. She'd touched it and stroked it, declaring it precious. It was precious to Harry Clewe. The toadstone was big magic.

7

Harry applied the power of the toadstone to his immediate domestic problems.

Firstly, the shocks in his bathroom.

He dropped the toad into his bath, flopping it from the neckerchief into the water. He was thrilled to see it swimming; it was indeed transformed in this new element. The natterjack strode through the water, propelled by powerful thrusts of its hind legs, sleek with muscle, quite altered from its previous pustular ugliness. The skin on its belly and flanks, which had hung in unhealthy folds when the toad was dry, became taut. When it bumped its nose on the side of the bath, it tumbled round and swam purposefully in the other direction. The golden eyes shone like searchlights on the bridge of a minesweeper. The toad's forearms were exquisite; it pulled through the water with its tiny translucent fingers. Transformed, the natterjack was a marvel, a fossil come back to life.

Harry knelt at the bath and watched for a few minutes. Then he stood up, reached through the door and felt for the switch outside the bathroom. He switched on the power, turned round and knelt at the bath again.

The natterjack was still moving through the water. But not swimming.

Every few seconds, the hind legs convulsed and thrashed so that the toad surged forward. Then it was still. The forearms stretched out, rigid and useless; the spasms sent the toad banging into the white enamel or spiraling under the water in a nose dive. In the center of those brilliant eyes, the pupils were no longer elliptical: they'd grown big, suffusing the gold with a glistening black. The toad was drowning. A string of pearly bubbles belched from its mouth. It sank to the bottom of the bath, where it lay on its back and quivered. Harry plunged his hand into the water. There was a jolt of power the length of his arm, a blow like a rabbit punch at the back of his neck. But he had the toad. He bolted to the living room and fell onto the sofa.

In no time at all, more quickly than Harry did, the toad recovered. It settled comfortably into the red neckerchief, apparently relaxed after its exercise in the bath. Its pupils resumed their original shape and size. Harry rubbed at the ache in his shoulder and jaw. He lifted the toad to his mouth and pressed his lips to the bumpy, brown head.

The magic would work for him. Switching off the power again, he took off all his clothes, including his wellington boots, and slipped into the bath. The natterjack sculled around his legs. It reassured him to see how smoothly and gracefully it swam, as though this were greater proof of his safety than the switch by the bathroom door. When he lay in the lukewarm water, the toad climbed onto the islands of white flesh and sat there, blinking and resting. It rowed through the gray, soapy water and pulled itself onto his slippery skin. Padding along an exposed thigh, tugging at the springy red hairs with its fingers, it nestled in his groin. It aroused him. He felt his belly stirring and his throat go dry. The toad swarmed on him, clasping with its forearms, just as he'd seen in the library book photographs. It smiled blissfully. Harry smiled too. The toad held on. It butted its face on him, it pressed with its velvet belly, it fluttered the delicate fingers... until Harry arched from the water, shouting the name of the girl he hadn't seen for a week but whose face and sweet golden skin he couldn't forget for an instant. The toad swam away, trailing a thread of silvery slime.

Secondly, the rats.

The rats were increasingly noisy at night. As it grew colder outside, they were more and more inclined to come into the cottage roof and warm themselves on the chimney stack. Harry would lie awake and hear their plodding footsteps a few feet above his head, separated from him by a sheet of plasterboard. Sometimes they would play like puppies, two or three of them, throwing a nail or a crumbled piece of brick across the roof space and wrestling for it. So the game went on, in the dust and rubble and the warm, dark shadows. Where there was a crack in the board or a gap around a light fitting, Harry could actually see the quivering pink snouts, sniffing the air of his bedroom. Showers of dust cascaded through. Then, exasperated and frightened, he would stand on his bed and hammer his fists on the ceiling, listening with satisfaction as the rats fled to the roof space elsewhere in the terrace.

The toad was precious. Sarah had found it and held it and given it to him. It might yet lure her back to his garden.

Before he went to bed, he put the natterjack in the roof space over his bedroom. He did this by pushing open a trap door in the center of the ceiling. When he flashed a torch into the cobwebs, all was silence and dust. Around the toad's body he'd gently attached a length of string which could slip neither forward over its forearms nor backward over its hind legs. Once the creature was settled on the red neckerchief, itself a precious thing that the girl had worn and had given him, he closed the trap door. The string trailed down to his bed. Tied around his wrist, it connected him with the toad; throughout the night, he could feel its movements, its pulse, its power, whether he woke or slept.

No rats. In the morning, when Harry retrieved it from the ceiling, the toad was peacefully dozing, replete after a feast of spiders. It was a mutually satisfactory arrangement. The rats no longer came to the roof space. To Harry Clewe, it seemed that the toadstone protected him from them... as it protected him from the dangerous wiring and might yet deliver the girl to him.

8

Harry's obsession with the toad and his brooding over Sarah were responsible for a sharp decline in his enthusiasm for gardening.

It was autumn. The middle of September saw an end to the enveloping warmth of summer. The mornings were misty and gray, wrapping the oak trees at the top of the hotel garden with silver cobwebs. It was much cooler. Harry was reluctant to get out of bed and into his damp, dirty trousers, into the wellington boots with crumbs of leaf mold inside them, into a shirt which smelled of smoke. Reassured by the tension in the string around his wrist, after another night undisturbed by rats, he would turn over and go back to sleep. Until then, he'd been perfectly punctual, arriving at the hotel at eight o'clock every morning and working until one o'clock in the afternoon. But now he'd lost interest in the hotel garden. It had been a novelty, after a year in Sudan and his convalescence in Shrewsbury. In reality, he'd made little impression on it. The wall was rebuilt and might be safe for a year or two, but it compared unfavorably with its predecessor, which had stood for a century until he'd brought it down with a crash. Otherwise, he'd spent weeks cutting the rhododendron hedges and making the garden tidy. He'd cleaned out the pond, which had been choked with a thick carpet of grass he'd cut away and peeled off like a massive bearskin rug. Underneath, there was a shallow pool of brown water, heaving with insect life reactivated by the sudden sunlight: skaters and boatmen zigzagged on the smooth, dark surface. He'd enjoyed that, and his hours in the smoke of the fire had passed pleasantly enough: the clucking of jackdaws, the aromatic smoke of the burning branches and the chance to browse in an old newspaper; the flycatchers and swifts and the stinkhorn.... The summer had gone by in a dream, quite unlike the bruising disorder of his classroom.

But he'd achieved nothing in the garden that a healthy Boy Scout couldn't have done just as well.

Now he was late for work again. The garden had changed. It was gray and chill. The grass was drenched with dew. Underfoot there was a mat of wet leaves. The jackdaws drooped on the glistening branches like black, decaying fruit. The bronze and copper of autumn were deadly metallic without the sun to break through the mist and light them up. Harry shuddered and trudged up the path. He didn't feel like raking in the sodden undergrowth, but he took some tools to the top where he could hide from the manager. He stopped at the pond. The water was as smooth as wax, apart from the scribbling of insects on it.

He knelt down and took the natterjack from inside his shirt. It was used to being there, relaxed in the neckerchief on the skin of his stomach. Sometimes, if it sensed that Harry was tense, the toad became tense as well; then he'd feel it swelling, rowing its legs, or excreting a blob of feces. But now it was quiet as a stone, with its eyes closed tight. Without the startling brightness of those yellow bulbs, the toad was as dull as an old turnip. He held it to his mouth and breathed some warmth on its head. The toad woke up. It squirmed in his hand, flicked its eyes open, flickered its tongue. Harry felt his stomach go loose with a delicious caving. He clenched his eyelids shut and dreamed of Sarah.

For the rest of the morning, Harry sat and watched the toad about its business in the pond. It lowered itself into the water, submerged apart from its periscopic eyes. It launched a series of raids on the insects in the mosses and weeds, gorging on the mayfly nymphs, the saucer bugs, the water scorpions. Then it would stride to the land again with rhythmic and powerful thrusts of its hind legs, so that Harry could help it out of the pond and put it in the long grass. When it was ready, the toad returned to the water. It reminded Harry of the sleek, fat Arabs, the Wabenzi, he'd seen around a swimming pool in Khartoum.

Inevitably, the time had come when the hotel manager was no longer satisfied with Harry's performance as a gardener. That day, the man climbed into the garden to see how the work was progressing. He was a small, dapper, middle-aged fellow whom Harry liked, a Lancashire businessman who'd moved into Beddgelert some years before. Harry appreciated that he'd been given the gardening job in a generous spirit, when it would have been easier for the manager to turn him away and hire someone more obviously competent. He would have felt guilty about his recent laziness, except that his obsession with the girl and the natterjack precluded any other feeling. Now, he whirled from the pond at the approaching footsteps and cringed with embarrassment at disappointing his employer.

"Late again this morning, Harry?" the man began. "You haven't done much the last few days, have you? What are you doing now? Just playing with the pond? I've a feeling I won't be wanting a gardener any more, now that you've tidied up the wall at the bottom. Come inside, lad. I'll pay you up to date and you can go home."

He patted Harry affectionately on the shoulder. "Don't look so glum!" he said. "You haven't done too badly, you know. But I don't think the gardening's really in your line, is it? What the hell have you done to your face? And your specs?"

Harry muttered a brief account of his fall from the rocks. He was sorry that the manager was disappointed in him. He explained the injury to his cheek, which was healing in such a colorful way.

"You've been in the wars, my lad," the manager said. "You should have stuck to schoolteaching. I expect you were good at that. Come on, leave all this dirty gardening to someone else."

Harry waited for him to start down the steps, before kneeling again to try and retrieve the toad. It had hauled itself onto an island in the middle of the pond. Harry judged the distance, about six feet from him, stood up and attempted a jump onto another stone which protruded above the surface of the water. Perhaps because of his broken glasses, he misjudged the leap. He hit the stone, swayed for a second, and, crying out, trod heavily into the pond. It was much deeper than he'd thought it would be, almost to his waist, and very cold. The bottom was slimy and uneven; he had to put his arm sharply into the water to try and steady himself or else he would have fallen over completely. With the splashing commotion, the toad was galvanized into action. It catapulted into the water and dived, leaving only a string of bubbles to show where it had gone. At the same time, the manager came back to see what was happening.

"Bloody hell, Harry! What are you doing? Get out of there!"

Harry said nothing. He blinked, standing stupidly in the pond as the waves lapped at his thighs. His arm was draped with icy green weeds. The cold was in his bones, sapping him. The heat drained from him. The power of the toadstone was gone, lost in the deep, green pool.

"I slipped," he eventually succeeded in saying. Then, having decided there was nothing he could do that would humiliate him further, he waded after the disappearing toad, moaning incoherently, putting both his hands into the water and dragging them through the weed.

"Just get out, for heaven's sake!" the manager snapped. "What the hell are you looking for?"

Harry ignored him. Miraculously, he felt between his fingers the familiar, wrinkled shape of his natterjack, which he raised triumphantly from the surface in a welter of greens and browns and splattering silver. The power, which he thought he might have lost for ever, flooded through him again. Oblivious of the other man's presence, concerned only that he'd found the precious toad, Harry brought it to his lips again and kissed it. His throat was thick with emotion. His eyes blurred with tears.

The manager starting shouting. He was frightened and angry; he'd never seen anyone kissing a toad before. Half a minute later, after the two men had grappled clumsily on the edge of the pond, the ex-gardener toppled the hotel manager into the water. Waiting only long enough to see that the man wasn't hurt and to settle the toad on his heaving stomach, Harry bolted down the garden steps. He dashed through the hotel and into the street. Water and weeds streamed from his trousers as he ran squelching along the pavement and jumped into his car. Trembling uncontrollably, hardly able to believe that he'd tumbled a grown man into a brown pond, Harry drove wildly from the car park and out of the village.

The bullet-hole crack in the top right-hand corner of the windscreen and the bullet-hole crack in his glasses fused in a kaleidoscopic sunburst. Besides, he could hardly see for tears. But, with the toad in the neckerchief hot on his belly, and the Wabenzi power under his right boot, he didn't need to see. He was flying! He hurtled through the valley mist and broke into a glittering heaven of clear, bright sunshine.

Calming himself before he reached his own village, he pulled into some rough parking at the side of the road. His panic had been transmitted to the natterjack. Even as he was exhilarated by his flight from Beddgelert, he'd been aware of the toad's discomfort. Stopping the car and switching off the engine, he unbuttoned his shirt. The toad was swollen tight, shiny and smooth; the warts and carbuncles had vanished. It was nearly twice its usual size. He put it down on the passenger seat. There it sat, with its fingers clasped across its chest, the hind legs bunched as though ready for a leap. Harry felt his stomach tingling; opening his shirt, he saw that his skin was blotchy and red, nettled by the toad's poison. Moreover, it had oozed a pearl of excreta onto the waistband of his trousers.

For all of this, instead of being repulsed by the creature, Harry loved the natterjack more. They'd shared a moment of danger. With the toad pressed against him, he'd felt the sting of its acrid sweat. It was a kind of consummation.

At home, he marshaled his thoughts. Once the toad had assured him that the water was safe, he removed it from the bath and set it on the neckerchief. It sat and blinked at him, framed by the silver columns of the taps, like a fat little god in an oriental shrine. Harry lay in the warm bath. The irritation on his stomach was gone. The water was soon brown with earth from the garden pond, swirling with strands of emerald weed. From inside his boots or a crease in his trousers, a number of aquatic insects had arrived in the bath; they stalked and sculled about, so light on their spindly legs and covered with the finest of hairs that they didn't break the surface, but trod as though they were on dry land. They were water measurers. Harry reached for the toad and held it close to the busy insects. It lashed out its tongue and they were gone. He replaced the toad on the spotted neckerchief.

While the water cooled, he assessed his position. He had no job. The rent on the cottage was due. The car was expensive to run. He was owed some money at the hotel, but he wasn't sure he could go and collect it, after his skirmish with the manager. Far more important, he hadn't seen Sarah for nearly a fortnight. The realization was a jolt to him, almost as strong as the jolts he'd had from the bathroom taps. Again he was filled with courage and determination by the proximity of the toad, as it beamed at him and licked its chops on the edge of the bath....

The power of the toadstone! The jewel in the head of the pustular toad!

If only he'd had it in school, when he was teaching! If only he'd had it in Sudan! To outface those gleaming, untouchable girls! To outface the big-bellied children with flies in their eyes! To outface the cripples he'd seen in Kosti and Kadugli and Khartoum, gnawing on discarded bicycle tires!

He surged with confidence. Gripping the sides of the bath, he stood up in a spectacular whooshing of water. He was strong! He was armed! That day, he'd pushed a rich man into a pond! How many people in Beddgelert had done that? How many in Wales?

Bath water and threads of weed coursed down his body. For once in his life, he was sure what he was going to do. With the toad in his pocket, he would go down to the hotel and demand the money due to him. If the manager paid, Harry would buy him a drink; if not, Harry would carry the little man into the garden and throw him into the pond again.

Then, in search of Sarah...

9

By eight o'clock that evening, it was dark outside. A fine drizzle was blowing in folds of mist from the surrounding mountains: the kind of drizzle that drenches everything and penetrates every corner of man and countryside and machinery.

Harry had paid minute attention to his appearance. For the first time since coming to Wales, he'd put on a collar and tie and a sports jacket. He'd shaved carefully and dabbed on a drop of cologne from a bottle he hadn't opened for more than a year, since his weekends under the head-mistress. Washed and combed, his hair blazed like a beacon. The bruises on his cheek were almost gone, faded to a faint discoloring of the skin. In clean clothes from top to bottom, with the tie uncomfortably knotted at his throat, in a whiff of talcum powder and aftershave, Harry stepped from the cottage and met a blanket of rain. The weight of the toad in his jacket pocket was wonderfully reassuring. He ran to the car, which was parked under cover in the nearby farmyard.

It refused to start. Time and time again he turned over the engine, but there was no spark. Not wanting to flatten the battery, he waited in the darkness of the shed with his hands between his thighs, before trying again. The engine churned and churned but wouldn't fire. Swearing very loudly, gripping the bundled toad in his pocket to try and feel the power of its pulse, he leaped out of the car, wrenched open the bonnet and randomly jetted a spray of damp-start into the sooted, black contraptions of the big engine. To his astonishment and delight, it exploded into life the next time he tried it. The noise made the corrugated-iron shed rattle and thrum. Wonderfully exhilarated, buzzing with the combined power of toadstone and Wabenzi, Harry drove down to Beddgelert. The rain swept over and around the topless car, so he was still quite dry when he parked in the shelter of the great black yew.

Checking his pockets for the two things most crucial to the success of the evening, his wallet and the natterjack toad, he ducked through the glistening, empty streets of the village and stepped unhesitatingly into the hotel. Only then, in the warm, softly lit reception, he felt the qualms in his belly that he'd come back to confront the manager.

But the toad was strong magic. Without noticing that Harry Clewe was standing damply on the doormat, the man came strutting out of the kitchen, on his way to the bar with an ice-bucket under his arm. He was immaculate in a light-weight gray suit, a white shirt with his initials embroidered on the breast pocket, and a lemon yellow tie. His suede shoes were silent on the deep carpet. For contrast, Harry caught sight of himself in a full-length mirror: his limp, shapeless schoolteacher's jacket with frayed cuffs and worn elbows, his baggy schoolteacher's trousers. Instinctively, he thrust his hand into his pocket and gripped the toad. It was as hot as a pie. The heat flooded his arm.

"Excuse me!" he called out. The manager looked up to see who was there.

"Harry!" the man exclaimed. "Harry Clewe!" He came forward, smiling warmly, running his eyes from Harry's feet to his gleaming red hair. "That's more like it!" he said. "The gardening didn't suit you, did it? Are you going back to schoolteaching? Come on, Harry, my lad! Let me get you a drink! I owe you some money, too."

As influential people do, he turned away without waiting for a reply, knowing that Harry would follow him.

Harry went into the bar. From the glances and whispers of the other drinkers, he could tell that the morning's incident was common knowledge; inevitably, in a village community, especially when the publican was involved. The manager appeared on the other side of the bar and rubbed his hands briskly together.

"Ladies and gentlemen," he announced to the whole room, "this is Harry Clewe! Harry threw me into the pond this morning. I always buy drinks for people who throw me into a pond. I like eccentrics, that's one reason... and being so small, I have to keep on the right side of dangerous folks! What'll you have, young man?"

He pulled a foaming pint and pushed it toward Harry, before turning to the till for a handful of pound notes. He counted them onto the bar.

"All square then, Harry?" he said. "I'd use the money to get your glasses fixed, if I were you. You did me a world of good this morning, you know. Life can be bloody dull in Wales. The whole village needs a good shake-up. It takes a madman like you to do it!"

The toad flexed and shifted. Enfolded in the spotted neckerchief, it dreamed of water boatmen and saucer bugs in a sunlit pool. Harry slipped the money into his wallet and gulped his beer. When the time came, he bought a drink for the manager and another for himself. Famous, heroic, he basked in his notoriety. He glowed with the heat of the toadstone in his pocket and the power it gave him. At ten o'clock on a rainswept September night, he shook the manager's hand and left the hotel, bent on the achievement of his second and far more important goal.

It was raining much harder. The village drummed in the downpour, the hills huddled in a blanket of mist. The river roared. The cobweb spray, which had drenched the car and made it so hard to start when Harry left the cottage, had become a deluge. The night was very dark. The streets were deserted. Harry stepped into the middle of the road and stood there until his jacket was heavy with water, until his hair was plastered to his skull. The rain ran behind his ears and into the collar of his shirt; it trickled into the small of his back, between his buttocks, among the coils of hair in his groin. Then, when he was so wet that there was no reason to try and shelter, he strolled through the village. The toad slept in his pocket.

It would be easy to find where Sarah lived. She'd only

said that she used a caravan in her uncle's garden, but Harry was sure he could locate her. He crossed the bridge, walked the pavement to the restaurant where she worked, and, in the orange blur of a streetlamp, he again reflected on the painting she'd done. It streamed with rain, gleaming as though it were freshly varnished, and the glare made it hard to see all the picture at once. Harry angled his head this way and that, trying to see the prince's face. More importantly, he squinted for the name of Sarah's uncle.

"Proprietor: Alf Butterfield," it said in one corner of the painting, the letters just big enough to read in a pool of blood. Good: not a Jones or a Williams or a Roberts. The address should be easy to find in a telephone directory.

So Harry splashed to the telephone kiosk, which was outside the post office in the middle of the village, and stepped inside it. Most of the windows were broken and every inch of space was covered with obscene graffiti, much of it misspelled. But the kiosk was brightly lit and the directory was intact. In a moment, he'd found the only A. Butterfield in Beddgelert and noted the address: a house nearby. He slammed the directory shut. But suddenly, shivering in his cold, drenched clothes, knowing that the girl he wanted was so close to him and yet so far out of reach, he felt his confidence draining away.

What would he do if he found her? What could he say, after his humiliation on the cliffs? What would he do if Patrick, the bare-footed climber, was there?

The stimulus of alcohol was deserting him. His body was frail and sticklike, trembling and brittle. His schoolteacher clothes were sodden. His glasses were broken.

Why had he come this far? What was he going to do next?

Leaning in the glare of the kiosk, surrounded by a teeming black night, he peered through the shattered lens of his glasses, through the shattered windows of the telephone box. Everything was blurred. His face was a distorted reflection of ill-matching splinters, a jigsaw of blank and bloodless features and a mat of dripping, gingery hair. The tension in his belly and his fractured vision spawned the first of the sparks in the corner of his right eye... the angel, a beautiful, bright angel bringing pain and wretchedness for Harry Clewe. He groaned horribly at the sight of it. He whipped off his glasses and clawed at his eyeballs, as though he might tear them out and extinguish the sparks forever. But the sparks wouldn't shift. The angel had come for him again.

He groped into his pocket, put the heavy bundle of the spotted red neckerchief on top of the telephone directory and unfolded it. There was the toad, its eyes closed tightly, locking the magic inside the potato ugliness of its head. With quivering hands, Harry picked it up... and the surge of strength it gave him was lovelier than morphine, the blotting paper of pain. His moaning became less feverish. He caressed the toad and blew softly on its skin. The moment it slid open the golden eyes, Harry was flooded with warmth. The jewel was unlocked.

The natterjack stretched itself awake in his hands. He held it to his forehead and pressed it there. It writhed on his skin, cool and dry and comforting. With his eyes squeezed shut, he fused his jumbled thoughts into a single image of the golden girl in his golden garden. Sarah, oh Sarah, oh Sarah... His fingers burned with the heat of her skin, as the toad swelled up. His head was on fire. Sarah, oh Sarah, oh Sarah... He smothered the toad to his face.

Until his knees buckled. He crumpled to the floor. Fireworks exploded in his head, his eyeballs rolled, his ears jangled with bells....

Real bells. The telephone was ringing.

Harry squealed. He opened his eyes, stood up and slapped the toad onto the directory. His vision had cleared and, as always, the disappearance of the sparks brought the first pulse of pain to his head. Snatching the neckerchief, he covered the toad with it. The ringing continued, harsh and loud in the brightness of the kiosk. Simply to stop the noise, Harry picked up the receiver and automatically put it to his ear.

"Who is it?" he croaked.

A voice said, "What are you doing in there?"

Harry leaped from the receiver as though it had scalded his ear. He whirled round and round inside the kiosk. Through the broken windows, everything was black, streaming with black rain. When he thrust his glasses onto his face again, he could see lights in nearby houses, the ghostly flicker of televisions. Someone was drawing the curtains in an upstairs room. With the blood beating in his temples, unable to resist the magnetism of the telephone, he picked up the receiver and whispered into it.

"Who are you? Where are you? Can I see you?"

There was silence. The curtains shifted in another house. A light went off further down the street. Then the voice came again. It was a woman.

"No, you can't see me. But I can see you. I've been watching you. Are you sick or something? Are you mad?"

There was a click and the line went dead.

He banged the phone down. Under the neckerchief, the toad was swollen as though it might burst into a thousand shreds of rubbery skin. Hurriedly, he thrust it into his pocket. Then he flung himself from the kiosk and ran as fast as he could along the pavement. Every lighted window he passed, every twitch of a curtain, was a torment to him. Slowing down, he had the presence of mind to note one of the houses as the address he'd found in the directory, and he saw the white mass of a caravan in the garden; no light in it, just a single lighted room upstairs in the house itself.

He sprinted on to where the car was dry in the dense shelter of the yew. As carefully as if he were handling a piece of antique glass, he placed the toad on the passenger seat. In the gloom, he could see it slowly relaxing, deflating until it was wrinkled and flabby again and its golden eyes were shut. Harry relaxed, too. To try and still his hammering head, he leaned out of the car door and inserted two fingers to the back of his throat. He retched noisily, barking like a dog, as he'd learned to retch when he was a little boy, and lost all the beer with a khaki-colored stew he'd had at midday. At last, at the seventh or eighth churning attempt, the car started. He drove out of the waterlogged valley and into the waterlogged hills, parking under the cover of the shed.

For a few more minutes he sat in the darkness and listened as the rain drummed on the corrugated iron roof, as the big, hot engine ticked and cooled, and then he went into the cottage.

"You deserve a night off," he said to the natterjack, when he went upstairs to bed.

Instead of putting the toad in the ceiling with the string around its belly, he made a nest for it with the neckerchief in the drawer of his bedside table. That night, the rats could have the run of the roof. He was too tired to worry about them. He stripped, dried himself on a towel and climbed into bed. Utterly drained, Harry Clewe fell straight away into a deep sleep.

10

Three mornings later, Harry drove into Caernarfon to have his glasses repaired.

He'd done very little since his dismissal from the hotel. He wrote to Lizzie, his beloved sister, who was recovering slowly and painfully at home after her riding accident, but he didn't mention Sarah, nor the natterjack toad. He hoped very much that Lizzie would write back. He walked the woods and the hills, with the toad inside his shirt. Under the birch trees there was the fly agaric with its fairy-tale red umbrella; in the pine forest, the gagging pungency of stinkhorn. Thousands of acorns choked the roadside gutters. It was a harvest time for the gray squirrels, which raced overhead in the sunlit oak branches. The jays were the bandits of the woodland, mustached and brazen. A barn owl, hunting in bright daylight over an open field, drifted and feinted like a moth, plunging into a clump of long grass; then it rose, with something squirming in its talons. A cormorant fished on Llyn y Gadair, the lake by his cottage, low in the water, lethal and black as a submarine. In the woods, Harry sat down and took the toad out of his shirt. He put it into the leaf mold for a feast of lice and ants and the delicate little snails whose shells it crunched like breakfast cereal.

But, because of his shattered glasses, the branches and their remaining leaves were a twinkling blur, through which the jays and the squirrels moved like ghosts. The only thing that stayed in focus, close to him both physically and in spirit, was the toad. He was delighted, then, to have his lens repaired. It meant that, ostensibly, he was another step closer to a complete recovery from his fall.

To celebrate his improved visibility, Harry gulped a couple of pints of beer in the Black Boy and then drove from Caernarfon as fast as the car would go. He knew the road well. All the world was lovely, sparkling in the glassy autumn air. The car sprang out of town and into the hills, the exhaust crackling so loudly that the sheep stampeded in the fields. There was a hot smell of burning oil and a trailing haze of blue smoke, so that Harry wondered how much longer the Wabenzi power would be with him. Faster and faster he traveled, foot hard down. He'd taken the toad out of his shirt and set it on the dashboard, where it blinked grimly and squatted against the howl of cold air.

A familiar vehicle came into sight ahead of him. He closed rapidly on it. It was Patrick's van. Unable to overtake through a series of narrow bends, Harry found his long red bonnet almost nudging the van's battered back door. Then he braked and dropped away at the sight of Sarah's helmet of golden hair, which swiveled until he could see her face dimly through the gloom of the window. It was his first glimpse of her since the day he'd been climbing.

Patrick must have seen the car in his mirror and said something to the girl, for she raised a hand and waved. Harry flashed his headlamps in reply, and at this the van accelerated so sharply that its tires squealed on the twisting turns of the road. Harry's heart began to thump. He squeezed the throttle enough to bring his car close to the van again. The road straightened, although it was still quite narrow. Harry drew back while the van labored noisily in front of him; it was hard to have a view from the left-hand-drive car. Seeing there was no oncoming traffic, he flashed his headlamps again, pulled out and floored the accelerator. The car gathered itself like a tomcat and shot forward.

Level with the van, driver's door to driver's door, Harry had a split-second's view of Patrick's grinning face, and there was Sarah as well, leaning across to wave.... Her mouth opened and closed. Her eyes flickered with alarm. Concentrating on the road, Harry realized that Patrick had swung out deliberately to try and stop him from overtaking. A telegraph pole flashed close to his offside wing. His tires were in the loose gravel of the verge. A bank of brambles lashed the length of the car. At this, the toad sprang from the dashboard. The impact was breathtaking. All its turnip-weight landed in Harry's groin.

Gasping, his eyes tingling, he twitched the car through the narrowing gap. He held the accelerator to the floor and the blue van shrank in his mirror. It disappeared in a comet trail of burnt oil.

Harry bellowed with excitement. He'd seen Sarah! He'd left the rock-climber laboring in his slipstream! The toad, landing in his groin, had given him the strength when he'd needed it. He had all the power and magic he'd ever craved!

Gradually he slowed down so that he could put the toad on the dashboard again. He wondered if Patrick and Sarah had seen it, lumped on the spotted red neckerchief. He didn't mind if they had: it wasn't a secret. The hotel manager had seen it, and so had an anonymous woman from a window overlooking the telephone kiosk in Beddgelert. Now Harry had seen Sarah again and he knew where she lived. Moreover, he had the toadstone, locked in the natterjack's head. He must use it while the power was good and while there was time.

It was the end of September. Soon the girl would be returning to London.

11

Harry sat in his garden until the evening grew dark and cool. It was a still, dry night. The sky was deep blue. Venus was bright over Hebog. A toenail moon shivered on the horizon of black mountains. There was a shuffle and click of hunters in the undergrowth, in the leaning branches of the ash tree: the hedgehog, turning pebbles for a meal of snails; the zigzagging of bats, folding a leathery wing. And the toad was alive with the coming of night.

Harry put on a navy blue pullover and dark gray trousers. He took off his tennis shoes and stepped into his wellington boots. Like the hedgehog, the bat and the toad, he was wide awake in the twilight. He would learn from the toad, to be a slow, silent hunter, as patient as the stones it resembled, deliberate and unhurried in his movements. That was the way it worked: no dash, no thrilling chase, but a prehistoric slow motion. This time, he wouldn't make the mistake of exposing himself in the light of a telephone kiosk. He was ready, in his dark clothing, to match the deepening shadows.

He drove slowly toward Beddgelert. There were no headlamps but his own; Harry and the toad were alone beneath the mass of Snowdon. The mountain road plunged into the valley, where the world was darker and darker, where he stopped in the pitchy gloom of the yew tree.

Leaving the car, he walked quickly along the pavement, moving in the deepest shadows of bushes and hedges, avoiding the orange glow of the streetlamps. He had no plan. With the heavy bulge of the toad in his trouser pocket, he determined only to try and see Sarah again, perhaps to talk to her if Patrick wasn't there. Simply to be with her and see the spark in her gray gull's eyes, the suppleness of her throat and her hands... His bowels loosened at the thought. As he walked past the glare of the telephone kiosk, he shuddered to remember his exposure inside it. The village was quite silent, apart from a tinkling of laughter from the hotel bar. He glimpsed the blue-gray burning of televisions in softly lit living rooms. In a minute he could see the house and the caravan he was looking for. He tiptoed closer, fondling the toad in his pocket. It was stretching its legs in the folded neckerchief.

Harry stopped in the coal-black shadow of a horse chestnut. The house was directly opposite him, with a downstairs room brightly lit; probably the kitchen, with the window steamed up. Someone was moving around inside the room, Sarah's uncle, burly and heavily bearded, drifting dimly here and there like a great fish in a muddy aquarium. The caravan, a white tourer, was parked in the front garden; there was a light inside it. Harry leaned on the horse chestnut, quite giddy with the idea that the girl was there. His throat tightened and his scalp prickled. Better still, there was no sign of Patrick's van. With a sudden surge of confidence triggered by the stirrings of the toad in his pocket and the almost unbearable proximity of the girl, Harry crossed the road and strode toward the house. He stopped at the garden gate, out of sight of the kitchen window, and stared at the light inside the caravan. And there she was.

The window was perfectly clear. Against the surrounding darkness, it was like watching the girl on film; the big square screen was in focus and full of color. She was sitting down, with a magazine open on the table in front of her, wearing the short-sleeved white blouse she'd worn in the restaurant, still with the pen and notebook in her breast pocket. Probably she had the blue skirt on as well, and the white socks. She frowned as she read, then quickly riffled the pages. Her hair fell down and hid her face as she leaned to look closely at a photograph, and when she sat up straight again she pushed it from her forehead with a smart flick of her fingers. Harry's stomach turned over at the flex of her brown, bare arm. Swallowing hard, he was about to step forward and approach the caravan door, when he saw her shut the magazine and turn her face to the window. She stared straight at him.

He froze, his chest pounding. Then he realized that she couldn't see him. From inside the caravan, the windows were black mirrors in which she'd see nothing but her own reflection. That was what she was looking at, although she seemed to be gazing directly into Harry's eyes. She examined her hair, bunching it tightly behind her head with both her hands. She angled her face this way and that, and Harry could see her tiny white ears and her brown neck. He gasped at a glimpse of the marbled whiteness under her arms; his throat ached at the tautening of her breasts against the schoolgirl's blouse. She let go of her hair and shook it loose. Coming very close to the glass, she inspected the corner of her nostril where the spot had been: the redness was almost gone. She bared her teeth at Harry, snarling like a stoat, and finally, seeing that she was pretty and young and irresistible, she licked her lips with a pink, wet tongue, winked at herself and then giggled with one hand to her mouth.

Charged with desire, Harry strode across the lawn toward her. The girl spoke to her own reflection... so that, puzzled by this, Harry stopped in the middle of the lawn. In answer to whatever the girl had said, Patrick sat up behind her.

The magic of the toadstone deserted Harry Clewe at that moment. The rock-climber's appearance was so sudden and unexpected that Harry's mind went blank. He was stranded on the lawn. There were no shadows to hide him. Patrick stood up, tousled and frowning and fiercely bearded, and moved from the caravan window to the door. The handle turned. He was coming out. Unable to retrace his steps to the safety of the street, Harry dashed forward and dived headlong underneath the caravan.

He lay there, with the blood banging in the back of his head, his chest heaving. It was very dark, but he could make out the two wheels on either side and the metal struts supporting the vehicle at each corner. A tangle of electricity cables and a transparent plastic water pipe ran to the house; there was a big blue gas bottle. The bottom of the caravan was no more than a few inches from his face, with the axle jutting near his face, caked with black oil; Harry had been lucky, in his panic, not to have cracked his head on it. Struggling to control his breathing, he lay on the hard, dry ground and waited for Patrick to come out. He heard voices, masculine and feminine, muffled so that he couldn't catch what they were saying, and then the door opened, shedding a shaft of light across the lawn. Patrick's bare feet stepped onto the grass. The door closed with a click and the garden was dark again.

Cramped flat underneath the caravan, Harry held his breath and watched the feet tread away from the house and stop, wide apart, at a flowerbed near the garden gate. After a few moments' silence, a powerful jet of urine splashed into the soil, foaming noisily until the feet adjusted and the jet was redirected onto the lawn, where it fell with no more than a hiss. The flow decreased and faltered, shorter and shorter spurts stopping in a dribble. The rock-climber turned and walked back to the caravan, wiping the spattered urine from his feet on the longer tufts of grass which had grown around the gas bottle, close enough for Harry to see the callused soles and horny toenails. As Patrick opened the door again, the column of light fell across the garden. The man stepped inside and shut the door, so that the caravan creaked above Harry's head. Then there was darkness and silence.

Harry relaxed. In the circumstances, he was very comfortable. It was good to lie on the dry, warm ground, where the light from the street and the house couldn't reach him. He stretched himself luxuriously. It was the closest he'd ever come to a state of toadness: in the gloom of a cavern in the garden rockery, safe from rat or heron or magpie, where no man could smack with a spade or spit with a fork. Safe, snug in a velvet black space, like a toad in a rockery, Harry closed his eyes and sighed contentedly.

The natterjack stirred in his pocket, recovering from the bruising impact of the dive to safety. It untangled itself from the neckerchief. It felt with its tiny fingers, thrust its long hind legs. At last it stepped from the pocket, onto the ground, and hurried away from the caravan, flickering its tongue around the edges of its mouth. It disappeared into the nearest flowerbed.

Harry heard the two soft voices above him. Perhaps the girl had gone back to her magazine. The caravan creaked as she or Patrick got up to draw the curtains, and then the garden was darker still. No more voices, only the flexing of the floorboards. Everything was quiet: the road, the house, the village... the whole world. A quarter of an hour went by. Patrick and Sarah lay warmly and silently together, unaware of the man who dozed only inches below them in the cobwebs and molehills of a gentle toad-dream. At last, Harry felt for the natterjack in his trouser pocket.

Gone. This discovery provoked an instant and painful reaction.

He sat up sharply and slammed his head on the axle of the caravan. There was an explosion of pain and a brilliant starburst inside his skull. Careless of being discovered, he scrabbled in the earth around him, groping for the natterjack. A second time, as he tried to roll over, twisting and writhing in the confined space, he cracked his head on the caravan, a hammer blow behind his left ear. Panic took hold of him. He was stuck. He couldn't get out. Yelling with a horror of the cavern which had seemed so comfortable a moment before, he tried to crawl onto the lawn. He heard voices and footsteps overhead. Something was tangling him, preventing him from rolling clear.... He grappled at the cables twisted round his legs. At last, with a louder yell, he wrenched himself free.

At the same moment, the lights in the caravan went out. Before Harry could struggle to his feet, the door flew open and Patrick jumped onto the lawn.

"Who the fuck...? Bloody hell, it's clueless Harry Clewe! Hey Sarah! Get some clothes on and come and see this! It's your schoolteacher friend, the daredevil rock-climber!"

He squatted over Harry, shirtless and shoeless, wearing only his climbing slacks. Jutting his bearded chin, he grinned so hard that the tendons in his neck stood up.

Sarah appeared in the black doorway of the caravan, wrapping a pink dressing gown around her. "What's going on?" she hissed. "Be quiet, Patrick! My uncle will hear you! What's happened to the lights?"

Then she saw Harry, as he got up from the grass.

"Harry?" she said. "Harry Clewe? What on earth are you doing here? Why have you pulled the cables out? What do you want?"

He couldn't answer. Shaking his head to try and clear the sparks inside it, he felt into the hair behind his ear. It was sticky with blood.

"What's the matter, Harry?" she said. "Have you hurt yourself?"

Her voice and the way she wound the dressing gown around her dispelled some of his confusion. He held out his fingers toward her, and the blood on them shone in the dark garden. Patrick stepped forward and jutted his face again.

"What do you think you're doing, Harry fucking Clewe?" he said. "Why are you creeping around Sarah's caravan? How long have you been here?" With each question, he jabbed very hard with his forefinger in the middle of Harry's chest. "Peeping through the curtains, were you? You dirty old schoolteacher!"

He continued to jab, forcing Harry backward across the lawn, until Sarah's voice cut through, harder and thinner than Harry had heard before.

"Leave him alone, Patrick!" she said. The man hesitated long enough for her to add more softly, "Come here, Harry, and let me have a look at your head."

Harry moved like a sleepwalker toward the girl. But Patrick gripped him by the arm and stopped him.

"No, you don't!" he said. "You're just going to piss off home and not come back! Get the idea, Harry? Try and start that clapped-out fucking phallic symbol of a car and go home! Stick your head in a dirty magazine! I'll knock it off the next time you come crawling round here!"

With that, he shoved violently with the flat of his hand against Harry's chest, so that Harry, still dazed, staggered three paces backward and sat down with a bump.

The girl stepped from the caravan door. "You bastard, Patrick!" she said, hissing the words and glancing anxiously at the light in the house. "Grow up, for heaven's sake! If you think you're impressing me, you're bloody wrong!"

She came barefoot over the grass and knelt next to Harry, with her thigh close to his face.

"Up you get!" she whispered to him. "Don't take any notice of Patrick. He's got a lot of hang-ups himself, hence his clever monkey tricks on the rocks. He's afraid of school-teachers, for a start. Come on now, get up!"

She took his hand and helped him to his feet. But, before he could say anything or free his hand from hers, Patrick was there again, wrenching them apart and propelling Harry across the lawn toward the garden gate. Sarah started shouting, tugging at Patrick's arms and swearing colorfully, so that Harry was encouraged enough to swing a half-hearted blow in the vague direction of the rock-climber's face. By chance, as the man was distracted by the girl, the punch landed heavily on his ear. But Harry had less than a second to congratulate himself on this unexpected success, before Patrick's fist struck him very hard on the bridge of the nose. Harry went down again, covering his face with both hands.

Everything was wet and stinging. The blow had driven the frame of his glasses into his eyebrow. His eyes flooded with tears. A gout of blood burst from his nostrils and into his mouth. There was a tremendous commotion — Patrick's

singsong bellowing and Sarah's high-pitched shouts —
which Harry ignored as he lay on the lawn, spitting the
blood from his lips. He sat up and fumbled for the neckerchief in his pocket, wiping his eyes and nose with it, putting his glasses back on in time to see the door of the house
swing open. Sarah's uncle strode into the garden, with the
same expression on his face that Harry had seen in the restaurant and on the painting outside it. He confronted
Patrick in the middle of the lawn. There was more and
greater commotion: the black-bearded uncle blustered and
roared, the blond-bearded rock-climber jutted his face and
jabbed the air with his hands. Harry had recovered enough,
although his nose was still pumping blood, to see that Sarah had skipped into the caravan. He stood up, gathering
from the trend of the shouting that he was only a periph-
eral source of aggravation: The big issue was Patrick's half-
naked presence in the caravan in the first place.

So Harry slid out of sight. Crouching in the long grass
behind the caravan, he searched for the toad. He held out
the spotted red neckerchief, as though it might lure the toad
to him, although the spots were stained with mucus and
blood; he rummaged in the drab remains of the summer flowers and felt under evergreen shrubs; he reached for stones
and clods of soil, deceived by the dull toad shapes... until
suddenly, by a magic he could never understand, he plucked
the pimpled, wrinkled natterjack from a flowerbed. The
magic flooded him again. He was recharged by it. Pressing
a single, delicate kiss to the toad's head, he wrapped it in
the neckerchief and slipped it gently into his pocket.

The shouting continued unabated on the lawn.

Harry ran to the garden gate and into the street. Patrick
and Sarah's uncle were too preoccupied to notice him. He
trotted along the pavement to the yew, where the shadow
was so black he could hardly see his car underneath it. Indeed, he groped for the smooth, cold metal of the bonnet,
felt for the doorhandle and slumped at the wheel... before

he realized that Sarah was huddled on the passenger seat. He could smell her in the darkness. Her dressing gown slithered on the leather upholstery. Her fingers came up and felt for his face.

"Home in a couple of minutes," he whispered hoarsely, slotting the key into the ignition. With the other hand, he squeezed the toad in his pocket, praying that the magic was still good.

It was. The car coughed and coughed and started. The lights blazed. Harry and Sarah and the natterjack toad sped out of the village.

12

Instead of parking the car in the shed, Harry stopped under the streetlamp outside the cottage. With a wriggling of her bare legs, Sarah stood on the seat and skipped over the dented, jammed passenger door. Harry fumbled with his house key.

"Hurry up, Harry," she said, so close behind him that he could smell her breath. "I feel a bit daft like this."

She was barefoot, wearing the pink dressing gown. But no one would see her. It was eleven o'clock; the village was silent and deserted.

"Mind the step down," he said, as the door opened. He felt for the light switch, and again she was pressed close to him in the chill front room. Her face was pasty and confused in the sudden brightness. Her vitality was quenched in the glare of the naked bulb.

"Not very homely at the moment," he said. "Soon make it cozy for you."

He drew her away from the door and made her sit on the sofa. "You're cold," he said. "Do you want some clothes to put on? Some slippers? And what about Patrick? Will he...?"

At this, she seemed to wake up again. She reddened, as though she'd suddenly realized how little she was wearing, and she pulled the dressing gown tightly across her chest and over her knees.

"Don't worry about Patrick," she said, shivering. "Not yet, anyway. Get the fire started. Then I'll clean your face for you. You've got blood in your mouth. You look terrible."

In the flight from Beddgelert, he'd forgotten the pain in his punched face. He took off his glasses; the right lens was crazed again, exactly as it had been broken by his fall from the rocks. He felt at the bridge of his nose, at his eyebrow, at the bleeding bump behind his ear.

The girl shuddered very violently, hunched in the cold, bare room. "Get the fire lit, Harry!" she said. "Let's have some warmth before I fix you up!" She sprang from the sofa and turned toward the bathroom. "Must go to the loo! I expect a roaring blaze when I come back!"

Harry moved like a cat. He sprang past her and flicked the switch at the bathroom door. She blinked at him, surprised at the panic on his face, and he quickly said, "The wiring's a bit buggered, I'm afraid. I always make sure the power's off when I use the bathroom. Don't worry, it's safe now. But it means there's no light in there. Just hang on a moment…"

He crossed the living room, reached for a candle on the mantelpiece, took it past the girl and into the dark bathroom. He brushed the taps with his knuckle: no tingle. He melted some wax from the bottom of the candle and stuck it firmly on the washbasin before lighting the wick. Straight away, the room seemed warmer, lit with gold and silver flames from the mirror and the gleaming taps.

"There we are," he said. "That'll do, won't it?"

Sighing with exasperation, the girl closed herself inside the bathroom.

Harry listened at the door, as he'd done the first time she'd come to the cottage: the rustling of her dressing gown and a few seconds' silence before the water fizzed and foamed in the toilet bowl. Imagining her sitting there, with the tiny hairs on her shins and her thighs as bright as sparks in the candlelight, he leaned his forehead on the door and closed his eyes. The toad squirmed in his pocket. His stomach turned over. The trickling noise stopped. Hearing the rattle of the toilet roll, he stepped silently into the living room and knelt at the grate; he busied himself with newspaper and kindling wood, watched as the flames flickered and licked at the thin, dry splinters; he balanced the pieces of coal from a bucket by the hearth, constructing a dome on the spars of blackening wood. Soon, within the dome, a blossoming core of fire… A minute later, he heard the taps running before Sarah came back into the room, rubbing her hands together.

"It's freezing in there!" she said. "And don't you have any hot water?"

She flung herself onto the sofa and held out her fingers and toes to the fire. She grinned the stoat-grin. "Come on, Harry Clewe, get organized! No light! No hot water! No fire! If you're going to kidnap me, at least let's have a bit of comfort!"

He explained that there would soon be plenty of hot water, because the fire heated the back boiler. The flames grew bolder, forcing through the coal, filling the grate with blue smoke. He reached for a log and rested it there: the wood began to hiss, and a long jet of steam burst from it. Soon it was running with flames, splitting from end to end with an explosive crack which spat a spark onto the carpet. Harry stood up and ground the spark out with his wellington boot.

"I'll go and get out of these boots," he said. He switched on a little table lamp and turned off the naked overhead bulb, to make the room warmer and softer. "That's better, isn't it? I won't be a minute."

Upstairs, he took the natterjack from his pocket. The power of the toadstone had worked again. The girl was in his cottage, naked inside her dressing gown, in front of his fire.... It was a miracle, considering the resistance he'd met. But he gulped with fear, thinking that the rock-climber might arrive in his van at any moment. Consumed with gratitude for the magic of the extraordinarily ugly, indescribably beautiful creature, praying that it might continue to protect him, he unfolded the toad from the neckerchief and kissed it tenderly on the top of the head, where the jewel was concealed by poisonous pimples.

Sitting on his bed, he reached for the length of string in the bedside drawer; he attached the string to the toad as he did nearly every night, slipping the loop over its head and pulling it tighter under its forelegs. He stood on the chair and pushed open the trap door in the ceiling, reaching up and placing the toad tenderly on its neckerchief in the dusty darkness of the roof space. No sound or movement; indeed, there'd been none since he'd first used the toad to keep the cottage free of rats. Silently, he closed the trap door. The string trailed

down, running freely through a crack around the ill-fitting
hinge. Normally he would tie it to his wrist as he climbed
into bed, to keep the connection even in his sleep; but now
he knotted it to the door handle of his wardrobe. There was
a little slack, so that the toad could move about and explore
in the cobwebs. Satisfied with this arrangement, Harry took
off his boots and put on a pair of slippers. It was better to
have the toad out of his pocket for the moment; he would
show it to the girl later, certain she'd be thrilled. It was something to hold back, like a trump card.

He went downstairs again and sat next to Sarah on the
sofa. They stared at the flames together.

"You're famous in the village, you know," she said. "Or
infamous, to be more precise. That business in the hotel garden, I mean. Everybody's talking about it. It makes your dra-
matic entrance into the restaurant seem pretty tame by com-
parison. What were you doing this evening, crawling around
the caravan? Why did you pull the cable out? Another of your
jokes, was it?"

For a dazzling moment, Harry was going to tell her... about
the beautiful bright angel he dreaded so much... about his
chaotic classrooms and the soft, white weight of the suffocating headmistress... about Sudan. About everything! That
he wanted her, that he loved her, that he had come to the
caravan to see her and talk to her and would do anything to
stop Patrick from having her back again! He would show her
the natterjack she'd found in the garden, in the spotted red
neckerchief she'd given him, and they could share the power
of the toadstone which had brought them together. Yes, the
toadstone was common to them, to Harry Clewe and Sarah!
It excluded the rock-climber!

But the moment passed, perhaps because, for the first time
in weeks, he and the toad were apart. Harry had made a mistake. Thinking to close on the girl, he'd lost his connection
with the natterjack. The power was cut off. Now, he hardly
dared look the girl in the eyes.

"I wanted to see you," he mumbled, ducking his head from her. "I had to. Can you understand that?"

The words were mealy and bland. His courage was gone. He was nervous of the girl and afraid of the rock-climber. She didn't answer his question. So he said, "What about Patrick? And your uncle? They must be wondering where you've gone."

She shrugged. The corners of her mouth turned down, crinkling the skin on her chin. "Well, my uncle might wonder," she said, "but I don't suppose he'll do any more than that. He's really heavy about my morals while I'm in the caravan, in his garden, on his property, but he doesn't care a damn once I'm off the premises." She put her palms together and snuggled her hands deep between her thighs.

"And Patrick?" Harry persisted. "Does he know where I live? He'll find us! He'll see my car! What will he do then?" His voice trembled, because of the cold and because he was frightened.

Sarah stared into the fire, saying nothing. Quick as a lizard, she moved suddenly forward and knelt on the rug. Her breasts were cream against the darker gold of her throat, and one of her thighs was naked in the firelight. She reached for another piece of wood and placed it in the flames, very deliberately with both hands, as though she were fitting a crown on the round, young head of a princess.

"I don't know about Patrick," she said at last, staring into the fire. "I go back to London next week. He's going climbing in Nepal. We've had our fun for the summer, and I suppose that's the end of it."

"But now!" Harry said, trying to control the squeal in his voice. "I mean now, Sarah! Tonight! Isn't he going to come looking for you?"

"Not unless he walks up here, he's not," she replied, looking round at Harry. "He's got the van up on bricks in Beddgelert, doing something to the brakes, I think. He'll sleep in it tonight. But I wouldn't be surprised if he turns up tomorrow, as soon as he gets the wheels back on. It might be a good idea if you're out of the way then, Harry, unless you want some more alterations done to your glasses. Shit, you're a mess! Let me have a look at your face."

She was on her feet and in and out of the bathroom in a few seconds, sitting beside him on the sofa, lifting off his glasses and dabbing at his forehead with a wet sponge. She pressed him backward, soaked the congealed blood from his nostrils and the hair behind his ear, squeezed the sponge on the bridge of his nose.

"I don't think it's broken," she said softly.

He closed his eyes as she swabbed at the incision on his brow where the frame of his glasses had cut him.

"And that's just a nick," he heard her say. "That's all the nursing you need."

Her dressing gown rustled. The sponge rolled onto the rug. She curled up her legs and leaned on him, with her head on his shoulder. He could hear and smell her breathing very close to his neck; he could feel the flutter of her hair on his mouth. The only other sound was the movement of fire in the grate, the guttering of flames, the puthering smoke, the crackle and hiss of burning wood and the collapsing of coal in a bed of embers. Harry felt his bones go loose, as though his body were melting into the cushions of the sofa.

Harry and Sarah sat like that for a long time, half-asleep in the firelight.

Suddenly, there was a long creak and a bang from upstairs. The girl stiffened, without sitting up. Harry opened his eyes and held his breath to listen. Something banged a second time in the room above, wood on wood.

"What's that, Harry?" she said, lifting her face from his shoulder. "Is there somebody upstairs?"

She was frightened. Her wide, gray eyes moved from his eyes to the ceiling and to the staircase. Her right cheek was lined with a map of sleep, reddened creases from leaning on Harry's shoulder. He raised his eyebrows, listened for another sound, reached for his glasses and fitted them to his tender nose. A third time something banged, more loudly, so that Harry prised himself free of the girl and stood up.

"Don't worry. It's just the wind," he told her. "I must have left a window open. Stay there and I'll have a look."

She swiveled on the sofa to watch him go. He went upstairs.

In the orange light from the street, he could see that the wardrobe door had been tugged wide open, to bang three times on the skirting of the wall. Now the string from the door handle to the ceiling was slack, although it trembled in midair. Before Harry could reach it, there was a scuffle near the trap door and the string jerked tight, slamming the wardrobe door once more on the skirting. At the same time, a patter of heavy footsteps ran to the corners of the roofspace; there was the skid and rattle of rubble, the sneezing upheaval of dust.

Harry grabbed the chair. He stood on it and thrust open the trap door. A cloud of plaster and cobwebs fell on his head, as the rats fled to the adjacent chimney stack of the next cottage. He took the string, which trailed into the darkness, and pulled it gently toward him. Blinking at the dust in his eyes and spitting the chalkiness out of his mouth, he peered into the shadows of the roof. He tugged the string. It was snagged on something; there was a dead weight on the other end. He reached into the gloom with one hand and eased the string, finding the red neckerchief at the same time. He draped it over his shoulder and continued to pull on the string.

At last he saw the toad. It was dragging through the dust, tumbling over and over like a drunk in a gutter, its limbs gangling loosely and coated with white powder, its eyes closed. Harry slipped the string from its body and trod heavily from the chair onto the bedroom floor. The toad was cold and still between his hands.

Before he could slip it inside his shirt or his pocket, Sarah was there, in the light of the landing. She spoke, before he could say anything by way of explanation or conceal the toad from her.

"The natterjack? I thought so. What's happened to it? What the hell have you done to it? Give it to me, Harry."

She came forward, small and neat and shining in her dressing gown, and she reached out her hand to Harry's face. He instinctively flinched, accustomed to being punched, anticipating more punches in the coming hours... but she didn't touch him. She lifted the neckerchief from his shoulder. She shook it hard and held it toward him, draped over her hands.

"Give me the toad, Harry," she said. "I shouldn't have given it to you in the first place. Give it to me!"

And before he'd understood what she was doing, he put the motionless body of the natterjack on its neckerchief and watched her enfold it tenderly, until it was quite hidden from the light and the dust.

She spun away from him, down the stairs. He quickly jumped on the chair and closed the trap door, jumped down again and followed her.

She went straight into the bathroom, where, between the washbasin taps, the candle was guttering in a pool of wax. The girl's hair gleamed, her teeth and eyes were bright in the failing light. Putting the bundle in the basin, she let the water run round the folded material. Then she handed the wet neckerchief to Harry, who stood dumbly behind her. She turned the toad in her hands, massaging it as though she were trying to get a lather from a piece of soap. Harry felt his bowels squirm, to see her smooth, brown hands on the slick, rubbery toad. The plaster dust streamed like milk, spiraling into the plughole. When the toad was clean, she bent low and examined it close to the light of the candle, peering minutely into every crease of its body.

"The skin is punctured here," she said. "Looks like a bite. It's alive, though. I can feel it pulsing in my hands."

She glanced up at Harry, indirectly, by means of the mirror, where he stood so closely to her that his thighs brushed against her dressing gown. Her face, reversed in reflection, was oddly, intriguingly different. The candle was almost out, drowning the wick in molten wax. The girl bent forward again. At the touch of her body on his, Harry put his arms on her waist. She stiffened a little, then ignored him, running more water on the lifeless toad. Harry felt her warmth through the dressing gown. It was all she was wearing; it slid on her skin as he moved his hands. He saw his own face in the mirror, shadows and flames and bruises of blood, and he felt the desire in his belly as he leaned harder on the girl, as her hands caressed the slithery toad. He lowered his face to her hair. Ignoring her squirm, averting his eyes from her suddenly uplifted, frightened, back-to-front face in the mirror, he enfolded her waist with his arms. He slipped his hands inside her gown. Unable to control himself, he cupped her breasts, tweaked her nipples.... She cried out, she writhed like a seal in his grip. But he couldn't let go. He couldn't. His head reeled at the wriggle of her buttocks against him. For a second, his eyes met hers in the mirror, and her mouth was wide open with anger and fear... and then the candle went out.

The girl slapped the toad into the washbasin, freed herself by lashing backward with her elbows, and fled from the bathroom.

Harry sat on the edge of the bath, gulping air to try and calm himself, mopping his face with the wet neckerchief. The room was dark and cool. He had a delicious surge of toadness, like the toadness he'd enjoyed beneath the caravan, to be quiet and safe in a silent, black hole. So he waited for a minute, until his breathing was steady again, until his desire had gone down, and then he stood up, took the toad from the washbasin, wrapped it in the neckerchief and bundled it into his pocket.

What a fool he'd been to put it in the roof! He'd been mad to cut himself off from it! But now he had it back again, the toad, the toadstone, the jewel in its head... and, although the beast itself was so limp and lifeless, he thought he could still feel the tingle of power go through him.

He went into the living room. Sarah was kneeling in front of the fire. She was crying. The tears ran down her cheeks and into the corners of her mouth, into the creases of her throat. She made no effort to control them or to wipe them away. Her body shook with silent sobbing.

Harry sat on the sofa. "Sarah," he said very softly. "Oh Sarah, I'm sorry. I didn't mean to frighten you. I couldn't help it. I'm sorry. Please forgive me."

He reached out his fingers to her cheek, but she recoiled as though she were nettled by his touch.

"Sarah, please!" he whispered. "Can't I touch you at all?"

She shuddered and replied, wringing out each word, 'No! Not like that! Not the same way you—" She stopped in midsentence, took a huge, quivering breath and smeared her face with the sleeves of her dressing gown.

"What way, Sarah?" he whispered. "What do you mean?"

She said nothing. She shrugged. And the shrug, effortlessly insolent, totally dismissive, was the trigger for Harry's anger. He took hold of her shoulders, twisted her face toward his, and shook her as hard as he could until her head rattled this way and that like a doll's. He bellowed at her, flecking her face with spittle.

"What way? What way? Why can't I touch you? What way do you mean?"

She went limp in his arms. He leaned very closely to her and whispered again. "What way, Sarah? Please tell me! Please!"

Blubbering, gasping for breath, she managed to tell him. It was she who'd watched him in the glare of the telephone kiosk. It was she who'd dialed the number from her uncle's house and spoken to him.

A minute ticked by. A dead, empty minute.

"Not like that, Harry!" she whispered, as he slumped on the sofa. Her breathing was steady again. "Not like you did with the toad! I don't want you to touch me like that!"

She stood up from the rug, sat next to him and picked up both his hands in hers. His were the hands of a corpse, blue and mottled, colder and deader than stone.

"It reminded me," she said softly. "Just now in the bathroom with the light and the mirror and so on, it reminded me of what you were doing in the phone box. You frightened me then, when I was watching you that night. I thought you were ill, Harry, or mad! I saw you with the toad and I was frightened... and that's why I was frightened just now as well. I saw you in the mirror, and you looked sort of mad again."

She was no longer afraid. She'd stopped crying, although her eyes were bleary red and her face was smeared with tears. She could see that Harry Clewe was lost and broken, that he was cold and lonely. Now it was Harry's turn to weep. He shuddered and mewed as though his chest might burst, as though his throat were burning... and this is what she did to comfort him. She prised his hands from his face. She opened her dressing gown, parted her smooth, brown thighs and slipped his hands between them. Then she squeezed her legs together.

"Don't be sad, Harry Clewe," she whispered. "Don't! You're a nice man. You're good and kind and funny. I feel comfy and safe with you, now. Don't always be sad, Harry Clewe. And please don't be angry with me..."

She leaned on him again, her head on his shoulder, his hands between her thighs. At last, Harry controlled his weeping. Like two unhappy children, their eyes wet with tears, they sat for a long time without speaking... until the fire was nearly dead. The toad was cold in Harry's pocket, like a dead thing.

Eventually, when the room was chilly again, the girl squirmed away and gently lifted Harry's hands from her. His palms were moist, where they'd been pressed to her skin.

"Go to bed now," she said to him. "I'll stay down here on the sofa. Have you got a couple of blankets I could use?"

With difficulty, Harry got up, knelt by the fire and rebuilt it with coal and logs.

"That'll keep going nearly all night now," he said, "so there'll be plenty of hot water in the morning. I'll get some blankets from upstairs."

While the girl was in the bathroom again, rinsing the smudges from her face, Harry brought the rug, eiderdown and pillow from his own bed and arranged them on the sofa for her. He put the guard in front of the fire, which was brightly flaming. Sarah came back in. Hoping she wouldn't ask him where the toad had gone, he asked her, "Do you need anything else? Will you be all right?"

They were both embarrassed, now that it was bedtime. The girl couldn't climb under the blankets while Harry was standing there, and Harry couldn't think of anything to say. He nodded goodnight and went upstairs.

He stood in his bedroom, holding his breath and straining his ears for any sounds of movement. He heard the click of the lamp as the girl switched it off, the creak of the sofa, the snuggle of blankets. Nothing more. Without turning his light on, in the orange glow from the street, he took off all his clothes, unfolded the red neckerchief and pressed the toad to his belly, skin to skin.

The creature was cold and still. It had no warmth, no pulse. It was dead. No, please, no... He banished the thought at once. Slipping under the single sheet of his bed — no pillow or rug, or eiderdown — he lay there and squeezed the toad between his thighs: as the girl had squeezed his hands between her thighs, to give heat, to give life, to give comfort.

1 3

The hours went by and he couldn't sleep. Sometimes he heard the rats in the roof, shuffling through the shadows, snuffling in the dust; they'd come inside for the warmth of the chimney, now that the nights were colder. The street was silent. There was no wind in the mountains, no wind in the dense black trees of the forest. Once, he heard the collapsing of the fire in the living room and saw the glow of flames up the stairs to his landing. He lay without moving a muscle, holding the toad between his legs. He shivered, without blankets, and he wondered if the toad, instead of being revived by his own heat, was filling him with its dead and clammy cold. No, not dead! He wouldn't let it be dead. He wanted the power in him, the power and magic of the toadstone. So he squeezed the natterjack in the fork of his thighs.

Three o'clock. Four. Five. Still he hadn't slept.

When he saw the sky lightening, he tiptoed downstairs, naked, holding the toad to his groin, and squatted by the fire to put another log there. The girl was breathing regularly, sound asleep, her face on the pillow turned toward the cooling hearth. She looked like a child: her hair was damp on her brow, her cheeks were hot, her mouth was open and moving. She could have been twelve or thirteen — not much older than his little sister Lizzie, he thought — lost in the complicated, mysterious dreams that children have. Harry stood on the rug, where the new heat from the fire was good on his buttocks and thighs, where the pink dressing gown had been tossed on the floor.

He knelt to her oblivious face and smooth shoulders, and he felt the caving in his belly that she was so sweet and naked and so close and she would never let him touch her. He leaned down, unable to resist, and gently kissed her cheek.

At that, as if by some miracle, the toad started to move. It swelled and flexed and filled with heat. It throbbed and writhed, alive with a hot, hot pulse....

But no. It wasn't the toad. It was Harry Clewe. The toad was cold and apparently dead. But it seemed to swell as Harry swelled, as he rubbed it and rubbed it between his legs.

The girl began to whisper. Her breath was hoarse. For a second she opened her eyes and stared at Harry and he sprang to his feet again, turning to try and hide himself from her. She closed her eyes. She was deeply asleep. With the taste of her skin on the tip of his tongue, with the toad on his belly, he returned to his bed. It was colder and lonelier than ever before.

At last he slept.

When he woke, he found that he'd curled himself into a ball. Something was moving in his hands, where he snuggled them between his thighs. There was a gurgling, drumming noise. He blinked, trying to surface from sleep into the chill, gray bedroom of a Snowdonian cottage. When he realized that the toad was stretching its legs and squirming and trying to crawl out of his grasp, he kicked the sheet off him and sat up.

The natterjack was alive, as limber and sinewy and rubbery-tough as ever. It sprang about the bed, it scuttled and burrowed and bounced, quite reborn. And Harry yelped with pleasure to see it. He danced round and round the little room, giggling barbarically, a thin, white, naked man, bursting with joy that the toad had come back to life.

At last, having watched for a delirious minute while it explored the tangled sheet, he picked up the toad and pressed its bumpy brown body to his forehead. His eyes swam with tears. It was a glorious moment.... The power flooded through him, an infusion of pumping new blood.

And the noise, the roaring and drumming noise? It was the running of hot water from the boiler.

Rummaging in the bed for the spotted red neckerchief, he knotted it round his throat. Then he tiptoed halfway downstairs, holding the toad to his groin like a bizarre fig leaf. Peering over the banister, he saw that the living room was empty. The rug and eiderdown and pillow were rumpled on the sofa. The dressing gown was gone. He continued down the stairs, squeezing the natterjack to him, and leaned across the sofa to touch the warm place where the girl had been lying. He crossed the room. Again, he listened at the bathroom door, leaning his forehead on it, his eyes tightly closed.

Sarah was in the bath. He heard the drumming of water from the taps, the thunder of bubbles and foam as the bath filled up. A fine haze of steam came under the door, warm on his bare feet. For a minute, the sound of the water obliterated all other sounds. But then he imagined her leaning forward and turning off the taps, because the noise stopped and there were gentle splashes and ripples as the girl relaxed in the bath. Harry clenched his eyes shut. He pictured her in the water. The image of her soap-slithery limbs, her golden skin glistening with bubbles, her shining, smooth body, her hair slick in the fog of steam... the image was so vivid to him that he mouthed her name and felt his tongue go heavy and dry. Unthinking, he let the toad swarm on his belly.

Oh Sarah, oh Sarah... His lips framed the words. She was sleek with water, scented with soap, lying in the bath on the other side of that door, while the toad swelled and throbbed on him. He must have spoken her name aloud, because the girl called out with a tremor of alarm in her voice, "Is that you, Harry? Are you up?"

Yes, Harry was up. He blinked his eyes open. The natterjack squirmed, and the power was in him. It pulsed in his head and every muscle of his body. It made his mind go blank. There was nothing else for Harry Clewe: nothing but the toad, his throbbing nakedness, and the girl just a few feet away. He pushed open the door and stepped into the bathroom.

There was a terrible scene. Harry trod into the steam-filled room, naked, erect, with the toad clenched in his fist.

His face was bruised and swollen from the punching he'd had. His hair was a tousled, gingery mop. His eyes were the dead-cold eyes of a shark... no spark, but the gleam of an uncontrollable lust. He banged the door shut behind him, and towered over the bath. Seeing the girl's silvery white breasts and her slippery brown thighs as she squirmed away from him, he was powerless to control himself. Dropping the toad into the water, he reached down for her.

They fought in the bath. She stood up and tried to beat him off with her fists. She jabbed at his eyes, she tore at his ears, she screamed as hard as she could scream. He trod into the water with her and used his height and sinewy strength to force her downward again... until, for a few ecstatic moments, he was stretched on top of her, deep in the hot foam with every inch of his nakedness on hers... "in amplexus" like the toads in the photographs he'd seen. He could feel her breasts on his breast, her belly on his, her long, silken thighs sliding against him. Ignoring her squeals and yells and furious spitting, he muffled her mouth with his own mouth and weighted her down in the water.

Suddenly the girl stopped struggling. She went limp underneath him, heaving for breath. Slowly the waves subsided. She smiled at him, running her tongue deliciously around her lips.

"Harry Clewe..." she whispered. "Oh Harry... Shall I give you what you want, after all? Come on, then...."

He felt her legs easing apart. She lifted her belly to his. She wriggled her hips, as though to let him inside her. One of her hands went down there, expertly aligned him and nubbed his swollen tip toward her.

"There..." she whispered. "Nearly there... Jesus, you're a big boy, Harry! Just one little squeeze, and you're there. One little squeeze, like this... Like this!"

Her hand reached back to his balls and clenched. She clenched as hard as she could. With an animal grunt, using every ounce of her strength, she closed her fist, ground her nails together and arched her body with the effort of clenching.

Harry wrenched himself from her, bellowing like a camel. He staggered to his feet astride her and stumbled from the bath in a blur of agony that brought a cascade of water onto the bathroom floor with him. The pain filled his head, where the lust had been. And when he saw that the girl was laughing at him, that she was lying in the deep water and flaunting her inaccessible nakedness by squirming the toad on her breasts and belly and the coppery curls between her legs, he went roaring out of the bathroom, grinding his teeth, clutching the place where the pain was worst.

There he stood by the dead fire, naked, quivering, dazzled by rage and humiliation. He cursed and spat and squeezed his eyes shut. He cupped himself where the girl had clenched her hand, and the pain seemed to drum inside his head. The noise grew louder. It welled from inside him and drummed in the little room. Until, when he opened his eyes and looked around him, he realized that someone was hammering on the front door.

He froze. The hammering on the front door continued, staccato and hard. He knew who it would be.

He moved quickly to the sofa, picked up the rug that Sarah had used and wrapped it around him. He shook some of the water from his hair, rubbing it out of his eyes with his fingers. Miraculously, the pain had gone. He'd forgotten it, in anticipation of confronting the rock-climber. He took a deep breath and opened the front door.

Patrick stood there, glowering, jutting his bristly chin before anything had been said. He'd parked the blue van behind the Mercedes-Benz.

"Where's Sarah?" he said, peering at the bruises on Harry's face. He frowned to see Harry dripping wet, wrapped in a rug. He snarled, seeing that Harry was wearing the spotted red neckerchief. "Where's Sarah?" he said again. "Did she spend the night here?"

"Yes, she did," Harry replied. "Come in."

Patrick stepped into the living room, lean and threatening in T-shirt and climbing slacks, ridiculously barefoot. He glanced around at the pictures and books, at the pillow and eiderdown on the sofa.

"There's nothing to worry about," Harry said, closing the front door. "She slept on the sofa, nice and warm in front of the fire, and I was upstairs, of course. We just talked, that's all. You didn't think I'd try and take advantage of her, did you?"

"So where is she?" the man asked.

Harry took a step toward the stairs. He paused and took another step. "She's in the bath," he said. "She won't be long getting out. Have a seat and wait for her, if you like. I'll go and get some clothes on...."

Harry trod up the first two stairs. He was shuddering with fear. His heart leaped when Patrick said sharply, "Hang on a minute! What have you been doing? Why are you so wet, and prancing around with no fucking clothes on? Eh? What the fuck have you been up to? Where is the fucking bathroom anyway? Where is it?"

"I've been in the bath, of course," Harry answered, hardly controlling the yelp in his voice. "That's why I'm wet. It's through there, just through the living room. Go in and see her, if you like. There's no lock on the door."

Then he was upstairs and into the bedroom in three enormous panic-stricken strides. In less than ten seconds he'd stepped into trousers and boots and wriggled into a shirt. He could hear the rockclimber tapping on the bathroom door. Reassured by the rattle of car keys in his trouser pocket, Harry glanced from the window to check that Patrick's van wasn't obstructing a rapid getaway in the Mercedes-Benz. His heart was pounding, his breath was short. He moved onto the landing, ready to fling himself downstairs and out into the street, to jump into the car and go hurtling along the valley as fast as the remains of the Wabenzi power would let him. He heard the rock-climber tapping on the door, calling, "Are you OK, Sarah? Are you there? It's me, it's Patrick! Can I come in?"

Harry waited until the man had gone into the bathroom. Then he leaped down the stairs and tore open the front door.

But he didn't go outside.

He heard a thrashing commotion, as though someone was throwing buckets of water all over the bathroom.

He heard screams, not full-throated screams, but muted cries through tightly clenched teeth.... a man's gurgling and gagging, a woman's bubbling squeal. As though the man and the woman were retching, spewing so hard that their chests would burst, inhaling water, drowning in an agony of tortured cramps... As though they were grappling and drowning, locked together in deep, hot, soapy water.

As though they were dying.

Harry listened, too stunned to move. It lasted for a long, long minute. Gradually the commotion subsided. The thrashing stopped and there were no more cries. There was a slowly lapping silence.

Harry tiptoed to the bathroom. He listened to the silence for another minute, pushed the door open and stepped inside.

The light was on. There was water all over the floor, so that he could feel the buzz of electricity even through his boots. Patrick and Sarah were in the bath. Neither of them was moving. She was completely submerged, held down by his paralyzed body. Her face was framed by golden hair. Her mouth was wide open, with a splendid silver bubble the size of a cauliflower somehow attached to her lips. As Harry leaned down to see, the bubble broke away and bobbed to the surface, bursting with a sigh. She stared through the gray water, frowning, as though she was going to ask Harry a very important question and had just forgotten what the question was.

Patrick lay twisted on top of her. He was looking at Harry as well, grinning his cocksure grin. Barefoot on the flooded floor, poleaxed by the current he'd switched on before stepping into the bathroom, he must have tried to pull the girl out of the bath and then collapsed on top of her. She'd pulled his head into the water, winding her arms around his neck. His hands were clenched to the edge of the bath. His feet floated to the surface.

Something was moving in the bath. The natterjack toad, thrusting its legs in powerful spasm, sculled through the water. It dived to the bottom, trailing a string of pearly bubbles.

Harry, numb at the sight of the man and the girl in his bath, reacted at once when he saw the toad. Resisting the urge to reach into the water and pluck the toad out, he felt for the switch outside the bathroom door and turned the power off. Then, in another moment, he'd rescued the toad from drowning... it was too late to save the man and the girl, even if he'd thought of trying to do so. He sat on the rumpled sofa in front of the cold fire, and, welling with love and tenderness, he kissed the toad until it writhed and wriggled in his hands.

14

Patrick was dead for ever. So was Sarah. But Harry, befuddled by shock, hoped for a miracle. After all, the toad
had been cold and limp and dead, and then it had come
alive again. He wouldn't believe that the girl was dead for
ever. She couldn't be. She would come alive again, as the
toad had. She was his, thanks to the power and the magic
of the toadstone.

And there was something he'd wanted to do for some
time, an idea he'd had weeks ago, almost as soon as he'd
first met the girl. Now he could do it. He got busy, quite
calm and unhurried and methodical.

He took off the red neckerchief and wrapped the toad
in it. Leaving it on the mantelpiece, he returned to the bathroom. He prised the rock-climber's fingers from the edges
of the bath, unwound the girl's arms from his neck, rolled
him to one side and freed the girl from underneath him.
The man carried on grinning, as if the whole business was a
huge joke he was looking forward to sharing with his friends
in the climbing fraternity... how he'd given the girl a shock
by surprising her in the bath. A soapy gray wave splashed
onto the floor as Harry bent down and grasped the girl under the armpits. She was very slippery and much heavier
than he'd thought she would be. With great difficulty, he
pulled her upright, so that her face burst through the surface with a spectacular cascade of water. Her hair was slick
on her head, like a neat, smooth, golden helmet. She lolled
against him. He wrestled her to her feet, all her warm, wet,
naked body leaning on him, and manhandled her out of the
bathroom and into the living room, where he let her fall
softly onto the sofa.

He went back to the bathroom for her dressing gown
and a big soft towel, and, returning to the living room, he
dried the girl, working very slowly and deliberately from her
feet upward. He dried her tiny white toes, her dimpled knees,

her coppery pubic curls, her pale pink nipples, her pale pink lips. He closed her gull's eyes. His lust was gone. He handled her with all the love and tenderness and respect he'd bestowed on the toad. When he'd rubbed her hair dry and carefully combed it, he fitted her into the pink dressing gown, tying the belt at her waist. She was ready.

His turn now. It didn't take long. He dried and combed his thick, red hair. He made sure he had money, glasses, car keys. He went outside and peered up and down the village street. It was deserted: no people, and no vehicles apart from the Mercedes-Benz and the blue van. It was a glorious autumn morning, high in the mountains of Snowdonia, and the only sounds in the crisp cold air were the croak of raven and the mewing of buzzard. Harry turned inside again, picked up the girl from the sofa and carried her to the door. He felt strong; the girl was light and manageable in his arms; the work in the hotel garden had hardened his muscles; the power of the toad was in him. With a deep breath, he stepped into the street and swung the girl over the jammed passenger door of his car, lowering her onto the passenger seat. In another ten seconds, he'd gone inside for the most precious thing of all, the bundled toad on the mantelpiece, come out again, pulled the cottage door shut and flung himself behind the steering wheel.

Keeping his breathing calm, he unfolded the spotted neckerchief and put the natterjack toad on top of the dashboard. He leaned over to the girl and strapped her firmly in place; she lolled, as though she were sleepy or drunk, so he slid her deeper in the seat and tightened the safety belt on her. Then he slotted the key in the ignition, groped at the toad with the other hand for all the magic it could muster, and turned over the engine.

It churned and churned. It coughed. There was a bang like a gunshot and a cloud of filthy black smoke blew out of the exhaust pipe. But the car wouldn't fire. Harry turned the key again. He squeezed the toad harder and harder. The engine cranked and wheezed. Another explosion, more smoke; a woman opened a window in a cottage down the street to peer out and see what was happening. Harry smiled and waved and the woman withdrew. He squeezed the toad so hard he thought it might burst in his hand, like an over-ripe orange. The engine turned over, slower and slower and slower, and still there was no spark in it.

He struggled to stay calm. He let go of the toad and leaned back in his seat with his eyes closed. When he heard a vehicle come into the village and stop nearby, he opened his eyes and saw the postman get out of his van and go into the village shop, come out again and start striding along the terrace with a sheaf of mail. The postman flipped the letters here and there, through this letter box and that, shuffling them in his hands to read the addresses. Closer and closer he came. As he crossed the road, glancing down at the last letter in his hand and up along the street toward Harry's cottage, he held up the letter and waved it, seeing Harry at the wheel of the big, red car.

For a few moments, Harry lost control. Gibbering like a baboon, he turned the ignition key again, churning and churning the engine. It banged more loudly than ever, an explosion that clattered a flock of pigeons from the fir plantation on the hillside. Ducking his head in the feeble hope that the postman might walk straight past without seeing him there, he turned the key and pumped the accelerator at the same time. The postman stopped at the driver's door and thrust a white envelope in front of Harry's face.

"Clewe? Harry Clewe?" he said. "There's a letter for you, from Shrewsbury." With a mischievous grin all over his face, he added, "Sounds as though the car's had it. I'd give up and wait for the village bus, if I were you. There's one due the day after tomorrow..."

Harry took the letter from him. One glance at the childish handwriting on the envelope, and the magic was in him again. It was another miracle! He looked up with a dazzling smile. The postman was squinting at the girl slumped in the passenger seat, blinking at the pimply brown creature on the dashboard. Harry gestured at the girl with his thumb.

"She's the one who's had it!" he said with a forced laugh. "She's dead this morning! The car's OK, it'll start next time. Thanks for the letter. It's from Lizzie, my little sister. Funnily enough, we're on the way to see her right now. That was a bit of luck, her letter coming just as we're about to set off."

He leaned to the motionless girl and slipped the letter inside her dressing gown. With a grin and a wink at the postman, who was still peering at the bundled toad, Harry tried the ignition again. The Mercedes-Benz shuddered into life. The engine fired with a rasping bellow, filling the air with sweet, blue smoke. Winking again at the postman, Harry eased the car forward and then turned it round at the further end of the village. He waited for a minute while the engine warmed up, until it stopped shuddering and spluttering, until it idled a burbling, even note. He adjusted the girl beside him. He settled the natterjack toad. He strapped himself in and straightened his glasses on the bridge of his nose. He floored the accelerator.

What a day! Harry Clewe was going home, to show his girl to little Lizzie! Beloved little Lizzie, whose letter had just arrived!

The world was a sparkling, gleaming, glittering place. The car seemed to fly. In the whirling wind, Harry's hair and Sarah's hair burned red and gold with all the red-gold fire of a blazing autumn. The sky was cold and blue, quite cloudless. The mountains were raw and clear. The air was so crisp, it nipped at Harry's nostrils and brought tingling tears to his eyes. He held the accelerator down. The road was dry and clean and the car reeled it in, drawing the horizon closer. He slowed down in Beddgelert, hindered by dawdling traffic and ambling pedestrians, and the engine sang in the narrow village street. People turned to watch the long, red convertible go throttling by, with the red-headed man and the blonde woman inside it. The hotel manager, strutting along the pavement, smiled and waved; Harry waved triumphantly back, his chest aching with joy. Sarah's uncle was standing at the door of the restaurant; he opened and closed his mouth, gaping like a fish, and flapped a tea towel to try and catch the girl's attention. She didn't see him. Harry accelerated out of the village, and the man shrank in his mirror.

It was colder up the Nantgwynant valley. The summit of Snowdon loomed jagged and gray, snagged with mist. The sun was low, spangling in the sunburst of the broken windscreen and the sunburst of Harry's broken glasses. He crawled behind an ancient bus. The road was very steep and narrow, climbing between dry-stone walls, and it was impossible to overtake, impossible to see ahead from the left-hand-drive car. He had to wait, almost nudging the back of the bus with his bonnet. The car didn't like crawling. Harry wrinkled his nose at the smell of burning oil. He tapped at the temperature gauge and the oil-pressure gauge, alarmed to see smoke from under the dashboard. Up and up the valley he crawled, caught behind the toiling bus, wafting with his hands as more and more and denser smoke came billowing into his face. The toad blinked its golden eyes and flexed its legs on the red neckerchief, as though it might jump away from the acrid fumes.

At last the road was wider, near the top of the pass, and Harry pulled out to make sure the way ahead was clear. There was room and time to overtake, although he could hardly see through the shattered, sun-dazzled windscreen. He slammed the throttle to the floor.

The car shuddered from end to end. It gathered itself, missed and missed and then suddenly surged forward. Smoke erupted from the exhaust — Bang! Bang! Bang! — and a cloud of smoke blew out of the dashboard.

As the car broke over the crest of the pass, and the bus was swallowed in a choking blue haze, two things happened at once. There was a tremendous, muffled explosion — something burst so violently that the Wabenzi bonnet bulged and buckled upward and flew wide open on its hinges — and the toad sprang from the dashboard, landing with a breathtaking thud in Harry's groin. Blinded by the great flapping sheet of metal, winded by the impact of the toad, Harry trod on the brake. The car slithered to a halt in the roadside gravel. Clutching the natterjack to his belly, instinctively reaching for the neckerchief and jamming it into his pocket, Harry tore off his seat belt, flung open his door and rolled clear.

The car was going up. A column of smoke rose from the engine and from the dashboard. There was a crackle of sparks as all the fuses blew. The first of the flames started licking at an oil slick which had spewed onto the road. Then the flames burst through the sooty contraptions of the engine, melting plastic and rubber and flex into a stinking, treacly ooze.

The girl sat calmly in all the smoke. Harry thrust the toad into his pocket, stumbled back to the car and leaned hysterically toward her. "Sarah! Sarah! Sarah!" he shouted, trying to grab her dressing gown, her hands, her hair, trying to pull her out of the seat. But she was a dead weight. He couldn't unstrap her. She lolled like a broken, boneless doll.

The bus had caught up and pulled into the roadside, fifty yards short of the burning car. Through his streaming, smoke-filled eyes, Harry saw the driver and the passengers running toward him. But he waved so violently, he screamed so hoarsely — "Get back! Get back! It's going up! Get back!" — that they stopped and gaped from a safe distance, shielding their faces from the increasing heat. They saw the red-headed man grappling at the core of the fire, wrestling to free a small blonde figure who was trapped in what would normally have been the driver's seat.

The stench of oil and rubber was overwhelming. Retching, gulping, gagging, at last he sprung the girl's seat belt. He lifted her by the dressing gown, dragged her upright on the smoldering seat and lumped her over his shoulder. He trod away from the car.

Blinded by panic, Harry lumbered up the hillside, higher and higher from the road. His eyes burned, his chest heaved with the effort of climbing, his throat was scorched by the fumes he'd inhaled. At last, unable to carry the girl any more, he dropped her in a bed of bracken. Far below him, the car was engulfed in smoke. The plume rose black and thick and unwavering, a hundred feet high.

And the flames! No longer confined to the oil slick and the engine, they leaped from one end of the car to the other. As Harry flopped the girl into the bracken and tried to steady his breathing, the petrol tank ignited. With a roar that echoed and echoed on the peaks of Snowdon, the car exploded. It blew into white-hot shrapnel, shards of splintered glass and spatters of molten rubber. It erupted in a ball of poisonous orange flame.

After the explosion itself, the wreckage burned evenly, a glorious autumn bonfire. Harry stood and watched, aghast; the sun winked into his broken lens, a spangle of sparks in his right eye. He took his glasses off and rubbed at his forehead. He'd forgotten the toad, but now, feeling it writhing in his pocket, he pulled it out and squirmed it on the bridge of his nose. With his eyes squeezed shut, he could see the arc of sparks: the angel of pain and wretchedness, summoned by the surge of adrenaline. And this time, the pain came at once, without waiting for the sparks to go away. His poor head, punched and scratched so often in the last few days, pounded so hard he thought it would split.

With a roar of anger, he flung his glasses as far as he could down the hillside. He pressed the toad to the bruises and cuts on his face. He held it to his brow, while the creature pumped its legs and writhed in protest. It started to swell. The blotchy skin tightened and tightened. It oozed a nettling poison. Still, maddened by the jangling and thudding inside his head, Harry rubbed with the toad. Leaving the girl in the bracken, he paced this way and that, groaning and wailing, stumbling on scattered boulders, all but blinded by the dazzling sparks.

Until his head seemed to burst in flames, as the car had burst into flames...

There was an explosion inside it, a blooming of red and white fire. He fell to the ground beside the girl, retching into the damp, cold grass. Then he lay still.

The fit was quickly over. The angel had come and gone in no more than a minute, the worst but the shortest visit he'd ever had. A wave of relief swept through him.

As his head and his vision cleared, he looked down to the road. The fire was still blazing; the bus driver and some of his passengers were running this way and that, flapping at it with their hands. One of them was struggling gamely, hopelessly, with an extinguisher. There was a great commotion. When the people looked up and saw the red-headed man high on the hillside, they started to wave. They clapped and cheered. Harry stood up and heaved the girl to her feet. Heroic, he cuddled the girl upright, clasped her to him, lifted her hand in his, and together they waved back, acknowledging the applause.

Gently, reverently, he laid the girl down again. Kneeling beside her, he found the body of the natterjack toad. He must have squeezed it dead. It was still and cold, like a rotten potato. The eyes were shut, hidden, locked away.

No jewel. No toadstone. Just a knob of rubbery flesh.

But the magic had been there. Harry had felt the power inside him. It had delivered the golden girl. It had defeated the rock-climber. Now, at the end, it had banished the angel of pain and wretchedness. He hid the toad in the long grass.

He lay down with the girl and cuddled her to him, nuzzling his face into her hair. He slid a hand inside her dressing gown, cupping a soft, warm breast. And there he found the letter. Lizzie's letter! He slipped it out and tore the envelope open.

And Harry Clewe was lying in the bracken, delightedly reading with his head on the dead girl's shoulder, as the first of the people climbed up the hillside toward him.

PART
TWObrittlestar

1

It was a morning in November, early in the 1970s. Harry Clewe emerged onto the deck of his boat, the *Ozymandias*.

He scanned the scene from the mountains in the west, across the sandflats to the distant dunes, to the Menai Strait and Anglesey and the open sea. The tide was right out of the estuary. The channels of the river burrowed through exposed mud, and on this mud there were congregations of feeding birds. He inhaled fiercely, the cold salt air reviving him from a befuddled sleep. All around him and above him was a silver-gray sky, flecked with cloud: a huge sky that made him feel he was no longer earthbound, but soaring into space. Blue mountains floated on a surf of mist.

He dashed below, tiptoed through the cabin as quietly as he could so as not to waken the young woman who was sleeping there, and he returned on deck with his binoculars. There was a flock of widgeon, shoulder to shoulder on the flanks of the river; cormorants, black and angular like spars from a shipwreck; innumerable gulls and waders; a pair of shelduck, handsome and plump, adjusting themselves like women at a swimming pool; a flotilla of swans; a heron, stalking for eels in the shallow pools; mergansers, those sleek, dandified divers.... All this in one sweep of the estuary, as, for the past six years, he'd surveyed it from the deck of the *Ozymandias*.

Harry focused on the gulls, whose whiteness was smudged by the crows which fell among them. It was a furious commotion. The birds rose in a black and white cloud, squalling and screaming, and dropped again to the mud at the ebb of the tide. He cursed the condition of the binoculars, for the lenses were smeared and sandy and fogged by his breath, and for a moment he rubbed at them with a spotted red neckerchief he tugged out of his pocket. But it made no difference. He was intrigued to see what was causing such excitement at the water's edge. He wondered what the birds had found, that they should squabble so violently. He wondered what the sea had fetched up.

He stepped off the boat and onto the sea wall. From there he negotiated the rusty, slippery rungs of the iron ladder which was bolted to the wall, lowering himself onto the foreshore. He stood on the mud and shingle in which the hull was embedded, unzipped his trousers and urinated; and then, satisfied with a rapid inspection of the boat's timbers, he picked his way across the shore, over the seaweed-slippery boulders, and through the rolled-up flotsam of grasses, branches and sun-dried vegetation. Once on the flat sands, he moved more quickly in the direction of the birds.

The gulls and the crows gave way to him, whirling into the sky. The crows rowed raggedly ashore, to the fields where flocks of curlew and oystercatcher were feeding, and the gulls crossed to the dunes. Harry looked about, to see what had attracted such a mob.

The birds had gathered on the skeleton of a horse. It had been there for as long as Harry had lived on the estuary, a landmark on the open sands which he'd often seen on his walks. The first time he'd found it, he'd thought it was the wreckage of a small boat embedded in the mud. The ribcage was intact, like a huge, vicious trap left by primitive men for the capture of bears or other men. Pieces of the vertebrae lay round about, sunk into the sand. Bones... brown, riddled, softened to the consistency of sponge. The skull... no more than a shell, stuffed with mud, which gaped and was good only for the burrowing of worms and crabs. This was the wreckage of the horse. Harry stopped there and touched the pieces with his foot.

The pools and puddles were squirming with life. He knelt down to see exactly what had drawn the gulls and the crows to the skeleton. It was a phenomenon that Harry had seldom encountered before: the brown water of low tide was alive with hundreds of brittlestars.

The brittlestar: a creature akin to the starfish, but so much finer and more fragile that it was more like a bizarre marine spider. He picked one up on the palm of his hand, where it writhed and convulsed, where it arched itself in spasm.

An extraordinary, prehistoric animal. No eyes, no anus; a disc of a body, brown and hard, like a crumb of biscuit the size of a sixpence, from which five arms extended. These arms were about four inches long, extremely thin and delicate, covered with tiny brown spines. Harry put his face down to it, watching the arms as they curled and shivered. The brittlestar lived in the waters of the estuary, feeling blindly in the shifting darkness, passing food from the tips of its tube-feet to the underside of its disc-body and expelling waste from its mouth. A simple creature, odd and primeval, moving blindly with the movement of the tides...

Here, attracting the birds to feed on them, were hundreds of brittlestars. Harry scooped up dozens and saw that there were many different sizes and colors, a tangled, knotted handful of blue and green and orange and yellow, of mottled and marbled brown and black. The gulls had returned, screaming overhead, and he felt the rain of their droppings on his back and in his thick, red hair. But he ignored them. He held the brittlestars in his hands, marveling at them. He was thrilled to find them so near to the mooring of the *Ozymandias*.

Standing up, he let the brittlestars drop back into the water, where they sculled among the bones of the horse. The crows and the gulls were hysterical around him, impatient for him to go. He walked over the sands toward the boat, keeping in his hand just one of the brittlestars, and he clambered up the iron ladder to the top of the sea wall.

He tiptoed across the deck and down into the cabin. Without making a sound, he put the brittlestar in a shallow tray of water with a bed of sand. It squirmed and meshed, exploring, and soon it settled in this pool which was no different from the tidal pool from which Harry Clewe had lifted it. Here it was safe from the birds.

Quickly, silently, Harry took off his clothes and dropped them on the floor. Slipping under the rumpled sheet, he nestled to the soft, warm, naked body of the young woman who was lying asleep in the bed. She groaned and stirred, because at first his skin was cold. As she awoke, they made love, tenderly, urgently, with a hectic passion. They shuddered together, two bodies fused into one.

Afterward, they kissed and fell apart. He pressed his face into her long red hair. "I've been on the beach, while you were still asleep," he whispered. "Look, little Lizzie, I've got something to show you...."

2

It had happened like this.

As for the tragic events of that autumn in the late 1960s, once Harry's migraine had gone and his head had cleared, he'd explained the accident in which the rock-climber and Sarah had died. He'd told the truth, simple and unembellished. Patrick had come to the cottage, angry and aggressive, to find the girl. Fumbling for a light, the man had turned on the power which had killed him and the girl in the electrified bathroom.

Harry, in deep shock, had taken the dead girl joy-riding through Beddgelert and into the hills. He could hardly remember it; it was a blur to him, a nightmarish blur of migraine and madness. In any case, he was blameless; he'd reported the faulty wiring to his landlord, but the repairs hadn't been done. And that was that. The coroner had recorded a verdict of accidental death.

Soon afterward, Harry had moved down from the mountains to the shore, a few miles south of Caernarfon. The *Ozymandias* was an old customs launch he'd spotted on the remotest edge of the estuary and bought for a negligible sum, the write-off value of the Mercedes-Benz. It would be a refuge for him, where he might live on his own and try to forget what had happened. He'd made the boat habitable with a little work on the decks to ensure they were watertight, by installing a wood-burning stove which heated the cabin and enabled him to cook, and by bringing in the books and pictures he'd had in his Snowdonian cottage. The only reminder of his pursuit of Sarah was the red spotted neckerchief, which he would carry in his pocket or sometimes slip under his pillow.

He'd never been cold on the *Ozymandias*, even in the worst of the frosts which clenched the timbers of the hull and made them groan and crack, in the worst of the gales which swept from the sea and made the boat shudder and moan like an old sow. It had been home for Harry Clewe, for six years on his own....

Until, one morning, a telegram had been delivered to him.

It was from Lizzie, his little sister; not so little, for she was eighteen now and had just started her first year as a student at the Royal College of Music in London. The telegram told him that their parents, from whom Harry had been estranged since the trouble in Snowdonia, had been killed in a car accident.

So Harry took a train to Shrewsbury for the funeral. Lizzie came up from London. Afterwards, seeing that she was stunned by the bereavement, Harry had suggested on impulse that she should come back to North Wales with him and stay on the boat for a few days before returning to her studies. That was how it started.

It had been dark when they'd arrived at the boat, pitch-dark at midnight in late October. After the train to Bangor and a taxi to Caernarfon, it was an hour's walk along the beach, hand in hand on the shingle and weed of the foreshore, before they'd reached the mooring of the *Ozymandias*. Harry led his sister through a bewildering darkness, without talking except to encourage her on and on. No moonlight, no starlight. No sound but their crunching footsteps, their own irregular breathing, the cry of a heron on the estuary... At last they were there.

"Now stand still, Lizzie," Harry said, his voice sounding loud in the still, cold night. "We're on the sea wall, where there's a bit of a bend in the shoreline. The boat's tied up right here. I'm going to leave you for a minute while I go on board and unlock and go down below to turn some lamps on. For heaven's sake, don't move. If you wander about, you'll step right off the edge and into the water. Luckily, with the tide high at the moment, the boat's floating to the top of the wall, so it'll be easy for us to climb aboard. Stay there now."

He let go of her hand, for the first time since they'd got out of the taxi in Caernarfon square. She heard his footsteps on the wall, and then groans and the slapping of water as he boarded the boat. She heard him jangling the keys, the click of a lock and the sound of his footsteps fading as he went down into the cabin. Suddenly, miraculously, there was a light. A spark became a flare and settled to the gentle glow of a paraffin lamp, visible to her through a little round window. As she grew accustomed to this light, the first glimmer she'd seen for more than an hour, Lizzie took a few cautious steps forward, feeling the smoothness of the sea wall beneath her feet. Harry emerged from the doorway onto the deck, his every movement altering the level of the boat, so that this new light, which might then have been the only light in the world, danced before her.

"Lizzie? Are you there?" He was squinting toward her, one hand to his eyes as he peered in her direction. "Come aboard. Take it carefully, there are ropes you have to look out for."

She stepped from the wall onto the deck. He took her hand again. The boat sighed under their weight.

"Welcome to the *Ozymandias*," he whispered. They stood still while the deck settled beneath them. "'My name is Ozymandias, King of Kings,'" he intoned. "'Look on my works, ye Mighty, and despair!' You'll get a good look at her tomorrow. The poem's by Shelley, fairly appropriate if you don't mind a masculine name for a boat. The poem goes on: 'Round the decay of that colossal wreck, boundless and bare the lone and level sands stretch far away.' In the morning you'll see what a wreck the *Ozymandias* is, and you'll see the lone and level sands when the tide goes out. Watch your head now, as we go below."

He led her down the steep, narrow steps into the cabin. The amber light from the paraffin lamp gave an illusion of warmth, after the cold blackness of the night. Lizzie stared around for a moment, then she gave a squeal of excitement and bounced onto the bed, sitting next to Harry. They'd come into a good-sized cabin, bigger than Lizzie's room in her hall of residence in London, except that the ceiling was no more than seven feet high. The walls were paneled with wood, from which Harry had scraped away some of the paint in one of his earlier attempts at restoration. The floor was bare boards. There were round windows at eye level, portholes without curtains. Most of the paint had been stripped from the ceiling too; overhead, there was a hatch, bolted shut. Opposite the rumpled double bed, there was a stove, black and pot-bellied, with hinged doors on the front, with room on top for a saucepan or a kettle but not both, and a black chimney which disappeared through the ceiling above it; on the floor beside the stove, there were some splinters of driftwood and some newspapers. At the forward end of the cabin, a low door opened into a tiny compartment in the bow of the boat.

Lizzie squirmed with delight, flicking her hair from side to side as she pointed her bright white face from corner to corner of the cabin. In spite of the bareness, the absence of anything homely or decorative, the cabin of the *Ozymandias* was clearly wonderful to her. The lamp made everything golden, even the dust and the cobwebs, the nakedness of the boards and the stubbornness of the yellowing paint. When the timbers groaned beneath her, when the boat sighed from end to end and scrubbed itself on the sea wall, she jumped up with a shout of laughter.

"Oh, Harry, this is marvelous!" she cried, her face radiant in the lamplight. "We could make this really lovely, couldn't we? Let's get the fire lit! Shall I?"

Kneeling, without taking her jacket off or slinging away her shoulder bag, she screwed up the sheets of newspaper, pushed them into the stove and built a flimsy structure of twigs which exploded into flames as soon as she applied a match. Harry watched her, happy to see that she'd forgotten her sadness, for the time being at least. She was a tiny figure, slight and frail in a dark blue fleece jacket, blue jeans and suede boots. Her mass of hair gleamed like copper in the firelight. Although she was of age now, she was still the little sister she'd always been, whom he'd loved and cherished so much. He watched as she added more and bigger pieces of wood, as the fire grew hotter and stronger.

"There! That's enough for tonight, to take the chill off!" she cried. "We can collect lots more wood from the beach tomorrow, can't we?"

She turned toward him, her face flushed by the heat of the flames and with the pleasure of making them. The flames were blue, because of the salt in the driftwood. The fire threw red and golden shadows on the walls of the cabin.

The boat moved gently on the falling tide, as Harry and Lizzie Clewe, tired after their journey and drained by the grief of their bereavement, snuggled in blankets for their first night together on board the *Ozymandias*.

3

When Harry awoke, there was a pale light in the cabin. It was a light he recognized, reflected from the sand and shingle around the boat, which told him that the tide was out. Apart from the channels of the river itself, the estuary was dry. He lay on his back and watched as the shadows retreated to their corners of the ceiling, where they would be trapped in the cobwebs until the fire was lit again. He sat up and rubbed his eyes, groping for his glasses on the floor beside the bed.

Lizzie wasn't there, although the place beside him was still warm and her bag was on a chair at the foot of the bed. Harry got up, still wearing the clothes he'd been wearing the night before, put on his shoes and climbed to the deck.

At first he couldn't see her. It was six o'clock on a gray October morning. Shivering, he scanned the foreshore with his binoculars, across the sands to the creek where the river ran into the sea, to the tough grass of the dunes on the farther side of the estuary. This time, for once, he ignored the gathering birds: he was worried that Lizzie was missing, so far from her home, so far from her studies, in such a remote, unfamiliar place. He wished, for a second, that he hadn't invited her with him: not for himself, but for her. With a shudder of anxiety, he realized that, as her older brother, thirteen years her senior and her only relation in all the world now that their parents were gone, he was responsible for her. Perhaps, instead of bringing her to Wales, he should have accompanied her to London and resettled her there, where she might purge her grief by immersing herself in her music.

But then there was a cry from the estuary. He saw Lizzie, a hundred yards from the boat, coming toward him on the foreshore. Her coppery hair was the brightest thing in the monochrome morning. She was waving to him and calling. He looked at her through the binoculars: she was smiling too. She approached slowly, for she was walking on the very edge of the foreshore, on the uneven footing of boulders and seaweed, through the flotsam and jetsam of timbers and bottles and bones and bundled grasses. Every now and then, balancing precariously on the slippery rocks, she squatted and turned over the tangles of wrack, examined a relic and discarded it, before straightening up and continuing toward the boat. Harry watched her, cursing the poor condition of the binoculars. He put them down and waited for her to arrive at the mooring.

Her footsteps rang on the rusted rungs of the ladder as she climbed from the shore to the top of the sea wall. Breathing hard, she crossed the deck to where Harry was sitting. He didn't turn to look at her when she paused behind him; she said nothing, because she was out of breath, but he felt her hand on his head. Her fingers, smelling of seaweed, cold and wet from the beach and the cold, wet ladder, ran over his ear and down his cheek to his mouth, where they traced the line of his lips.

"Look what I found, Harry, among all the other wonderful things on your wonderful beach!" she whispered, leaning her head close to his. "What on earth is it? Is it a sea spider? Is there such a thing? Or only in the weird and wonderful world of Harry Clewe? Look, Harry! What is it?"

They took the brittlestar into the cabin and placed it in a shallow tray of water, with a bed of sand. Lizzie lit the fire. Straight away, that first morning, she began to make the *Ozymandias* more like home.

4

For a start, Harry and Lizzie tramped the shoreline many times, from the *Ozymandias* to the mouth of the estuary and back again. The priority was fresh water. They took a bucket to the brook, filled it and manhandled it, laughing and shouting as they stumbled over rocks and weed and up the iron ladder, so that Harry could deal with the chemical toilet in the forward cabin. Then they washed, shyly, negotiating the space around one another, giggling, not saying much.

The high-water line was littered with driftwood, and they came and went with armfuls of it, spars and branches which were white with salt, bleached by the sun, dried to brittleness and ready for burning. As they walked, Lizzie enquired about everything she found and saw, because everything was new to her. She was fascinated by the washed-up jellyfish, some of them a yard across, translucent and slick like gobbets of melted plastic. There were turnstones, very tame, very businesslike, working the weed for the insects in it. Harry showed her the mergansers, proud of them and pleased that they were there, and he hoped that Lizzie might see the peregrine he'd seen before, which terrorized the starlings from the cowpats in the fields and dashed among them, dangling a yellow claw. She picked up shells: winkles, whelks and wentletraps, cockles, razors and piddocks. She knelt and rummaged in the mattress of sea lettuce, bootlace and bladder-wrack, the great clumps of eel grass like heads of human hair. She found bones, the skulls of birds and sheep; the foot of a swan, the wings of a tern, the long, thin, down-curving bill of a curlew. A rubber glove, protruding from the mud, made her squeal. There were no more brittlestars, only the one she'd found that dawn and brought back to the boat as a trophy.

Hungry and dirty but very happy, they walked along the seashore to Caernarfon. Now they could see the way that had been so black the night before. Across the strait,

Anglesey was easy and green; inland, the mountains of Snowdonia rose bare, a fortress of wet, gray slabs. The castle was ochre in the winter sunlight, many-faceted like a nugget of gold. Harry held his sister's hand, and he could feel through the touch of her fingers the thrill of excitement she was experiencing.

They separated for fifteen minutes at the town's swimming pool, meeting again after their showers, and from there they went shopping for essential supplies for the *Ozymandias*. By mid-afternoon, on a day that nipped around the nostrils and set their faces tingling, it was time to step out fast, back toward the boat. The tide was rising in the estuary, driving the feeding birds closer and closer together on the exposed sandbanks. The air grew colder, so that Harry hesitated at first, when Lizzie asked if they could pause to look at the little church in the fields just a hundred yards from the shore. But then he led her toward it, among the slow-eyed cattle.

The church of St. Baglan squatted against the prevailing wind, rooted into the earth. Surrounding it, protecting it from the weather and the livestock, was a dry-stone wall, splashed with white, orange and scarlet lichen; and there were sycamores, stripped of their foliage, warped by the gales. Harry led Lizzie through the lych gate and into the churchyard. The wind had got up. The jackdaws brawled from the trees and were tossed like rags across the fields.

Lizzie moved from grave to grave, apparently careless of the cold. She bent to the stones, pushed aside the long grass and the brambles to read the inscriptions: the epitaphs of sailors and tide surveyors, shoemakers and candlemakers, schoolmasters and sea captains, of their wives and children. She called out to Harry, to kneel at the family grave of one John Hughes, his wife Laura and their six children, and she read the names aloud, her voice trembling.

"Look, Harry! Laura, Ellen, John, John, John and Robert... They had six children and not one of them survived two years! Here's another one the same," she said, turning to the next stone. "Ann Ellen, Catherine Ellen, Robert Griffith, Robert David, Jane Ellen, Gwen Ellen... six more children in the same grave! The children of R and J Williams of Cefn Ynysoedd, Llanfaglan, and none of them reaching the age of two! How awful! What on earth happened to them, Harry?"

By now, her thin white face was pinched with cold and her eyes were watering.

"Well, look at the dates," he answered, kneeling beside her and hugging her close to him. "They're not really so old, Lizzie, considering that the church dates from the twelfth century. In fact, if we come back some time when it's unlocked, I can show you the lintel over the doorway which has been dated to the sixth century, just after the end of the Roman occupation. But these children were dying in the diphtheria epidemics in the middle of the last century. If one of them got it, they all got it. There was a very high infant mortality rate in those days, with or without epidemics."

He could feel her shivering now. "Look, Lizzie," he said, "if we don't get you inside quickly, you'll catch your death. Then I might as well leave you here in the cemetery, with the little bones of the Williams children..."

She shuddered, grimacing with laughter at the horror and the humor to be found in the leaning, lichen-encrusted headstones.

"We'll come back another time," he told her. "You can spend as long as you like here."

He led her around the church, trailing his fingertips on its flanks as though it were an old horse, and they walked to the seashore track.

There was an early, threatening dusk by the time they approached the *Ozymandias*. The sky was prematurely dark, darkening with an ugly bruise. The sea crept over the mudflats. The masses of weed, half submerged in the shallows, black in the twilight, were like corpses, the nibbled and bloated bodies of drowned men which had been washed into the estuary. The swans fed among them, with growls and croaks. Over the open fields, a barn owl was hunting, quartering like a pale moth, dropping to the long grass to gorge on beetles, to linger in the hot, sweet breath of the cattle. It wafted to the hedgerow, where it stared its terrible moon-face and felt for flesh with its talons. All traces of the sun were gone.

Arriving at the boat, Harry stepped down first onto the deck, which was a yard or more below the level of the sea wall, and he helped Lizzie on board. "Good," he said. "We're just in time. Let's not go below just yet. Let's wait for a minute."

Gazing into the darkness, they heard the whispering of the wind in the dunes, the rumble of surf in the open sea, and the comforting conversation of a thousand duck. At this further corner of the estuary, there were no lights from cottages or farms: only a towering sky, a gathering twilight, a man and a woman on the deck of their boat. They waited together. The boat groaned. They felt it stir.

"Now!" Harry whispered, ducking his face to the girl's. He squeezed her to him. "Now, Lizzie! This is it! Can you feel it? The *Ozymandias* is waking up again!"

At that moment, the tide, which had been stroking the hull of the boat, lifted it gently from the sand. The boat shivered from one end to the other, seemed to stretch itself like an old dog, and then there was a wonderful feeling of weightlessness. The *Ozymandias* was afloat once more. Harry and Lizzie were no longer earthbound. They were sailing through an infinite darkness, following a ballooning moon to the very edges of the world.

5

That evening and that night, in the lamplit, firelit cabin, they continued their voyage, further and further from the day which had brought them suddenly together again. There was no talk of their parents, although they were thinking about them. There was no talk of Lizzie's music, her cello, her studies; no talk of London or Shrewsbury, which were faraway places in a distant, foreign, dimly remembered country. The wind got up. The moon was muffled by cloud. At sea, there was a storm which drove a swell into the shelter of the estuary. There was nothing to be seen from the portholes, for the blackness of the sky and the ocean was a kind of blindness.

The stove grew hot on a feast of firewood. The fuel, spitting salt, burned bright-blue flames, and soon the cabin was warm. Harry and Lizzie ate soup and bread and cheese, drank coffee laced with whisky. As the storm became fiercer, they blew out the lamp and lay on the bed, covering themselves with blankets. The *Ozymandias* wrestled at its mooring ropes, groaning and cracking, the timbers flexing like muscles unaccustomed to the work. It rode the tide. In the firelight, Harry and Lizzie listened to the wild wind and the booming water, imagining the world outside tossed into mad, blind, turbulent motion.

Rougher and rougher... they held each other tightly as the cabin rolled, as the boat banged on the sea wall, as the ropes stretched and sang. Noisier and noisier... they gripped hard, their faces deep in one another's hair. When the fire died and neither of them moved to revive it, the cabin was also black. So they lay together that night, huddled in the roaring, pitching darkness, as though they were the only living things in the grip of the storm.

Lizzie woke Harry with a whisper the following morning. The wind had dropped. The boat stirred fitfully with the chop of the waves, but the storm was over. It had turned to rain, whose watery gray light filled the cabin. Lizzie, sitting on the edge of the bed with the tray of shallow water beside her, was whispering over and over, using the word like a charm to wake her brother — "brittlestar, brittlestar, brittlestar" — and stirring the sand so that the strange, antique creature squirmed around her fingers. She grinned down at him, her face brilliant, her hair like a flame, as he sat up and peered shortsightedly to see what she was doing.

"The brittlestar!" she said. "It's our lucky charm, Harry! It guided us through the storm, when there were no other stars to guide us."

He turned sleepily toward her, blinked into the tray and then buried his face in the blankets again. "We stay in bed on days like this," he mumbled. "We stay in bed all day...."

So they did. The rain continued its gentle drumming on the roof of the cabin. The *Ozymandias* nestled to the sea wall as the breeze died to nothing. By midday, after Harry had got up to rekindle the fire — not a difficult task with plenty of dry wood and the ashes still warm from the night before — as he and Lizzie leaned together under the weight of the bedding, they felt the hull of the boat settling on its cushion of mud. Then there was stillness, a returning to earth. When Lizzie got up to look from the windows, she reported a landscape of flat, gray sand, a gray horizon and a huge, gray sky, a population of scurrying gray birds whose names she couldn't remember... and rain, a soft, unrelenting rain which gave everything a curious light, the gray-white glimmer of pearl.

The rain stopped, late in the afternoon. The sky cleared in time for a brilliantly orange sun to sink onto the dunes, a sun which flattened on impact and ignited a gigantic bonfire, whose embers glowed and flared and died.

Later that night, Harry took Lizzie onto the deck.

"Come and see the stars," he said. "Maybe I can give you a little guided tour."

They put on all the clothes they had, bundling themselves against the cold. Dressing, the two of them out of bed for the first time that day, they watched one another and smiled shyly, touching unconsciously in the confined space. Sometimes their hands met, as their eyes met.

On the deck, they nestled under a blanket, leaning back to see the sky. She grinned and grimaced when he brought out his battered old binoculars, but Harry insisted she should try them. "You're right, Lizzie!" he laughed. "These are the ones Mum and Dad bought me when I graduated from university. That was ten years ago, back in '62. I was twenty-one and you were just eight. What a memory you've got! I had them with me in Sudan, when I was teaching out there, and that's when I started using them on the stars. It was the clear skies in the desert that got me interested. Go on, try them! Even low-powered binoculars, even my ancient gritty binoculars, make a terrific difference."

The deck of the *Ozymandias* was a good place from which to observe the stars. The only distraction was a faint orange glow from the town of Caernarfon. There was no blurring from streetlamps, no smoke from houses or factories. Harry and Lizzie were away from all that on the deck of their boat, grounded on the wet, black sands of the wide, black estuary. They stared upward, holding their breath, and the stars were a glittering powder, like sugar crushed into a deep, blue-black carpet.

"The trick is this, Lizzie," he whispered. "Don't look straight at the stars. Look slightly askew, just a fraction to the side of the one you want, and you'll get a better focus. Edgar Allan Poe explained it in one of his stories, 'The Murders in the Rue Morgue,' I think it was: 'To look at a star by glances, to view it in a side-long way, is to behold the star distinctly; the lustre grows dim as we turn our vision fully upon it.' Let's start with Orion."

He glanced at his sister's upturned face. She was quivering with excitement. So he showed her the Hunter, a giant figure sprawled on his side, the magnificence of his bejewelled belt and the mistiness of his sword.

"Now, from there it's best like this," he said, and he drew her eyes straight down the line of the belt to the brightest star in the sky, Sirius, the Dog Star. "The one above Sirius is Procyon. So you already have three constellations, if you take in the smaller clusters around those distinct stars: you've got Orion, Canis Major and Canis Minor."

Onward and upward they moved, to the Twins, Castor and Pollux, in a sweeping curve to glorious, yellow Capella, and from there to Aldebaran, the eye of Taurus.

"That's an easy circuit," he whispered, "with Orion's Belt running one way to Sirius and the other way to Aldebaran. It points you round some of the clearest constellations."

She was breathless. When he leaned closer toward her, so close that he brushed her hair with his lips, she continued to gaze into the heavens.

"And there's lots more, little Lizzie," he said very softly, where her neck was very warm. "Lots and lots more..."

She was training the binoculars on the gaseous nebula in Orion's sword, on the fiery redness of Betelgeuse, discovering that Castor was white and Pollux was yellow, meeting the bloodshot eye of Aldebaran, gasping at the loveliness of the Pleiades.... Harry watched her.

"Perhaps," he whispered, nuzzling into her upturned collar, "perhaps one day I'll have a telescope on board the *Ozymandias*. A telescope, maybe the next time you come and visit, and then it'll be like flying. What do you think about that, Lizzie?"

She lowered the binoculars and turned her eyes to his. "I think it's all wonderful!" she said, and she buried her face into his coat before continuing, as though there were things she couldn't say without hiding herself from him. "I think the *Ozymandias* is wonderful! I think your estuary and your beach are wonderful, and all the odd creatures you've shown me!"

Then her voice was muffled against his clothes, as he looked down on the thick, red mass of her hair. "The stars as well, Harry!" she said. "You've brought me here and shown me everything, all these things I'd never seen before, things I hardly knew existed." Her shoulders started to shudder. She took a long gulping breath and said, "You make me feel so safe and happy here, Harry, so happy that I'll never want to..."

"Never want to what?" he asked her. But she didn't answer. She wept. He felt her body relax almost to bonelessness. He held her closely, and he gazed from her star-bright hair to the stars themselves. At last she spilled what was left of her grief, which she'd tried to hold back at the funeral in Shrewsbury. Sobbing, she mourned her mother and father, and she mourned the passing of her childhood years, which were gone for ever. Her parents' death had marked her transition into adulthood.

She wept for a long time, pressing her face into her brother's body. Even when she stopped, she didn't finish what she'd been going to say to him.

There was a perfect, unearthly silence that night. The wild-fowl settled to roost, folding their wings with a whisper. Not a breeze, not a cloud, but a clear sky and a crackle of early frost... a frost that gripped the air and squeezed it dry, that tightened like a thin steel trap. Harry and Lizzie lay on the bed, their faces to the fire, feeling its warmth on them. Apart from the flutter of the flames, the only sound was the creak of the boat's timbers. It seemed that the world and all its inhabitants were holding their breath, to conserve some inner heat. Brother and sister slept deeply, unconscious of the cooling fire, moving more closely together. They didn't feel the nudge of the rising tide and the shiver of the *Ozymandias* as the boat eased from the mud. They slept dreamlessly....

While Orion wheeled overhead. While the heron hunched in its cloak, while the fox limped across the fields, while the salmon surged to the river's mouth... While the sky and all its stars leaned on the earth.

In the morning, Harry awoke with a shudder of cold, alone in the bed. In his sleep, he'd turned to the wall of the cabin, so his opening eyes saw nothing but a blank of white and blistering paint. When he rolled over, he saw Lizzie kneeling by the stove, her back to him, busy with newspaper and splinters of wood, preparing to relight the fire. He watched her without speaking, her slim, boyish figure in one of his big, baggy pullovers, her bare white legs and feet, the toss of her bright-red hair in the gray light. He remembered what day it was: Lizzie had been with him on the boat for three days. She was startled when he spoke, because she hadn't heard him turning to look at her.

"Good girl," he said, making her jump. "Get it lit and then hop back into bed. The cabin will soon warm up again."

She grinned at him over her shoulder. The twigs crackled and spat as the newspaper exploded into flames. She built a scaffold of driftwood on the brand-new blaze, kneeling to watch the flames take hold.

"Come on, come back to bed," he said, and she slipped in beside him. "Enough of a fire to warm up the cabin a bit, for when we get up. We mustn't be late setting off. It's an hour's walk into Caernarfon and then at least half an hour on the bus into Bangor. Your train goes at midday."

She didn't say anything. She was burying her face in the blankets, as she'd buried her face the night before, and he sensed she was preparing to speak. But when a minute passed in silence, while he stared through her hair at the growing fire, he added, "Well, you've left me plenty of wood for this evening, when I get back here after seeing you off to London." He nudged her, making her look at him. "You'll visit the *Ozymandias* again, won't you, Lizzie? At the end of your term? Come for Christmas, if you like."

She fixed him with her clear, dry, intelligent eyes. "Oh yes, dear Harry, I'll be here at Christmas," she said quietly. "In fact, I'll be here this evening. You see, I'm staying on the *Ozymandias* with you. I'm never going back to London."

6

Indeed, it was Harry who found himself on the London train that afternoon, while Lizzie stayed on the boat.

They'd spent the morning in exhausting, numbing debate. He was astonished by her refusal to return to college. She was hurt by his sudden, impulsive decision to go instead of her, to talk to her tutor and the warden of her hall of residence, to leave her on her own to mull over her extraordinary decision.

She wept as, big-brotherly, Harry reminded her of all the work she'd done to win her scholarship at the Royal College of Music, how she'd worked and worked since she was a skinny little ten-year-old, bending her tiny body to the cello without missing a single day, including Christmases, birthdays and holidays throughout her childhood and adolescence. She wept as, trying to bring her to her senses by touching the wound of her present grief, he reminded her of the unselfishness, the sacrifice of their parents, whose only thought had been the future of their exceptional daughter. She wept as he reminded her that, in winning her scholarship and her place at the college, she'd won a chance that others had worked for, whom she'd beaten into disappointment.

But she was stubborn. He couldn't dissuade her. The fire went out and the cabin grew cold again, but they wouldn't seek warmth and comfort under the blankets. They sat apart, shivering. They sat in silence, distanced from one another, clenched up.

The morning passed. At last, Harry said gruffly, "Well, if I don't get moving, I'm going to miss that train," and he started to dress. While he gathered a few things, Lizzie grew calmer, smearing the tears on her face, breathing more deeply and steadily, and she dressed too. They didn't touch, maneuvering carefully in the confined space of the cabin. Without glancing at her, hoping he'd made her change her mind by threatening to leave without her, he said, "Are you coming then, Lizzie? I can travel down to London with you and make sure you're all right, if you like."

But she replied, her face averted from his, "No, Harry, I'm not coming. I'm going out on the beach to start collecting some more wood for the stove, if you're really going to leave me here all on my own."

Coincidentally, they were ready at the same time, both dressed, their red hair tousled after a night under the blankets. Harry was going to London; Lizzie was going to gather driftwood from the seashore. It was exactly the opposite of what he'd envisaged.

"At least," he said through gritted teeth, acknowledging with a shrug and a weary sigh that she wouldn't alter her decision, "at least have the goodness to walk with me into Caernarfon, won't you? On the way back you can collect all the bloody firewood you can carry."

As they walked, he told her that he would talk to her tutor and make things straight for her, for the time being. He would go to her hall of residence, let himself into her room and stay overnight there; he would talk to the warden the following morning and then return to Wales with some of her clothes and, most importantly, with her cello and her music. By now they were touching again, hand in hand on the boulders of the seashore track.

"I don't want the cello!" she said.

They stopped walking and faced one another. Her eyes gleamed cold, and her lips were white with anger.

"You needn't fetch it for me! Listen, Harry, I know how much it cost and how Mum and Dad saved up to buy it for me, and how they saved for all my expensive tuition. I know all that and I loved them for it. I'll always love them, remembering everything they did for me. But I've finished with the cello. Even if you bring it up here to the *Ozymandias*, I'll never touch it. It's dead for me."

She grimaced, shuddering at the thought of it. "Ugh! Bits of dead wood, all twisted out of shape and embalmed

in layers of polish! I hated the tension of it, as though it
would snap into splinters at any moment... shatter into lots
of ugly, sharp spikes. That's what it started to feel like for
me. I never told Mum and Dad, and I never told you, Harry,
although I nearly did in one of the letters I used to write
to you. I just kept working, holding the cello between my
legs, feeling the tension in it building and building, waiting for the thing to burst into pieces and then all the spikes
to fly off and stick into me. I know it sounds horrible and
silly and ungrateful, but that's what it felt like. Can you
imagine it, Harry? Can you?"

She paused for a moment and took a deep breath. She
wrung her brother's hands, and her fingers were icy on his.
Her sharp little face was very white, pinched with cold,
blanched by the brightness of her hair.

"Please, Harry! Please don't bring the cello back!" she
implored him. "We'll think of something to do with it later,
but for the time being, leave it in its case, in my room. Then,
if it happens to shatter, with all that tension wound up so
tight for so long, it can shatter inside its case and not hurt
anybody with its flying spikes!"

She looked up at her brother's bewildered, frowning face
and she laughed. "Harry, my dear Harry, the things I want
are here," she said softly. "Now that Mum and Dad are dead,
the cello's dead, too. For the first time in years, since I was
nine or ten, I'm free of it. It's a great feeling! All I want is
this bit of a beach, this washed-up end of the estuary, where
a river goes trickling into the mud... and then the sea comes
in, all fresh again, cleaning up and bringing odd things with
it. Not exotic things, but pieces of lives, real lives. Birds or
fish that have really flown or really swum. Not like the cello,
holding its breath in its velvet-lined case."

She smiled at him, and her eyes glistened with tears. "I
want to be here with you, Harry," she said, "on your silly
old boat. Mum and Dad thought you were mad or lazy, coming to Wales, wasting your time after all that expensive

schooling and university and teacher training, but I didn't. I could see that you were alive and breathing, doing what you wanted to do. And I always thought that one day I'd escape and join you, wherever you were. So here I am, alive and breathing! That's why I want to stay here instead of going back to London. Don't bring the cello back, Harry! Please don't!"

At last she stopped, out of breath after this gushing confession. They started to walk again, along the beach toward Caernarfon. Harry didn't speak, until, as they crossed the Seiont footbridge opposite the castle and paused for a few moments to watch a cormorant which was fishing in the river mouth, he said to her, "Listen, Lizzie. I'm going all the way to London and back to do these things for you, because you're my little sister, because I love you... and, now that there's just the two of us in all the world, because I'm responsible for you. Do you understand that? I'll bring the cello back with me, and then it's up to you. You can do what you bloody well like with it. Smash it up for firewood if you like. But I'm bringing it back here. All right?"

So they parted in Caernarfon square, where Harry caught the bus to Bangor. "You've got money?" he said to her. "You've got the key to the boat. You've got food. I've got your room key for the hall of residence, and the name of your tutor. For heaven's sake, look after yourself! Keep warm and dry and I'll be back tomorrow night."

He held her tightly, squeezing her so hard that he could feel her bones against his, as though she were a part of his own body. "Lizzie," he whispered. "Silly, stubborn, pigheaded Lizzie! Lizzie, my little love..."

7

The expedition was a horror for him. He hated the city. He hated the idea of leaving Lizzie alone on the estuary. By late afternoon, the train was approaching Euston Station. The landscape was appalling: acres of blackened industrial dereliction, scorched earth which even the willowherb refused to colonize; vast areas abandoned as graveyards for all kinds of twisted and rusting wreckage; on every space on every soot-caked wall, a scrawl of obscene, humorless graffiti; huge, sky-blotting hoardings; glimpses in the half-light of cramped and crabby lives in dark terraces, where the only illumination through a haze of exhaust fumes was the jaundice of neon.

The train got in. It burrowed into a black, booming hole. Harry crossed London in rush hour. Swept downstairs by a swarming, faceless, breathless mob, bullied onto escalators, he was crushed into the carriages of tube trains, where the oddest of intimacies took place: people who wouldn't speak to one another or look at each other were forced into a clammy union of buttocks and bellies and breasts of every age, shape, size and ethnic origin. Finally, after a walk through a maze of ill-lit streets lined with plastic rubbish bags and cankered plane trees, he sneaked into Lizzie's hall of residence, found her room and let himself into it.

It was cold and empty, smelling of bleach. Only the cello, leaning in one corner, and Lizzie's clothes in the drawers and wardrobe reminded him that she'd been there.

He sat down on her bed, and a wave of desolation swept over him. He imagined her alone on the *Ozymandias*, under a wide, starlit sky, hearing the cries of the curlew, watching a blue flame in a salt-spitting fire... while he had come to London.

And, next day, there were bewildering things to be done.

Lizzie's tutor was first of all speechless, and then very angry. While Harry stood meekly in the book-lined study, having given an account of his sister's whereabouts and state of mind, the man paced furiously around him, flinging questions into the air without waiting for answers or explanations. On a boat? A *boat*? What on earth was she doing on a boat? In Wales? Why Wales? It occurred to Harry, as he remained silent and glum, that it was Wales that infuriated the man more than anything else; if he'd said the boat was in Devon or Sussex or even on Skye, the tutor wouldn't have minded so much. But Wales! The man repeated the word with distaste, as though it were an unpleasant condition like piles or athlete's foot. And where was her cello? Why hadn't she had the courtesy to excuse herself, to write or telephone? On a boat? In Wales? Why?

At last the man was forced to pause for breath. Harry managed to repeat that Lizzie was recovering from the shock of her parents' sudden death, that she was taking the opportunity of enjoying a break she'd never had since she was ten years old. He suggested that it wasn't such a bad thing if she enjoyed the break a bit longer before returning, refreshed, to her work with the cello. But when he left the man's study, he felt as though he'd been mauled by a grizzly bear.

He returned to the hall of residence, where he thought it would be an easier matter to talk to the warden, to unlock Lizzie's door again and take out the cello and a few clothes. It wasn't. The warden was suspicious. She was a burly, middle-aged woman with a wall-eye, who insisted on telephoning Lizzie's tutor to confirm that this tousled young man was really the student's older brother, who might reasonably have access to the girl's room and walk away with a valuable musical instrument. There ensued a conversation between the tutor and the warden about the extraordinariness of the student's removal to a boat in Wales.

Again it was the Welshness that rankled. When at last the woman put the phone down, she squinted at Harry, barely satisfied by what the tutor had told her, and said, "So, she's in Wales. I wondered where she'd got to. In Wales..." Leading Harry along the corridor to Lizzie's door, she continued to mutter the word, repeating it over and over, as a child might savor a new obscenity it had picked up in the playground. Harry blew the dust from the heavy black case in which the cello was locked. One of the woman's eyes followed his every movement as he gathered an armful of socks and underwear from a bedside drawer and packed them into a bag; the other eye watched the ceiling.

Somehow he wrestled the cello and the bag across London. He wanted to get out of the city as quickly as possible. As the train accelerated into open country, his spirits rose. He leaned back in his seat and thought of the warm, gently rocking cabin of the *Ozymandias*.

8

It was nearly midnight as he walked the last hundred yards along the seashore toward the boat. It was dark and cold, but he was warm enough with the effort of trudging from Caernarfon with the bag and the cello. A tall, unwavering plume of smoke rose from the chimney of the *Ozymandias*, and a light glowed at the portholes. Lizzie unlocked the door when he knocked on it and they hugged each other breathless on the swaying deck. She winced when she saw the cello, but said nothing. They went below.

She'd transformed the cabin. Harry stared around it, surprised and impressed. "Good Lord, Lizzie!" he exclaimed. "You've been busy, haven't you?" There was fresh white paint on the walls and the ceiling. Bright curtains hung at the windows, a bright, thick rug lay on the floor, and a colorful quilt lay on the bed. There were flowers in jugs, seashells and unusual pebbles in saucers. The fire burned hot in the stove, throwing out golden flames, and the driftwood stacked in the corner exhaled a breath of the beach.

"It's terrific!" he said. "What a job! And I was worried that you mightn't be all right! It looks as though you can cope pretty well. But have you spent a lot of money?"

They sat down. He was relieved to get out of his coat and drop the cello. The boat rocked on a rising tide, stirred at its moorings. Lizzie assured him that everything she'd bought was from the charity shops in Caernarfon, the rug and the quilt and the remnants she'd used for the curtains, and the paint had been on special offer from the do-it-yourself store.

"Don't worry anyway," she said. "There's plenty of money in my account. Mum and Dad made sure of that, to supplement my grant. And what about the will? We're going to be quite rich, the two of us. Aren't we?"

He told her about his meeting with her tutor and her warden. "I only stalled them, you know," he said. "That's all. We can't just leave it like that. You've only just started the course. They're expecting you back, sooner or later. I practically promised them you'd go back, and I promised that in the meantime you'd be here sawing away at the cello, practicing just as you're supposed to be doing in London. Before I left your room, I checked that there's plenty of music in the cello case, as well as a few spare strings, your bow and rosin, so there's no excuse for not practicing. You ought to telephone your tutor, that's the least you can do. This is all marvelous, of course." He gestured around the firelit coziness of the redecorated cabin. "It's all marvelous, Lizzie, but..."

Here, his words dried up. He remembered the horrors of London, the stinks and the dirt and the faceless mobs, and how relieved he'd been to escape. Must his sister go back there? Must she bind herself once more to a regime she hated, straddling the cello with her thin, white legs, bending her body to it?

"But what?" she said, with a tiny, mysterious smile on her face. "But what, Harry? Come on, let's put this horrible thing away."

She took the cello, lugged it into the forward cabin, propped it up beside the chemical toilet and closed the door on it. She sat on the bed, very close to him, and leaned her smiling mouth toward his mouth.

"But what, Harry?" she whispered. "You don't really want me to go back to London, do you?"

So a second weekend went by. There was no talk of music, the cello, the Royal College. Harry and Lizzie shelved all that and let the days and nights look after themselves. They remained silent on the whole subject, as though it would go away and leave them alone. Every other day they walked into Caernarfon for showering and shopping, and it was then that Harry's stomach seemed to buckle at the sight of a telephone kiosk, while Lizzie would tug him past it with a determined smile on her face. She wouldn't phone.

Another week slipped by, October into November. Gradually, in their minds, the idea of Lizzie's commitment to studying in London became dimmer and dimmer, like a dream they'd almost forgotten, a dream which only nagged a little in their memories. The time dissolved into nothing. It didn't matter what day it was. Harry and Lizzie were engrossed with one another: with their exploration of the estuary for fuel and for treasures, with the tides and the rhythmic movements of the *Ozymandias*, with the shifting patterns of the birds on the sands, with the fixity of the stars in the sky....

The sky. The seas and the river and the shining mudflats were merely a reflected fragment of it. In the mornings, it was a towering white vault, raising a foam of cloud. In the afternoon, it was a canopy of beaten silver, which silvered everything beneath it. In the evenings, there were flames, as though, just over the horizon, a huge city were besieged and burning. And at night, there were stars on a background of black emptiness.

The *Ozymandias* was a speck. Harry and Lizzie were mites, clinging so hard together in the swaying, creaking darkness of their boat that they became one mite: microscopic, but alive, breathing and warm under an icy heaven.

A month passed since their parents' death. And soon, as natural as breathing, as warm and as soft as their breath in the firelit cabin, Harry and Lizzie were lovers.

9

Harry continued to nurse the idea that Lizzie might yet return to her studies in London. She might go back after Christmas to start the new term, and these weeks on board the *Ozymandias* would have been a curious episode, a time in which a brother and sister had fallen in love and become lovers in a way which neither of them could have foreseen or prevented.

But for Lizzie, the matter was closed. She wore an expression of fierce, formidable happiness. It seemed to say: "I was once a child in the care of loving but repressive parents... now I'm an adult with my own life to lead. I was once bound to a carcass of highly polished, tightly clenched wood... now I live and move freely under a huge sky."

She would smile determinedly as she marched ahead of Harry on the shore, as she bent with a cry of excitement to something quaint or bizarre in the debris of the high-water line, as she stumbled over the slippery boulders with an armful of driftwood. The tilt of her chin and the glitter of her eyes were defiant; here was a joy she would not relinquish to anyone. It was a joy she shared with Harry. Since it was Harry who'd initiated her removal to this wild, open world of seas and skies, so she loved him. She loved him with a passion that made her giddy.

The feeling was mutual. He was dazed just by watching her: by the movement of her bright, red head or the flex of her slim body. When she turned on the beach, pointed her little white face at him and flashed a smile, his head would reel. To hold her close and love her in the rumpled blankets of their warm cabin was to feel the rest of the world dissolve into nothingness, whether the *Ozymandias* was becalmed on a bed of mud or riding a driving swell. Harry and Lizzie were utterly absorbed in one another and their place. Still, sometimes, he hoped that she might one day lay a finger on the cello again.

A postman came with two letters. He was disgruntled, obliged to cycle down the narrow, muddy track to the foreshore, but the address was on the envelopes and it was his duty to deliver. One of the envelopes, originally postmarked in London, was addressed to Miss Elizabeth Clewe at the family house in Shrewsbury, to be forwarded if possible. Someone had redirected it to "The *Ozymandias* (a houseboat), The Estuary, near Carnarvon, North Wales." There were two notes inside it, from Lizzie's warden and her tutor, which Lizzie read out loud, her voice ringing clear and high in the little cabin.

The warden, the wall-eyed woman whom Harry had met, had written to say that the student's belonging were safe for the time being in her allotted room, but there was a waiting list for places in the hall of residence and another student would be admitted in the New Year if Lizzie had decided not to come back.

Her tutor wrote:

"Dear Miss Clewe,

Since I've heard no news of you since your brother's visit, I assume that you will not be taking up your place at the College, at least for this term. What a pity! We are putting on the Dvorak cello concerto at Christmas and would have loved to have heard you play: a great and glorious work! While I am concerned that you are well, following the tragic loss of your parents, I should remind you that your scholarship was contested by a number of other young musicians, who might have grasped the opportunity with more seriousness and maturity. I sincerely hope that you will consider..."

Lizzie stopped reading. She snorted with a strange, uncouth laughter, crumpling the notes in her hand and tossing them into the stove. Her smile remained intact, as hard and as cold as ice. For her, the matter was closed.

"Well, Harry? What's in the other letter?" she asked him. "Come on, open it. I think it's from Daddy's solicitor."

She was right. The other envelope was postmarked in Shrewsbury, addressed to Harry and Elizabeth Clewe, their names juxtaposed as though, instead of being brother and sister, they were husband and wife. The letter was about their parents' will. At first they read it quickly, skimming the lines for the gist. Then, stunned into breathlessness, they slumped on the bed and reread the letter very slowly. It made no difference to Harry, who'd never expected an inheritance, who'd assumed he'd been cut off a long time ago, alienated and estranged from his disappointed parents. But it would have made a difference to Lizzie.

There was no money. Although the Clewes had kept up appearances, maintaining the house in suburban Shrewsbury, financing Lizzie's private education and expensive music tuition, there was nothing left, now that they were dead, to benefit their beloved, brilliant daughter. Nothing. The Clewes had been broke, or rather, living precariously on the brink of being broke. They'd lost catastrophically on the stock market. The house was mortgaged and re-mortgaged to the hilt. There were no insurance policies; the solicitor reported bleakly that these had been cashed to see Lizzie through her last few years at school.

At last, after a long silence, Lizzie said, "'I'm glad, in a way.'"

Harry's mouth fell open. He stared at her, agog, and she burst out laughing, the same snorting, uncouth laughter with which she'd greeted the letter from her tutor.

"Well, don't look so amazed, Harry!" she cried. "Did you think I was going to break down crying? A spoiled little heiress, heartbroken because she hasn't inherited a fortune from Mummy and Daddy?" She crumpled the solicitor's letter and tossed it into the flames. "There! That's the end of it! It's all gone! We're on our own now, Harry. We're adrift on the ocean, on board the *Ozymandias*. It's what I wanted. I told you that, didn't I? Don't you remember? I told you! It's what I wanted!"

She flung herself at him. She hugged him so hard that all his breath was squeezed from him. Still laughing at what she'd said and her brother's dumbfounded expression, she forced him backward on the bed. She smothered his face with her hair. So they lay panting, their bodies joined, and the boat seemed to rock as they rocked, as though they were drifting away from their moorings, further and further out to sea, further and further from the world they'd known. Yes, they were adrift, adrift together.

Harry hugged Lizzie as hard as she hugged him. His heart seemed to rise in his chest, to swell and burst with the love he felt for her. He stared through her hair, which was soft and fragrant on his face, and he blinked through the tears in his eyes. Yes, oh yes, he wanted her with him, alone, adrift... but the letter from her tutor confirmed that the option of her returning to London was still there, if she should choose to take it. He was torn, terribly torn, between wishing she might resume her studies, to nurture her talent instead of letting it waste away, and wanting her to stay with him for ever on board the *Ozymandias*. As her brother and her lover, he felt the dilemma like a stab of pain inside him.

10

It was the beginning of December. Both the brittlestars, the one that Lizzie had found on her first morning and the one that Harry had brought in from the squalling of gulls, were dead. They'd died in their shallow tray. Lizzie had taken them out of the water, thrown the water away, and kept the brittlestars with her other relics of the beach, the bones and feathers and shells she'd brought in and arranged prettily around the cabin. The brittlestars dried and stiffened. They were fragile wafers of the squirming, sinuous creatures they'd been, as dry as biscuit, as dead as ice. Lizzie kept them on the shelf in the corner, where Harry's bird books, poetry books and star books were neatly stacked together.

Harry's flute was there too, in its case, almost invisible between the top of the shelf and the beams of the ceiling. He hadn't touched it for years, although, in his schooldays, he'd been a competent flautist. Mischievously, thinking of Lizzie's cello left silent and neglected in the forward cabin, he reached for his flute one evening, as he and Lizzie sat in the cabin together. She was flipping the pages of a magazine. She didn't glance up as he lifted the long, slim, black case from the bookshelf and opened it on the bed.

The flute shone cold and silver in the firelight. As Harry leafed through a sheaf of sheet music, he saw, from the corner of his eye, that Lizzie was watching him. She was pretending not to, but her breathing was altered. There was a tension in her, as though the chill of the flute had touched her across the quiet, warm cabin.

"It's years since I had a go with this," he said. "I was in the school orchestra, you know, at Wrekin. I bet we sounded bloody terrible, wheezing and scraping! I got to grade eight, though. I used to think I was quite good, until you came along, my brainy, brilliant baby sister, and showed me up."

She didn't say anything. She curled herself into the chair, kicking off her slippers and folding her legs beneath her, and pretended to be engrossed in reading. As she dipped her head to the magazine, her long red hair fell around her face like a screen. She was hiding from him.

"I'll be a bit rusty, I expect," he went on. "My fingers will have seized up. And the flute might be rusty too, although it's been in its case all the time. Let's have a go." He tried a scale, licked his lips and tried again, pleasantly surprised by the tone of the instrument. "Hey, it sounds all right, doesn't it, Lizzie? Quite nice acoustics on board the *Ozymandias.* What do you think?"

She looked up at him, flicking her hair from her face. Her smile was different, somehow askew. "The tone's fine," she said. "When you've got it warmed up, I expect the tuning will improve. I hope so, anyway." She dropped her head to the magazine.

Undeterred, Harry continued to work. He practiced scales and exercises, ran through some of the pieces he'd studied years ago, as a sixth-former in public school. He impressed himself with the way he could still play, although he fluffed and fumbled here and there. His eyes met Lizzie's as she moved around the cabin to refuel the stove or make coffee. The anxiety caused by the unexpected appearance of the flute, its exhumation, diminished over the course of the evening, as the surprise wore off and Harry's sensitivity to pitch became keener. Lizzie relaxed again. She dropped the magazine, lay down on the bed and listened as he played. So he grew more and more confident; at first, he'd been nervous with Lizzie as his audience. He steeled himself to the grimace on her face when he was clumsy. He ignored her flinching at his wayward tuning. He played on, sensing her initial misgivings turn to tolerance.

At last, when he stopped and shut the flute and the music into the case, he lay down beside her on the bed. He whispered into her hair. "Now, that didn't hurt too much, did it? Are your delicate little eardrums still intact? Or is that another piece of your intactness that your big, bad brother has stolen from you? It hurts a bit the first time, but I promise it gets better and better...."

It was the first of successive evenings when he practiced with the flute. However, Lizzie made no move to touch the cello, which remained in its case, in its corner, beside the chemical toilet. He wondered how he might encourage her to play again.

11

They agreed to split up for an hour, the next time they walked into Caernarfon. The Christmas lights were on in the streets. The shop windows were bright with decorations. When they came out of the sports center after their showers, Harry and Lizzie met a darkening afternoon, the pavements glistening under orange neon lights. It was cold, a raw cold which clenched around their wet heads.

"Maybe I'll have a browse in some of the shops," he suggested. "On my own. I've got an idea for your Christmas present. A surprise, of course."

And she answered with an enigmatic smile that she might have a surprise for him too; she would go off to make some enquiries about it. So they separated, having arranged to meet later in one of the tea shops near the castle.

He went into a newsagents, to place an advertisement in the window. Handwritten on a postcard provided by the shop, among the other advertisements offering flats to let, cars and motorcycles for sale, rewards for the return of lost cats and jewelry, it read: "Tuition in flute and musical theory. All standards, from beginners to grade eight. If interested, leave phone number in the shop." The card cost him a few pence for the week, and the shopkeeper agreed to keep a note of any enquiries until he called in again. This accomplished, having decided to keep it a secret from Lizzie pending a response, he strolled the busy streets of the town and blinked at the twinkling windows until it was time to meet her.

She was already there, in a corner of the tea shop, her hands closed around a mug of coffee.

"Did you find what you were looking for?" she asked, as he sat down and ordered another coffee. "Aren't you going to give me a clue about my present?"

He shook his head. It was hard to talk, because the place was hot and crowded and there was a television blaring: a war film, in black and white, was reaching an explosive climax. Harry sat opposite Lizzie and explained that she'd have to wait until Christmas morning for even a glimpse of what she might get. The film ended. There was a splendid feeling of relief in the tea room that the screaming of shrapnel and the rattle of machine-gun fire were over. The credits rolled on a background of monochrome flames.

"No," he said, now that the place was quieter. "No clues about Christmas. But I might have some other news for you soon. It's a secret. What about you? Did you order my present? Have you been sitting on Santa's knee in his supermarket grotto?"

She nodded, smiling into her coffee. "You'll have to wait too. It's a secret. Meanwhile," she went on brightly, reaching down to a plastic bag on the floor by her feet, "I've got some decorations for the *Ozymandias*. Can we get a bit of a tree and some holly? There must be lots in the hedges along the seashore."

In this way, they began their preparations for a Christmas on the boat. The only reminder of another world, a previous existence, was Harry's practice on the flute. Otherwise, their absorption in one another and their isolation on the estuary gave the increasing feeling that their past had been a dream, whose detail, once so sharp and graphic, was blurring. For Harry, all his schooldays and university days, his time as a teacher in England and Sudan, the short, eventful period he'd spent as a gardener in Snowdonia and his mad pursuit of the blonde Sarah... it all seemed to fade from him. It was dissolving into nothing, as a dream dissolves, as the memory flickers and fades like old newsreel. For Lizzie, this was a new world. Only the flute reminded her of where she'd come from. She was adrift with her brother, her lover, on a wide sea, under a wide sky.

In such a small space as the cabin of the boat, it took no time to make it festive. With candles, with the festoons of tinsel that Lizzie had bought, with holly and mistletoe raided from the hedgerow, they made a cozy Christmas nest. They couldn't find a suitable tree among the wind-warped sycamores along the seashore: their one concession to conventionality in such an unconventional setting would be to buy one, as though they were a young couple mortgaged into semidetached suburbia. This was high on their shopping list, the next time they walked into Caernarfon.

So they separated, to be reunited later, having showered, having accomplished their mysterious errands among the press of Christmas shoppers. By four o'clock the afternoon was dark, with a heavy sky leaning on the streets and the black slab sides of the castle, but the shops were loud with music and laughter, ablaze with lights. Having bought a tree, Harry carried it like an enormous brush in front of him, sweeping a path through the milling crowd. And he was pleased to find there were three replies to his advertisement. Removing his postcard from the newsagent's window, he went to rejoin Lizzie.

Stepping into the tea room, he was met by a blast of heat and noise. Every seat was occupied; there were people standing, there were children and pushchairs and dogs; red-faced, sweating waitresses fought their way from table to table. This time there was a rugby match on the television, turned up against the din of voices. Harry, newly scrubbed and shaved, his glasses misted in the sudden steam after the cold air outside, stood at the door and peered around for Lizzie; he felt clumsy, claustrophobic, bundled in too many clothes, clutching the tree. About to turn and leave, he heard her voice calling his name. Whipping off his glasses, he spotted her in a far corner, where she was sharing a table with some other customers. He struggled toward her, brandishing the stiff branches of the tree and its battery of needles.

He squeezed onto her chair, jamming the tree beside him. "This is bedlam!" he bellowed, the words barely audible in the uproar.

She was giggling at him, having watched his entry into the tea room and his maneuvers toward the table. Her thigh was hot against his. Her hair, washed and blown dry in the sports center, gleamed like copper, and her face was flushed with laughter and the warmth of the crush.

"Bloody Christmas!" he shouted, but she couldn't hear him. "Bloody Christmas!" he mouthed at her, thrilled to see her so happy. It was impossible to talk, so he reached for the spotted red neckerchief he happened to have in his pocket and concentrated on wiping the steam from his glasses. There were children crying, a dog was barking; a try was scored and the commentator was shrill amid the thunder of a distant stadium. The windows were running with condensation. But Harry was happy. Crushed into the corner of an overcrowded cafe, with no hope of service, sharing his space with bad-tempered strangers and the prickles of a small conifer... it was grand, so long as he was with Lizzie.

With a swig from her mug of coffee, he reached for a paper napkin, spread it on the table and took a pen from his pocket. He winked at her, and wrote on the napkin: "I've got news for you."

The volume of the television seemed to increase, and so did the clamor of the room. It grew hotter.

Lizzie read the note, took the pen from him and wrote her reply: "I've got news, too."

He produced the postcard he'd placed in the newsagent's window and slid it to her. As she was reading it, he scribbled on the napkin:

"Got three replies! We'll be rich!"

She read this too. She glanced up at him, her face momentarily clouded, for the flute was the only thing which nudged her memories of a life before the *Ozymandias*. But the cloud passed. As she reached for the pen again, she gripped his hand warmly. There was another message to write. Still the room was hotter and noisier and more crowded, with more customers forcing in. Lizzie was writing on the napkin, and Harry could smell the shampoo on her hair as she leaned toward him. When she'd written the note, she folded it once, folded it again, flashed a look at the family who were sharing the table to discourage them from watching, and then hesitated with the napkin in her hand. She held it to her lips, and again there was a cloud on her face, a shadow on the gleam of her smile, as though she might change her mind and withhold the note from him. At last, when Harry put out his hand, she took an enormous breath and proffered the piece of paper.

He unfolded it and read. She'd written: "I'm pregnant."

So the two of them sat at their table, perched on a chair in a corner of that hectic place, holding their breath, watching one another's eyes. Harry read the note again, neatly printed on the white napkin. For a few moments his mind was blank. All the noises of the room faded into a rushing silence, as though he'd been sucked through the porthole of a ruptured airliner and was tumbling through an emptiness of cold, thin air. Then the room came back. Lizzie was smiling, and the brilliance of her smile fell on him. He reached for her cup and gulped the dregs of coffee from it. Taking the pen from her fingers, letting his fingers linger on hers for a second, he wrote on the napkin: "I love you. Let's go home."

Somehow they managed to extricate themselves from the tea shop. The struggle with the tree caused a mixture of hilarity and petulance, invoking a squeal of alarm from a waitress as the friction of the prickles on her nylon pinafore produced a flash of static electricity. It was nothing compared with the charge which was going through Harry, the current which coursed through him from the folded napkin he'd pushed into his pocket.

Soon, they'd walked around the base of the castle, which was floodlit into sharply angled relief against the black sky. They crossed the Seiont footbridge to the other side of the river mouth. Harry held the tree by its stump and let the branches trail behind him; his other hand gripped Lizzie's hand.

Six o'clock. A December evening. The air was mild and damp. The sky was a single, impenetrable cloud: no moon, no stars. They walked in silence until the lights of the castle had vanished behind them and they'd entered a world of utter darkness. Only the whisper of the waves on the foreshore, the cry of a heron, which flapped away from the sound of footsteps. The rustle of the bristles of the Christmas tree...

After a while, Lizzie spoke. Her voice was soft, disembodied. "This is just like the first time you walked me along here, Harry," she said. "Do you remember? Not a light in the world. Just you leading me along. I couldn't see a thing then, and I can't see a thing now. It seems ages and ages ago."

"It's only two months," he replied. "That's all. Two months since Mum and Dad were killed. It's extraordinary, isn't it, that something like that should have started something like this? As though their death should start a new life for the two of us."

"Three of us," she whispered. "There'll be three of us, by the end of next August...." Her grip tightening on his, she huddled to him and clung to him as a wave of panic folded around her. "Oh, Harry, what on earth would Mum and Dad have thought of it? What would they have said? What would they have done? Oh, Harry, will it be all right? Are you glad for us, Harry?"

He hugged her until her panic was gone. The shiver of cold she'd felt, like an icicle stabbing between her shoulder blades, melted quickly in the warmth and strength of her brother's body. Holding her, he stared into the darkness, where the sea was black and the sky was black, where the weed whispered in a black current.

"Yes, Lizzie, I'm glad for us," he said. "Don't worry. We've done nothing that's wrong, whatever Mum and Dad might have made of it. Don't think about them. They're gone now. It'll be all right for the two of us, for the three of us. Come on now, home."

They continued to walk. Their only points of reference in the blindfolded night were the touch of each other's fingers, the crunch of the shingle beneath their feet, the dragging pursuit of the tree.

In the cabin of the *Ozymandias*, they set the tree firmly in a corner, wedging the stump between barnacled boulders from the beach. Harry revived the fire with some twisted tentacles of ivy he'd found drying on the high-water line. The driftwood spat. There were blue flames and the golden glow of the lamp. Lizzie was decorating the tree. She hung tinsel on the branches; she knelt and stood and knelt again with all the excitement of a child in the coming of Christmas; she frowned and smiled with the gravity and the joy of her task. The boat moved on the swell of an ebbing tide.

"Now, what's missing?" she said, narrowing her eyes, squinting at the tree. Moving close to her, he could smell the scent of her hair, the pungency of burning ivy, the resinous fragrance of pine needles.

"We've forgotten something," she said.

She wriggled free from his embrace. "I've got it!" she cried triumphantly. "Our talisman, which has brought us so much luck so far!"

In a moment, she'd moved to the bookshelf, crossed the cabin, stretched upward and down again with the speed and lightness of a cat. "There!" she said. "Done it!"

The brittlestar dangled from the topmost point of the Christmas tree.

12

Lizzie's pregnancy began well. That is, at first it changed nothing.

Its announcement seemed a natural part of Christmas, the exchanging of gifts. There was a marvelous feeling that perfectly matched their joy and their apprehension at the news: that, for the moment, nothing was different. There was still time for the careless, carefree irresponsibility of a Christmas together before they need do anything differently or begin to think differently. They wanted the baby... but not yet, not for a long time. And the summer was a long way away. If there'd been any lingering idea in Harry's mind that his sister might yet return to her studies, it was now dispelled.

For the time being, they told no one. There was no one to tell. Their union and their privacy on the *Ozymandias* were ensured. They were castaways, that Christmas. They sailed alone. They navigated by the brittlestar.

But, on New Year's Day, when the *Ozymandias* was set down on the mud by the ebbing tide, there was something oddly unnerving in the thump and the creak which shuddered the boat. The stillness, after a night of gentle, rhythmic motion and the sensation of traveling a great distance, announced that the voyage was over. As the boat settled, a shower of dead needles fell from the tree. There was rain, a driving drizzle which obscured the dunes and the estuary and smothered the mountains, and trapped the day in a curious, suffocating opacity. Christmas was nearly over.

There were more days of rain, and for Lizzie the business of gathering driftwood became a chore instead of a game; thrown beside the stove, there was a tangle of damp twigs, to which the seaweed still clung. The fire smoked. It sizzled and sulked, giving little warmth, filling the cabin with a faint, pungent haze which made her eyes sting. She spent her mornings and evenings on the bed, making a feeble concession to wakefulness by sitting up, wrapped in blankets, instead of lying down and sleeping. For her, the afternoon expeditions to town were tedious, in the face of the wind and the wet.

Christmas was really over when they took down the decorations. All of a sudden the cabin was bare. The glamour was gone. Where there'd been tinsel and streamers, there was the woodwork which Lizzie had slapped with paint; where there'd been a tree like something from a child's picture book, there were floorboards furry with dust. Harry snapped the tree into pieces and fed it to the fire, giving the room a short-lived burst of cheer. Lizzie swept up the needles and they were sparks among the flames, flung fast up the chimney, quenched by the smoke of whining, wet wood. She took the brittlestar, and the other brittlestar which had been on the bookshelf, and pinned them to a beam on the ceiling. From there, they released a fall of salty crumbs.

There were things to be done, to shake Harry and Lizzie from their lethargy.

"You must write to your tutor," he said to her. "To your tutor and your warden. It's only fair, Lizzie. It's a matter of courtesy. Just write to them, or let me write the letter for you, telling them you're definitely not going back to college."

It was the first time the subject had been voiced, ever since Harry's visit to London, and now the words hung heavily with the smoke from the fire.

"Make a clean break," he went on. "Once the letter's written and posted, you can forget all about it. Maybe it's not such a bad decision, although people will think it is and say it is — you know, a waste and so on. You'll still have the talent and the potential, won't you? All of that's still there, isn't it? It hasn't gone away."

He thought for a while, watching Lizzie's head turned away from him, the blankets pulled up to her face. "But it's just the way it's happened," he said, "the way events have overtaken us, starting with Mum and Dad's accident. All the love and the time, the money too, that Mum and Dad put in — none of that's been lost. But things have happened to change our lives, to change your life more than mine, I suppose. We couldn't have foreseen any of this."

He leaned down to her and made her look at him. He whispered to her, "Whatever anyone says, I can tell you, Lizzie, that I'm happy to have been overtaken like this. But we must write to your college. Come on, let's do it now. There's no shelving it."

Suddenly businesslike, she sat up and said, "You're right, Harry. We'll write to the college, straight and simple. We don't have to explain to them or justify anything." Frowning, she added, "But we need to go and see a doctor, about the baby. We need to hear him say that everything's all right."

She paused, parrying his puzzled look. Then she said, "Hadn't you thought, Harry, that we ought to check up pretty fast? Neither of us knows much about all this. Well, do we? And there is something just a bit unusual about our pregnancy, isn't there? Well, isn't there?"

She was right. They knew nothing. Harry composed a letter to Lizzie's tutor, informing him in blunt, no-nonsense terms that, for personal reasons, she wasn't going to resume her studies at the Royal College of Music. Lizzie signed the letter. They enclosed a note to her warden, authorizing the disposal of the few things she'd left in her room in the hall of residence. So it was done. Having posted the letter in Caernarfon square, they went together to arrange a visit to the general practitioner who'd confirmed Lizzie's pregnancy.

"I can see you right now," the doctor said, ushering them into his surgery. "You've caught me just before I set off on my rounds. Time for a quick chat and then we can fix a proper appointment for another day, if you like. Come in and sit down. About the pregnancy, I suppose?"

"Yes, doctor," Harry said. "We need to ask a few questions."

"Well, Mr. Clewe, there's really nothing to it." He was a young Englishman, fresh-faced, clean-cut, not long out of medical school. "You're both happy about the news?" he said.

"Yes," Lizzie answered. "We're very happy about it. But we need your opinion about..." She paused, wringing her fingers in her lap, dropping her head to hide behind her curtain of hair.

"About what, Mrs. Clewe?" the doctor said. "Fire away and I'll do my best."

"Well, that's the point," Harry put in. "Lizzie isn't Mrs. Clewe. We aren't married."

"Of course we aren't married," Lizzie blurted, without looking up. "We're brother and sister. That's why we've got the same surname. Harry's my brother." She pulled herself upright, her cheeks pink, her eyes bright, and said in a steady voice, "We love each other very much and we want the baby. But we're not sure if it's all so straightforward in our case."

The doctor flushed too. He blinked very rapidly and leaned back in his chair, glowing. "How interesting!" he murmured. He frowned, flustered. "It's really very interesting," he said, "but I don't think there's anything to worry about. No, Mr. Clewe, and er, Miss Clewe... I'm pretty sure there needn't be anything out of the ordinary, from the medical point of view. Let me see what I can remember, just off the top of my head."

Rattled, he talked briefly on the subject of consanguinity, the effect of a close blood relation on the offspring of such a union. He spoke as though he were spouting some half-digested information he'd learned by heart in case the subject came up in his final examinations. Occasionally he glanced at his watch, speeding up his delivery when he saw what time it was. Recent studies in both Japan and the United States, he was saying, had shown that the chances of damage to children resulting from consanguinity, even from the closest relationships such as brother and sister or father and daughter, were negligible; only ignorance and superstition had created taboos. Indeed, there were some societies which positively cultivated inbreeding in order to maintain a pure stock, to preserve existing hierarchies; conversely, in other societies there was such a fear of it that the law had made certain unions illegal.

The doctor, smiling now, gaining in confidence as he remembered more of his recent studies, had started to sort some papers into his bag. He was preparing to set off on his rounds.

"So, you have nothing to worry about," he concluded. "Your union isn't illegal, although, admittedly, a certain taboo exists. You'll learn to live with that, I'm sure. Finally, what you really wanted to know is this: the horror of resulting damage to children is nothing but an old wives' tale. How's that?"

He stood up. So did Harry and Lizzie.

"I've got to dash off now," the doctor said. "But don't hesitate to call in again, if you want to. Have a word with the receptionist and make an appointment for another time."

Harry and Lizzie emerged into the town square, into the chill drizzle of a new year.

The rain had come on again that evening, obliterating any other sound from the seashore. The boat was stuck in the mud. The fire filled the cabin with smoke, the whining of wood and the popping explosions of bladderwrack. Lizzie lay on the bed, ignoring the magazine beside her. Harry reached for his flute. Cocooned in the *Ozymandias*, listening to the spitting driftwood and the perpetual patter of raindrops, he felt another night come tiptoeing into the estuary; it stole across the dunes, crept in with the same insidious stealth as the flowing tide... to enfold the boat in darkness.

Harry played scales. He practiced exercises. Concentrating hard, he continued to work. When the *Ozymandias* was lifted from the mud, it seemed that for the first time neither he nor Lizzie noticed it: the moment passed unremarked. Harry was intent on a troublesome phrase, where both the fingering and the breathing eluded him, and he repeated it over and over. Lizzie glared at the ceiling, saying nothing, until she could stand it no longer.

"For heaven's sake, Harry!" she hissed. She stood up so quickly that the cabin rocked with the suddenness of her movement. "Can't you read it? You're making it sound bloody impossible!" She snatched the music from in front of him. "Let me have a look, before you drive me completely crazy."

He submitted, craning up at her while she scanned the sheet. She seemed to fill all the space. She was all he could see: She eclipsed the fire and towered to the low ceiling. Then she said, "It's not exactly difficult, is it? Look, you've marked your breathing in the wrong place. That's what makes it so hard for you. Try it again, the whole phrase without a breath until you get to bar seven." She dropped the music onto the bed.

He put the instrument to his lips. His mouth was dry. His fingers quivered slightly as they hovered on the cold machinery. As he began to play, Lizzie remained standing over him. And when he faltered again, his hands and his breath refusing to coordinate, she spat a single, unlovely word he'd never heard her use before and she snatched the flute from him.

"Can't you read?" she shouted. "Or are you just bloody useless?"

Without another glance at the music, she played the entire phrase from one end to the other, without a pause for breath.

"Like that!" she snapped, thrusting the instrument toward him. "If you can't do it, Harry, then leave it, please! Otherwise I can't bear it!" She spun away from him, up the cabin steps and onto the deck.

He attended to the stove. He placed among the flames some pieces of an old chair he'd found washed up, to which the seaweed had attached itself. The weed turned from black to gray, until its blisters burst with a spattering like distant gunfire. He squatted there, feeling the warmth on his face, and he wondered where the chair had come from, what kind of rooms it had been in and who'd sat on it before it had been thrown away, arriving as driftwood for him to gather on the shore. The flames grew hotter, driving him onto the bed.

As he'd expected, Lizzie soon came back, because the rain was still falling hard. She knelt by the fire, her hair sequined with droplets. She shivered suddenly and very violently, so that the water flew from her head and fizzed into the flames. Having returned from the deck, she filled the cabin again. There was something powerful about her, which Harry had felt as soon as she'd arrived at the *Ozymandias*, even when it had seemed as though he'd had the ascendancy, on his boat, on his estuary, in his world. Now the power of her personality flooded the cabin of the *Ozymandias*, pervasive as the pungency of sizzling kelp.

Overshadowed by her temper and her quicksilver demonstration with the flute, he took up the instrument from the bed. At last, he ran smoothly through the troublesome phrase.

13

Harry's pupils came one by one to the boat, once he'd arranged their lessons and negotiated his fee on the telephone. They were beginners, and Harry was sure he was competent to instruct them; but he was nervous at first, more nervous than they were, until he relaxed and concentrated on the work. The novelty of being on a boat on the shore of a wide-open estuary, especially in the evenings when there was a swell and the darkness grew noisy with rain or wind, clearly intrigued the students; so that, even before he'd proved his ability as a teacher, Harry felt that he had their interest. The *Ozymandias* lent him a little glamour, an eccentricity which impressed his visitors.

For the arrival of the first pupil, Lizzie had taken pains to make the cabin especially attractive, with flowers and seashells, the rug and the quilt lit up by the flames of a good fire. Moreover, she'd slipped a ring onto the third finger of her left hand; she noticed that Harry had noticed, and they nodded at one another without saying anything.

Frank was a man of forty, who drove out of Caernarfon and down to the shore in a Morris Minor. He had shoulder-length black hair, very thick and flecked with gray, and he always came in the same blue jeans and khaki combat jacket. He was goggle-eyed when he first stepped into the warmth and light of the cabin, reluctant to break the spell by taking his flute from its case.

"Hey, this is beautiful, man!" he drawled. "A great place you've got here!" He stared around, rearranging a crooked smile on his face, and said at last, "Hey, you don't mind, do you?" before performing the ritual of rolling a joint on the sheet music he'd brought with him.

For Frank, whose hair and dress were the uniform of a harmless nonconformity, these visits to the *Ozymandias* were evenings of loose, inconsequential chat with Harry Clewe and his fragile young wife, who smiled enigmatically as she knelt by the fire and lowered her coppery head to the flames... a chance for Frank to talk about music, of his travels in Afghanistan, Alaska and the Amazon basin, of poems and stars. The boat was the quintessence of the Wales he'd come looking for. His flute playing was breathy and muted; it suited Frank, just as the *Ozymandias* and its gentle restlessness suited him.

Lizzie watched and listened, apart. She said little, nor did she accept the proffered joint, although she followed the intricacies of its preparation with a gleam in her eyes and her nostrils flared at the heavy perfume. Harry smoked, and he countered the strangest of Frank's Third World reminiscences with his stories of Sudan. Lizzie maintained her alertness. She was vigilant, however garrulous her brother might become.

Dewi cycled from Bontnewydd, the nearest village. Sixteen years old, the boy was so tall that he could hardly stand upright inside the cabin, but held himself like a huge, skinny question mark until he was persuaded to sit down. His face was a minefield of spots, some of which had exploded and left a deep, raw crater, others charged with poison and ready to blow at the slightest touch; for this reason and the spurt of growth which had made him so conspicuous, he was excruciatingly shy. If Lizzie met his eyes, he would drop his head and glow until his ears were purple. If she smiled at him, he would recoil as though he'd been scorched. But Dewi became confident with the flute, blushing at Lizzie's words of praise, not knowing that she was outstandingly qualified to judge his musicianship. When the boy left, she had kind words for the teacher too, and this made Harry happy.

The third of the pupils was an Englishwoman in her late thirties. Her name was Helen Ince. She arrived at the mooring in a silver Daimler. She had dark, sleek good looks. She smoked a tiny cigar. During the preliminaries to her lessons, when there was general conversation about the novelty and charm of the *Ozymandias* and about living in Wales, she recounted the circumstances of her recent divorce from a barrister, the sale of their house in Kingston-upon-Thames and a flat in Chelsea. With her share of the proceeds, Helen was able to start a new life. Now she was in Wales, the owner of a substantial house on the seashore, not far from Caernarfon, with money left over for living and for work on the property. She'd always wanted to learn the flute. She opened a case and flourished a very expensive instrument.

"Well, what do you think of her?" Harry had asked Lizzie after the first of Helen's lessons, when the woman had driven away. "Pretty glamorous for these parts, isn't she?"

And Lizzie had shrugged, with a sniff and a pout, answering, "Money, of course. Expensive clothes and hair, and that's expensive perfume she's wearing. Flashy car. I didn't think much of her. She'll never play the flute, I can tell you that much."

So, as the dark afternoons and evenings of January slipped by, the cabin of the *Ozymandias* was left with the lingering scents of its three weekly visitors. The fragrance of marijuana remained when Frank had gone, and Lizzie was mellowed by the man's rueful nostalgia. After Dewi, there was a faintly chemical odor of whatever treatment he was using on his face, and Lizzie had enjoyed watching his progress. Helen Ince swept out in a haze of perfume, while Lizzie affected indifference.

14

Winter was hard. Harry was used to it, after years on his own aboard the *Ozymandias*. Lizzie wasn't. The weather wore her down. The drizzle drove deep into the hull of the boat. Rain found a way through the roof of the cabin, dripping with a fizz onto the hot stove. The winds, which had started in the coldest and dreariest corners of the world, hurtled over the dunes, raising an icy spray from the estuary which spattered the portholes with salt. Either the *Ozymandias* lay on the black mud and simply shuddered, or it rode the swell, bucking, trembling, ramming the wall so that the buffers squealed and groaned. Harry and Lizzie were warm enough, as the stove consumed wet wood, but the fog of smoke gave Lizzie headaches and made her eyes stream. Harry tramped the shoreline for fuel, bringing in planks and spars and branches that never quite dried before it was their turn to go into the flames; meanwhile, the salt water dripped from them and ran across the floorboards. Days went by when the world was blanketed in the mist which rolled in from the sea, and then Harry and Lizzie would stay in bed, rising periodically, rubbing their eyes at the sting of smoke, to feed the stove, to make coffee, to cook beans, to use the toilet in the dank darkness of the forward cabin. They lay enfolded in one another's limbs, in a thrall of lethargy induced by the winter weather, rousing themselves to sluggish action when Frank or Dewi or Helen was expected, so that once more the *Ozymandias* became a bright and welcoming place.

In its case, the cello warped and split. It was racked with damp. It seized, like an athlete crippled with arthritis. Abandoned and broken, it was a dead thing.

Snow covered the mountains. On the coast, although it bore the brunt of the winds from the Irish Sea, it didn't freeze, even if a snap during the January and February afternoons seemed to threaten a frost. When Lizzie was dispirited, Harry would try to hearten her by the example of the migrant birds whose presence on the estuary proclaimed that these were milder, more sheltered shores than the ones they'd been forced to leave.

"See how lucky we are!" he would say, aiming his battered binoculars out of the portholes despite the drumming of rain on the roof. "Relatively speaking, this is an easy climate! Look at those birds out there — all kinds of waders, some of them weighing no more than a couple of ounces, which have flown thousands of miles to get here, to escape a real winter in Iceland, Greenland, Norway or even Russia. All we've got is a bit of rain to put up with."

Before Christmas, there had been fieldfare and redwing from Scandinavia, which pillaged the hedgerows for berries: theirs was an invasion, followed by looting. Now that the hawthorn and the rowan were bare, these handsome thrushes worked the land for grubs, among the lapwings and oyster-catchers, the starlings and gulls. On the water, a dozen swans had arrived one night from Siberia; they were Bewicks, elegant, aloof, with cold yellow faces.

But Harry's jovial references to colder and wetter countries did nothing to alleviate the dreariness of the *Ozymandias*'s mooring on the estuary. He sensed that Lizzie was sinking. She huddled before the stove and stared into its smoldering fire. February was drowned: it was a month of rain and mist, when everything was clammy. The sky no longer towered like the vaulting of a great cathedral; it flapped like a wet, gray blanket on a washing line. The horizon shrank to a line of matted dunes, beyond which the thunder of surf was only a part of Lizzie's smoky headache. The days blurred together.

She grew impatient with the flute lessons, and with Harry's persistent good humor when his students were due.

"Who's coming tonight, maestro?" she would ask. "Are you going to end up stoned with Frank or intoxicated with the loveliness of Helen Ince? At least with Dewi we get a bit of music... using the term loosely, of course."

And Harry would try to disguise his wincing with a smile, turning aside her jibes. "Fair's fair, Lizzie," he'd say. "You know young Dewi's in love with you. You can tell by the way he flares up whenever you look at him. And so I'm in love with the glamorous Helen. As for Frank, he's in love with himself and his idea of exploring the cosmos in Wales. But tonight it's my tryst with Helen. We're going to make sweet music together, right here in front of the fire."

Then, realizing the clumsiness of his banter, seeing Lizzie's face begin to crumple, he would hold her very tightly and rock with her on the bed. "Come on, my real love," he'd whisper to her. "Cheer up! In a few weeks the winter will be gone and everything about the *Ozymandias* will be as wonderful as it was when you first arrived. In fact, it'll be better: the spring is lovely here. And don't forget, we have an exciting summer ahead of us!"

They would kiss, separating at the crunch of tires on the gravel of the sea wall, rearranging themselves for the footfall on deck. "Meanwhile, Lizzie," he would add, "these lessons are paying for a present I'm getting for you. Maybe next week I'll collect it."

Inevitably in such a confined space, her discomfort was transmitted to Harry and his pupils. She would sit in a corner of the cabin and pretend to read, trying not to flinch at the beginners' ineptitude. Frank didn't mind. He simply guffawed to see how she winced; she could go so far as to cover her ears with her hands without really offending him. For him, it was a pleasant evening on board the *Ozymandias*, of which the flute lesson was just a part. However, Dewi was especially vulnerable. Lizzie never interfered, because she could hear that the boy was competent and conscientious, but she could still unnerve him with a glance or a sharp intake of breath.

She bristled in the presence of Helen Ince. It was a torment for Lizzie to have her in the cabin. It wasn't only that Helen was a woman whom Harry clearly found attractive; the little space was not enough for her and Lizzie together. During the lessons, Lizzie huffed in her corner. She would get up and fling herself about, feeding the fire or making the coffee with such a clatter that Harry would have to say, "Can you hold on a moment, Lizzie, while we do this bit? It's quite tricky. Maybe I'll make some coffee when Helen's finished her lesson." Or else, if the wind and rain allowed, Lizzie went on deck those evenings, with blankets, binoculars and one of her brother's star books, so that Harry and Helen could relax and sit more closely together on the bed. They would hear Lizzie moving overhead, and feel the swaying of the boat. Lizzie followed her route among the constellations, and even the stars would shudder as she fixed them in the dark tunnels of the binoculars, as she heard the fumblings on the flute below. Coming downstairs when Helen had driven away, she found the cabin warm, the quilt rumpled, and the air giddy with the woman's perfume.

Lizzie brooded on her inactivity. She seldom joined Harry on the beach. She would hear him returning to the *Ozymandias*, feel the lurch of the boat as he came aboard, watch him drop a load of driftwood by the stove. Then, instead of straight away slipping under the blankets with her, he must stack the wood to let it dry more quickly, he must fetch water from the basins on deck, he must empty the chemical toilet... She knew these were things that had to be done, as he'd done them for himself all his years alone on the boat; but it irked her to see him so busy while she grew lumpish.

And it troubled Harry, as Lizzie became increasingly reluctant to stir from the fireside, that she'd merely exchanged the regime of her adolescence for this confinement on the *Ozymandias*.

15

In the first week of March, Harry announced that he would return from his walk into Caernarfon with the present he'd mentioned before.

"Soon be spring," he said as he prepared to leave on the shopping expedition, while Lizzie stayed behind. For weeks she hadn't accompanied him into town, although on her last visit she'd been to the clinic and was pronounced fit; the baby was scheduled to arrive at the end of August. All was well with her pregnancy, in spite of her earlier anxiety. The concept of consanguinity was mentioned here and there by the young doctor and then put aside; it was treated like an interesting but worthless antique, something to be brought out of the attic, gently ridiculed, and returned to the attic until the next time someone asked to see it.

Harry said, "It looks as though we've seen off the worst of the winter. I've saved up a bit to get something that'll make life easier for us, something we can both use. Do us good too."

So it was that, having taken the usual three-quarters of an hour to walk into town, he returned in less than fifteen minutes — on a bicycle, with the shopping slung in a basket on the handlebars.

Lizzie came on deck, summoned by the ringing of Harry's bell. She shivered in the thin afternoon sunshine. Her hair, once so bright, was dull and dark around her face. The roundness of her stomach was already pronounced. She shuddered at her brother's high spirits, for he was rosy with the exhilaration of his ride along the seashore track. He propped the bicycle against the wall while he handed the shopping to her, and she put the bag down on the deck.

"Come and have a look!" he said excitedly, helping her ashore. "It was advertised in the newsagent's window. It only took me ten minutes to get back from Caernarfon! Now that the weather's improving, either of us can go into town whenever we want, instead of feeling as though we're stuck out here. It's an easy ride, dead flat all the way!"

He tilted her pale, pointed face up to his. "I know it's been dismal for you, Lizzie, the last couple of months. It was bound to be, if you think about it, spending the winter on a boat in the middle of nowhere. I've got pretty used to it; I've even got to like it, in a funny sort of way! You haven't been out at all. Now there's no excuse!"

He grabbed the bicycle and tinkled the bell. "Lots of air and exercise this spring! Even in your condition, as they say! There's no reason why you can't have a slow and gentle ride along the shore now and then, and into Caernarfon. Well? What do you think?"

As soon as he let go of her chin, she lowered her eyes and looked away. She shrugged her shoulders.

"What's the matter, Lizzie?" he said. "Aren't you pleased? I got it for you." He took hold of her chin again.

"I can't ride it," she said softly, meeting his eyes. "I've never been able to, so it's not much good for me." Seeing his surprise and disappointment, she added, "But thank you, Harry. You'll be able to use it, won't you, in and out of town?" This time it was her hand that went to his face and touched his lips.

"You never learned to ride a bike?" he asked her, incredulous. "You must have! Didn't Dad ever show you? Didn't you ever have a bike at home?"

"Dad tried to teach me once, but he didn't have much patience," she answered. "Anyway, I was always too busy with my music, and with horses, at least until my accident. No, Harry, I never had a bike. It's just something I never got round to...."

"Well, I'll show you," he said in a brisk, no-nonsense voice. "Look, it's a nice small one, a lady's, without a cross-bar. Just right for you. Come on, Lizzie, I'll show you."

But she refused to go near it. With more shrugs and shakes of her head, she tried to elude him, and both of them affected a desperate jollity which masked her fear and his impatience. They appeared to laugh, wrestling with one another, but it was the laughter of stubbornness, through clenched teeth. He picked her up and swung her; he carried her from the deck when she'd retreated there, he carried her and swung her kicking legs. Her giggles started to crack. His encouragement was losing its playfulness. At last their efforts at good humor collapsed. As he heaved her toward the bicycle, which stood waiting against the wall like a patient donkey, she wriggled so hard that he was forced to drop her. She sat heavily on the ground. He stood over her, panting.

"You're being childish," he said, his voice shaking. "You could at least have a go. Any child can ride a bike. It's not normally considered a difficult thing to do. If you can ride a bloody great horse, for heaven's sake, then surely you can manage this!"

She glowered up at him. Before she could reply, there was an unmistakable sound from along the track, the whirring of wheels and the crunch of tires on gravel, as someone else approached on a bicycle. As Lizzie got to her feet and they both stared into the distance, they saw the bicycle appear and come fast toward them. They recognized the lanky, angular figure of Dewi. He skidded expertly to a halt.

"Hello, Mr. Clewe," he said, dismounting. He nodded at Lizzie, mumbled, "Hello, Mrs. Clewe," and ducked his head from her, as though she might assault him with a smile. "I just called by to see you, Mr. Clewe," he went on. "I can't make it for my next lesson, I'm afraid. There's some sort of a do on at school and I've got to be there. I thought I'd call in to excuse myself."

"That's fine, Dewi," Harry replied. "We'll give it a miss this week. Thanks for coming to tell me."

"You've got yourself a bike," the boy said. "A lady's." This reference to Lizzie initiated a furious blush, starting on his mottled forehead, suffusing the raw blistering on his nose and chin, draining to his neck. His complexion was worse than ever: he had a face like a pizza. "Good idea, Mr. Clewe. It's no time at all from here into town." He blurted the words, relieved to see that Lizzie wasn't looking at him.

"That's right," Harry said. "Ten minutes or so. But I'm afraid Lizzie — er, Mrs. Clewe — doesn't like it much."

She scowled at him and blushed, not as violently as Dewi had done, but longer, the color persisting as he said, "I was trying to persuade her to have a go, just now, as you arrived. But without success." To her he added, "Come on, love. Me and Dewi will help you. It was a stroke of luck, wasn't it, having this young man turn up on his bike to give us a hand? What do you reckon?"

Dewi grinned, his self-confidence rising with this appeal to his expertise. For once, he managed to address Lizzie directly, without blushing. "Can't you ride a bike, Mrs. Clewe? That's amazing! I've never met anyone before who couldn't. It's easy! We could teach you in five minutes."

Unable to refuse, Lizzie allowed herself to be seated on the bicycle. She essayed a smile, but it disfigured her face like a scar. "Don't let me go, please!" she cried in a trembling voice. Her knuckles whitened on the handlebars, and Harry could feel the quivering of her body when he placed a steadying hand on her back.

"You'll be fine," he said. "Try to relax. Just sit there. You don't have to do anything else. You've got me holding you this side and Dewi on the other. Now, we're going to walk you very slowly along the track. All right, Dewi? Off we go..."

This they did. If the curlew had lifted a quizzical eye, if the heron had turned its dagger head, they would have seen the ludicrous progress of three people and a bicycle along the edge of the seashore, the three of them bound together by their concentration and the skeleton of the machine to resemble some extraordinary crablike creature which might just then have emerged from the sands. But the estuary ignored them. The crackle of drying weed absorbed the ticking of the wheels. Harry muttered reassurance; Dewi crouched like a mantis; and Lizzie sat bolt upright, like a princess flanked by eunuchs. She was terrified. A flock of peewits somersaulted from the fields, clapping their black and white wings as though to applaud her passing, but she didn't see them. After a hundred yards, Harry said, "We'll turn round now and head back. Maybe a bit faster this time." He exchanged a nod with Dewi.

Harry and Dewi accelerated to a trot. "Keep your feet on the pedals, Mrs. Clewe!" the boy was saying. "Look straight ahead, not down at the wheel!"

So the crab-creature scuttled, faster and faster, until, at the signal of another nod behind Lizzie's back, its pairs of legs seemed to break from the body... and Lizzie was traveling unsupported. Harry and Dewi jogged behind her, without a finger on her or the machine. She stared into the cold wind, narrowing her eyes. When she sensed a growing silence, she dared to glance around, to confirm what her ears had suggested: that the footsteps on the gravel were receding and she was alone, yards ahead of her supporters, gaining distance as the bike gathered speed. She squealed, her feet slipped off the pedals, and she veered toward the shore. Although Harry and Dewi were no more than six feet from her back wheel, they were too far away to grab her, to alter her downward course. The bicycle wobbled as it left the track. It bucked on the pebbles and threw its rider as it struck the uneven, unmoving boulders. Lizzie toppled from it with a loud cry.

She wasn't hurt. She'd landed on the soft and pungent rolls of weed which the tide had left along the length of the shore. A cloud of flies roared around her, disturbed from the mat of warm vegetation. But she was winded, unable to catch a breath until Harry manhandled her to her feet and pushed her head between her knees. When at last she could breathe, she sobbed.

He walked her to the *Ozymandias*. Dewi sped into the distance on his own bicycle, pumping the pedals so that the machine zigzagged violently and then vanished around a bend in the track.

Harry held Lizzie's heaving little body to him. Her sobbing subsided and turned into anger. With her face against his chest, she cried out, her shouts muffled and wet.

"I told you I couldn't do it! I said I couldn't! Why did you have to try and make me? I said I couldn't do it, didn't I? But you had to make me, to do your teaching thing! You can't resist it, can you, Harry? Always teaching something... even things you're not very good at yourself!"

She wept, in anger and shock and embarrassment, without lifting her face from his body, as though she couldn't bear to look at him. "Always teaching! Why don't you put another card in the newsagent's window? 'Harry-clever-clever-Clewe: introductions to sex, astronomy, birdwatching, flute and bicycle!' Do you think you'd get plenty of people to practice on?'"

She started to control herself. She threaded her arms around him and squeezed, nuzzling into his shirt to wipe away her tears. "Oh Harry, my love! Oh Harry, oh Harry! I can't hold you hard enough! If I could hold you as hard as I want to hold you, I'd squeeze all the breath out of you!"

"My little Lizzie," he said into the top of her head, tasting her hair on his lips. He stared across the estuary. It was darkening into twilight. The dusk was cold, and the surf roared beyond the distant dunes. "My little Lizzie," he whispered.

16

As the toad had been the talisman of Harry's infatuation with Sarah, so the brittlestar was a talisman for him and Lizzie.

Lizzie had found one on her first morning on the estuary; Harry had found another a few weeks later, by which time brother and sister had become lovers. For a while the brittlestars had meshed in their shallow tray of water, linking their limbs and moving together as Harry and Lizzie did. Once dead, the creatures had dried on the ceiling, pinned to the beams. The brittlestar was a symbol of Lizzie's transition into womanhood: her separation from her parents, her first home away from the family home, her first love, her first man.

She'd never found another one, although she looked. There were common starfishes among the huge, translucent jellyfish and the dismembered remains of crabs which the sea had left behind. But never another brittlestar. The spring tides didn't oblige by bringing one. While the brittlestars still dangled in the cabin, Lizzie's search for another was desultory, casual, something to give a focus to her occasional walks on the beach. Then, one morning in April, as the *Ozymandias* lifted from the mud with the rising water, the brittlestars broke from the ceiling, fell to the floorboards and shattered into thousands of dry, salt splinters.

Lizzie was dashed. All of a sudden, it seemed overwhelmingly important to her to find another brittlestar, which would hang above her as she and Harry lay on their bed and guide them through the coming months. Its absence assumed the focus of her growing despondency. In spite of the arrival of spring, which Harry had hoped would have lifted her spirits, Lizzie became increasingly depressed.

There was the business of the bicycle. Instead of being glad that Harry was more mobile, Lizzie felt sour. The contrast between her confinement and his mobility was something that rankled. Nearly six months into her pregnancy, she was weary, although regular checks had always shown her to be surprisingly strong for one so little and pale and apparently fragile; the enforced lethargy of winter was replaced by a disinclination to move. It seemed unfair that, having bridled at the narrowness of the cabin during the gales and squalls of the new year, she was still a prisoner now that the weather had improved. Of course, she joined Harry in and out of Caernarfon for her showers at the sports center; but the walking gave her pains in her back, and she was self-conscious about her ballooning belly in front of strangers. Sometimes she accompanied him simply for the exercise, for the loveliness of the seas and the skies was still a wonder to her; she was thrilled by the movement of the birds and the tides. However, as far as the fetching of supplies was necessary, it made sense to say, "No, I'll stay here, Harry. It'll only take you ten minutes on the bike. At the rate I go these days, it's more than an hour if I come with you. Go on, I'll stay here...."

He'd bought the bicycle to get Lizzie out of the *Ozymandias*, not for his own convenience; but the result was to compound her immobility. He sped along the seashore with a basket full of clothes for the launderette. It was a short enough journey to justify the bringing of fish and chips or a curry from the takeaway restaurants. The bicycle made a considerable difference to the convenience of living on the boat. But it irked Lizzie.

Often, when Harry returned from town, he would find that Lizzie wasn't there. She spent hours along the beach, leaving soon after the nudge of the hull on the mud told her that the tide was out, and she searched for the brittlestar. So he would sit with his back to the cabin and scan the estuary with his binoculars until he spotted her distant figure, very tiny on the wide, wet sands, bulked in jeans and baggy sweater, moving slowly in black wellington boots. A flock of gulls blew around her, the duck rose with a roaring of wings. Lizzie was a speck... even in the circle of his binoculars, she was an ant, creeping and stopping and creeping again. She looked downward, always. For her, there were no gulls, there was no sky. Her only interest was in finding another brittlestar.

That evening, as the light faded, Harry rode steadily back to the *Ozymandias* with his basket of clean clothes swinging on the handlebars. A plume of smoke rose from the boat's chimney. Inside the cabin, Lizzie was lying on the bed, staring at the ceiling. She hardly flickered her eyes as he came down the steps.

"No luck?" he asked.

She didn't answer.

He started to take out the clothes and hang them over the stove. In spite of the fire, the cabin seemed dull, suffocatingly domestic with the clothes hung up to air. There were no flowers; there'd been no flowers for weeks. "No luck with the brittlestar?" he asked.

She rolled over listlessly and looked at him. "The other way round," she said.

He frowned. "What do you mean?"

She sighed, as though she were struggling to communicate with an imbecile or a foreigner, rolling back to stare at the ceiling again. "I mean, dear Harry, the other way round. You said, no luck with the brittlestar. On the contrary: no luck without the brittlestar." She patted the bed, so that he sat down beside her. "Had a busy time in the big city?" she asked.

He kissed her. To his surprise, she recoiled from him and buried her face in the quilt.

"What on earth's the matter?" he said. "Oh, come on, Lizzie, don't be such a grump! Stop moping! Our luck's been great so far. We've got each other. We're both in good shape. The spring's come and—"

She interrupted him. "Did you think the ride home would blow that smell away?" she said, her voice muffled by the blankets.

Puzzled, he sat up. "What smell? The beer? Yes, I had a beer while the things were in the wash. I always do. Better than just sitting there watching the clothes go round and round. What's the matter with you, Lizzie?" He took her by the shoulders and turned her face toward him. She wrinkled her nostrils.

"It's not the beer," she said, grimacing. "I don't mind the beer. But I don't like who you go drinking with. Can't you wash it off? It's horrible!"

It made no difference, thereafter, to explain to Lizzie that he'd bumped into Helen Ince and they'd gone for a quick drink together. "I always go for a drink while the clothes are doing," he said. "This time I just happened to see Helen in the square and we dropped into the Black Boy for half an hour. Nothing very sinister about that, is there? Everybody who's been in the Black Boy tonight will be reeking of her perfume, not just me! All over Caernarfon at this very moment, men are having to explain it away to their wives and girlfriends. She'll probably get banned from the pub if she causes this much trouble."

So he laughed it off, winning a rueful smile from Lizzie. "I promise you, my love, all my trysts with Helen are conducted right here, under your beady eye, and under the—"

Too late to stop himself, he gestured vaguely in the direction of the ceiling, where a couple of drawing pins stuck into the wood were the only reminders of the strange, rare creatures that Lizzie had fixed there. Again, she buried her face from him.

So the bicycle remained a source of irritation in her mind, that he was so free while she was torpid. Furthermore, from that time on, no amount of banter could quite remove its link with Helen Ince. In the same way that the woman's perfume lingered, so her name inevitably arose, as a joke that was more than just a joke, whenever he cycled to town. Indeed, there were times over the following months when Harry and Helen met in Caernarfon, not always by coincidence.

17

Physically, Lizzie remained in excellent health throughout her pregnancy. Her spirits, however, continued to sink.

Having thrown off the strictures of her music, she found herself confined on board the *Ozymandias*. At first it had been an exchange she'd been glad to make, to be with Harry on the boat, as though the two of them were sailing, free and alone, away from everything that had been so oppressive. Now she was discovering that the widest horizon and the tallest sky could be a cage. Having set aside the cello, to which she'd been harnessed throughout her entire adolescence, she began to feel that she was in harness again: the thing that was growing inside her, beating with her pulse, kicking against her, reminded her of the way she'd borne the cello, how she'd borne it for so long that it had seemed to become a part of her. Now the cello was twisted and cracked, garroting itself in the darkness... while the thing was alive inside her, squirming blindly.

Worse, much worse, there was guilt.

It gnawed at her. It drained her. What would her mother and father have said, if they'd known what had happened? The idea was a horror for her. Despite Harry's efforts to reassure her, Lizzie conceived the nightmarish vision of her parents visiting the *Ozymandias*.... The more she imagined it, the more realistic the nightmare became. She was on the edge of her nerves. She listened for the crunching of tires on the gravel, as though a taxi would arrive with her parents in it. Her eyes grew wide, the sockets grew hollow. She would leap with terror at the sound of an engine, which usually turned out to be a light aircraft or a boat. On the evenings when either Frank or Helen was expected for a lesson, when either the Morris Minor or the silver Daimler would roll up to the mooring, she would leap onto deck to confirm who it was. It made no difference to Lizzie that her mother and father were dead, that their bodies were cinders blown into the air. For her, they were alive. She dreaded their visit.

There was an evening when Harry and Lizzie had been sitting quietly in the firelight, until the beam of a headlamp shone through the cabin window and a car came to a stop on the seashore track. By then, Lizzie was up and pacing, her face contorted in a mask of tears. She wailed, out of control. She wriggled from Harry's arms as he tried to comfort her. She flashed her eyes around the cabin for a hiding place, and, at the slamming of a car door and the approach of footsteps, she flung herself blindly into the forward cabin, locking herself in.

There she squatted, a hunted, haunted creature, on the seat of the chemical toilet. The boat swayed as someone came on board. She held her breath and quivered in her lightless confinement, with only the presence of the cello, its dusty black shape like a child standing silently in the corner, and the squirming tumble of the child inside her....

As the *Ozymandias* settled under the weight of its visitor, as the caterwauling of gulls drifted over the water and filled her ears with grief, Lizzie was entombed: Lizzie and the cello and the child, entombed in a dreadful darkness.

"It's Frank!" Harry called to her. She wept with relief, until she was exhausted by weeping. At last, weak and thin and wanly smiling, she emerged into a haze of marijuana smoke. Frank had come to rearrange a lesson, as Dewi had once done.

She remained in a state of barely tolerable tension. Harry could do nothing to relax her. Her trembling reached a climax one evening in the middle of June.

Dewi had come for a lesson. Harry reckoned that the boy's progress over the past months had been remarkable. They were on good form, combining to perfect a duet, an arrangement of English folk songs they'd written together. Lizzie listened from her corner, rocking herself in a chair, her hands clasped across her belly. Having played the piece from beginning to end without a pause or an error, Harry and Dewi beamed at one another with satisfaction. It was the end of the lesson.

"Well, Lizzie? What do you think?" he asked. He and the boy were putting their flutes away. "Give us your professional opinion."

Dewi scrambled to his feet, ducking his head to avoid the ceiling. For him, the idea of inviting the young woman's judgment was excruciating, and he was keen to leave. "Look, Mr. Clewe, I'd better be off," he blurted, his face crimson. "I've still got my homework to do...."

"It was very nice," Lizzie said. "A nice little arrangement, nicely played." She paused, to let the platitudes sink in. "But there's a danger, isn't there, in writing your own arrangements for yourselves to play? Well, isn't there?"

Harry glanced at Dewi, with a grin which was supposed to be reassuring. "Is there, Lizzie?" he asked. "What do you mean? Surely it's good exercise? And good fun?"

She stared into space, affecting puzzlement.

"Fun?" she said, frowning as if it were a word she'd never heard before in all her life. "Fun? What's fun got to do with it?" Her voice went thin and cold. "The point is, that when two very ordinary musicians arrange music for themselves to play, they make very ordinary music. They're bound to. Consciously or not, they write an arrangement which is comfortably within their own limitations. They can't help it. Now, it might be fun, as you put it, to write and then practice for hours and hours a banal piece of music, which, whether you thought about it or not, you wrote especially to suit your own limitations and mediocrity... but it's a waste of time as far as stretching and improving Dewi's musicianship is concerned. Yes, it might be fun. But it just panders to your own ordinariness. Worse, it gives Dewi a false sense of achievement. Do you understand what I'm saying?"

After a pause, in which neither Harry nor Dewi spoke, she added, "Fun's all right. It depends what you want to get out of it. But work's a different thing altogether."

Harry managed a smile. He followed Dewi onto the deck. The boy was downcast. "See you next week," Harry said to him. "Don't worry about what Lizzie was saying. Maybe there was no fun in her music lessons, but there will be in ours. You're doing fine. Better than fine. You're doing really well." He waved the boy away, still smiling. But he was angry with Lizzie.

"You did ask me," she said, preempting his outburst as he reappeared in the cabin. "If you don't want my opinion about your musicianship or your pupils' musicianship, don't ask me. Heaven knows, I always got the blunt truth from my teachers."

"But can't you see how sensitive Dewi is?" he shouted at her. "I'm not worried about any barbs in my direction, I can tell you that! By the time I was eighteen I knew what my limitations were! I soon found out I was never going to be a bloody genius like you were supposed to be!"

"By the time you were eighteen?" she retorted, her eyes blazing. "Is that when you found out? You mean no one had the ear or the gumption to tell you before that?"

She leaned forward and put her hot little face close to him. "That's exactly what I was trying to say about Dewi. Stretch him, Harry! Push him! Make him work! But don't always send him away thinking he's the bee's knees, when he obviously isn't. I had good teachers. They hurt me sometimes. They always told me the truth. If you think you might be a good teacher one day, now that you know you can't play, you can at least tell your pupils the truth!"

Breathing hard, both hands on her swollen stomach, she leaned back.

Harry bent to her and put his own hands on top of hers. She was as warm and round as a pudding. He was still angry with her, but he controlled his voice and spoke softly. "Listen, Lizzie, my love. I'll do the lessons my way. How you learned your music and how I learned mine are poles apart. But here we are on the *Ozymandias* together. I know what you think of my so-called musicianship. I won't ask you again for your opinion of my teaching."

He straightened up, his hands cooling. His voice rose and shook. "But at least I have the guts to do something with my music, knowing it's so bloody ordinary! All the music you ever learned has been locked in the bloody toilet for a year! Best place for it! That's where all the waste goes!"

Seconds later, he was on his bicycle and accelerating hard along the track toward the glow of the town.

The effort of cycling drained his anger. By the time he reached the footbridge under the bulk of the castle, he was calm. He imagined Lizzie alone in the cabin of the *Ozymandias*; she would be crying, as she'd cried so often in the past few weeks. For a second, he almost turned round and started to cycle back again, but then he rode across the bridge and locked the bike to the railings on the quayside. It was a long time since the matter of his incompetent teaching had been aired, and despite what he'd said about his immunity to barbs, the old hurt was touched. He would wallow a little. As he'd sometimes done in his year as a probationary teacher, and as a well-meaning, ineffectual volunteer in Sudan, he would console himself with beer.

He sat in a smoky, noisy corner of the Black Boy. Six pints later, he'd spent the price of Dewi's lesson. He'd spent his melancholy too.

Relieved, he rode slowly and somewhat unsteadily along the seashore track. It was a still, cool night. The vague summer constellations made up in their shimmering delicacy for what they lacked in definition. He drank the salt air. Stopping to urinate, he discovered that the silence was prickling with tiny sounds, the secret shadow life of the hedgerow, the fields and the foreshore. He cycled on, upright and alert in the saddle. He paused a hundred yards short of the mooring, thinking to walk the rest of the way. Wheeling the bicycle beside him, he approached the *Ozymandias*, pleased to see from the lighted portholes that Lizzie must still be up. He stopped again.

There was music, coming from the boat.

Harry leaned the bicycle into the hedge, not wanting the crunch of the tires or the ticking of the wheels to give away his arrival, and he tiptoed on the grass verge toward the *Ozymandias*. Whenever he paused, he heard the music of the cello drifting to him like something from a dream, a part of his own breathing and the thud of the blood in his head. He crept nearer. The playing was deep and mellow and measured despite the condition of the neglected instrument. When he stood on the seawall and looked down on the soft light of the curtain drawn across the porthole, he exhaled softly, trying to still the pounding in his temples until he'd silenced every sound of the summer's night except the sound of the cello. The sighing of the surf subsided. The estuary itself seemed to hold its breath.

The playing increased in volume and intensity. The bruising of the bow on the strings became a rapid chopping and stopping, like angry voices in an angry crowd. The bow worked faster and faster, more and more aggressively, used like a hatchet to split up the music. Harry felt himself clench. He ground his teeth until his jaws were aching. Staring up at the dim stars, he watched the sky begin to whirl as the music grew giddier and more frenzied. The bow assaulted the cello, flaying it, raking it, relentlessly sawing. And the constellations billowed, in time with the ugly, discordant, jagged sound which came from the cabin of the *Ozymandias*...

Harry squeezed his eyes shut. He lifted his hands to his ears to blot out the noise. It was a horror. He felt impotent, as though, through the walls of a hotel room, he could hear the perpetration of a brutal rape and was powerless to stop it. At last, when it seemed that the bow must have hacked and bludgeoned the cello into pieces, there was silence. For a second or two, there was a silence such as that sea and that sky had never heard before, an ebbing, throbbing absence of sound. Then, as Harry opened his eyes and relaxed the clenching of his fists, he let the music of the night wash over him: the roar of the surf, the breeze in the leaves of the hawthorn hedge, the whisper of an incoming tide. Nothing more from the boat.

He stepped onto the deck and down to the cabin.

Lizzie was quivering on the bed, her eyes wide open but unseeing. She didn't turn her head as he came in. She lay on her back with her nightdress pulled up and held the cello on top of her, her legs gripped around its body, her hands around its neck. Oblivious of his presence, she rocked her hips against the polished wood. She thrust upward. She clenched harder with her legs... faster and faster she continued the rhythmic thrusting. The sweat stood on her chalk-white face and glistened in the hollow of her throat. The cello slithered on her wet belly. Until she rolled her eyes and only the whites were blindly staring... her mouth opened in a series of dry croaks which accelerated into a long, hoarse yell... and, at the same time, she arched herself upward, grinding the cello between her thighs.

There she remained for a long second, her body lifted from the bed. With a rattling exhalation which seemed to go on and on for ever, she subsided and lay still. She breathed evenly. Finally, she turned her face toward Harry, smiled the smile of an angel, and closed her eyes.

Straight away, she was asleep. Harry lifted the cello gently from her, wrapped it in the blue silk scarf in which it was always enfolded, and put it in its case; the bow as well. With a warm towel he wiped the sweat from her face and body, rubbed at her hair which was plastered in wet, red strands around her temples, and then he covered her with blankets.

He took off his own clothes and slipped into bed. Holding Lizzie in his arms, he was soon asleep too.

18

From that day, a curious calm fell over Lizzie and remained intact to the day of the birth of her child.

Curious, because for Harry it was somehow more disquieting than her previous tension had been. The angelic smile remained on her face. Her jaunty defiance filled the *Ozymandias* and spilled across the estuary. It was unnerving for Harry, to see her transformed like this in the space of a few hours, to see her continuing calm as the days went by.

She said simply, "No, Harry, that was just an aberration," when he asked her if she would take out the cello and play it again. "I must have weakened that night, after what you said about the waste. Now that I've got my strength back, the cello stays in its case. Anyway, the damp has wrecked it. It's split and warped." She added, "But you might find a use for it one day," and then refused to explain what she meant.

It unnerved him that nothing unnerved her. She was unflappable. She seemed to have dispelled the nightmare about her parents' coming to visit. She humored Frank, encouraging him to talk about his travels in South America, flattering him into a feeling of avuncular seniority; she went so far as to draw on a joint, a concession which won him over completely. She apologized to Dewi for her waspishness, tapping her belly as though to blame its contents for her graceless behavior, and she praised him for the progress he'd made. She was friendly to Helen Ince, with tea and cakes to sustain her through her lesson. Once more, there were flowers in the cabin of the *Ozymandias*, willowherb and yarrow and the viper's bugloss she'd picked from the hedgerow.

Lizzie smiled through the final weeks of her pregnancy, utterly calm, utterly relaxed. She clasped her hands across her stomach. She glowed with health, but there was a chill in her invincible glitter that made Harry shiver. She radiated a mysterious resolve: some irrevocable decision had been taken, and the certitude of it flooded her with strength. At the same time, she distanced herself from her brother, her lover, the father of her child. She was moving further and further off. And Harry felt, with a shudder of helplessness, that he would never have her back again.

19

The baby came sooner than expected.

Harry was woken by the movement of the boat and by the dancing of shadows on the walls of the cabin. His first impression, which reminded him why he'd been sleeping so deeply, was the lingering fume of marijuana — the previous evening, Frank had been for his lesson. The stove was blazing, although it was a sweltering night at the end of July, and in the firelight he could see Lizzie standing at the foot of their bed. She was a tiny, pale, elfin figure in nothing but a nightdress, with her belly ballooning and big. She turned to Harry, startled to see him awake, and he could see that she was sweating; her face was glistening like moist cheese. Strands of hair were plastered to her temples.

He lifted himself onto one elbow. "Lizzie? Are you all right? What time is it?" She was opening and closing the door of the forward cabin.

She glanced around. She had the cello. For a moment, she tried to conceal it from him by holding it behind her body, before realizing he was wide awake and had already seen it.

"Don't move, Harry," she whispered, smiling weakly. "Not just yet, anyway. The baby's coming, quicker than I thought it would. But there's still a bit of time."

Startled, Harry sat up and peered into the firelit darkness to see what she was doing. "Don't worry," she was saying, her face turned away from him. "I'm not going to play."

She wasn't talking to Harry. She'd taken her cello out of its case, unwound the blue silk scarf from it, and now she was turning the machine heads to loosen the strings. She removed the bass string completely and dropped it, shining and sinewy, onto the cabin floor. It squirmed in the corner.

"There," she said. "That must be better for you. A bit late, I'm afraid, but better late than never. All these years you've been wound up tight, fit to burst. There, all that tension has gone now."

She leaned the cello against the bed and sat down, with her little white hands pressed to the bulge of her belly. Her smile was thin, like the smile of a lizard, and her eyes were cold, like the eyes of a gull.

"I'm all right," she said to Harry. "I didn't want to wake you yet. It's two o'clock. I was restless. Remember what it says in the book about the tremendous surges of energy I'm supposed to have when it all starts happening? Makes a change from my usual laziness! I found myself awake, realized it was starting, and I just couldn't stay in bed. I suddenly thought of the cello, all wound up in its case, and had a terrific urge to unwind it. Daft, isn't it? I don't know why exactly," she added with a shrug of bony shoulders. "Just a whim, I suppose."

The boat stirred. It was a big tide that night, one of the highest of the summer. The timbers groaned against the sea wall; water and silt lapped in the bilges. Outside, on the estuary, all was still, as it had been throughout the hot, airless summer. There was hardly a cry from the distant dunes. Harry and Lizzie had been becalmed for weeks — hard weeks for her, who was so pale and frail. The lunging, the squirm of the baby had left her exhausted. Now she sat, clammy-cold with sweat, on the edge of the bed. She was out of Harry's reach.

He sat up and leaned over to touch her. "It's so stuffy in here, Lizzie," he said. "Why on earth have you got the stove going like that?"

She felt icy, although the cabin was ablaze with firelight.

"We're going to need hot water, aren't we?" she answered. "I stoked up the stove, trying not to wake you. I'll put the kettle on it now."

But, as she stood up, small as a child except for the weight she was bearing before her, she gasped and clutched hard at her stomach. Harry sprang from the bed and quickly laid her down on the rumpled sheets where he'd been lying.

Things were happening very fast. The chapters of the books he'd read for just this moment, describing what should be done at different stages, now flickered their densely worded pages through his mind. Socks? That was something he remembered: however hot a woman might feel in labor, her feet would be freezing, due to a diminishing circulation of blood. While Lizzie lay down and tried to relax, to calm herself and her breathing for another contraction, Harry found his thickest socks, and tugged them onto her feet. Tea? The kettle was on the stove, which was too hot to touch.

"How long have you been up, Lizzie?" he asked her. "You should have woken me!"

When she had the breath, she said that she'd been up for an hour, refueling the fire before turning her attention to the cello. She spoke to him from a distance, with a glitter on her. She was the center of things, the focus of everything that was happening and about to happen. She eclipsed him. The smile she smiled, even as she gulped for air, seemed to drain him. The force with which she inhaled left little oxygen for him. All the firelight fell on her. When she said, with a quiver of excitement in her voice, that the waters had broken and then commanded him to bring her some towels, Harry was so grateful to be involved in what she was doing that his eyes stung with tears. And when she told him to call for an ambulance, he got straight into his clothes and onto the deck of the boat, fumbling to unlock his bicycle, accelerating as hard as he could into the darkness of the seashore track, in pursuit of the feeble, zigzagging beam from his lamp.

The night was warm around his face and neck. He covered a mile in a blankness of oblivious exertion before he realized with a pang that he'd left without giving Lizzie a kiss or a word of encouragement, without even saying goodbye. He cycled steadily on, toward the lights of the town.

Close to him, on his left, the waters of the Menai Strait were soft and full and silent on the shore. The tide was so high that the swell moved in the grass at the edge of the track. On the gravel, where the wheels of the bicycle were evenly crunching, there glistened the heavy, wet clumps of seaweed which the waves had put down; as he rode over them, there was a tender yielding, the gentle explosions of rubbery bubbles. The night was very dark. Across the strait he could see the lights of a house, faint among the trees of Newborough Warren, and sometimes the headlamps of a car swung and scythed through the high-banked lanes which tunneled in the fields of the island. The water was black as oil, and just as still; only the dimmest reflections of the stars were quivering there, like a powder of sugar spilled on a deep carpet.

Harry peered above him. The constellations weren't clear, because the summer heat had spread a haze across them. But, as he hurried on, as he felt his breath coming hard and a trickle of perspiration between his shoulder blades, he saw a meteorite flash across the sky: a blazing star which spent itself on the horizon of the Irish Sea... as though it had fallen and been quenched, extinguished, before sinking as cold, dead fragments to the darkness of the depths. The meteorite was gone in a second or two. Harry continued to cycle, having seen it appear and disappear.

It was three o'clock in the morning.

Caernarfon Castle loomed before him, its floodlighting switched off. Only then, as he came to the mouth of the river, he remembered with a shock like a punch to the stomach that the footbridge had been swung open hours before, at eleven o'clock, and would be left open all night so that the fishing fleet could come and go. He fought down a wave of panic. A hundred yards from him, brightly lit against the slabs of the castle, there was a telephone kiosk; but he couldn't cross to it. He breathed deeply and cycled on until he reached the first bridge upstream, crossed the river and hurried through the sleeping outskirts of Caernarfon. The detour had cost him a quarter of an hour.

His conversation with the maternity unit at St. David's Hospital, Bangor, lasted a minute and then Harry's coins ran out. But in that time he'd informed them of Lizzie Clewe's imminent delivery of a baby and they'd assured him of the immediate dispatch of an ambulance, once he'd described the whereabouts of the *Ozymandias*. Slamming down the receiver, he remained inside the kiosk, sweating from the exertion of the dash into the town, from the stress of the hurried conversation. The square and the streets and the castle were in darkness. Harry hesitated, reluctant to step out of the comforting brightness. He braced himself against the cowardice that wanted him to pause, so that, by the time he returned to the boat, the ambulance might already be there.

In the windows of the kiosk, he saw his own reflection, his pale face, the gingery, disheveled hair, the puzzled, bespectacled eyes. How bewildered and inexperienced he looked! It suddenly seemed such a long way home, with the tide lapping close and black beside him: a burrowing journey into darkness. Something in Lizzie had chilled him. He shuddered with a spasm of cold, in spite of the warmth of the summer's night. He shivered to feel so separate from her, excluded from what she was doing, from what she was going to do.

For another moment, the glare of the telephone kiosk held him. He avoided his eyes in the mirrored glass, winced at the fear on his face. Then he spilled out, mounted the bicycle and bent to the business of returning to the *Ozymandias*.

Soon, the lamplight beckoned from the cabin of the boat. A plume of smoke rose into a still sky. The sea was up, so calm that the reflection of the stars was steadier than the stars themselves. As Harry dismounted and threw the bicycle onto the sea wall, he felt that all must be well: this was their home, so quiet and cool, on such a lovely, lovely night.

He stepped onto the deck and set the whole cabin rocking. He went quickly down the steps, into the cabin.

Lizzie was in front of him, upright, swaying, her head and face covered with the blue silk scarf she'd unwound from the cello. For a second, it looked as though she was dancing in the center of the room, in her nightdress and socks... dancing, with her arms at her sides, her body moving in time with the flickering firelight.

But she wasn't dancing. She was hanging.

"Lizzie? Lizzie, what are you...?" Harry took a step forward, unsure of what he was seeing.

Lizzie was hanging from the ceiling of the cabin. The bass string of the cello was wound around the beam and around her throat. Her feet were swinging about six inches above the floorboards. Her hands clenched and unclenched. The front of her nightdress was red and wet with a gout of blood and there was blood on her legs. She turned and swayed before him, as though she was dreamily dancing... The blood hissed when her legs touched the stove.

With a wild cry, Harry lunged at her. Embracing her, holding her to him and trying to lift her with one arm, he reached to the ceiling and scrabbled at the knotted wire. Through the folds of the blue scarf, wrapped round and round her face, he could hear her gagging, gurgling whispers. Her hands felt into his hair, her freezing fingers were on his lips and in his mouth. He sawed at the string with a knife, and the room was filled with the jagged and violent resonance he'd once heard from Lizzie's playing....

But he couldn't cut it. He couldn't undo the string from around the beam.

Exhausted, sobbing, he folded his arms around her body and cradled her. His face was buried in her breast. Her hands fell from him and swung. He sobbed and sobbed until her whispering stopped. Until at last he stepped away from her, releasing her gently when the string took all the strain. It hummed a deep, sonorous hum. She sighed a long, rattling sigh.

Among the blankets of the bed there lay a child, very tiny, very gray. His mind completely blank, Harry bent to it and pressed the tip of his little finger into its mouth. The baby flinched and gave a mewing cry. Now that its mouth was clear, it continued to cry. Harry made sure that its face wasn't covered, rearranging the blankets around its body, and he watched how the baby's coloring changed quickly from gray to a suffusion of pink. It was a girl, with an angry face and a wisp of silvery hair.

Lizzie had stopped the swaying dance with which she'd greeted Harry's return to the boat. She was still. She was silent. Her socks were burned through and the soles of her feet were blistered black and stinking, because she'd stood on the stove before stepping into the air, as a means of driving herself to do it. Now, the shrouded, dangling figure slowly turned. The string buzzed. The cello leaned in the corner. In a spasm that set her dancing again and invoked a wail of horror from Harry, the afterbirth slithered down Lizzie's legs and slopped onto the floor. It signaled that everything was done.

Harry held the baby. She was hot, bawling lustily in a huddle of blankets. He lay with his daughter and hid his face, and they were crying together when the ambulance arrived.

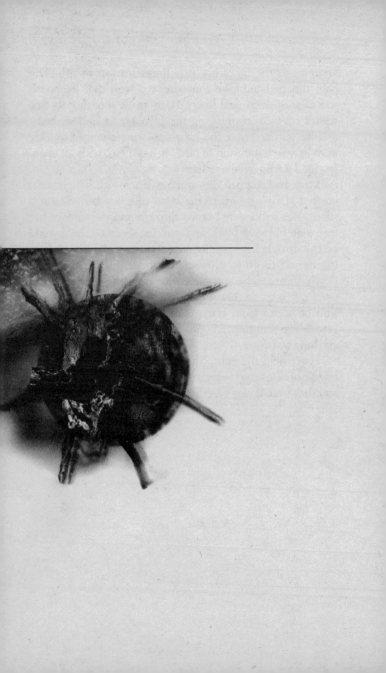

PART THREE star-splitter

1

In the hospital, Harry Clewe was taken to see Lizzie's body.

She'd been washed. Someone had brushed her hair. It was beautiful, gleaming red, falling smoothly from her forehead and her temples. Her face was no longer suffused with blood, but her lips were blue. Harry couldn't see the damage that the cello string had done to her throat. Considering the trauma of her death, her expression was calm. But she was cold and broken. He looked at her face and her little hands, at her puffy, stupefied frown and the whiteness of her wrists and fingers. She was broken, like the things she'd found on the seashore, dead and bleached, scoured by the sand and the tumble of waves on barnacled boulders. She'd found things like this before, between the tidelines, on the foreshore where the boat was moored: things that had once been vital and vigorous, until they were quenched.

The doctors covered the body with a sheet.

Not far away, inside the same building, separated from the remains of her mother by a long corridor, the baby continued her lusty squalling. Her birth and her mother's death had occurred within a matter of minutes: the life had passed from one to the other. The baby bellowed, newly created, her tiny limbs rowing and pumping in a flush of energy, as though the force was burning within her like a stoked-up boiler and driving her with a dynamic strength. Her silvery hair gleamed. Harry was taken to see mother and baby: the one used up and empty, no more than a husk; the other alight with a newly ignited fire of life, ruddy and hot and enflamed.

But the baby wasn't so perfectly whole as her vigorous crying suggested. She was as blind as a stone.

The doctor explained this to Harry in the privacy of a reception room. He was the same young doctor whom Harry and Lizzie had consulted several months earlier. Called to the hospital especially to counsel Harry, to help him through the trauma of Lizzie's death, he'd thought to do this by contrasting the stillness of the corpse with the vigor of the newborn child. Now he struggled to account for the baby's blindness.

"You asked me, Mr. Clewe," he stammered, "to explain any possible problems associated with your union with your sister. Perhaps I should have mentioned that if the consanguinity were to throw up any... any, er... any kind of deformity or disability — and this is extremely rare — then the disability would most likely be of this sort. That is, a weakness in the eyes, or even, tragically, complete blindness. In this case there's albinism too, an absence of pigmentation. That's another unfortunate result of the inbreeding."

He cleared his throat, pinched the bridge of his nose between his thumb and forefinger, and took a deep breath. His voice broke.

"I'm really very sorry," he said, "for your sister's death and your daughter's disability. Of course, I'll do everything possible to try and help you, and to see that the baby continues well."

Harry felt no grief at Lizzie's death. He felt no joy at the birth of the baby. He felt no anger at the news of the baby's blindness. Only, at that moment, he was tremendously sorry for the doctor. He reached out and touched him, folding his hands on the young man's hands. Then his mind went blank.

Seeing this nothingness in his eyes, the nurses put Harry to bed.

The case was referred to the coroner, a kindly, twinkling, gray-haired man who came to Harry's bedside a few days later. He made the procedure as painless as possible. Briefly, he explained that there was no suspicion of foul play: he was convinced that Lizzie had stepped from the stove into thin air. The scorching of her socks and feet was evidence of this. From his own examination of the body, from his study of the photographs and measurements that the police had taken on board the boat, he was satisfied that the two legal requirements for the recording of a suicide had been met: one, that the deceased had done the deed herself; two, that she'd meant to kill herself. There was no need to know why she'd done it. There would be no interrogation, no nightmarish cross-examination. All he wanted from Harry, who'd identified the deceased as his sister, Elizabeth Clewe, was her address and the date and place of her birth.

Harry blinked up at the soft-spoken, avuncular gentleman who was sitting at the hospital bedside. Knowing why Lizzie had killed herself, that the guilt had gnawed at her like a worm inside a plum, he was tremendously relieved that he wouldn't be asked to explain it.

"These days," the coroner said, "we don't even use the old chestnut about 'the balance of the mind being disturbed.' I've seen a lot of cases like this: believe it or not, nearly three hundred suicides during my thirty years as coroner, and a good number of them caused by the guilt engendered by the closeness of a union such as you had with your sister. It's not uncommon. But it's none of my business. No doubt it's something you'll think about, on your own." He patted Harry's hand. "Don't worry, Mr. Clewe," he said. "No one's going to come prodding and prying. I'll conduct an inquest, of course, but I won't dwell on your relationship with the deceased. It won't be reported in the press."

So the inquest was a formality. The coroner signed Lizzie's death certificate, recording a verdict of suicide. For a while, the doctors insisted it was best for Harry to remain in hospital. When at last he was discharged, he committed himself to the years ahead, to the blind child he called Zoë.

2

He returned to the *Ozymandias*. Helen Ince drove him from the hospital and out to the estuary. Lizzie hadn't liked her, but Harry liked her, and now she was the only friend who'd come forward to offer support and consolation.

"Will you be all right, Harry?" she asked him as he climbed out of the silver Daimler. "Do you want me to come inside with you, to see if everything's OK?"

He shook his head. He managed to thank her, although he felt numb at the prospect of stepping aboard again. She leaned to him and brushed his cheek with her lips. Her scent made him feel a little giddy. She drove away.

He went below, for the first time since he'd cycled breathlessly back from the town and found Lizzie.... Swallowing a bubble of nausea at the memory, he squeezed his eyes tightly shut to erase the image of the dancing, dangling, shrouded, blood-splashed figure. He stepped into the cabin.

The environmental-health department had done a good job, as the kindly coroner had promised they would. More than that: not only had they removed all trace of the ghastly scene, but they'd restored the place to the bare emptiness of the days before Lizzie had moved in, to the days when Harry had been living on the boat on his own. By way of her spectacular death, Lizzie had brought blood and gagging and the stench of scorching flesh to the cabin; all of that was gone, dissolved in the ammoniac whiff of disinfectant. Prior to that, she'd brought laughter and warmth and the bright disarray of wild flowers; all of that was gone, too.

Harry sat heavily on the bed. The cabin was scrubbed raw. He searched in vain for a single sign that Lizzie had ever been there, then lay down and stared at the ceiling. Had he imagined her? Had she been a dream? Had that night been no more than a nightmare, whose horror would fade from him, whose reek would soon be forgotten?

No. The beam was rubbed into a deep groove by the action of the cello string with which she'd hanged herself. Harry remained on the bed, gazing upward, and he shuddered with a terrible cold to think how the string had scored her throat. So Lizzie had been there, although now she was gone.

And the cello leaned in the corner of the cabin, silent, sullen, warped by the damp after months of neglect. Harry left it there. He tore his eyes from the groove in the beam, lest it assume the focus of his attention. It mustn't do that. He must be strong enough, stronger than Lizzie had been, to beat the onset of a fatal depression. He went on deck.

The heat haze of an August afternoon.... The tide was right out of the estuary, and on the mud there were large numbers of feeding birds. As ever, he dashed below and returned to the deck with his binoculars. There was a furious commotion. The birds rose in a black and white cloud, squalling and screaming, and dropped again to the mud at the ebb of the tide. He cursed the condition of the binoculars, because he was intrigued to see what was causing such excitement at the water's edge. He wondered what the birds had found, that they should squabble so violently. He wondered what the sea had fetched up.

His spirits rising, his heart pounding, he leaped off the boat and onto the sea wall. As fast as he could, he slithered down the rungs of the iron ladder and dropped onto the foreshore. With a shout, he crunched across the shore, sprang over the grasses and branches and sun-dried vegetation that the tide had left behind, and he sprinted on the flat sands in the direction of the birds.

He bellowed, he clapped his hands, he whirled his arms. He cackled a strange, mirthless laughter. The gulls and the crows beat away from him as he splashed knee-deep into the warm salt pool where the skeleton of the horse was lying.

Bones... brown, riddled and rotten... The ribcage, like the

spars of a sunken boat... The skull, stuffed with mud, burrowed by worms and crabs... This was the wreckage of the horse. Harry rummaged inside it, giggling and shouting.

The pool was squirming with hundreds of brittlestars. He scooped them up, a tangled, knotted handful of them, and felt their writhing on his fingers. The gulls had returned, screaming overhead, and he felt the rain of their soapy droppings on his back and in his hair. But he ignored them. He held the brittlestars in his hands and marveled at them, thrilled that they'd come to this place, so near to the *Ozymandias*, where Lizzie had searched and searched for so long....

Then he remembered the shooting star he'd seen, on the night of Lizzie's death, the night of Zoë's birth. He'd seen it fall into the sea. Here it was, cooled into fragments, the shards and smithereens of a meteorite.

Standing up, grinning to himself at the fanciful notion, he let the brittlestars drop back into the water, where they sculled among the bones of the horse. He walked over the sands, toward the *Ozymandias*, keeping one of the brittlestars in his hand, and he carried it with him to the boat.

As he'd done before, and as Lizzie had done, he put the brittlestar in a shallow tray of water, with a bed of sand. It squirmed and meshed and burrowed, disappearing from sight. Harry smiled, knowing that it was there.

He spent the night on the deck of the *Ozymandias*, for it was too hot and stuffy inside the cabin; he dozed in the cooler air of the estuary, lying back with his binoculars trained on the sky. He cleaned the lenses with the red spotted neckerchief — a piece of his life before he'd come to the *Ozymandias*, before Lizzie had come to him there — and he gazed at the hazy summer constellations, dreaming of the difference that a telescope would make, remembering the hours that he and Lizzie had passed with the old binoculars on the old boat.

No more meteorites, no more showers of sparks into the sea.... He smiled to himself, running his fingers through his hair. It didn't matter. Down in the cabin, the brittlestar was limber and lithe in shallow water. And, coming home soon, Zoë herself, as brilliant a silvery spark as any that had swept the sky on her birthday.

3

Lizzie was buried in the cemetery of the little church nearby, no more than a hundred yards from the seashore and the mooring of the *Ozymandias*. The sycamores were in heavy leaf, the branches hardly stirring, coated in fine white dust after weeks without rain. The ancient headstones leaned askew; some of them had fallen to the long grass, swallowed by a tangle of nettles and dock. Lizzie had loved the cemetery. She'd browsed the epitaphs, felt at the cold slate with her fingers, reading the inscriptions on the children's graves which she'd found so poignant. That winter, when the sycamores were stripped of their foliage, she'd brought Harry here. Now she'd come to stay.

It was a glorious morning in August. A lark was spiraling in the tall, blue sky, no more than a speck, releasing a torrent of song. The trees sighed in a breath of breeze. The church basked in the sunshine, as still and hot as a boulder. Out at sea, there flickered the blue and white sails of yachts and windsurfers, like a flock of exotic wildfowl. A lovely morning and a lovely place: Harry and the minister; the sexton watching from a distance, leaning on his spade...

Harry stood over the damp pit into which the coffin had been lowered. There was a plain headstone, recording nothing more than the name of the person inside the coffin, among the older stones which were splashed with rust-red lichen and on which the gulls and the crows had dropped mussels to crack the shells, where the long grass was littered with feathers and bones.

Bones, bones and more bones, Harry thought: the tiny white bones of Lizzie Clewe, his sister, his lover, the mother of his child. The earth and the gravel slid from the spade and clattered on the coffin, until it was quite covered and the pit was filled.

Remaining there alone, at last he managed to weep. Kneeling on the wet earth, he wept so loudly that the cattle

lifted their gormless heads to see him. The peewits somersaulted away. The lark abandoned its jigsaw-puzzle song. He
wept until he thought he was too exhausted to weep any
more. Then he continued to weep.

A month had passed since Lizzie's death and Zoë's birth.
Harry had at last achieved something of the catharsis afforded by tears. Moreover, he'd had time to organize the
Ozymandias for the homecoming of his baby daughter. In
the hospital, he'd been quizzed by representatives of the social services about the suitability of the boat as a home for
a child, a disabled child, and about his competence as a father to cope with her on his own. While conceding that
his incestuous union with the mother wasn't necessarily a
bar to his custody of the child, they'd stressed that Zoë's in-
terests were paramount, that they could order her into care
if Harry's custody were deemed inappropriate.

He'd convinced them that all would be well. He had an
income from his music teaching, work he could do at home
while simultaneously taking care of Zoë. Since leaving the
hospital, he'd had help in substantially refitting the boat,
the most radical alteration being the connection of piped
water from the nearest farmhouse; the cabin was warm and
weatherproof. Harry made the point that, as far as the baby's
disability was concerned, there were no more difficulties,
in the early months at least, in the care of a blind child than
there would have been if she were sighted. He'd attended
the usual post-natal classes, along with a number of simi-
larly inexperienced single parents, and there was nothing
to suggest that he couldn't be just as efficient as they were
in the care of a baby daughter. Of course, there would be
regular inspections from social workers and health visitors.
In the meantime, work was complete on the *Ozymandias*.
Harry was ready to receive Zoë home.

Lizzie was in a box, cold in the cold ground. No more
lunging for her, no more writhing and squirming. It had

murdered her. The baby bellowed in Harry's arms when he picked her from her cot to take her from the hospital. She kicked and raged against him. Her pale, empty eyes met his. There was something on her mouth like a smile, and a crowing in her voice.

4

Zoë was asleep when they came to the boat. She slept throughout the journey in the ambulance, and she slept as Harry settled her into her home. Her face was wrinkled, like the kernel of a walnut; she was wrapped in the blue silk scarf which had enfolded the cello and had enshrouded Lizzie, and which Harry had especially reclaimed from the coroner's office.

The boat now swayed and soothed her, as it had swayed with the dangling of her mother. Harry ducked his head from the low beams, averting his eyes from the groove that the wire had made. He got busy, to avoid thinking too much. The baby continued to sleep for hours after the ambulance had gone and after the evening had turned to night. On the falling tide, the *Ozymandias* rocked gently. The night outside was hot, a soft summer's night which held the boat warm and moved it so that the baby slept. Harry went up the steps and onto the deck.

There was a splendid summer sky. He lay back with his old binoculars and followed the constellations from one wonder to the next. The great triangle of Vega, Altair and Deneb was brilliant above him. Even through the gritty lenses, Vega was gorgeously blue, a sapphire directly overhead. Altair, high in the south, flanked by fainter stars, led him to the nearby cluster of the Wild Duck. Straining north, he came to Deneb, the first-magnitude star in the constellation of Cygnus; he moved on, using it as a pointer through the body of the Swan to the double star Albireo....

And there he settled himself with a sigh. Albireo: the loveliest double star in the sky, a primary of golden yellow with a turquoise companion. He gaped. He goggled. Had he ever seen anything so lovely?

The lenses became misty, clouded by his own breath. Infuriated, he smeared them on his shirt, wiped them with his fingertips, but there remained a film between him and the perfect clarity of the sky. He closed his eyes. Still there was silence from below. He remembered how he and Lizzie had sat together on the deck, when he'd shown her the winter constellations. She'd smiled at the puniness of the binoculars against the vastness of the heavens, and they'd speculated about the telescope they might have one day on board the *Ozymandias*. What wonders would they see? In winter, how stupendous were the Hyades and the Pleiades and the great gaseous nebula of Orion's sword? And in summer, if Albireo was so fine in the smears of the binoculars, what marvel would they see through the lenses of a powerful telescope?

They? Harry opened his eyes. He'd thought: they. But Lizzie was gone. Below, in the cabin, there was his daughter, for whom a telescope would be a nonsense. Nevertheless, even without Lizzie to accompany him, even with Zoë, whose presence might prick him with guilt, he would see great things if....

Standing up, he turned from the sea and faced inland. The bulk of the mountains was lost on the black sky. But, in the direction of the town, there was an orange glow on the horizon, much brighter than the glow of the castle's floodlights: another fire in Caernarfon, the third in the same week. The local newspaper had printed a letter from someone who claimed that the spate of fires was caused by the recent eclipse of the sun, quoting an account from the *Gossiping Guide to Wales* to the effect that "in the years 1542 and 1567, when the sun was eclipsed, the town suffered very much by fire; and after the latter eclipse of the two, the fire spread so far that two hundred houses in Caernarfon were consumed."

Harry trained his binoculars on the distant horizon, and there were flames in the warm darkness. Knowing that these fires were the natural and unfortunate result of a long, dry, hot summer, he smiled to think that the eclipse of the sun might be blamed for them. He smiled to think of his silvery spark of a daughter, asleep in the cabin, whose birth had been presaged by a shooting star and whose homecoming was now celebrated in solar eclipse and blazing fire. Wherever she'd come from, this meteoric child, and whatever she might turn out to be, her arrival had been marked by the sun and the stars....

He went downstairs, into the silence of the cabin. Zoë frowned up at him, surfacing slowly from sleep; she rowed her arms a little and held out a fist clenched into dimples. He prepared her feed, in anticipation of her waking. He pondered the dreams of a newborn baby, a baby who'd been born out of one tumbling darkness and straight into another, for whom, perhaps, the cabin of the *Ozymandias* was indistinguishable from the womb. He prepared for her waking.

Still distracted by his star-gazing, he bent to inspect the brittlestar in its tray. He couldn't see it.

He put his face to the surface of the water and breathed on it, disturbing the mirror-stillness into ripples. There was no other movement. With his finger, he stirred softly in the bed of sand. But the brittlestar wasn't there.

Zoë was waking. He heard her spit and mew. Ignoring her, he peered into the tray. He noticed there was a splash of water on the chest of drawers, and a trail of water and sand on the polished wood. He followed it to the books, thinking to find the creature hidden among them, like a spider in a dark and dusty crevice. Zoë was squirming under her blankets. Still he left her.

He picked out a book, having seen a tiny, bristle-covered tentacle protruding from its loose pages, and he sat with it on the bed. Bending forward to the heat of the stove, whose door was ajar so that the flames could light the cabin, he opened the book and found the brittlestar pressed wetly on the print. He tenderly took it out, holding the disc of its body between his fingertips, while the tendrils flexed and felt for a grip on the smoothness of his nails, and he replaced it in the tray. It sank to the sand. He sat with the book in the firelight. Zoë had started a keening wail.

On the pages, the outline of the brittlestar was marked with sea water. It faded in the warmth of the stove, as he leaned even more closely to read what was written: one of their favorite poems, which he and Lizzie had read and re-read together. This was what the brittlestar had marked for him: a message from Lizzie. Or a message from Zoë...?

It was a narrative poem by Robert Frost, the story of a man who "burned his house down for the fire insurance and spent the proceeds on a telescope, to satisfy a lifelong curiosity about our place among the infinities...." The man called the telescope the star-splitter, "because it didn't do a thing but split a star in two or three, the way you split a globule of quicksilver in your hand with one stroke of your finger in the middle...."

Zoë was wide awake now. She wrestled under her blanket. Harry felt a sudden and familiar stillness fall the length of the boat, as the *Ozymandias* settled on the sands. Minutes must have passed, time for him to read the poem again. If this was a message from Lizzie, or from Zoë, or from mother and daughter in cahoots, then what should he do? What did they intend him to do?

Harry ducked swiftly across the cabin and reached for the cello in the corner.

Inside the case, with the cello itself, there was a sheaf of music, a bow and its rosin. He lifted the cello out. Very gently, he examined it in the lamplight and the firelight. Zoë had set up a caterwaul, which he hardly heard. He caressed the cello, running his hands sensually over its curved flanks; he turned its back and its belly this way and that, and the curl under the russet colors of the varnish rippled like flame. He ran his fingers up and down the neck, stroked the perfect black smoothness of the fingerboard and the simple machinery of the pegs; the tailpiece, in ebony like the fingerboard and the pegs, was quite uncluttered. By contrast, the scroll was bizarrely, beautifully carved in the shape of a human fist, as though it were clenching the strings tightly.

The instrument was exquisite, lovingly made and lovingly used. But now it was a silent thing which Harry turned from hand to hand. The bass string was missing. The other strings flapped loosely. After a winter of neglect, the lower bouts were split and the neck was out of alignment.

Among the sheet music, there was a Christie's auction catalogue. As Harry picked it up, it fell open at a page marked with some slips of paper. By now he was oblivious of Zoë's yelling: if she'd climbed out of her cot and seized his arm, he wouldn't have noticed her. There was a color photograph of Lizzie's cello, and he read the accompanying description by holding the catalogue closer to the stove:

Lot no. 243. An interesting Italian violoncello, labeled JO. BAP ROGERLUS BON NICOLAI AMATI DE CREMONA ALUMNUS BRIXAE ANNO DOMINI 1681. The two-piece back cut on a slab of poplar wood; the table of strong medium grain widening to broad on the flanks; the varnish of a brown color on a reddish ground. Uniquely, the scroll carved into a human fist, clenched. With certificate of Charles Booth, Nelson, Lancashire, dated April 1934, stating the instrument to be the work of a pupil of Nicholas Amati, one of the founders of the Cremona school.

The slips of paper, which he now unfolded, were the verification of authenticity referred to in the catalogue, a receipt from Christie's for a successful bid of £5,750, and the instrument's current insurance certificate. As he read, his hands trembled. The bow itself, whose photograph he also found in the auctioneer's catalogue, had been bought for £700: it was stamped with the maker's name on the shaft, L. Tourte, and was insured on the same certificate as the cello.

Harry stared long and hard into the fire. Behind him, in her cot, Zoë lunged and screamed. Her face was lined like an old glove, her sightless eyes squeezed shut, her hair a gleam of silver. Wrapped in the scarf in which the cello had been wrapped, she boiled with life... while Lizzie was dead and gone. In front of Harry was the cello whose bass string was missing; above him, the beam which had been scored by the missing string. He turned from Zoë again, back to the fire, to give it his full attention.

The message was in the poem. He would interpret it literally.

First, to fuel the flames, he fed the sheet music and the auction catalogue to the stove. Into the quickened heat he tossed the rosin, consumed in one explosive hiss that filled the cabin with a sweet and heady perfume. Then he laid the bow on the bed of fire. The horsehair vanished. The bow buckled and flared; its one straight grain, selected from tons of the knotty pernambuco, charred into the blaze. The tortoiseshell nut, the mother-of-pearl head, the silver mounting... the fire swallowed it all.

Zoë breathed more easily, rolling her eyes at the ceiling, inhaling the exotic fumes. Harry reached for the cello itself, and picked up the hatchet from beside the stove.

He turned the ebony pegs to loosen the three remaining strings. Continuing to unwind them until the strings were detached and each one could be extracted from the peg box, he weighed the hard, black screws in his hands, knocking them together like pebbles. Then he threw them into the stove. Without hesitating to see how they burned, he stood up and pressed the cello into a corner of the cabin, to exert as much pressure as necessary to snap the neck from the body: this he did, the maple groaning against his weight as he leaned on it and held the neck in both hands. He forced his knee down; there was a sharp crack like the firing of a starting pistol and the neck was broken, with the simultaneous separation of the ebony fingerboard. He worked with a curious combination of joy and guilt, of exhilaration and furtiveness: a childish joy in the splintering of wood, and guilt in the vandalism of a thing that had been so lovingly created and so lovingly used. Unraveling the strings to free the neck completely from the body, he fed it to the stove. The fist burst into flames... soon it was blackened and charred.

There remained the shapely brown torso. Harry placed it on the floor, on its belly. With a glance and a smile at Zoë, who lay breathlessly still as though she were listening to the undoing of the cello with the same relish that her father was enjoying, he put his foot on the back and stepped down hard. The poplar collapsed. Turning it over, he did the same on the belly, easily shattering the wood between the f-holes. In order to see inside, into the entrails, he took the hatchet and smashed the bouts, splintering them to find the all-important label. Amati de Cremona, 1681! He hacked furiously and wildly at the carcass of the cello. And he heard himself laughing, a dry, manic, high-pitched laugh, to see how the purfling was broken, to see how the bee-stings were burst.

Time and again, striking aimlessly at the wreckage, the hatchet rose and fell. In the dancing shadows, it was hard to see what he was hitting. Until, exhausted and almost hysterical, Harry dropped the hatchet, threw all the remains of the cello into the fire, and squatted in front of the blaze to watch it burn.

Colors! Blue and green and golden flame! Perfumes! A breath of bitter-sweetness! The mysteries of coloring and varnish, the gums and resins used in infinite combinations by the great Italian makers of the sixteenth and seventeenth centuries... no more than a sigh from the mouth of the stove for Zoë and Harry to savor before it vanished in the air of the cabin.

By now the heat was intense. Nothing remained in the flames to suggest the sweet curves of the cello or its deep autumnal glow. It was all gone, in the stove, with so much humbler wood that he'd gathered from the mud of the estuary.

Harry was stunned by the heat, and his face had been scorched by sitting so close for so long. He stood up, crossed the cabin and looked down at Zoë. She was still quiet, breath-

ing evenly through the little O of her mouth. Her eyes, unwavering, stared into him when he leaned over her cot.

"Come with me, Zoë," he whispered to her. "I want to
show you, while you're so peaceful. And while it's so warm
outside." He lifted her up and carried her onto the deck of
the boat.

The fires on the horizon were gone. The stars were dim
behind a veil of cloud. Harry inhaled the sea air, after his
search for the brittlestar and the discovery of the poem, after his destruction of Lizzie's cello. He wanted, somehow, to
show the child her home, on her first night aboard the
Ozymandias. Although she could see nothing, she might
know the bigness of the estuary; she might taste the tang of
salt, hear the rumble of surf on the further side of the dunes.
He wanted no more than that.

Zoë had begun to fidget in his arms. He couldn't see her
face, but she was starting to moan again, softly, insistently.
It was well past the time to feed her; they'd both been distracted from it.

Below, Zoë smiled at him, unblinking. Harry met her
stare, but somehow, its fixity was too much for him. He
looked at the brittlestar. It moved blindly in a swirl of sand.

5

The woman was sound asleep, breathing evenly, very warm and very soft, with her back and buttocks pressed to his. She smelled different after a night in bed with him; her scent was quite altered. Harry lay for a while, long enough to be fully awake and to remind himself what day it was. The cabin was still dark, but he could see the sky lightening, changing from black to blue, from gray to silver. It was cold. Contrasting with the scent of the woman's body, there was the sharp, resinous tang of pine needles.

He slipped out of bed without waking her. Zoë was sleeping, too. Squatting, he reached for some wood and placed it in the stove, the weight disturbing the pale-gray ashes into a tumble of bright-orange embers. There would soon be a good fire to take the chill from the morning.

Harry quickly and silently dressed, his breath white. When he was ready, he crossed the cabin to Zoë's cot and leaned over it. He whispered into her tiny, unconscious face. "Happy Christmas!" he said. "Your first! I'll be back soon, with luck!" He went up to the deck of the *Ozymandias*.

It was a morning of torrential rain, heavy and unrelenting, the drops hammering into the sand flats of the estuary. There was no horizon in any direction, only a blanket of dense cloud. No birds: the impact of the rain was too much for them. Clumsy in his waterproof jacket and trousers, Harry clambered down the ladder from the top of the sea wall and onto the beach, negotiating the slipperiness of the boulders on the foreshore. The tide was right out. The sands were ribbed and polished, corrugated like the roof of his mouth. Soon he was a hundred yards from the boat, the rain loud on the hood of his jacket, where he stood alone in a world of jumbled, unsettling sensations.

No tall sky, only a lowering ceiling of rain. No calling of gulls and waders, only the noise of the raindrops on his head, as dinning as the din of machinery in a factory. His face was cold, he exhaled an icy breath. He licked his lips, and he could taste the woman as he tasted the salt in the air. He thought for a moment, as he altered his focus on this altered world, that perhaps it would be like this for Zoë, for whom every sound and taste and texture and vibration was altogether new. Sightless, she would adjust her perceptions of the environment, like the ghost-blooms of the bindweed which opened and closed and breathed so blindly in the hours of an altering darkness.... Exhilarated, disoriented, he trudged further into the morning, pushing aside the curtain of rain.

He came to the skeleton of the horse, knelt beside it and felt among the riddled bones. His fingers ached in the icy, green water. But he was lucky. Again the brittlestars were there, writhing between his hands. Tears of relief welled in his eyes, blurring his vision, stinging with salt. Blinking them away, he stood up with a single, perfect brittlestar on the flat of his palm. He'd wanted it so much on this day, more than he could rationally have explained to anyone... except perhaps to Lizzie. But there was no Lizzie. There was Zoë. And he'd wanted this thing for her.

Almost overwhelmed by relief, Harry slipped the creature into the pocket of his jacket and walked quickly through the rain.

The cabin of the boat was warm now, after his walking and his dousing on the estuary. Careful not to waken the sleeping woman nor to disturb the sleeping baby, he tiptoed to the Christmas tree and looped the brittlestar to the topmost point with a piece of thread. The creature shuddered and arched itself, its tentacles writhing as though to burrow to the safety of sand. But it dangled in dry air. Harry freed himself from his clothes. Naked, he moved to the tree, felt the needles hard and sharp on his belly, then he crossed the cabin and slipped into bed beside the woman. Pressing the length of her body with all his coldness, he breathed into her hair and inhaled her perfume.

"Happy Christmas, Helen," he said.

Zoë awoke as he and Helen were making love. The child howled, her cries as vigorously rhythmic as the cries and the lunging of the man and the woman. The baby settled to a steady wail as they subsided; she'd spent some of her raucousness in sympathy with them, who lay spent together in rumpled sheets.

"Zoë needs feeding and changing," Harry mumbled, with his mouth in the woman's soft, dark hair.

"So do I," Helen replied. "I've got people coming to my place who expect a sleek hostess and an elaborate Christmas dinner. You leave me all sweaty and tousled, you do. I mustn't stay much longer."

This was always Helen's signal to move, since their first lovemaking on board the *Ozymandias* after one of her flute lessons in October. It suited them both, for her to go away in the silver Daimler to her polished and scented house, until the next time she came for a lesson or for the lesson to be no more than a part of their foreplay. They had bodies that contrasted and yet were complementary: Harry, thirty-two years old by now, was hard, thin and white; Helen, four or five years older, was ripe, soft and full. They were satisfied to fall apart and continue separately, differently, at least for the time being.

She'd asked Harry to come to her Christmas lunch; he'd declined, using the baby as an excuse. Helen was a warm and loving woman, who'd been supportive over the past six months; her presence was a great comfort to Harry. Now she watched him change and feed Zoë, she who'd never had a child. He managed the baby well, holding her with an expertise as relaxed as his expertise with Helen. The woman watched, her eyes soft. She saw the flame-haired man and his silveryhaired, sightless daughter, and she saw the groove in the beam of the ceiling from which the mother, Lizzie Clewe, had hung.

She'd never asked about Lizzie's death, and Harry was grateful for this. Only, one day, catching him in pensive mood, she'd said, "Well, my love, Lizzie's gone, for ever and ever. But she's left you with Zoë. That's something to be thankful for. She meant to finish herself off and she made a pretty thorough job of it, from the rumors I heard. But she meant the baby to be born first, before she did it. It's all a mystery to me. I thought it was traumatic when my husband walked out on me, but it's nothing compared with the way your wife left you. Maybe, sooner or later, you'll tell me what happened. In the meantime, keep it to yourself, as long as you can bear it...."

She didn't know the peculiarity of Harry's relationship with Lizzie. She didn't see the writhing thing that dangled from the top of the Christmas tree; she hadn't missed the man while he'd been searching the sands. She was outside the orbit of the brittlestar.

"So, it's just the two of us," Harry said to Zoë when Helen had gone. "A year ago, it was just me and your mother. Now it's just you and me. Our first Christmas together on the *Ozymandias*."

That afternoon he lay on the bed, listening to the diminishing rattle of rain on the deck. He watched the brittlestar curl and stiffen.

When the rain stopped, the skies were lit with a curious wash of watery sunshine. This, and the lifting of the boat by the incoming tide, had the effect of reviving him from his daydream; the sunlight and the weightless wallowing of the whole cabin made him feel that he was airborne in a silent airship, high above the dark clouds.

"Let's go out," he said to Zoë. In no time, she was snug in her carrycot and he was ready in a coat. He took her onto the deck, onto the sea wall, and continued with her along the seashore track.

Having decided where they were going, in the desultory brightness of a Christmas afternoon, he paused several times to drop onto the beach and search for trophies. No, not trophies; they were gifts that he gathered. Zoë rolled her eyes at the sky. She fretted while her father made her wait. He found the skull of a curlew, clean and dry; he found razor-shells with the luster and colors of enamel; he collected the egg cases of rays, the remains of cuttlefish. All of these things he placed carefully in the carrycot, at the baby's feet. He took them away from the shore, across the fields to the church and the cemetery where Lizzie was buried.

He put the carrycot on the grave beside Lizzie's. Weeping, but nursing the happiness he felt at the closeness and the wriggling warmth of the baby, he arranged the Christmas gifts around Lizzie's headstone.

"From both of us," he said, through a blur of tears. "These are from me and Zoë."

The baby bellowed, her face crumpled and hot, but she didn't squeeze a tear. Together they cried, the man silent and shuddering, the child in angry spate, until the afternoon was too dark and too cold for them to stay any longer, and they returned to the *Ozymandias*. When Christmas was over, Harry vowed, when the tree was consigned to the fire, he would bring the brittlestar to the grave as well.

This he did, as he tried to do on subsequent Christmas Days.

6

In the meantime, he had the telescope.

He'd been surprised and relieved at the ease with which he'd completed his claim on the cello's insurance policy. In an accompanying letter, he'd explained the circumstances of Lizzie's death in just enough detail to suggest the horror he'd experienced, saying that the instrument had gone missing from the boat during the time he'd been in a state of shock in the hospital. The Caernarfon police obliged with a certificate supporting his claim, and the insurance company paid in full.

So, not many weeks after his gleeful destruction of the exquisitely crafted, three-hundred-year-old cello, Harry took delivery of a telescope, superbly hand-built in polished brass and lacquered gunmetal by Ernest J. Elliot of Broadhurst, Clarkson & Fuller, which two men maneuvered with difficulty into the *Ozymandias*. The equatorial mounting, on a steel pedestal which the men bolted into the floorboards, cost £170. The telescope itself, a four-inch refractor in a tube nearly five feet long, cost £2,765. With delivery and installation, Harry Clewe had spent £3,000, half the value of the cello. In this way, like the man in Robert Frost's poem, who'd burned down his house in order to purchase a telescope, he had his own star-splitter.

And from the start, Zoë conspired with the tides to thwart her father's observation of the night sky. Her howlings seemed to say, "If I can see nothing at all, not a thing but a wall of blackness shot with random dazzles and sparks, then why should I let you see any more?"

The best nights for star-gazing from the *Ozymandias*, with the telescope thrust through the hatch in the cabin roof, and Harry reclining comfortably in a specially sited and tilted easy chair, were the nights when the sky was cold and clear, when the boat was still on the mud of the estuary. Those were the nights when Zoë bellowed. She writhed. She turned from pink to purple and pink again with the effort of bellowing as stridently as possible. There were no tears. Each time Harry went fuming to her cot and leaned over to comfort her, she uttered a little croaking chuckle and smiled a wrinkled smile. She stared at him with her empty eyes. As long as the tide was out and her world was still, she found the strength to shout and wrestle. Perversely, when the boat was up and moving, enough to prevent the use of the telescope, she was quiet.

"At first I thought it was me she was objecting to," Helen said. "But it's the bloody telescope she can't stand. Of course she can't! She already hates the thing."

Helen and Harry spent a good deal of time in bed together. The flute lessons were all but forgotten, although the woman still brought her flute and music with her when she came to the boat. Usually the instrument stayed in its case. Now the telescope dominated the cabin, its black and weighty frame like a gibbet. It was a cold thing, pointing coldly into a cold sky. It had no warmth at all.

"What a monstrosity!" the woman said, who was so warm and soft. "Why on earth do you want such an ugly machine as that in here? Can you use it properly?"

Harry told her that he could, although he sensed already that he'd bought a highly complicated instrument he might never fully understand. Perhaps he'd spent too much on something he could never use. The thing was too big, too awkward, wrongly sited; worst of all, he admitted to himself, he was really quite ignorant of astronomy. He could have done just as well with a good pair of binoculars, for a mere ogling of the stars....

He lay close with Helen as she slept against him. He felt the heat of her sweetly sweating body and he thought uneasily of what he'd done. The burning of the cello! A glowing thing, lovingly used for three centuries, touched by living hands, cradled by gentle limbs... it was destroyed in the flames of the stove so that Harry Clewe, who knew so little, could own the cold, black tube and stare into cold, black space. He lay with his face in Helen's breast, so that the telescope's angular deadness was forgotten in the soft, white warmth of the woman.

"You what?" she gasped. "Smashed it and burned it? The cello? In the stove? You did what?"

She'd been incredulous, almost speechless, when he confided in her and described what he'd done. She'd stared into the fire as though she might see the bones of the instrument there, the charred skeleton. But not a trace remained.

"A poem? What bloody poem? Show it to me, for Christ's sake!"

She read the poem, and she gazed from the flames of the stove to the gantry of the telescope. She continued to read, in silence. At last, shaking her head in disbelief, she put the book down and reached for him, pulling his head to her breast and rocking him to her, as though he were a bewildered child in need of womanly comfort.

7

Helen continued to come to the boat, although Harry never went to her house. Her fragrance lingered in the little cabin. She was fond of him, kind and loving and supportive. He needed her and trusted her. Zoë must have sensed her, understood that the perfume was somehow akin to the movement of the tides, in its coming and going, its headiness and gradual dissipation... another element of the days and weeks that went by.

Frank came too. For him, the telescope was the most wonderful finishing touch to the magic of the *Ozymandias*. In much the same way that Helen's flute lessons had been abandoned in favor of sex in front of the open stove, Frank was inclined to ignore his flute in order to pass another evening in a haze of marijuana. Harry submitted, as he submitted to Helen, gladly, resignedly; he inhaled the giddying smoke while Frank talked of Machu Picchu and the Nazca lines, of all things and all places that were truly cosmic. Frank swooned in the easy chair, one eye against the polished tubing of the telescope; and Harry, with only a little more understanding of the machine than Frank had, feigned expertise, naming stars and constellations, adjusting the lenses, so that Frank might think him as serious an astronomer as he seemed to be a flautist. But Harry knew that the telescope, although it afforded some spectacular observations from time to time, was really beyond him.

Frank was content with goggling at the moon and the glittering Pleiades. So Harry didn't admit to him that the instrument was inappropriately installed in the first place. The equatorial mounting was wrongly set up; indeed, its adjustment was all but impossible; handcrafted with enormous precision, intended to be based on a concrete plinth for complete stability, the telescope was wasted on the shifting swell of the *Ozymandias*. Harry knew this, and it made him feel stupid. He didn't tell Frank or Helen. Still, he thought, doped into apathy, there were beautiful things to be seen through the lenses of the cold, black machine, albeit more by luck than by judgment.

Dewi became confident with the flute. The lessons progressed and he improved with all the work he did. He was the only student who really persevered with his lessons, in the weeks and months which ran into years in the aftermath of Lizzie's death. His complexion improved as a year and then another year went by. He arrived and left punctually and expressed no interest whatsoever in the telescope. Only, he looked around the cabin as though he still expected to meet the straight, clear eyes of Mrs. Clewe, the young, pretty, red-headed woman who'd winced so hard at his clumsiness with the flute. But she was gone, in extraordinary circumstances he'd barely grasped from local gossip. She was gone, although sometimes when he glanced up, his face burning, he seemed to hear her intake of breath.... Harry heard it too, because the boy's mannerism was infectious. But Lizzie was no longer there, pretending to read by the stove. Zoë was there.

So Helen came, and Frank and Dewi. Who else? What else?

The gulls came. The gulls, which had lured Harry to the skeleton of the horse, were drawn to the boat, to the child, Zoë. When the days were fine, he put her in the carrycot on the deck. The gulls beat around her. The first time it happened, he dashed to protect her from them, to wave his arms like a madman and shout unlovely words. But when he saw that they were oblivious of him, that he might as well have been invisible, he withdrew and watched from the stern of the boat. The gulls rose and fell around the cot, calling hoarsely into the child's face, buffeting with their powerful wings. The deck was white with droppings; the cot was splashed, and Zoë had the splatter on her cheeks. She was grinning. She chortled and crowed. Her eyes were aglitter with a brightness that Harry had never seen before, as though her blindness were dispelled, as though the shells of

her eyes were stripped and she could see the pearly creatures which dived and screamed around her. She was quite
separate from him.

Zoë had summoned this noisy congregation: Harry was
excluded from it. She was more a part of the estuary than
he could ever be, like the shooting star which had fallen
there. And so the gulls fell to her.

Harry adjusted himself to her routine, his days and
nights in tune with hers. He managed her, earning the
praise and approval of the people who visited to see how
he was coping; the child was warm and well fed, clean
and strong. A social worker came, a young woman, brisk
and severe and very Welsh, determined to find fault and
to report to her superiors that the Englishman, Harry
Clewe, and his home, the Ozymandias, were quite unsuit-
able for the upbringing of the blind child. She stayed for
an hour, angling her peaky, birdlike face this way and that
around the cabin. But there was nothing wrong with the
man or the place. The Ozymandias was neat and bright,
scented with flowers and a hot stove. Harry, with a regular income from his teaching as well as a little nest egg
from the claim on the cello, was managing a good deal
better than most of the other single parents on the local
authority's books, who lived in the damp, dilapidated
council houses on the outskirts of Caernarfon. So the
young woman warmed to Harry Clewe, over coffee and
cakes, in front of the crackling fire.

The coroner dropped by, genial and well-meaning, to see
how Harry was coping. Standing on the deck of the
Ozymandias, he squinted at the sunlight on the estuary. He
watched the heron as it stalked in the shallow waters, held
his breath as the bird stabbed into a pool and came up with
an eel, which squirmed and writhed in the dagger beak. The
man smiled, looking around at the distant dunes and the
foam of surf on the horizon. "Are you all right, young man?"
he said, gripping Harry's hand. "Yes, I can see you are...."

Harry was all right. Surrendering himself to the demands of Helen and Frank and Dewi, applying the mighty great eye of the telescope to the changing constellations, he found that the weeks passed.

And so did the early years of Zoë's life. He made her a bed of her own, screened into a corner of the cabin. Soon she knew every inch of the boat. Even on the deck, around which he'd constructed a solid, surrounding barrier, she learned to crawl and then to totter as adventurously as if she could see.

The years slipped by: four years, five years, six years. In the evenings, the child lay and listened to the music, inhaling the scents in the air. She stared at the ceiling, fixing her eyes on the wooden beam and its deeply scored groove, as though she could see it on the empty black screen inside her head. She sensed the presence of the telescope, the star-splitter, for which the cello had been put to the fire. Breathless, dry-eyed, strangely silent, she would listen to her father's flute; along with the cries of the curlew and widgeon, it was part of the everyday music of the estuary which she was unconsciously assimilating and learning to recognize.

Zoë would gaze about the cabin, grinning. Her silvery hair was the brightest flame in the room. She swiveled her eyes from the groove in the beam to Harry's face. And she would laugh, a dry, hoarse laugh, outstaring him. He flinched from her.

8

The little girl was sound asleep, breathing evenly, very warm and very soft, with her back and buttocks pressed to Harry's. He lay still for a while. He saw the sky beginning to lighten through a winter dawn, heard the rain fall loud and heavy on the decks of the boat. The cabin was cold. There was the sharp, resinous tang of pine needles.

Without waking the girl, he slipped out of bed and squatted in front of the stove. Under a blanket of ashes as fine and as gray as dust, there was still a glow of embers. He teased them, prodding with a piece of wood into the core of the heat, and he built a scaffold of dry spars for the fire to climb. It would soon take the chill from the morning.

He quickly and silently dressed, his breath white. The telescope loomed in the gloom, a heavy, hard gantry draped with a sheet. Under the covering of the sheet, there was a sudden shifting and beating of wings which were straight away quiet again. Harry held his breath, and once more there was a stillness in the cabin. The only sounds were the rain on the roof and the increasing crackle of the fire. Ready to go out, he leaned over the bed and whispered into the girl's unconscious face, "Happy Christmas, Zoë! I won't be long." He went up to the deck of the *Ozymandias*.

He immediately saw that he'd mistaken the tide. The hull of the boat was embedded in the sand, and this motionless solidity had woken him for the same scouring of the estuary he'd religiously performed on Christmas dawn for the past six years. But this time, Zoë's seventh Christmas and the seventh Christmas since Lizzie's death, Harry was too late. The tide was coming in fast. It had already covered most of the mudflats, apart from a few shrinking expanses on which the feeding waders and shelduck were forced closer and closer together. The water was rising through the boulders and weed of the foreshore, lifting a scum of coffee-colored bubbles, inching toward the hull of the *Ozymandias*.

Morose, Harry stood on the deck and stared into the rain.
No horizons to a gray and saturated world. No sky, but a lowering of drenching, gray cloud. The rain drummed loudly and
hard on the hood of his waterproofs. There was nothing he
could do this Christmas morning but watch the rapid and in-
evitable vanishing of the mudflats. The birds gathered and
huddled, until they fled in flocks: the smallest waders, the
dunlin and the knot, in a volley of silver arrows; the curlew,
hawklike, gull-like; the shelduck, dignified to the brink of
pomposity. And once the birds were gone, as the boat groaned
a groan of futile resistance before rising from the sand, there
was no dry place remaining on the estuary.

He went below, the rain coursing from the folds of his
waterproofs and onto the rugs. The cabin was already much
warmer, or so it seemed to him, who'd been standing in the
lightening dawn.

Harry and Zoë exchanged presents in front of the fire,
close to the scented pine needles, under the nodding tube
of the telescope.

"But Daddy," said Zoë, once the cabin was strewn with
wrapping paper, "we didn't get anything for Tycho, did we?
Poor old Tycho! We forgot all about him! Come here,
Tycho! Come on, come to me!"

From its perch on the telescope, whose gunmetal finish
was spattered with white and yellow droppings, the jackdaw beat across the room and landed on Zoë's wrist. The
bird folded its wings. It sidled and ducked, its black and gray
plumage in stark contrast to the little girl's colorlessness. She
was so bright, with her white face and arms and her bob of
silver hair, that the jackdaw was like a smut on her. Its black
feet clenched into her skin. Its beady black eyes glared into
her eyes.

Its beak was broken. The jackdaw had been blown onto
the deck of the *Ozymandias*, where it had lain, shattered and
ragged, until Zoë picked it up and carried it inside. Oddly
passive in her hands, it quickly recovered its senses. At last,

lulled into submission by the girl's tenderness and firm handling, the bird had consented to Harry's repair of its beak with glue and a sliver of hard wood he'd whittled into shape. In the course of the repair, which worked well and was still in place this Christmas, more than a month since the arrival of the jackdaw in an autumn storm, he'd told Zoë about the sixteenth-century Danish astronomer Tycho Brahe, who'd had his nose cut off in a duel and had rebuilt it himself out of gold, silver and wax.

"You and your stars, Daddy, and your silly telescope!" she'd said. "But Tycho's a good name for him, isn't it, with his beak broken and mended?"

Now, the bird balanced on her arm and cocked its head toward the fire. It had become quite tame. It responded with uncanny readiness to the girl's voice. Their eyes met.

The jackdaw sprang from her wrist. With two strokes through the air, it settled once more on the telescope. It lifted its tail and eased a mute onto its handmade, exquisitely engineered perch. Zoë laughed, a jangling, discordant laugh like the chimes of the jackdaw, guessing what the bird had done.

"Poor Daddy!" she giggled. "Is Tycho making more of a mess on your telescope? Anyway, Daddy, what are you doing every night, pointing that thing through the roof and into the sky? I keep asking you what you think you can see with it. Tell me again, please, Daddy! What do you see in your funny telescope that I can't see?"

And when he explained, as she'd had him try to explain so many times before, about the hugeness of the black space which seemed to be so empty until you saw everywhere there were stars like flashes of white light and blue light and countless sparks and glimmers... then she would shrug, fixing him with her unseeing stare and paralyzing him with a smile. "Oh," she would say, "so you mean it's just the same for you, Daddy, as it is for me?"

The jackdaw shot its droppings the length of the telescope. It pecked at its reflection in the wide, unblinking eye of the lens. And Harry began to realize that, with all the power of the machine he was struggling to understand, perhaps he could see no more of the heavens than the blind child could.

In the afternoon they went together to the cemetery.

Zoë held her father's hand and walked beside him, but often she slipped his grip and skipped ahead. She'd learned to move easily on the foreshore, to work among the boulders with the systematic concentration of the turnstones, searching for shells and pebbles whose shape fitted her hands. In spite of her blindness, or because of it, she had the gift of economy of movement and of effort; she seldom wasted a step by stumbling. It gave her grace, just as the birds were unspectacularly efficient on the shoreline. She found shells to offer at the shrine of her mother's grave; she hung herself with necklaces of pungent weed with which the headstone would be decorated. Feathers and bones fell to her fingers.

Harry watched, having taught his daughter to identify such things by touch. She knew the egg masses of whelks, and would crunch them delightedly and explosively in her hands; she could distinguish the mermaid's purse of the dogfish, horny and smooth, with twisted tendrils, from the hairier capsules of the thornback ray. There was the clicking of stones as she worked among them, the rustle and pop of the rubbery weed. Yes, she was as easy as a bird on the foreshore, as natural a part of the estuary as the birds themselves. Harry watched her bright head bobbing. He saw her pause and bend, straighten and move on, saw that she was always listening to the sounds of the sea and the air and the skies around her. Sometimes she turned to him, knowing exactly where he was, and she beamed the whiteness of her face.

In the graveyard she did not weep, although Harry did. She smiled as she felt his cheeks and his wet eyes, as she pushed her cold little fingers into his lips and touched the tears there. Then she traced the letters on the stone, spelling out her mother's name and leaving a wetness which quickly dried in the winter wind. She would ask the questions she always asked, her stare so unwavering that Harry blinked from it.

"Is Mummy really here, Daddy? In the ground?" Arranging and rearranging the weed and the seashells she'd brought, she'd say with a giggle, "That's silly, Daddy! Putting Mummy in the ground! Why did you do that?"

She followed the flight of the gulls, which had accompanied the man and the little girl to the churchyard. The birds blew in from the shore, to dice among the bare branches of the sycamores, to swoop among the headstones where the child knelt. She gazed at them, imitating their cries with mews and bleats of her own. When the peewits tumbled by, turned this way and that by the wind, she clapped her hands loudly, over and over, not with the regular beat of applause but irregularly, syncopated, in time with their clapping wings. The wind fell around her and found that she was like the wind, nerveless, bloodless, who didn't need to see in order to understand the ways of the birds.

Harry shivered, watching her at her mother's graveside, for she already knew more about the estuary than he did, about the birds and the tides and the broken things that the sea fetched up... about the stars themselves. She seemed to know the mystery of her mother's death, how the woman had gone into the damp soil.

Thinking of this, he shivered again. Zoë looked down from the whirling peewits and into his face, as though she could see his punched and puzzled expression, and she said with a quick smile, "Let's get you home, Daddy. You're cold, aren't you? Let's get you home before you catch your death! Come on, Daddy! Come on!"

She took her father's hand, stood him up, led him from the cemetery and down to the seashore. She guided him back to the *Ozymandias*.

The afternoon grew dark. The tide was falling. He saw that, by the time the sandbanks of the estuary were exposed again, it would be the early night of winter. So there would be nothing on top of the tree this Christmas, no guiding star.

Together they sat on the bed, with the heat of the fire on their faces, feeling the dropping of the boat as the sea went out. Zoë played with her new toys, dolls and bears and gadgets she could dismantle and rebuild with her nimble fingers. The jackdaw was nervous; it sprang from one end of the telescope to the other, its claws loud on the metallic surface.

"Sit still, Tycho!" the child called out, pointing her face at the bird. For a while it was quiet, folding and refolding the black wings and preening its breast with the home-made beak. Zoë said little; she had none of the prattle of other six-year-olds. She listened. She and the jackdaw heard sounds from the night outside that Harry couldn't hear. He found himself excluded when the bird and the girl would suddenly stiffen and hold their breath together, and he knew that they'd caught a cry or a whisper from the distant dunes which was lost to him in the huge, rumbling silence of the estuary. Now, tired of playing, she lay with her face in the blankets of the bed. She asked another familiar question.

"When was Aunty Helen here, Daddy? I can smell her perfume on your pillow."

"You know when she was here, you monkey!" he replied, prepared to be defensive. "She comes in the mornings, when I've taken you to school. She often comes, for a chat and sometimes for a flute lesson. She was here the other day, when you were at your Christmas party."

The child sniffed long and hard, testing the air with a quivering rodent's nose. She wagged her finger at him. "Only me allowed!" she said sternly. "Daddy's bed is for Daddy and me! No one else!"

She paused, and before she asked the next question she put up her hands to his mouth, in order to read his expression.

"Do you love Aunty Helen, Daddy? Like you loved Mummy? Will you put Aunty Helen in the ground too?"

At this, before Harry could frame an answer, the jackdaw launched itself across the cabin, where it battered at the Christmas tree with its wings and scrabbled with its prehensile feet. Showers of needles fell to the floor. Motes and mites swirled in the firelight, the dust from the bird's feathers. The jackdaw clacked, as it spattered mutes like gouts of yogurt.

"There's nothing there, Tycho!" Zoë cried. "There's nothing there! Wait, Tycho! Wait!"

The bird fluttered to the foot of the tree. Panting, ruffled, it hopped into the corner and hid.

"Time you got ready for bed, little madam!" Harry said, resorting to conventional paternal authority. "There's lots of hot water for you. A quick shower and off to bed. Your own bed, that is, Miss Bossy-Boots! And that's another Christmas Day all wrapped up!"

The girl obeyed. Under the shower, with the soap shining on her little body, with her helmet of hair quite white in the spray of water, she spluttered, "Off to bed in my own bed, Daddy! But can I come and get into yours, if I wake up in the middle of the night? Can I?" For this was what she often did, sleepwalking to him and crawling into his bed, to be there when he woke in the morning... very small and very hot, her head damp against his shoulder.

"Yes," he said. He dried her with a warm towel. Seeing her in her pajamas, tucked into bed with a Christmas bear, he loved her with a love like a flame he could feel in his belly. She was his Zoë, who baffled him with her fey, unearthly wisdom, who was quite beyond him, who was bright and alight and out of reach, like the sparks he was only beginning to see through the telescope. His Zoë. He would love and cherish her for ever. His eyes tingled as he leaned down to kiss her goodnight.

Just then, she asked a new question, staring fixedly over his shoulder at a point on the ceiling of the cabin. "Daddy, how did Mummy die?"

Harry sat up, blinking. Unblinking, the girl stared past him. Unblinking, the jackdaw peered from under the tree. It bounded across the floor and sprang up to the telescope, where it settled with a shuffle and a scratch. Zoë ignored the bird. She asked again, "How did Mummy die? Did something kill her?"

Harry's mind went blank for a moment. Until he saw before him, as harsh and as glaring as an overexposed photograph, as though Zoë herself were projecting the image onto a screen inside his head... the horror of Lizzie's death. It was as vivid as the real horror, so real that his nostrils stung with the stench of burning blood and scorching skin.

He heard himself saying, woodenly, "She died when she was having you. You were born and she died, almost at the same time. There wasn't enough life for both of you. You took it all...."

The horror faded, folded and vanished. He looked down again at the child. She was staring straight at him. Silently, she was laughing.

9

That same Christmas night, Harry was woken by the bird.

Usually, once the lamps were out, once he'd gone to bed and the cabin was lit only by the glow of the stove, Tycho would settle to sleep, the beak and the eyes hidden under one wing. Harry woke to hear the jackdaw springing from one end of its perch to the other. The fire had burned down. He'd been asleep for several hours; in the darkness, he guessed the time at one or two o'clock in the morning. The boat was motionless, beached. Apart from the curious agitation of the jackdaw, there was no other sound or movement.

Then he heard Zoë beginning to stir, and he saw her in the dim light of the dying fire. She pushed back the blankets of her bed and swung herself to a sitting position. The bird gave a single muted, metallic cry. It bristled its black feathers.

"Be quiet, Tycho!" the girl whispered. "You mustn't wake Daddy!"

She stood up, stretched, and seemed to peer across the cabin. Harry watched her, trying to maintain the regularity of his breathing so that his wakefulness wouldn't disturb or frighten her. She was asleep, he thought; she was sleepwalking to him, to creep into the security and warmth of her daddy's bed.

But she didn't come. She reached to the foot of her own bed for a jumper and pulled it on, tugging it over her head. A moment later, she'd clambered into a pair of trousers, putting them on on top of her pajamas.

"Quiet, Tycho!" she hissed, because the bird was shivering with excitement to see her tiptoe toward it. It shot a mute which ran like milk the length of the telescope. The little girl stepped into her boots, knowing exactly where they were; she knew the position of everything in the room.

"Now!" she breathed. She pointed her face directly at her father's face. She stiffened as she listened as hard as she could. He lay and watched her, continued his rhythmic breathing.

"Come!" she said. The bird reached her shoulder in one easy spring, landing with open black wings which extinguished the firelight on her hair. The black claws gripped. With the jackdaw balancing on her, she moved silently up the steps and was gone, the door closed behind her. She left a shiver of cold air where she and the bird had been standing.

Harry followed her. By the time he was on deck, barefoot, wearing nothing but an old shirt, the girl was already halfway down the iron ladder on the sea wall. She worked herself backward, her feet and hands quite sure on the slippery rungs, down and down onto the boulders of the foreshore. There she paused. She wiped her hands against her thighs. Somewhere in the darkness, the bird also moved, with a beat and a waft of sooty wings, with a cracking of its powerful legs. Harry could see very little. He heard the crunch of Zoë's boots among the shingle, the bubbled explosion of seaweed, and he sensed her making her way from the wall. His eyes were bleared with sleep, unaccustomed to the gloom; but, without hesitating to put on boots or trousers, he pursued his daughter down the ladder and onto the beach.

There, the darkness seemed to lift. Having painfully negotiated the barnacles, the treacherous unevenness of the boulders and the weed, finding himself more comfortably barefoot on the level, hard sand, he saw that the pitchiness of the night was diluted by a reflection from the sky onto the mudflats. There was no moon. The stars were hidden behind a cover of cloud. But the estuary seemed to gather and hold what light there was, and he could see the outline of the child quite clearly ahead of him. Even the jackdaw was visible, a fluttering shadow on the night-gleam of the sands. He felt neither the cold around his bare legs nor the aching of cold in his feet, as he stepped after Zoë and the bird which circled her. Once, she stopped and spun to face him, poised for listening, so that he also stopped... but he couldn't make out her expression before she turned away and continued to walk faster and further from the boat.

"Here, Tycho!" she cried. "We're here!"

Harry was close enough to hear her. The clouds were suddenly split, like an old sail, and there was a wash of nightlight which caught the child's cap of silvery hair. She was kneeling. The bird fell raggedly beside her, spiraling down and disappearing into her shadow. Harry crept forward, as silently as possible, placing each footstep firmly on the ribbed sand. He heard her whisper, "Come on, Tycho! See what you can do!"

Zoë knelt among the wreckage of the dead horse. Around her, jutting from the mud, the ribcage was a palisade of black bones. She tugged at a segment of vertebra, which resisted until the gristle disintegrated, and she held it aloft. Quickly a pool formed and filled the hole she'd made. She dropped the bone with a splash. A frail and tiny figure, she knelt in the remains of the horse, pulling aside the spars of the skeleton, dismantling it. She worked faster, more breathlessly, apparently exasperated, until suddenly the bird reappeared and flapped heavily upward. It wheeled up and up. The girl tilted her head as though to follow its labored flight.

"Tycho! Tycho!" she cried, her voice shrill. "Come down, Tycho! Come and show me!"

And the bird, like a crow with a mussel which it wants to crack on the rocks below, hovered before dropping something from its beak, a thing which fell with a slap on the sand where the horse was embedded. Tycho followed its prize downward. Before the bird could land, Zoë had scrabbled in the brown bones and was on her feet again. In the light from the torn clouds, Harry could see the exultation on his daughter's mouth. There was a spark in her eyes.

She strode toward him, straight past him, so close that he could smell her clean hair and hear her breathing. The jackdaw's wings wafted at his face. But, for the girl and the attendant bird, he didn't exist. He wasn't there that night. There was only the shattered horse from which the sea had retreated, and the search among its ruins.

"Zoë?" He repeated the word, but the child marched onward without pausing or turning, unerringly in the direction of the *Ozymandias*. The bird flew ahead of her, chiming. Harry's cry — "Zoë! Zoë!" — the single sibilant word he called until the girl was almost gone, was lost on the wet sands. He forced himself into action, for he was standing numb and stupid, looking from the figure of the disappearing child to the remains of the dismembered skeleton, and he set off at a run, skirting widely past Zoë so that he could reach the foreshore before she did. He overtook her; he scrambled across the rock pools and the weed, hobbled over the high-water line of driftwood and jellyfish and plastic bottles, and, clambering onto the gravel track which followed the edge of the shore, he sprinted as hard as he could along its grassy verge. Out of breath, his head clearing enough for him to realize the oddity of racing through a Christmas night in nothing but a flapping shirt, he stepped from the sea wall and stood panting on the deck of the boat.

He'd beaten her to it, just. He could hear her footsteps as she approached the ladder, the rhythmic gonging of her boots on the rungs, her breathing coming closer and closer. The jackdaw landed beside him. Moving very quickly now, careless of the noise he made, he tumbled down the steps into the cabin. In seconds, he'd thrown a bit of kindling wood into the stove, to make some light as much as for the heat, and he snuggled under the blankets of the bed. There he lay. He struggled to steady his breathing. He faced the fire and awaited Zoë's arrival.

The bird came in first. It settled with hard claws on the telescope and straight away leaned into the lens to peck at its own reflection. It folded and refolded its wings around its body, like a man trying on a raincoat.

Zoë was there a moment later. She stepped out of her boots at the foot of the stairs, careful, even in her sleep, to leave them exactly where she'd found them. "Shhh now, Tycho!" she whispered. "Wait! Just wait!"

Barefoot, she climbed onto the easy chair beside the telescope, and she felt the air near the ceiling of the cabin. Her hand waved and hung, finding nothing but space; for a second it fingered the beam, where a groove in the wood provoked her gasp and a highpitched giggle, and then it brushed the bristles of the tree. She held the topmost branch with one hand, she fumbled in the pocket of her trousers with the other. She dangled a thing that squirmed and arched itself, something wet. Nimble, unhesitating, she twisted the tentacles of the brittlestar among the needles and stepped down from the chair, leaving the creature twitching on the Christmas tree.

"Not yet, Tycho!" she hissed sternly, because the jackdaw had sprung to her shoulder. "Not yet! Get down!"

She knocked the bird to the floor, where Harry couldn't see it. She took off all her clothes, jumper and trousers and pajamas too, and in the new warmth, where the kindling was ablaze and lighting the cabin with golden flame, she ran her hands the length of her body. She was thin and hard and perfectly white: even the fire could not color her. Only her hair and her eyes caught the sparks. She smiled, and she stared straight at her father. She stepped to the bed, his bed, and slipped into it.

There was a long silence. The jackdaw was back on the telescope, motionless, hunched, unblinking. The fire had settled, after the crackling ignition of the twigs. The little girl's head was close to Harry's, and, as he breathed, her hair stirred like anemones in a rock pool. She seemed to sleep immediately, pressing herself hard and hot against him, because her eyes were closed and her breathing was heavy and regular. He stared at the ceiling, at the groove she'd touched with a squeal of pleasure, and he watched the brittlestar writhing on the tree. Their Christmas star, he thought, which Zoë had found, which might guide them through another year.

Zoë had stopped breathing. Her body was tense. The jackdaw had stopped breathing, too. Harry held his breath and waited for something to happen.

Then the child spoke, expelling the words with all the breath she had inside her. "Now, Tycho! Have it! Have it!"

The jackdaw sprang into the air. It crossed the cabin with two beats of its wings. And its beak, the beak that Harry had meticulously remade, hammered at the brittlestar. The bird hung on the tree, a tattered black star, obscene among the tinsel and trinkets. It scrabbled on the needles with its sharp claws. It clacked harshly, hoarsely, dissonant as a broken bell. The home-made beak broke into the body of the brittlestar.

Until the child cried out, "Enough, Tycho! Enough!" Straight away the jackdaw fell to the floor, from where it leaped effortlessly to the telescope. There, with eyes like beads of blood, it preened its breast. It wiped a morsel of fish-flesh from its beak.

Harry didn't move. He'd been frozen by running half-naked on the cold sands. He'd been stunned by the spectacle of the child in the bones of the horse, stunned by the heat of the child's body on his, by the firelight and the dancing shadows... by the lunacy of the bird, the ragged black star which had tarnished all the gew gaws on the Christmas tree.

All this had paralyzed him. He was on the edge of nightmare. He knew that, if he moved, he would be in it.

While Zoë was asleep, as lovely as an angel in his arms, Harry watched her and the fire and the jackdaw through all the hours of a troubled night. He saw the brittlestar dangle, a dead and broken thing which Zoë had used and then destroyed. He dared not sleep, in case the nightmare should come for him.

10

There was a false spring that February. The world basked in still, warm sunshine. All over the hedgerows, the ivy berries hung in heavy, blue-black handfuls, as tempting as sloes, whose symmetry was out of place in the untidiness of a countryside emerging from winter. Deep within their fortress of hawthorn, snowdrops flowered, pale and drooping: bridesmaids for a wedding unexpectedly called off. Daffodils stood up, too fast and too tall, and collapsed, crumpling their golden faces. The mistle thrush challenged from the top of the tallest tree. The robin sang a watery song. Inland, in the shelter of rolling fields, it seemed that spring had really come, where the sheep in their shaggy overcoats knelt and nibbled at new grass. The lapwings were a quick, metallic green in the sunlight. Jays went swashbuckling through the dense foliage of holm oak, whose leaves gave them cover and were an illusion of a faraway summer.

Even on the shore, there was a stillness and a warmth which suggested that another winter was over. These were days when Harry Clewe cycled by the beach and through the lanes and it was marvelous to be alive, when he shook off his preoccupation with Zoë.

In the mornings, he rode into Caernarfon with the child behind him on her pillion seat, to leave her at school. There, it seemed, she was hardly disadvantaged by her sightlessness. She had specialized help and was learning to read Braille. And then there was an opportunity for shopping in town, for joyful careering on the bicycle, for the prearranged meetings with Helen on board the *Ozymandias*.

Once, their lovemaking had been prolonged and vigorous. There'd been a time, when Zoë was a baby, when Harry and Helen had abandoned the charade of the flute lesson with such alacrity that their clothes were strewn all over the cabin, when their skins were smooth with sweat in the flames of the fire. Through the long nights, fueled with gin or red wine, oblivious of the tides, they'd ignored the cries of the baby and made love.

It was different now. Theirs was a perfunctory coupling, only possible in Zoë's absence. There was something almost surgical about it: they dealt with one another, they operated with efficiency and swiftness and then they were finished. Helen's clothes were neatly folded on the easy chair. She remained as perfumed and powdered, as she lay on the bed and exhaled the smoke of a post-coital panatella, as she'd been on her arrival.

"So," she said. They were side by side, on their backs, without touching. "I'd better get going." Neither of them moved. "You'll be off to collect Zoë, won't you? And I've got things to do this afternoon."

Harry rolled over and spread the palm of his hand on her cooling belly. "I'm sorry, Helen. We don't have the time that we used to, do we? You know how touchy Zoë is, about me and about you too. She's very possessive about me — a perfectly normal thing, I suppose, for a child growing up without a mother. And living as we do, on the boat."

"I can't tell whether she likes me or hates me," the woman said, putting her hand on top of his hand. "That little white face! That little smile! Those eyes! There's no way of telling what she's thinking. And, although she's so small and so young, she seems to fill up the cabin, fill up all the space. There's no air left for anyone else to breathe. She's like a cuckoo chick, pushing everything else out of the way, consuming all the energy around her...."

Helen turned her face to Harry's. "Can't you feel it?" she went on. "She can't see, but she has a kind of... I don't know what to call it. A kind of vigilance about her, as though she's waiting and watching and choosing her moment... I don't know what for. She's all tuned up, waiting. She's already changed you, my love. She's taken something from you. She has that kind of magnetism. It's draining."

Harry said nothing. It had been like that with Lizzie, on board the boat, during the last weeks of her pregnancy. Suffocating, stifling... yes, draining, until all the air was sucked out of the sky, sucked out of the cabin, until it was harder and harder to breathe. He and Lizzie had been unusually close, unnaturally close. Their closeness had spawned the guilt which had haunted Lizzie to self-destruction. Harry said none of this to Helen, although sometimes he felt driven to confide in her. One day he would tell her everything. Now he glanced over her naked shoulder at the splashed and spattered telescope.

"Yes!" she said, following his eyes. "And that bloody bird too! It's hardly conducive to uninhibited sex, having that thing as a spectator. Bloody voyeur!"

At least this time the jackdaw had been fairly passive, remaining on its perch and silently preening while they'd stripped and lain down and spent their lust. "It doesn't seem so interested today, thank goodness," Harry said. "Maybe it's because of the warm weather and the stillness after the winter. It's not so excitable."

"Nor are we," said Helen. "It's got nothing to do with the weather. The bird's just bored with watching us, that's all." She spoke over her shoulder. "Sorry, Tycho. Not much of a show today, was it?" The jackdaw croaked, expelling an arcing mute which dripped from the telescope and onto her clothes. "Oh, shit!" the woman whispered, hiding her face in Harry's throat.

They lay together a little longer, without talking. He watched the bird. It watched him. The previous week, it had been so agitated at Helen's arrival and the subsequent flurry of undressing that he'd tried to catch it and throw it out of the cabin. Helen, naked, shielding herself with a pillow, had retreated fearfully to one corner, while Harry, also naked, had pursued the bird and tried to trap it in a blanket. At first it had been funny. Helen had laughed until tears ran down her cheeks to see the man's thin, white body leaping and twisting after the tumbling black rag of the jackdaw. He'd grown angry. His erection had faltered. As the bird became hoarsely hysterical, it shed feathers, it croaked until its voice was cracked, and the room was rank with its spurted droppings. The woman's tears of laughter turned to tears of helplessness....

When at last the bird was caught and bundled onto the deck, Harry and Helen had collapsed together on the bed, careless of the messes they lay in, and they'd gripped each other hard until their anger was replaced by passion.

They were alone, truly alone, because of the frantic removal of a shabby crow and because the vigilance of a sightless child was temporarily avoided. This was the pattern of their lovemaking. It was chilly, daylit sex: sober, timetabled, shadowed by a beady spectator.

There was a frost in the air when Helen came the next time. By then, February had fooled the country into premature growth. Among the cladding of ivy, where already there was a luxuriant greenness of dock and sticky willie, Harry bent to inspect the tiny blue flowers of speedwell, to see the primroses' buttery yellow. The still air was scribbled with clouds of gnats. From the bicycle, his shadow was long, swaying before him down the lane. The hedgerows were ablaze with gorse, climbing with a new growth of nettles and foxgloves. The mistle thrush chattered, though not a blackbird sang, nor was there yet the bravado fanfare of the wren. The warm sun urged the farmers into activity: fields were ploughed, with a rejoicing of gulls in the tractors' wake; hedges were cut, chewed into neatness by noisy, hungry machines; everywhere there hung the sweet tobacco smell of silage.

Still, as Harry pedaled from Caernarfon back to the *Ozymandias*, having left Zoë at school, he could taste the frost. The sky looked dry and hard.

Helen was sitting in the Daimler. The window hummed open. She simply said, "Get the bird out first, will you, Harry? Then I'll come inside. I've brought a present for you and Zoë. It's a sort of antidote to the crow."

Soon, she saw the jackdaw flung onto the deck, where it extricated itself from the folds of a blanket and hopped to a perch on the sea wall. Carrying a big bunch of flowers in one hand, holding a wicker basket in the other, the woman stepped into the cabin. Her nose wrinkled.

"Jesus, Harry! This place is getting a bit high, isn't it?" she exclaimed. "What with the mess the bird makes, and all that stuff as well. She's bloody taking over, Zoë is! What a stink!"

The telescope and the floor around it were white with droppings, although Harry had made desultory efforts with newspapers to keep the corner tidy. He seldom used the telescope; it was a machine to be tinkered with, adapting it to his own limitations rather than exploring its potential. In any case, the jackdaw had established squatter's rights on it, and on the easy chair too. The other "stuff" offending the woman's sensibilities was Zoë's growing collection of trophies from the seashore, the prizes she carried home from her walks on the beach, which she kept and processed in the cabin before taking them as offerings to her mother's grave. Around her own bed, the child had draped a curtain of seaweed, shining and green where it was fresh, black and pungent where it had been hanging for a week or two; bluebottles droned drunkenly from it and butted the windows. Among the inoffensive and beautiful relics she'd put at her bedside — pebbles, shells, feathers and the clean, white skulls of seabirds — there were pieces of the horse's skeleton, saturated to the consistency of wet biscuit, whose crumbs stank of the most fetid mud in the estuary.

And bones. Zoë was a collector of bones. That simple grave in the nearby churchyard gave her collecting a kind of focus: there were bones under the ground, and the child brought more bones that she'd found on the shore, bones which the sea had fetched up. Her mother's grave had become a shrine, or a reliquary.

Harry had seen it happening over the years, noticed the awe with which Zoë approached the headstone, and how her wonderment, spontaneous at first, had gradually become more studied. She assumed the air of a priestess. She laid her offerings with a great and otherworldly reverence. She repeated and refined her questions as though they and the appropriate responses were an important part of the ritual.

Yes, Zoë was the guardian of the bones. In this way, once more, she excluded her father. He'd seen the development of this absorption. Now it extended to the boat, where they lived so closely together. The *Ozymandias* was the anteroom to the shrine.

"You're right, Helen," he said lamely. "She has spread out a bit, hasn't she? Kids are like that. Didn't you collect all sorts of odds and ends when you were little? It's just untidiness, after all."

"No, I didn't!" Helen replied. "I didn't collect horrible things like that." Shuddering, she sat on the bed, without taking off her coat. "Bones and seaweed and bloody bird shit all over the place!" When he sat beside her, she recoiled from him. "And you don't smell so good, either," she added.

"The roses are lovely," he said. "The scent helps in here."

He'd put the flowers in a big earthenware jug, the one which he and Lizzie had used for carrying warm water onto the deck to wash their hair, in the old days before the installation of the shower.

"They're gorgeous, Helen!" he said. "You're right, they're an antidote to Tycho's messes. What's in the basket?"

"Well, actually this is the present I was talking about," she replied, "not the roses. The roses are just a temporary relief from the stink. This is supposed to be a bit more permanent, to give Zoë a healthier interest than that revolting crow of hers. Have a look. If you think it's a bad idea, just say so and I'll take it back."

A kitten was nestling in the straw inside the wicker basket. Harry lifted it out. It was a black and white scrap which lay on his open hand, tiny and helpless.

"I got it from the farmer who delivers eggs to me," Helen explained. "He was going to drown it otherwise. What do you think? It's a bit more lovable than that bloody bird, isn't it?

If Zoë took a fancy to it, you could get rid of the crow and she'd hardly notice it was gone. Then you could clean out the bones too, and all this morbid paraphernalia which seems to go with her interest in Tycho. Well?"

Tycho was at the window. It rapped with its home-made beak. It pressed the bulb of its eye to the glass, watching the man and the woman while Zoë was absent. It remained there and peered in, tapping sometimes, blanking the window with ragged, outspread wings, while Harry and Helen made love. Even as they lay together, in a spasm of indifferent coupling, the woman was distracted by the jackdaw, and her gaze moved from the man's face to the corners of the cabin. When she settled on him, she rose and fell mechanically, as though she were trotting a predictable horse. He came. She didn't. She was goose-pimpled throughout.

Dressing quickly, she said, "I don't know if I'll be here again this week. Maybe I can make it next week. I don't know. Since I can't come here at night any more, I'm not sure when I'll be able to." She spoke the words in a rush, feigning briskness as she bent for stockings and shoes, without looking at Harry. "I'll come by some time and see if the kitten's a success."

She was soon gone. He remained on the bed, the blankets hardly disturbed. The sea smell of weed was too strong for the fragrance of roses, obliterating the woman's perfume too. It absorbed the sea scent of sex.

Harry had already christened the kitten before collecting Zoë from school that afternoon. He went to his poetry shelf again, reminded of something he'd read. There was a poem by Seamus Heaney about kittens being drowned in a tin bucket — "scraggy wee shits," the poet called them. Taking the kitten out of the basket, seeing it spit and sneeze as it squinted through newly opened eyes, he thought what a scraggy wee shit it was and what a narrow escape it had had. So he named it Seamus. And of course, he didn't explain to Zoë how he'd come by this name.

The child held the kitten to her face and sniffed it. She even licked it. She stared into a faraway distance, smiling with a bubble of saliva on her lips as she inspected the tiny creature. Finally, unable to bear her silence any longer, Harry said, "Well, Zoë? What do you think? Isn't he cute? Do you want to take care of him? He's so feeble and helpless... he's only a week old, I think. Well?"

"And the flowers?" she asked. "Are they from Aunty Helen, too?"

She inhaled the woman's perfume, which must have been so strong to her. She put the kitten on the bed, where it crawled clumsily on the blanket, snagging its needle-sharp claws.

"Is that why Tycho had to go outside, Daddy?" she asked. "Because Aunty Helen was here? That's not fair! Tycho lives here, Aunty Helen doesn't!" The child made for the door of the cabin, saying over her shoulder, "Can Tycho come in, now that Aunty Helen's gone? Now we've got a pet each, Daddy, haven't we? You can look after Seamus, and I'll look after Tycho. I wonder if they'll be friends...."

She grinned dazzlingly and went out. Harry shivered. Despite her gleam of hair, although she burned so hot, Zoë left a swirl of frost in the air. And he thought, perhaps Helen had been right: this child drew all the heat, sucked all the energy. He shivered again, his body chilled, and he nestled the kitten to his face.

11

Helen had meant the kitten to be more permanent than the roses. After all, roses are soon dead, and then they're thrown out.

In the meantime, Zoë had nothing to do with the animal. Harry fed it with milk and kept it away from the jackdaw, the two most important measures to ensure its survival. The little creature soon became adventurous, exploring the cabin with springs and pounces and a scrabbling of its claws; the jackdaw watched from its perch on the telescope, bending a baleful eye, cocking a zany head. Harry took Zoë to town, brought her back again, and, as they cycled the seashore track, the bird came too, matching its cries to the cries of the child. Tycho was in constant attendance. The jackdaw was a shadow of her.

Frank came for his lessons, for his scanning of the stars through the increasingly dusty lenses of the telescope, for his evenings of slow, smoky conversation. The lure of the telescope wasn't the only reason why his music lessons were sometimes suspended: he was uncomfortable under Zoë's sightless but highly critical scrutiny. He tried to laugh with her when she laughed, when she snorted and giggled at his fumbles on the flute; she sighed when he bungled, and he smiled gamely. But her stare, so vacant and yet so keen, made him wince. So he would put down the flute with a self-deprecating shrug, and roll a joint instead. They would spend the rest of the evening, Harry and Frank, simply talking; or rather, it was Frank who talked about his travels in Afghanistan and Turkey, about the Yukon and the Amazon, while Harry listened and dozed.

Zoë and Tycho watched the two men. When the girl fell asleep, the bird remained vigilant. Harry cuddled the kitten, where it hid its eyes from the eyes of the crow, and he hardly noticed when Frank stood up and left the boat. But he wondered, before he too was asleep, how many more times Frank would come to the *Ozymandias*, to endure the stare of the blind, unblinking child.

Dewi persevered. For him, the cabin of the *Ozymandias* had been a haven, away from the jibes and jeers of school, and Harry was happy to see the youth relaxing, more inclined to talk and to enthuse unselfconsciously about the music. In the first four or five years after Lizzie's death, Dewi had worked hard at the flute and made progress. He'd felt safe on the boat, because no one was watching him....

But now there were eyes on him after all. It was worse than school. The eyes never left him: even when the child was in bed, asleep, there was the bird on the telescope. Dewi continued to work with his teacher, but his concentration was gnawed away. The youth flinched from Zoë's brilliant stare. He blazed like a beacon at the sound of her laugh. How much longer would he endure it? Who was this child, from whom nothing was hidden?

So, Frank and Dewi might soon be gone. And the roses were dead.

One afternoon, Harry cycled from Caernarfon with Zoë on the pillion seat. Tycho was overhead. This was the child's domain, the wide estuary. The tide was out, the sky was tall, there was frost in the sky. She sat behind her father with her hands on his waist, and she scented the air, tasting the salt and sand on her lips. She heard the rush of wings when the starlings rose from the cowpats in the fields; smiling, she turned her sharp little face toward the sound. She heard the growling of shelduck on the mudflats, and she growled as deeply as her childish voice could manage. When the black-backs looked up from the dead thing they were dismembering, she met their dead, chill, yellow eyes with her own chill eyes. There were oystercatchers, as dapper as men in dinner jackets, whose fluted cries she could mimic. There was nothing on the estuary, to the distant dunes and beyond, that she hadn't sensed and seen in the infinity of her imagination. She was a creature of the estuary, of the sea and the salt and the skies.

Now, without speaking, transmitting her excitement by the pressure of her grip on Harry's waist, she sat behind him on the bicycle and appraised her world. Tycho beat alongside.

Minutes before they arrived at the mooring of the *Ozymandias*, Harry could see Helen's car parked there. He didn't say anything to Zoë, so it was extraordinary to feel the child bristling, to feel how fast her pleasure in the place and the frosty afternoon drained. She stiffened. She scented the air, sniffing like a setter. Harry helped her off her seat, and he could feel the cold in her brittle frame.

"Aunty Helen's here!" he said cheerily. "I didn't know she was coming today. She's dropped in for tea, I suppose."

The child didn't reply. She and the bird went on deck. Harry leaned the bicycle into the hedge and walked across to the car.

"So, you've still got the crow," Helen whispered, squeezing his hand and kissing his cheek as they followed Zoë onto the boat. "I was hoping you might have got rid of it by now."

The woman smelled gorgeous. Her hair was dark and sleek. Her skin was flawless.

"I just thought I'd come by and see how you were," she said. "I was watching you coming along on the shore, the two of you on the bike and that bloody thing circling around like a vulture...."

Stepping onto the deck, she called out to Zoë, and the child smiled, although she swerved from the woman's kiss with a little snort and a shudder.

"Can we leave Tycho outside, please, Zoë?" Helen asked her. "You know I don't like him. Please, while I come in for a cup of tea? I'm longing to see how the kitten's getting on!"

"Seamus is all right, so far," Zoë said, staring across the mudflats. "That's what Daddy calls him. He's Daddy's pet, not mine. But thank you for the roses, Aunty Helen. They're lovely."

At her own mention of the flowers, Zoë grinned, her eyes glittering, as though the idea of them in their earthenware vase was suddenly something novel.

"Yes, they're lovely, Aunty Helen!" she said again. "Come and see!" She led the way into the cabin.

Below, it was warm and comfortable. Harry had stoked the stove before cycling into town to fetch the child. But the room was steeped in the smells of the things that Zoë had brought in, the seaweed and driftwood, the mud-sodden bones. Helen's perfume was the only sweetness. Instinctively, he leaned toward her as she took off her coat, and the movement of her clothes released a fragrance that made him giddy; he'd forgotten, in the fortnight since Helen's last visit, when she'd made the gifts of the kitten and the roses, how much he wanted this soft, generous woman. He put his face to her hair, inhaling. His hands went to her waist and her breasts. Laughing, she pushed him away, because the child was gazing at her with hard, empty eyes.

"But the flowers!" Helen cried. "Oh, Zoë, I'd hardly say they were lovely! They're dead, aren't they? They want throwing out!"

The child moved to them, past the mouth of the stove, and reached up her fingers to the smooth, rounded fullness of the vase. She caressed it, turning to her father and grinning, as though in mockery of the way he'd touched the woman.

"But I like them like this, Aunty Helen," she said. "I like them dead. They smell nicer, I think."

"They want throwing out!" the woman said. "There's nothing worse than dead flowers!" She glanced about the cabin. "Well? Where's the kitten, then? What did you say you'd called him?"

"Seamus," Zoë said. She was struggling to lift the vase of dead roses, with her arms around its body, toppling it toward her. She panted over her shoulder, as Harry went to help her, "I can manage, Daddy! Leave me! We're not going to throw them away just yet. If you don't like them any more, I'll have them in my corner, by my bed. I like them like this!"

She'd lifted the vase. She crossed the cabin with it, avoiding the obstacles of telescope, bed, chair and stove, and pushed her way through the curtain which screened her part of the cabin. Hidden from view, she called out, "Show Aunty Helen the kitten, Daddy! I'm putting these roses with my other things." They could hear the child arranging and rearranging the trophies in her collection.

Harry took the kitten from its basket. He and Helen sat on the bed together, feeling the heat of the fire on them, and she cooed over the antics of the tiny creature. In a fortnight, it had become cutely mischievous, a bundle of fur which sprang at the woman's hands, pouncing at the bright-red varnish on her nails. Harry snuggled to the woman's side; she smelled so good and warm. Zoë was behind her curtain, humming to herself. The jackdaw was outside.

"Isn't he lovely?" Helen said, holding the animal to her face. "Imagine what was going to happen to him! Where did you get the name from, Harry? It'll suit him one day — it's got a kind of roguish, swashbuckling sound, hasn't it?"

Without saying anything, he smiled and stood up from the bed. He took a book from the shelf, found the page he wanted and handed it to Helen. She quickly read the poem. With a shiver, she closed the book and put it down. "You and your poems!" she said. "That's pretty horrible, 'scraggy wee shits...' But I can see what you mean. After all, the farmer said he was going to drown the wretched thing."

She leaned to Harry and breathed into his mouth. She touched his teeth with the tip of her tongue.

"You and your bloody poems!" she whispered. "Reading all kinds of bizarre messages into them! What with the cello and the telescope, and now the kitten! Well, at least we've saved Seamus from poetic fulfilment, or whatever you thought you were doing with the other poem."

She shifted herself to him, pressing her body on his. "It's a pity Zoë can't vanish for a while, isn't it?" she said. "I didn't come just for a cup of tea, you know...." Her mouth was sweet and wet on his mouth.

"Maybe she can," he managed to reply. He withdrew from her embrace and called softly to the child. "Hey, Zoë, what are you doing? Why don't you go outside? The tide's right out. You and Tycho might have some luck on the beach.... I was out there earlier on, and saw a whole lot of mermaid's purses at the foot of the sea wall. Some of them have got the tiny dogfish inside them, not yet hatched. You'd soon find them, not far from the bottom of the ladder."

Zoë emerged from behind the curtain, sucking her fingers. She smiled and held out her hand to him.

"Blood!" she said. "Those roses have got sharp prickles, haven't they? They might be dead, but they still sting!" She put the wounded fingers into her mouth again. Speaking around them, she said, "I'll go and see if Tycho's all right. We'll go on the beach a bit. Give me the kitten, Daddy, and I'll put him away for you. He can have a little lick at this, if he wants."

Darting between the man and the woman, her face alight, Zoë offered her hand to the kitten, which sprang to it and rasped at the saliva and blood with its sandpapery tongue. She scooped up the animal and hugged it to her, the first time she'd shown it any sort of tenderness since it had been on board the *Ozymandias*.

"Come on, Seamus, come with Zoë," she said, nuzzling her face into its fur. "You can come into my corner if you like, and see all the things I've collected. See the roses...."

A moment later, she'd taken away the kitten, disappeared behind her curtain with it, reappeared with her coat and skipped up the steps of the cabin. There was a gust of cold air when she'd left. Her footsteps rang on the deck and her voice was high and clear as she called for the jackdaw. Then there was silence. Harry and Helen slipped off their shoes and moved closely together on the bed.

"You're a funny pair, aren't you?" the woman whispered. "You and Zoë, with your odd collections. You with your poems and your stars, collecting them like relics in a dusty museum; Zoë with her bones and her dead roses. What are we going to do with you?"

She slipped her hand inside his shirt, running the razor edges of her nails over his chest. Just then, the silence in the cabin was broken by the faintest of scrabbling sounds, no louder than the flutter of the fire, like the skittering of mice behind a skirting board. Helen cocked an ear, lifted her face from his so that her hair swung fragrantly on his lips.

"What's that noise? Mice in the bilges?" she asked. "Seamus is going to earn his keep one day...."

The woman shrugged and bent her mouth to Harry's throat. He strained to hear, but Helen's breathing so close to him and the friction of her clothes against his made it impossible to tell where the noise was coming from. There'd never been mice on the *Ozymandias*. Perhaps it was the patter of wagtails on the deck. He ignored it.

Helen's breathing became louder. She moaned when he wriggled his hand inside her blouse. She was on top of him, all her weight was on him, and he was giddy with her scent. Nevertheless, he was aware of the scrabbling sound, which was louder now and faster. The mouse, if that was what it was, was somewhere in the cabin, scratching with its tiny claws for the biscuit crumbs which Zoë must have left at her bedside. Harry managed to clear his face from Helen's hair. While she groaned, while his fingers teased her nipples, he listened.

They both looked up at the next noise. Something had fallen over in the corner behind Zoë's curtain. There was a tumble and a thud as some sort of object was dislodged.

"What is it, Harry?" the woman whispered, her face flushed. "Is it the kitten? Didn't Zoë say she'd put him away in the basket?"

They lifted themselves reluctantly from the bed. Together they tiptoed across the cabin and peered through a gap in the curtain. There were dead roses on the floor, and droplets of water on the bedside table. The earthenware vase was shuddering, so that the remaining roses trembled and rustled. Thrashing and writhing among the stems, a string of black, wet fur snagged on the thorns.

Harry darted forward, Helen beside him. For a second they peered into the stagnant water. They saw the surface bubbling, heard the scrabble of claws on the inside of the vase. They watched the spasms and twitches of that string of fur. They felt the flying droplets on their cheeks... until Harry picked up the vase and emptied its contents onto the floor of the cabin.

Too late. The kitten had been jammed in head first, with only its tail above the surface of the water. Now it lay still, shining like a wet glove, glossy and dead.

"Jesus Christ!" That was all Helen said. She knelt in the pool of water and touched the animal's slick, black and white fur. When she turned it over, water pumped from its mouth... water and blood. She looked up at Harry as though she was going to say something else, ask a question, but a tap at the window of the cabin drew her eyes from his. They both glanced up to see that Zoë was there, squatting on the deck to press her face to the glass. She rapped with her knuckle. Tycho was there as well, tapping with its beak.

The child was grinning, with a gash of a smile on her mouth. Her eyes were glittering. She stood up. Harry and Helen, transfixed by the stares of the child and the bird, listened as her footsteps ran the length of the boat, and they caught her tinkling cry when she summoned the crow. They heard her feet clanging on the rungs of the ladder, from the top of the sea wall onto the shore.

Helen stood up too. Her flush was gone. White-lipped, trembling, she adjusted her clothes and put on her shoes. She got ready to leave, in silence, breathing deeply to control her nausea. Her only gesture was to pick up the poetry book which Harry had shown her, to hold it for a second and frown, before slinging it, as hard as she could, at the other books on the shelf. He watched her, barefooted in the pool of water in which the roses and the kitten had died. Helen didn't say another word. Harry was speechless, too: he watched from the deck as the big silver car hurtled up the lane, and he clenched his hand on the dead animal.

It was very cold on the estuary, sheltered from the Irish Sea only by the distant dunes. He could hear the roaring of the surf on the further side. A tremendous shiver took hold of him, shook him from the crown of his head to the base of his spine. He saw Zoë, who'd fled across the mudflats, with Tycho in conspiratorial attendance; there they were in the gathering twilight, far out on the exposed sands. In a spontaneous gesture of rage and helplessness, that the child was beyond his understanding and control, he flung the body of the kitten as hard as he could away from the boat, across the boulders and weed of the foreshore, where it splashed into a shallow pool. It was a gesture of disgust and defiance. He would not be beaten by Zoë. He would not be gnawed to emptiness by the energies of the child, as Lizzie had been. Zoë would not eclipse him....

Straight away he regretted his impulse. Somehow, Zoë had sensed what he'd done, because he heard her cry and saw how she sent Tycho wheeling skywards with a wave of her arm. The jackdaw was despatched. It beat quickly toward the boat, toward the pool where Harry had hurled the kitten.

Too horrible... He hurried below, racked with cold and the fear of an imminent nightmare. He couldn't watch, as the bird dropped like a rag. It applied its beak, the beak that Harry had made, to the tiny corpse.

12

The spring passed into summer. Zoë had alienated Helen. The woman didn't return to the *Ozymandias* after the murder of the kitten. Sometimes Harry saw her by chance in Caernarfon and they would pause for a talk over a drink or two in the Black Boy, but she didn't visit the boat. Helen's reference, many months before, to the cuckoo chick which ousts the competition from the nest in order to monopolize all the energy around it, seemed to have been apt. The woman couldn't share that little room with the child: the confines of the cabin were too narrow; there wasn't enough space and air for her and Zoë.

Harry was feeling the same kind of threat himself, not only in the boat but on the wide expanse of the estuary. There was nothing that Zoë hadn't claimed for herself. He felt squeezed by her, even in the vastness of the sand flats and under the towering sky: a feeling he'd first experienced on the night of the child's birth, when Lizzie, gasping for breath in the exertions of labor, had snatched the air from him, gulping so hard that he could barely breathe for himself. Remembering that time, he thought he understood what had been happening: the imminence of Zoë's birth, which quenched Lizzie so utterly that the young woman was destroyed, had drained him even then. Now seven years later, the child was marshaling her strength by sapping his. She'd murdered her mother, as surely as she'd murdered the kitten. Harry knew this. He watched the bright, blind child throughout that summer and determined to resist her.

One incident marked Zoë's seventh birthday and the seventh anniversary of Lizzie's death, which might otherwise have passed unnoticed in the hot, slow days of another hot, slow summer.

Zoë continued to enjoy her relationship with Tycho, their solidarity excluding Harry; and the gulls would fall to her, as they'd done in the earliest months of the child's life, when they'd screamed around her cot on the deck of the boat and had one day delivered the jackdaw to her. Tycho was the only smut in the snowstorm of gulls. Often, if the man and the child were walking on the seashore track or cycling to and from the town, they were followed by the gulls, the droppings like sleet on their shoulders. Zoë stared upward, laughing. The jackdaw beat in the blizzard of birds.

They walked to the churchyard on Zoë's birthday. Harry carried flowers; Zoë brought a razor-shell so sharp that she'd cut her fingers in prising it from the foreshore. She knelt at the graveside. When she traced the letters of her mother's name, she didn't leave tears, but a smearing of her blood. Harry put down his flowers among the dry, black seaweed that the summer sun had crisped, among the crumbs of crabs and cuttlefish. He sat in the long grass while the child disappeared to the corners of the churchyard, exploring with the crow.

It was a day like the day when he'd buried Lizzie. The sun was on his back. The sycamores were dense with leaf, white with dust, and above them a lark was lost in the infinite blue. On the estuary, the sails of dinghies and windsurfers were as brilliant as butterflies on buddleia. The little church was a hot rock, a meteor that had fallen and been embedded there; the gravestones were the splinters of its impact.

Zoë had a special gift for the grave. She ran toward her father, calling shrilly, holding out some treasure she'd found. It was indeed a treasure, quite unexpected this far from the ebb of the tide.

"A brittlestar, Daddy!" she shouted. "A brittlestar! Tycho was pecking at it, over there, in the nettles! Look at it! Look!"

Astonished, he took the creature from her fingers, which were dirty with blood and grass stains. The brittlestar was broken, with only two of its arms intact on the disc-body, and so dry that these remaining tentacles disintegrated to dust in his clumsy fingers.

"Good girl, Zoë!" he whispered to her. "We haven't seen one of these for a long time, have we?"

His words were clumsy too, after seven years with the blind child, but she'd grown used to this blunder from him and from her contact with children and teachers at school; she simply smiled, and she licked at the blood on her hand.

"A long way from the sea, isn't it?" he said. "How could it have got here? What do you think, Zoë? A brittlestar in the undergrowth of our churchyard!"

He knew she knew the answer. He submitted to her wisdom. She led him from gravestone to gravestone, even to the deepest thickets of the cemetery and the heaviest shade of the sycamore.

"Seashells," she said, pointing with eerie accuracy. "All over the place. They're mussels, aren't they, Daddy? And they've all been dropped by the birds. By the crows mostly. Tycho himself might have brought some of them."

She leaned her father on the wall which surrounded the church and the graveyard, where his eyes were drawn to the glitter of water, the horizon of dunes, to Anglesey and the glare of the open sea. The tide was well in, but on the foreshore, where the waves left rolls of weed, where jellyfish and other dead things were fetched up, there were stones, graded into boulders and pebbles and shingle.

"Are there any crows now, Daddy?" the little girl asked. "On the beach? Are they working?"

A number of carrion crows were swaggering among the rocks and seaweed. They jimmied into every crevice with their weighty, black beaks, searching for a morsel. And up they floated, with a spring of their muscular legs and a shake of their sooty wings, so that from a height of ten or fifteen feet they could drop a mussel and smash it on the boulders. Then the crows fell down, like huge, spiraling cinders, to prise open the shattered shells.

"They come up here too," the child said. "When it's very windy they get blown this way, over the field, to use the stones in the churchyard. Listen, Daddy! What's happening now? What is it? Is it a black-back? Here it comes!"

A herring gull flapped from the foreshore, pearly in the sunlight. It labored for a few heavy beats of its wings before gliding effortlessly across the hedge and low over the meadow. It held something black and wet in its beak. Approaching the bank of sycamores, the gull flung itself skywards, gained the height to clear the trees, and made an arcing pass over the roof of the church. It released the object it was carrying. With a clatter and a bounce, the mussel skidded down the old, uneven slates and fell silently into the grass of the grave-yard. Immediately, the gull was back to claim its prize... but, as it swooped between the headstones, it saw the man close by and swerved away with an ugly croak.

Zoë, with the help of Tycho, found the mussel and picked it up. It was split. Yellow and pink flesh oozed through the broken shell. She dropped it onto a slate slab.

"See, Daddy?" she said. "Whose grave is this one? Are there bones here too?"

"Henry Albert Griffiths," he read. "Candlemaker of Caernarfon. He died in 1783, about two hundred years ago. Yes, Zoë, Mr. Griffiths's bones are here, under this stone. For all these years, the gulls and the crows have been eating their breakfasts off him. One of them must have dropped the brittlestar. Let's leave it with Mummy, shall we? With my flowers and your razorshell?"

They were shattered, desiccated, the remains of the brittlestar. Zoë shrugged at her father's suggestion, but humored him by sprinkling the crumbs of the creature on the grave. He watched her, and he remembered the meteorite that had fallen close by, on this very day, seven years before. So, he thought, there were still some shards to be found.

Zoë grinned at him, as though she knew what he was thinking. She put down the cold, dead thing and led him from the churchyard, guiding him with the pressure of her hot, strong hand.

13

"And Frank?" she asked him one evening. "Won't he come any more either?"

It was November. The summer had passed. Zoë had continued to prove that she knew the seashore as well as her father did, or better. Yet there remained one thing he could still monopolize, which was beyond her piercing intelligence: a black, metallic thing he'd neglected for months, which was now encrusted with the accumulated droppings of a jackdaw. For Zoë, the telescope was out of reach. Harry took comfort in this. At least there was something he could claim for himself, which she could never usurp.

Now, as a winter's night enfolded the *Ozymandias* and they were snug inside the cabin, he sat before the open stove and pondered the machine: spattered white, stuck with feathers and a down of dust, it was in a filthy condition. For this, he found himself thinking once more, the cello was put to the flames. And again, as always, his thoughts ran from the burning of the cello to the poem that had provoked it; from there, to the groove in the beam where his beloved Lizzie had swung. The child sat beside him. The heat of the fire fell on her bright face.

Knowing the answer, as she always knew the answer to all the questions she ever asked him, she repeated, "And what about Frank, Daddy? Will he be coming again, do you think?"

"No, I don't think so," he replied.

He'd already explained that the youth, Dewi, had had the last of his flute lessons, having long ago left school and gone away to college in Chester. With Harry, the boy had briefly bloomed. Then he'd withered, been blighted. For him also, the cabin had been too small a space to share with the child. Zoë had smiled when Harry told her that Dewi had gone. She snuggled closely to her father, and he could feel the heat in her body, the glow reflected from her cap of silvery hair. She knew she needn't ask about Helen. Her nod at Tycho, her gesture in the direction of the earthenware jug, were signs of her self-assurance, her certainty that the woman was gone too.

And Frank? The time came when he simply hadn't turned up for his lesson, and that was weeks ago, when the *Ozymandias* was becalmed in the dead calm of summer. The estuary had started to stink. The mud was exposed to a baking sun, the weed was crisped and burnt and writhing with big, black flies. In the shallow, brackish water, there were dead fish floating: bellies swollen until the gulls broke in with their beaks, eyes staring and glaucous until the magpies had them. The sky was white, a hot poultice on a wounded place. Tourists came, and came and came, leaving the shoreline littered with condoms... Frank stopped coming.

The boat had been a novelty for him. Years before, he'd patronized Harry and Lizzie Clewe, playing the dusty traveler with tales of his adventures with the Pathans in the Khyber Pass and the Waorani in the rainforests of Ecuador. But Lizzie was gone. And now there was the child: a blind child, who'd changed quickly from a bellowing baby into a little adult — yes, an adult only seven years old, who smiled at the things Frank said, who smiled a grimacing smile at his stories, who stared sightlessly, unblinkingly, across the cabin at him. He was unmanned. His nerve went, on those sweltering summer's nights, when Zoë and the jackdaw laughed together, not as one, but antiphonally, at his bleared perception of the stars. At last, unable to bear her scrutiny, realizing with the onset of middle age that his travels were old hat, sensing that the cabin of the *Ozymandias* held a mystery more disquieting than all his accumulated and largely bogus cosmology, he was gone.

"No, Zoë," Harry said. "I don't think Frank will be coming any more. Why? Did you like him? What did you think of our friend Frank?"

She laughed, a chiming laugh not unlike the cry of the jackdaw. "He was funny, wasn't he?" she said. "The smell of that funny smoke! He was a bit of a show-off, wasn't he, Daddy? Not very clever at all! Why isn't he coming any more?"

Harry shivered. In spite of the fire, the cabin was cold. Zoë snuggled to him and they leaned more closely to the mouth of the stove.

"Oh, I don't know," he replied. "He got fed up with us, I suppose. He's got other friends in town and he goes to talk to them instead."

The room seemed very small. The fire was not the focus of it: the flicker of the fire on the child's face was the focus, from which all other things took their light... as Harry did. He spun in Zoë's orbit, as giddy as a moth in the flame of a candle.

"Frank was funny with your telescope, wasn't he, Daddy?" she said. "He said he could see things in it that even I know aren't there! He made it up, to show off to you! He couldn't really see anything!" She turned up her eyes to him. "Could he, Daddy?"

He didn't answer. He could feel the heat from her face reflected onto his.

She said, "I told the class about the telescope today. Mrs. Henderson made me stand up and tell them all about the *Ozymandias*. It was my turn to do a little talk. I told them about the telescope and I said that my daddy sometimes let me look through it. I made that bit up. They all laughed at me! Even Mrs. Henderson was laughing! So I sat down and wouldn't tell them any more."

A long silence fell between them. There was a booming tide, but the night was still and cold. The mooring ropes creaked, stretching and straining. The fire burned evenly. It warmed the cabin and heated the water in the tank to an occasional, ill-tempered rumble.

"Daddy?" Zoë said, and then she held her breath to get his fullest attention. "Daddy? Can I look into the telescope? Please? Don't laugh at me, Daddy. Can I? Will you show me what's in it? Please? You could show me like the books I use at school, couldn't you? Just a little bit? Please, Daddy?"

He stared around the walls of the cabin, into their flame-shadowed corners, focusing and refocusing his eyes to reassure himself that what he was seeing was only a trick of the light. The place was shrinking about him, the room was closing in... it felt as though the tide had filled up the cabin, as it filled the swirling rock pools, to sweep away everything and everybody that was too weak, everything that wasn't prepared to cling....

The *Ozymandias* rose and fell on a gentle swell. It was full of Zoë. All the light and the heat were concentrated in her. All of it was hers. The grave of her mother was hers, for she was the custodian of the bones. All the estuary was hers, where the birds beat around her bright head. And now the telescope....

"But, Zoë," Harry heard himself saying, his voice lame and bewildered. "But, Zoë, what do you mean? How could you possibly do anything with the telescope? How could you? I really don't see how—"

"Show me, Daddy!" There was a brisk finality in her voice. "Show me the stars! Starting tomorrow night! No excuses! It's winter now, getting cold and frosty, and you've told me it's best for the stars when it's cold and frosty. You can show me while it's frosty, starting tomorrow! Bedtime now!"

Without another word, stretching up her mouth for a goodnight kiss, she slipped into his bed and snuggled herself down. Harry gazed into the diminishing glow of the stove. He fed it with driftwood until the flames roared again. Soon, forced to concede that the fire wasn't the most powerful source of energy on board the *Ozymandias*, he crawled into bed beside Zoë.

14

Returning from town the following morning, having left Zoë at school, Harry stopped near the church and leaned the bicycle into the hedgerow. The track was strewn with seaweed, driftwood, plastic bags, and right into the hedge there was flotsam from the previous night's high tide. There'd been an early frost. He strolled onto the beach, across the heavy boulders nearest the track, over pebbles and shingle, and onto the flat sand of the estuary. He was looking for something, not the brittlestar this time, but handfuls and pocketfuls of shells. The sand was scattered with them. He bent to examine them, choosing the smoothest and best, the winkles like human fingernails, polished, translucent, varying in size from that of a man's broad, ribbed nail to a woman's carefully sculpted ellipse. When he had enough, he returned to the bicycle and rode the rest of the way to the boat.

There, in the cabin, he spent the entire morning in the planning and making of a scale map of the night sky, of the autumn and winter constellations, so that Zoë might be able to form some kind of a mental picture of what he could see through the telescope. He painted part of the wall a uniform midnight blue, and, while it dried, he sorted the shells for size and color. He found a tube of glue with which to fix the seashells onto the wooden paneling of the cabin where Zoë would be able to touch them.

About to start, he'd had such a shameful thought come to him that he'd bolted to the deck for fresh air, otherwise he would have vomited. He'd disgusted himself. The notion had occurred to him, oozing from some dark and slimy corner of his mind, that he might deliberately construct a false map, a travesty, a fake, so that... so that what? So that the child might not... might not what? It had nauseated him to think what he could have done to deny the blind girl her access to the stars. Gulping an icy lungful to clear his head, he'd gone below again, where he lost himself in the construction of his map. Zoë's map.

Accurately, painstakingly, lovingly, he made it. It seemed to him to be a beautiful thing that he made. It thrilled him. He could barely resist the temptation to describe it to Zoë as he cycled her home that afternoon.

"The tide was right up last night, Daddy!" she called out from behind him, where she sat in her pillion seat and held tightly to his waist. "There's seaweed everywhere! Go on, Daddy! Faster! Faster! Pop the seaweed!" The frost-dried bubbles exploded under the tires of the bicycle. "Did you remember what I asked you yesterday, Daddy?"

"Maybe I did and maybe I didn't, young madam!" he interrupted her cryptically, panting over his shoulder as they sped along. "Wait and see!"

He realized the foolishness of what he'd said when she laughed and punched him playfully on the back. The child was in high spirits, sensing the imminent divulgence of a secret. But he wouldn't give it away until night-time, when he'd be ready to point the telescope through the hatch in the cabin of the *Ozymandias*. Until then he would say, whenever he saw that Zoë's inquisitiveness was bringing her close to finding what he'd prepared for her, "Mind that bit of wall, Zoë! The paint's still wet! I only gave it a fresh coat this morning, while you were at school."

She glanced at him, smiling, the blind eyes settling on him for a moment and continuing past, arcing around the room like searchlights. Harry inspected his handiwork and was pleased. He'd cleaned the telescope too; Tycho's claws were loud on the polished metal.

The night fell, with a mighty clang of frost. When all was still, when the cabin was warm and quiet, Harry prepared to look at the stars.

"Now, Zoë," he said. "What was it you were asking me last night? Something about the telescope, wasn't it? Let me get the hatch open and we'll be ready."

She snuggled to him on the easy chair. She lay breathless beside him. He aimed the telescope skyward and swung it on its silent swivels, to see what he could see.

"Lovely!" he said. "Perfect! No cloud to hide the stars from us. Not too bright a moon to dazzle us, but bright enough to dampen the fainter stars so that we can see the major constellations clearly. Now, this is always the best place for us to start...."

In the very center of his vision there hung a single star, Epsilon Orionis, the middle of the three stars that made up Orion's unmistakable belt. He locked the telescope on it.

"We'll leave that there for a moment," he said. "Right, Zoë, up you get. I want to show you something. Over here, come on."

He led her by the hand across the cabin, guided her to the wall he'd prepared for her.

"There... put your hand up, both hands, like so... that's it!" He lifted her fingers to the three white, smooth seashells he'd fixed a few inches apart, the line they formed running slightly downward from right to left. "What can you feel, Zoë, stuck to the wall?"

"Winkles," she answered straight away.

"Yes," Harry said. "Winkles. Three in a line. Three dots. Imagine they're the stars I can see right now in the telescope, in a straight line but angled down a bit to the left. Stay there." He hurried back to the easy chair and put his eye to the lens. He said, "Now I'm going to swing about and find some more stars, and I'll tell you which way I'm moving so that you can follow me. They're all on the wall in front of you, big shells and little ones, different colors even, so that I can try and explain to you what they're like. All right, Zoë?"

He glanced over to her. She had her fingers on the three seashells. She was holding her breath, with her eyes tightly closed. "Good girl!" he said. "Here goes!"

He quickly explained that what she was touching was supposed to be something like the belt of a man, a great hunter, that it helped to identify the stars by remembering these ideas even if they were rather hard to imagine.

Sternly, she said to him, "I can imagine it, Daddy. You know I can."

He directed her from there, upward, straight upward from the left-hand star until she found a much bigger winkle.

"Betelgeuse," he told her, "or Beetlejuice, if you like. A huge orange star which I'm looking at right now, and which you're touching with your fingers. You're touching it, Zoë! Isn't that wonderful?"

It was working. She was quivering with excitement, her face set in a tight smile, her eyes clenched shut.

"So that's one of the Hunter's shoulders," he said. They found the other shoulder, Bellatrix; they returned to the belt; they moved down to the big stars, or winkles, which were his feet and established the scale of the constellation.

"It *is* like a man, Daddy!" she cried. "A skeleton, anyway! His bones in the sky! His belt and his shoulders and feet!" Again she ran her fingers from shell to shell. "Can you see him, Daddy? Like this?" She paused, her fingers hesitating on the wall, then she squealed with laughter and turned to her father, opening her eyes wide. "What's this? I think I've found his... yes, it's his willy! Just under his belt! Have a look through the telescope, Daddy! Can you see it too?"

Her fingers returned to the cluster of tiny shells he'd placed a few inches beneath the belt, and she giggled tremendously.

Harry laughed too, fixing the Great Nebula in front of him, a magnificent, mysterious cloud of gases. "That's not his willy, you silly madam! It's supposed to be his dagger, or his sword," he told her.

So they laughed together, and he was thrilled that she'd found the nebula before he'd swiveled down to it, even if her interpretation of its shape and position was different from the ancient Greeks'. Her hunter had taken shape. Zoë felt for his bones on the wall of the cabin.

That evening he saw more wonderful things through his telescope than he'd ever seen before. Zoë was showing him.

Quite close to the floor, as though it were appearing over the horizon of black dunes, she found Sirius, the brightest of all the fixed stars and therefore the biggest seashell on the wall.

"Sirius is the Hunter's dog, so we sometimes call it the Dog Star," Harry said. She came to Procyon, "known as the Announcer," he told her, "because its arrival each night tells us that Sirius will be up soon afterwards. Imagine all of this swinging slowly upward, each evening, from the floorboards to the ceiling and moving overhead. That's what it's like."

They traveled on together to the Twins, Castor and Pollux, for which she had to stand on a chair. Almost at the ceiling, she stretched as tall as she could for the wide, ribbed shell he'd put there, which signified Capella, in the constellation of the Charioteer.

"Get down again," he said. "You'll find some lovely stars about head height, not much higher than Orion's shoulders, but a bit further this way. Just a pace nearer to me. That's it! There!"

At the same time, he was training the telescope into space until he found what he was looking for: the Pleiades. He explained to Zoë that these were the Seven Sisters, perhaps the most beautiful and most delicate cluster of stars in the entire night sky. They'd never looked so fine before as this time with Zoë. Through the lenses of the telescope, the stars were brilliant, cold and distant and untouchable. And yet, in the same room where Harry Clewe lay in the easy chair and felt the warmth of the stove on his legs, his daughter was chuckling with pleasure at the touch of her own Seven Sisters, a cluster of tiny white seashells stuck to the panels of the wall.

There was more. They completed their circuit of the winter constellations, through the Hyades and the Bull, returning to Orion's Belt. Harry remembered how Lizzie had thrilled at the same journey, seeing the stars through the pitted and gritty lenses of the old binoculars. Now Zoë could have some kind of understanding of what her father could see. She was up and down, from the floor to the ceiling, on and off the chair, as she went round the circuit again. She found more stars, some shells she hadn't found the first time, and she asked him their names.

"Thank you, Daddy!" she said, nestling close again. "They won't laugh at me in school now! Mrs. Henderson won't laugh when I tell her I've been star-spotting with you. I love your shells, all over the walls. They make the *Ozymandias* seem more like a spaceship than a boat on the water, as though we're on board a rocket ship, flying with the stars all around us."

They cuddled, father and daughter, under the nodding black barrel of the telescope, before the shadowy black wall on which the seashell constellations were fixed. The jackdaw was asleep, its head under its wing. Harry and Zoë giggled together, confiding in one another. They went to bed in the glow of the stove, falling asleep as one person.

15

Such was the success of Orion, whose seashell skeleton dominated the cabin, th   by the following May another part of
the wall was studded with winkles. Zoë became familiar with
the Plough, fingering the polished surfaces of the seven big
shells which Harry had arranged there. He'd included Alcor,
to make the double with Mizar in the center of the Plough's
handle, a double known as the Horse and Rider.

"He must have fallen off," she said, more to herself than
to him, as she felt the two components of the double, two
winkles separated by inches of empty wall.

She frowned as she worked her imagination around the idea
of the Bear, flashing her father a smile as though she had a better suggestion for a name. At least the Lion made sense; she
understood the Sickle that comprised its head and front quar-
ters with the big star, Regulus, and could appreciate the shape
of its haunches to its tail, Denebola. It started as a joke between
the man and the child, her questioning of the constellations,
that such a scattering of stars, or indeed seashells, could have
come to represent the creatures and objects and people they did.

With the Plough, the Lion and the Crab, together they
swiveled to the Crow and the Water Snake, and that section
of the wall was as thoroughly explored as the earlier map he'd
made. Zoë's skepticism was a customary ingredient of their evenings with the stars.

"I know they don't really look like or feel like the things
they're named after," he told her, pretending to be cross, scuffling with her in mock exasperation. "They're ancient names.
They're characters from legends, old stories that people used
to tell one another hundreds of years ago. We've got to call
them something, Zoë, so that we can learn to recognize them.
So yes, a bear! Yes, a lion! Try again, and let your imagination go free! After all, you found Orion's willy pretty quickly,
didn't you? But you can't go renaming the whole sky — not
with that sort of name, anyway."

"Can't I?" she said, with an expression of such wisdom on her face that he could only shrug and look away.

Another wall was completed in August. She ridiculed Hercules, who seemed to be flailing with panic at the proximity of the Serpent. "Not much of a hero!" she sniffed, feeling the shells, her eyes tight shut. "He's terrified!"

"And down a bit, Zoë, down to the Crown," Harry whispered. "How lovely that is!"

They came to Boötes, supposedly the Bear Driver. "Well, I can just about make you out," she muttered to the wall. "But I'm afraid your bear's gone missing. I couldn't find it anywhere when me and Daddy were looking for it on the other wall. Just a few bones, that's all...."

As she knelt on the floor, she could feel the head of the Scorpion emerging; and she humored her father by fleeing in a pretense of terror, cuddling to him on the easy chair, where he reassured her that the sting in the tail was safely out of sight below the horizon, buried by the distant dunes.

Through November, the final map was built: the flattened W of Cassiopeia, in which the demon Algol lurked, and close by, the spiral nebula of Andromeda. To Zoë, this extragalactic system, more than two million light years from the *Ozymandias*, was a dusting of the tiniest periwinkles, as fine as sand on her fingertips. She could touch it. The Swan beat across the heavens, its long neck outstretched, exciting her to an agitation of hopping and clapping which wasn't entirely devoid of sarcasm: for this was a creature on her shell maps that she could truly identify.

"Just like the swans on the estuary, Daddy!" she cried, imitating their flight by thrusting forward her head and holding out her arms. "Great big wings making that whistling noise with every flap, and then landing on the water with a whoosh! That's a good one, Daddy! No need to think of another name for that one!"

Saying this, she fell suddenly quiet, dropping her vigorous and noisy beating, and she returned to the wall.

"Go on, Daddy," she said. She knew that her father was

watching her instead of looking through the telescope. "Where shall we go next?" she asked him. "This way?" She fingered the Eagle and flashed him a broad smile. "I suppose it's a bit like an eagle," she conceded, "if it's gliding with its wings wide open. Yes, Daddy, let's call this one the Eagle, shall we?"

Harry blinked at her magnanimity, her empty, invincible stare. "Yes, let's," he said.

And back into Taurus, toward the Pleiades, which signified that the year had changed, that the sky had rolled around them and was once more stretched vast and silent above the *Ozymandias*, just as it had been when the first shell map was fixed into place....

The whole cabin was painted blue-black, from floor to ceiling, and was studded with seashells. That year of star-gazing had quickly passed. There'd been no visitors; no Frank, no Dewi, no Helen. Zoë and Tycho presided. The night skies were captured, brought inside, painted and glued on the walls. The room was dark, the shadows relieved only by an encrusting of shells: winkles of different colors and sizes and shapes, more lustrous as the days and nights slipped past because of the polishing of Zoë's fingertips and the heat of her breath on them. She'd said that the *Ozymandias* was a spaceship. Harry watched her as she read and reread the maps, over and over again.

Past her eighth birthday, the little girl, blind and brilliant, moved silently around the cabin, her lips working soundlessly as she continued her exploration. Sometimes, when she paused and she could tell that he was watching, she would turn to her father with that smile, with her fingers to the wall, holding her breath, whispering to herself. And he wondered what she was saying, what words she was mouthing.... She held a secret of her own, which she wasn't prepared to divulge. He didn't ask, lest she refuse to answer.

Instead, afraid, he turned his face from hers and from the beady glare of the crow. What was her secret? What did the constellations mean to her, that she should retrace them so many times and smile like that?

16

The star maps continued to enthrall Harry too. He grew more expert with the telescope, with the result that more and more details were added to the walls of the cabin. Where there'd been empty space between the skeletons of the constellations, he put clusters and clusters of shells. For him, the heavens had become ever more fascinating; the cabin of the boat was the universe encapsulated, its vastness brought within reach. For Zoë, the room was densely encrusted with winkles, like a rock pool, every corner and crevice studded with barnacles. She continued to explore.

But Harry couldn't judge how she really felt about their stargazing. Was the *Ozymandias* just a kind of playhouse for her, which she enjoyed as any eight-year-old girl would do? Or had she really transformed it into her starship? Had she the imagination to let herself fly, through the agency of her sensitive fingertips? Harry couldn't tell.

However, enigmatic as she was, she didn't disguise her misgivings. They'd laughed about the constellations, the discrepancy between the shapes and the names. As the walls filled up, she laughed less and frowned more.

"What's the problem, Zoë?" he asked one evening, sensing her exasperation. "Is it getting too difficult, too cluttered?" He squinted at the map. "It's getting harder to make out the major star groups, isn't it? I could take some of these off again, if you like, to keep it simple. What do you think?"

"No, Daddy!" she giggled. "It's not too difficult. I can see more and more now!"

She stood in front of the wall. With arms outstretched above her head and then down to her waist and knees, she ran her fingers fast and nimbly over the accumulated shells.

"So many!" she murmured to herself. "So many and so far away! Light years away, hundreds of light years away!" She turned to him, very serious and grown-up. "But they're really not like this at all, are they?"

Harry knelt before her. His stomach fluttered as though it were gnawed hollow. "What do you mean, Zoë?" he said softly.

"Well," she said, "they might look like this in your telescope, but... I mean, do they really look like this? Do they, really?"

"Yes, they do," he answered. "Just like this."

"Well..." She turned to the wall again, her teeth and tongue glistening. Her smile quivered. Her eyes beamed past him, to all the corners of the cabin.

"Well, Daddy," she said at last, "they might look like this and feel like this. But isn't it just a sort of joke you've made for me? Sticking them on the wall? All flat?"

She took a huge breath, which sucked the breath from him and left him giddy.

"That's what I mean!" she went on. "They're really not like this at all!" She gave a squeal of a giggle. "You told me that all these stars are whizzing around at top speed, at different speeds and in different directions. Didn't you? And of course they're all at different distances from us. Whizzing around all over the place! So, you've done it all wrong! Haven't you?"

She put up her hands to his face, stroking him as though he were a daft old dog.

"Poor Daddy!" she laughed. "You've stuck them all! You've stuck them all flat! They're all stuck!"

Harry managed to laugh too, gulping for air at the same time. Her fingers were burning his cheeks.

"But how else could I have done it, Zoë?" he said. "There isn't another way, is there? This is how they look to us, from here. We can't fly up there, among them, and see them any differently, can we?"

"Can't we?" she said.

She drifted from him, creating a space between them which was suddenly cold. She spoke quietly to herself, excluding him.

"So that's why the names are all wrong!" she was whispering. "Of course! The names make everything stuck! The stars, stuck on the wall with glue!"

Her snorted laughter, full of contempt, made Harry shiver.

"Maybe I can..." She was whispering too quietly for him to catch her words, moving more rapidly around the room, from wall to wall, caressing the clustered seashells with the flats of her palms. "Yes, maybe I could..."

She'd forgotten her father's presence on board the *Ozymandias*. With a rattle of its claws, the jackdaw sprang from the telescope and onto her shoulder, where it nuzzled the home-made beak into her silvery hair. Harry was superfluous. Zoë and Tycho floated together from one constellation to another. She fingered the shells, muttering to herself and to the bird.

From this time, the cold distance between Harry and his daughter grew bigger and bigger. Her claim to the stars would sap his strength. Perhaps soon, he would know how Lizzie had been drained, until she was broken and dead. Or perhaps he would be able to resist. He sensed that the end must come quite soon... that one of them, Zoë or himself, must be lost.

Zoë was the blind astronomer. She could see more than he could. She could fly, while he was earthbound.

A few nights later, he discovered her in flight and saw how high she flew.

He woke from a deep and dreamless sleep. Accustomed to the rhythm of the boat on the tide, or its stillness on the mud, he was woken by the child's footsteps. He sat up in bed. The cabin was very dark; the fire was almost out. Zoë was a dim figure who paced from one wall to another, where she paused and murmured, running her fingers over the clustered seashells.

He lay back and watched her for a while, thinking that she'd got up to come to his bed for the rest of the night and had stopped briefly for the pleasure of touching the maps.

However, something in the jerkiness of her movements, the stopping and starting, the feverish shaking of her head, made him uneasy.

"Zoë," he called softly, careful not to frighten her. "Zoë, get to bed now. It's the middle of the night."

She ignored him. It was only when he stood with her, when he put his hands on her shoulders and had no response to his whispers in her ear, that he realized she was still asleep.

"Zoë? Can't you hear me?"

She moved from him to another wall. Following her, he knelt to catch something of her mutterings.

With wide sweeps of her arms, encompassing two or three of the constellations whose shapes and names were so unshakably fixed in Harry's mind, she ran her hands over the shells. He could hardly make out her words, because she whispered and hissed them; and, having only just woken up, he couldn't yet grasp what she was doing. She stepped lightly sideways and let her hands stray across the wall. She gave a little chuckle, standing away from the maps and staring at them, her eyes moving from the floor and to the ceiling, open and unblinking. With a sigh, she stepped close again, so close that she could touch the shells not only with her fingers but by laying her cheek on them, leaning her body on the wall so that the shells pressed into her chest and stomach and thighs. She caressed them with her lips, licking for the tang of salt, muttering as though she were praying... she held herself harder and harder to the wall. She whispered as she eased herself along. The shells rasped and tugged at the material of her pajamas. She stretched as high and as wide as she could until her hands were deep in the clustered constellations, until her face and body were more and more a part of the wall's maps. She was flying, in her sleep....

Retreating from her, Harry sat on the bed. He remained there for an hour, for two hours, while Zoë continued her flight. She reinvented the sky from one end of the year to another, from one corner of the *Ozymandias* to another. She was among the stars, flying. Meteoric, she was the shooting star he'd seen on the night of her birth. She saw the stars from different angles and perspectives and from ever-changing distances. What had seemed to be a belt of stars, neatly equidistant from Earth, was exploded into the vastness of space. There was no belt. Of course there wasn't. No bear. No swan. No scorpion. Of course not. She'd pierced that plane. She was through it and beyond it.

Flying... so that the stars might also fly, their patterns shifting, the image altering. The sky was a kaleidoscope. The bones were there, but the skeletons shifted and blurred and could never be fixed, could never be named for more than a moment. Could never be stuck!

Zoë careered from wall to wall. Harry sat and watched, dazed into torpor. Sometimes he caught a word, when the child glimpsed something so new and exciting that she stepped from the shells with a cry of surprise. What did she see? The berry bunches of ivy, the flock of redshank, the cuttlefish, the dogfish, the jellyfish... the ray with a whiplash tail. Snowdrops drooped in a bed of nettles, a blackbird shuffled the dead leaves. Harry caught the name of Tycho, the jackdaw whose ragged, excitable flutterings she'd glimpsed in deep space. Viper's bugloss, sticky willie, no longer entwined in the hedgerow, had their places in the sky.

Zoë reinvented the constellations, drawing her images from the seashore and the nearby lanes. The stars were no longer stuck. She flew, a blazing meteorite. Harry Clewe, who couldn't fly, watched her and listened. Zoë was the blind astronomer; her blindness released her imagination. His was clenched tightly shut.

Eventually she grew tired. But there was one more discovery to be made. She leaned wearily on the wall. Her hands groped everywhere. She was searching for something and becoming exasperated at not finding it... for it was a rare thing, seldom found except with luck and perseverance.

"Where? Where? Oh, where?" she was muttering, frowning, rearranging the infinity of shapes and permutations that came to her mind's eye through the touch of her fingers and body and lips on the seashells. "Oh, where is it?" Then she smiled. She whispered with a bubble of saliva on her mouth. "The brittlestar! Among all the other stars!"

Exultant, rapt, her eyes ablaze, she turned and came padding past Harry, barefoot on the rugs and floorboards. There was blood on her pajamas, constellations of blood, because she'd pressed her body so hard to the shells. There was blood on her mouth. She clambered into his bed, where she was accustomed to sleeping, and snuggled among the blankets. Asleep. Still asleep. As she'd been sleeping in her dream flight to the stars....

Harry moved aside. She hadn't acknowledged him at all, although she would come to this warm place he'd made. He went to the stove, which he refueled with wood. In the flamelight, as he felt the heat on the back of his legs and balanced himself to the lift of the swell, the cabin was extraordinary. All the walls were black, decorated with seashells of white and silver and the loveliest, palest blue. On every shelf or ledge, among his precious star books and poetry books, were more shells; feathers and bones; bottles of different colors and shapes; driftwood, gnarled and salted and cast up; seaweed, black and brown and green, hung from the beams. The telescope, a scaffold where the jackdaw perched and fidgeted, the claws like needles on the gleaming gunmetal...

An extraordinary place, the cabin of the *Ozymandias*! And outside, the sea and the sky, a huge black night which rumbled with the thunder of a distant surf!

Extraordinary... except that Harry Clewe was stuck. Stuck, like the shells on the wall. Was that as far as he could ever see? No wonder Zoë had snorted with contempt. He'd stuck the stars on the wall with glue! She'd asked him: do they really look like that? Do they really look like that in the telescope? And he'd said yes! Oh, Christ!

Now he snorted with contempt for himself. He could

spout a bit of poetry. He could play a bit of music. He could spot birds. He could poke into rock pools and stare at the stars. He could identify things, label them and file them away in the museum of his mind, all dead and dry in a dusty darkness. That was all he could do. That was the accumulated expertise of Harry Clewe.

The telescope mocked him. It told him nothing about the stars. While the crow unfolded its head from under one wing and glared at him, Harry found himself pacing the cabin. He riffled the pages of his poetry books, remembering the messages he thought he'd found there. He reached to the beams, where the wood was deeply scored. He stared around at his ultimate folly: the walls on which the stars were stuck with glue... the prison of his paralyzed imagination.

In dread of waking Zoë, lest she stare at him and smile and mock him more, Harry crawled under the blankets. He didn't think he could tolerate her eyes on him.

17

From then on, Zoë flew nearly every night.

It followed the same pattern. Harry would be woken by the girl's soft, barefooted movements in the cabin; he would watch her effortless, ecstatic star flights; and, an hour or two hours later, she would brush smilingly past him, to occupy the warmest part of his bed.

And he remembered, with a laugh so bitter that he could taste the bile in his throat, how he'd worried, long ago, about the effect that the presence of the telescope might have had on the blind child... that Zoë might have felt excluded, that Zoë might have felt disabled, disadvantaged in the shadow of the telescope. He'd thought of constructing a false map, to deny her access to the stars... and of course his maps were false, all of them. When he stared into the barrel of the sophisticated, handmade machine, he saw no more than a wall. It was all flat. There was no distance. So much for mystery. So much for wonder. Where was the wonder in a wall studded with seashells?

Harry knew the answer to that question. The wonder and the mystery were in Zoë's head.

Nevertheless, she persisted with the charade of conventional star-gazing, as they'd done for weeks and months before her progression to space flight. During the long evenings which had once been so comfortable, father and daughter in a cozy conspiracy, he endured her mockery. Because, in wakefulness, she reverted to the old scheme of things, as though to humor him. Sweetly childlike, the smiling child whose hair was gleaming and silver, who padded from chart to chart as softly as a kitten, who smelled of soap and shampoo and of white, clean skin, Zoë would urge him to the use of the telescope, reversing the roles so that it was she who led him from one constellation to another, naming them and their component stars: the old names, without a flicker of dissent.

Harry acquiesced, too limp to resist her brisk authority. Around him, in the cabin that had once seemed so quaintly glamorous, he saw the stars glued on the walls. In the tube of the telescope, he saw the stars glued on the walls. For him, the mystery was gone. And yet he and Zoë continued with the list of labels, the dusty legends, the dry and crumbling bones... a menagerie of skeletons.

Only at night, for Zoë to slip effortlessly through the flatness of those walls, to rocket into a space he was powerless to imagine. From this he was excluded. Wretchedly, he sat on the corner of his bed, night after lonely night, and he watched her. His effacement was almost complete.

His bed had been requisitioned. The boat was a spaceship from which he could see nothing. The telescope was blinkered, spattered with bird shit. Lizzie's bones were in Zoë's custody. He'd thought the stars were his, like coins in his collection, but now they were tarnished beyond polishing. He'd thought the estuary was his, but he no longer dared identify the birds or the berries or the wild flowers, lest the child correct him; every cry from the dunes was a challenge he now shirked. He attempted the flute, exhuming it from its case, but it was a chill, unforgiving thing, and the child grimaced at the noise it made.

Sometimes he went onto the sands, while the girl was at school. Head down, hunched under the hugeness of the sky, deaf to the distant sea, he stalked the mudflats. The dead horse was still there, broken into many pieces. He pushed aside the ribcage with his boots. Kneeling in the oil-black pool, he tugged at the vertebrae, twisting the gristle. But there was no brittlestar, although the child could find it in a dream, in her sleep, in the thundering spaces of heaven. For Harry, there were no shards left, no fragments of that meteorite. Unable to compromise, he rejected the starfishes that he found, hurling them away with a backhanded flick of the wrist or tossing them skyward for a gull to catch.

The birds ignored him. They continued to feed, un-ruffled by his slow-moving, dull-brown presence, as he trod with his boots on the mud and kicked the clumps of weed. It was a vast place of sea and sand and sky. Harry Clewe was a speck on it.

18

"Where's Tycho?"

That was the first thing Zoë said when they stepped into the cabin that afternoon. It was January. Harry had struggled along the seashore track, cycling into a fierce, freezing wind, with the child on her seat behind him. The tide was coming in fast, the estuary was white with spray. They'd been unable to speak on the way home, against the roar of wind and water. He'd bent into the cold, with an icy rain on his forehead, and Zoë was huddled behind his back. It was a tremendous relief to be inside the cabin, where the fire was hot. Harry threw off his coat and knelt with his face to the stove. The *Ozymandias* ground on the sea wall, lifted higher and higher as the tide rose, and the groans of the timbers grew louder.

"Where's Tycho?" she asked again. "He's not here. And he wasn't outside with us, on the ride from school. Where is he, Daddy?"

He turned to look at her. Still in her coat, her hair speckled with raindrops, she peered about the cabin and she sniffed. She listened for the rattle of sharp claws. Moving past him to the telescope, she reached to its barrel and felt into the droppings; she bent to the floor to do the same thing. They were all dry. She went to the bed, where she sniffed the blankets.

At first, Harry didn't reply. He made busy with the fire. With the hatchet, which always leaned by the stove, he split some driftwood, the spars splintering under the blade. That morning, he'd evicted the jackdaw from the boat. He'd been daydreaming on the bed, when Tycho flapped in with a trophy from the beach: a sheep's eye, gouged from a swollen carcass, which the bird had lifted to its customary perch on the telescope and started to peck, holding the slippery ball in one foot. This was too much. At the sound of the pecking, seeing Tycho with juices on its beak and breast, Harry had sprung from the bed and driven the bird outside. It hadn't been seen since.

"It's going to get rough later on," he said. "There'll be a really big tide tonight. A neap, that's what they call it."

The girl snorted. Having established that the bird wasn't there, she was standing quite still, pointing her eyes at her father.

"No, Daddy," she said, with a little twist of a smile. "A neap is a smaller tide than usual, not a bigger one."

The boat shuddered under a shock of wind and was borne upward. It squealed against the wall.

"You put Tycho out?" she asked. "This morning? And he hasn't come back at all?" She brushed past him, and the spray from her hair hissed on the stove. "I'd better go and find him then, hadn't I?"

She was up the steps and out, before he'd thought of anything to say. The cabin was dense with the smell of weed and the reek of Zoë's disapproval.

Uneasy, but determined not to follow her immediately, Harry continued to rebuild the fire; there would be hot water for the evening and a hot stove for the cooking. He took up the soiled newspapers from the floor, burned them, replaced them with clean ones. The more objectionable remains of the horse he also put into the flames. With a damp cloth he wiped the length of the telescope, which was encrusted with droppings. All a bit late, he thought ruefully... long after Helen was gone and might never come back, long after she'd been driven away. He looked around the cabin.

Books, a lot of books, of which he'd read and understood so few. Books about stars, too baffling, too difficult, demanding too much concentration and commitment; books of poems, which he seldom opened except to remind himself of the messages and prophecies he'd thought they contained...

His battered binoculars, through which, years before, he'd learned the stars in an African sky...

A red spotted neckerchief, stuffed under his pillow, faded and washed out, a piece of a previous life he'd had, a life and a love which had all but consumed him, which now he could hardly remember...

His flute case, locked, a coffin for his dead music...

The telescope, recently requisitioned by a crow...

The seashell constellations, as dead as hundreds of human fingernails, stuck to the blue-black walls of the cabin...

So much baggage, surrounding him.

And Lizzie was gone: his sister, his partner, his lover, the mother of his child. She'd been murdered. The scar on the beam was a reminder of the wounds on her throat.

He shook himself from this daze and averted his face from the stupefying heat of the fire. Zoë was gone, too, into the storm.

The late afternoon had grown dark. Now and then, as the boat lurched up and down, as it scraped its buffers against the wall, a flurry of spray rattled on the windows. The estuary was swollen and choppy. The rising waters foamed white. Harry was worried about Zoë, although she knew the shoreline as well as he did, or better, and was accustomed to being out there alone. He put on his waterproofs and clambered onto the deck.

The tide was lapping at the top of the sea wall, so that, for the first time in all the years he'd lived on the *Ozymandias*, he could step downward from the deck and onto the shore. He adjusted the mooring ropes, as the boat was riding so high. Glancing along the track, he saw the sea forcing onto it and rising still; soon it would be impassable, the water would be through the hedgerow and into the fields. He strode away from the boat.

The cold took the breath from him. There was frost in the air, a pummeling wind. A hundred yards, two hundred yards along the shore, and then he turned and looked back at the hulk of the *Ozymandias* as it darkened into gloomy dusk. Horizontal, the smoke from the chimney raced inland.

The light at the portholes surged and fell. Afternoon became evening and was suddenly night.

No sign of Zoë. When he bellowed her name, the word vanished in the noise. Not only the wind and the sea, but the rasping agitation of the hawthorn hedge took the word from him and tossed it away. She was out there, somewhere, and it needed an effort of imagination to remind himself of the darkness she always inhabited, the irrelevance to her of daylight and twilight and pitch blackness; Harry was disoriented by the night, especially in this buffeting, but for Zoë it was another day of high winds across the estuary.

He battled onward, head down, tugging at the hood of his jacket, occasionally shouting, and when he came level with the gate from which the path crossed the fields and led to the churchyard, he leaned on it with his back to the sea in order to regain his breath. The wind pinned him against the gate until he swung clumsily over it, his waterproofs creaking, and he was driven to grassy, higher ground and the shelter of the cemetery wall. He ducked behind it and sat down. There was total darkness, a marvelous lull, while the gale bellied about him and left him quite untouched. The sycamores groaned, thrashing their leafless branches. But, with his shoulders on the bulging boulders, Harry had found a still place at the center of a tumultuous world.

It was a roaring world in which voices were lost. He crouched and listened. There were cries, gulls perhaps, or curlew. He pulled down his hood and strained to hear... yes, a cry, clear and high above the broil of the wind in the branches. But not a bird. He could hear a child's voice and the single word it was shouting. "Ty... cho...!" Each syllable took a full second. "Ty... cho...!"

Harry lurched to his feet and stumbled on, bent double to keep his head below the top of the wall, until he reached the corner of the churchyard. There he met a blast of wind, a faceful of salt spray. It carried the cry more clearly to him. As he squinted into the howling darkness, he caught a movement in the field beyond, something white and shifting. A gull, grounded by the force of the storm? A sheet of blowing newspaper? Its purposeful progress told him it was Zoë, the glimmer of her hair: it was Zoë, bareheaded, resolute, a field away from him, working back in the direction of the *Ozymandias's* mooring.

Wanting to overtake her, he ran toward the shore, where he thought it would be quicker to use the gravel track than to negotiate the fields, with all their ditches and fences. However, when he reached the gate, he saw why the girl had opted for the inland route. The sea had covered the track. The tide had broken through the hedges, through the tumbledown stone wall, and still the water drove in. There was no alternative but to follow Zoë. At least he'd seen her, had heard her, could assume that she was safe.

And so Harry discovered how it might feel to be blinded, for his senses were flummoxed....

He tumbled into drains, chest-deep in ice water. He blundered on barbed-wire fences. The ground collapsed beneath him, and he slithered in reedbeds and dew ponds. He was lashed with spray; the sting of salt was on his lips and in his eyes. There was blood on his hands. And always that roar, the sea or sky or both together, a torrent of dinning, deafening noise.... He was drowning in darkness. It took the ground from under his feet, snatched the breath from his mouth. Sometimes he glimpsed the child's hair, the only bright thing in the world, a beacon to guide him home. He followed it. He thought he cried out, but he couldn't hear his own voice; he thought he heard the child, but it must have been the wind. Sheep fled before him, cattle stumbled close, and these creatures were like boulders that shifted around him. There was no horizon from which to take a bearing, no silence against which the intensity of sound could be measured. His own footsteps, the beat of the blood in his head, the rhythm of his breathing... all of these were out of time. Somehow, by pursuing the bobbing body of the child, he reached that corner of the field which was nearest to the mooring of the *Ozymandias*.

Here the child was lost. It was the first time Harry had seen her like this, when the world she'd learned and remembered was so altered that she no longer recognized it. Things had changed since she'd left the boat. The tide was over the track. Where there should have been sea wall and the rough gravel that bordered it, now there was a boiling race of water. It surged through the hedgerow. With each sucking withdrawal it abandoned mattresses of debris; with each roaring charge it brought more of this foaming flotsam. The *Ozymandias* rose high, all but lifted on top of the wall; only the tightness of the mooring ropes prevented the boat from being dropped and broken. He came up behind the girl. Together they stood in the corner of the field. Side by side they faced the flying spray.

He pulled her to him, holding her cold, wet body. She was shivering violently. Her teeth were chattering.

"Come on, Zoë!" he shouted, putting his mouth to her ear to make her hear above the noise of wind and water. "Daddy'll get you home safely! It's not as deep as it sounds! Come on!"

He picked her up. She was as light and as limp as a lamb. His bones seemed to flood with exhilaration: the child's helplessness and disorientation fueled him with strength. Having followed her this far, in mud and darkness, now he would carry her to safety. He timed the rushes and retreats of the waves. Waist-deep, he strode through the skeleton of the hawthorn with Zoë in his arms. He steadied himself against the force of the undertow, reassured by the track underfoot, and waded onward until they were beside the hull. The boat bucked in front of him. It strained at the ropes with a creak and a groan, so that he staggered from it in case the child should be struck. He touched the edge of the sea wall with his foot, and he knew they were lost if he stepped too far, where they would surely be smashed and drowned. There was no way of boarding. The sea tore against his legs. It welled to his chest and the *Ozymandias* reared above him, a huge black mass that was going to topple and crush them; then it rolled away, controlled by the restraining ropes. So this went on for what seemed like hours, man and child cowering under the hull of the boat. Zoë lay against his chest as though she were dead.

At last the wind began to drop. The cloud cover frayed, split enough for a little light to leak through, and then tore open, revealing a bright moon.

"Right, Zoë!" Harry shouted. "Now we can do it!"

He lifted her easily and laid her on the deck of the boat. The storm was dying. The tide was falling, having peaked in the flooded fields. Making sure that the hull was clear of the wall, Harry loosened the ropes so that the *Ozymandias* could drop to the mud as the sea level dropped; then, moving quickly, he clambered aboard and carried the child below. She was a dead weight.

Nothing was amiss in the cabin; only a few fronds of weed had fallen from the ceiling and a few books had tumbled from the shelves. Putting Zoë on the bed, Harry knelt swiftly to feed the stove and left its door wide open to warm the room. He tore off all his clothes, flung them down and rubbed himself very hard with a towel. Then he turned his attention to the girl.

"Zoë?" he cried. "Little Zoë? Are you there?"

He bent to her. Her face was as cold as marble. Her lips were blue. Her hair was plastered about her head like a silver skullcap. When he began to undress her, she moaned and moved and her hands pushed abstractedly at his, to try and prevent him. He persisted, relieved to see her stirring, and soon he'd removed her shoes and socks, her trousers and pants, and was beginning to pull at her jacket. At this, she wriggled, tossing her head and murmuring, "No! No, you can't! He's not...!" but the words were too faint for him, no more than a whisper against the crackle and spit of the fire.

She wrestled from him, her arms locked across her chest. She continued to mutter and chatter.

Feeling the icy cold in her limbs, Harry tugged at her. "Come on, Zoë! Out of these clothes! Look, I've taken all mine off! Let's get yours off too and get you warm in bed! Come on, Zoë!"

The child, whose eyes had been tightly shut until then, suddenly blinked up at her father. She held that piercing, pale stare throughout the ensuing struggle, grinding her teeth loudly together. He avoided it, turning his face from hers, as he gripped both of her tiny wrists in one of his hands and tore open the buttons of her jacket with the other. She screamed through locked jaws. She flailed her naked legs.

"Livening up, are you, young madam?" he shouted, very angry but encouraged by the heat he could feel in her. "Well, keep on kicking and we'll soon have you warm again! These clothes are coming off whether you like it or not!"

She writhed hysterically, but he held her down easily with one hand.

"All right, you little bitch!" he bellowed at her. "If you want a fight you can bloody have one!" He heaved himself onto the bed and sat astride her, bearing down on her thighs with the weight of his body. She was trapped. "Got you, you witch!" He was panting heavily, unable to control his breath. "Now..."

A prisoner, she silenced her scream and lay still, her chest pounding, her eyes fixed on his. They remained like this for a minute, the naked man straddling the half-naked child. The boat moved gently on the moving swell. The cabin of the *Ozymandias* was a warm, swaying place. The shadows and the flames were dancing while the man and the child were motionless.

"That's better," he said, lowering his face to hers. "Have we finished our little tantrum?"

Still he held her two hands in one of his, pressing them to the pillow, pinioning them above her head. With his free hand he started to undo her jacket. "You're absolutely soaking, Zoë, my love. Don't you think it's a good idea to take these things off?"

She maintained her unblinking stare. She lay limply beneath him as he tugged at her clothes. A tiny smile formed on her mouth, and her tongue appeared, like the tongue of a lizard. She licked her lips until they shone. She moved her hips very gently, very softly, arching her body off the bed so that her belly was pressed into his. Her smooth, wet skin slithered on him. Aware of his nakedness on her, Harry felt his mouth go dry... until, a moment later, seeing with horror and amazement that he was aroused, he sprang away from her and stood quivering by the stove.

"Jesus Christ, Zoë! What the hell are you doing to me?"

Her smile hardened. It marked her face like a wound. The child sat up and opened her jacket. Something was moving inside her shirt, a squirming, fluttering thing....

Harry recoiled from it and from the child. She grinned at him with a dry chuckle. Her shirt was moving, for there was something inside it, something alive or barely alive.

"For fuck's sake!" he cried out. "What the fuck have you got?"

When Zoë lifted her shirt, the jackdaw was there, a sodden black rag on her white belly. It was a broken thing. Slick with rain, tattered and shattered, the bird was dying. With its remaining strength, it sculled its wings, clawed for traction on the child's skin, and the beak opened and closed in silence. The jackdaw slid down her thighs. She kicked it from her, and it fell to the floor of the cabin.

"I found him in the long grass, Daddy," she said. She could hardly speak, because her smile was fixed so hard. "I found him by Mummy's grave. Tycho's going to die, isn't he, Daddy?"

Harry said nothing. His body ached with cold. He flinched from the bird, which was panting and glaring, and he flinched from Zoë. She swung from the bed and stood up. She tugged the shirt over her head and was perfectly naked, her thin, hard body quite white in the light of the flames. She shone her face at him.

"Isn't he, Daddy? Tycho's going to die, isn't he?"

She stooped to pick up the bird. She held it by the neck, in her right hand. It dangled. Its wings didn't move, but it rowed feebly in the air with the black claws. Zoë cracked it like a whip, once. Water flew from it. Harry felt the droplets on his face and heard the hiss as they hit the stove. The child rattled the bird at him.

"He was going to die, wasn't he, Daddy? Well, now he's dead."

She sat on the bed and laid the bird in her lap. She spread its wings across her thighs. The black thing was the center of her. She caressed the drenched plumage, with her head down... she'd forgotten the man, her father, who stood naked and speechless and shivering on the far side of the cabin. Lifting the jackdaw's beak, she stroked it with her fingertip. She preened the feathers. Then she lay down, and with the wreckage of the bird against her belly, a black smear on her colorless skin, she rolled herself into the blankets. Straight away she was asleep, her breathing deep and regular.

Harry went to Zoë's bed in the corner. He didn't want to touch her or be touched by her. He watched the firelight through the curtains of seaweed. Eventually, curled up very small, he also slept.

19

Much later that night, Zoë made her final flight through
the seashell constellations.

Harry was woken, as he'd been woken so many times
before, by the sound of her footsteps as she moved about
the cabin. The fire had burned low. Still naked, she went
gently from wall to wall and pressed herself to the shells,
until there were pinpoints of blood on her chest and belly
and thighs where the winkles had pricked. He didn't try
to stop her or persuade her back to bed. She was asleep,
although her eyes were open and staring. As ever, he
watched the child's journey through the stars... this child
whose blindness had released her, for whom blindness was
a gift.

But this time was different. She was shaking her head,
alternately frowning and giggling at the falsity of the charts.
They were ridiculous. Sometimes she stood away from them,
hands on naked hips, as though she could really see the maps
on the walls in front of her, and she shook her head as if
she could hardly credit the naiveté of this primitive plan-
etarium. And what did she do then? She spun from the wall,
an expression of tremendous resolution on her face, and she
reached for the hatchet by the stove.

Harry didn't try to stop her. Why should he? He also
knew that the maps were false. Why should he have tried
to prevent the child, as she stepped lightly from constellation to constellation and smashed the winkles with accu-
rate, rhythmic blows? She felt for the shells with her left
hand, one by one, for she'd learned their exact positions from
her father, and she dealt them each a sharp, unerring tap
with the flat of the hatchet. They shattered. The fragments
fell to the floor. Harry lay curled in the corner, and he
watched. He almost got up to help, to abet the destruction;
but the child needed no help. She was swift and efficient.
In a matter of minutes, all the shells on all the walls were

broken. The stars he'd translated from the skies to the cabin were gone, their smithereens dropped to the horizon. Dead fragments of dead stars...

Zoë looked suddenly drained. Her body, ghostly pale in the dying firelight, seemed to droop. When Harry crossed the cabin and guided her to bed, he felt the cold in her. She was as cold as stone, like a dead, cold stone. The heat was going from her. The energy was leaving her.

Soon she was wrapped in the blankets again. Harry bent to kiss her, and the touch of her lips was like ice. However, she breathed evenly, without shivering. He left her to sleep, now that she'd done what she'd got up to do. Treading gingerly, barefooted on the splintered seashells, he put the hatchet by the fire. The blade was powdered with white dust, but the edge was very sharp.

Harry woke to silvery daylight. Aching in all his bones, he peered with bleary, mucous eyes from under the blanket. And the thing he saw was pure nightmare. He ducked his head from it. Shuddering like a spastic in the darkness of the covers, he wailed with horror....

A figure was hanging from the ceiling.

Paralyzed, sweating, with his knees to his chest, Harry hid himself. There was no sound in the cabin, only the chatter of his teeth and the moaning he couldn't contain. He squeezed his eyes shut, and the images blurred and fused; the graphic, monochrome picture of Lizzie as she'd hung from the beam, her head enfolded, her white and bloody nightdress, her feet in the socks which were blackened and burnt... and the thing he'd just seen, a smaller figure, swinging, silently rotating....

These two pictures flashed on the screen in his head, branded on the inside of his eyelids. Trembling, he saw every detail. The stench of scorching came to him, triggered by the twin visions, and he could hear the gurgling of the garroted girl. He was inside the nightmare. It had come for him.

Until he felt a hand on his head, and a sweet little voice said, "Daddy! Daddy! What's the matter, Daddy? Are you having a dream?"

Zoë pulled the blanket from him. She smiled like an angel. "Were you dreaming, Daddy? Was it something nasty?"

He looked past her, around the cabin. She seemed to follow his stare, but she laughed when he flinched from the thing he'd seen. He rubbed the sleep from his eyes until he could focus clearly.

"I hung them up, Daddy!" she said with a giggle. "They were soaking wet from last night. I hung them up while you were still asleep."

Her clothes were there, that was all, dangled from the beam and drying in the warmth of the fire. There was a pool of water on the floorboards. Harry uncurled from the tiny bed and stood up, stretching himself tall again.

"I hung up Tycho as well," she said. "I've been making things tidy. Come and look!"

As though he were blind and she were sighted, Zoë escorted her father about the cabin. She brushed him past the hanging clothes; he ducked from the broken body of the jackdaw, which she'd fixed to the beam with a pin through one leg, whose disheveled plumage was steaming as it dried. The child had swept up the wreckage of the seashells. She was pleased with her work, quite radiant, although her hand was cold.

"We can take Tycho with us today, can't we, Daddy?" she said excitedly. "It's lovely outside! I've been on deck! It's very frosty, but it's lovely. We'll take Tycho with us!"

As soon as he was dressed, they went out, along the seashore track. The frost had bitten. The fields were white over. Even the foreshore was frozen, the weed was silvered and the edges of the rock pools were blurred with ice. It was beautiful and cruel. Father and daughter walked side by side, their footsteps crunching on the gravel, and they negotiated the debris which the unusually high tide had left behind. The hedgerows were choked with driftwood and dead grass, all of it whitened by the frost. The thin, sunlit air pinched around their nostrils. In the fields, the cattle were like furnaces, the steam pluming from their muzzles.

Beautiful, the frost... and cruel. Every stone in the grave-yard was shaggy with white fur. The long grass, once so rank and pungent, was cast in ice, a statuary of steel; overnight, all its blades had been sharpened. Dock leaves were cleavers. Nettles were bayonets. A lone foxglove, a survivor from the autumn, was a single silver sword. The snowdrops were as keen as stilettos. The cemetery, whose soft, secret corners had been tangled with wild flowers, was now the boneyard of a battlefield. The dead were buried, but their weapons remained behind.

On Lizzie's headstone, where the letters of her name had been cut so deep, the frost defied the child's sensitive fingertips. Zoë knelt, as she always did. She felt for the words, as she always did. But the frost had erased them. Nevertheless, there was no mistaking the grave. All around it, as though the tide had really reached so high, there was sea-weed, so dry that it crumbled at Zoë's touch; there were bones, whose bone whiteness was fettled to ice whiteness, the skulls of godwit and heron, as different as tweezers and dagger; the egg cases of rays, split by the cold; the gaping shark mouth of dogfish; even, among the accumulated gifts at the grave, the bits of the brittlestars.

Poor things they were, the segmented arms a powder of cartilage, the disc-body ground to dust. They'd come from the estuary, the shards of a shooting star that had signaled the death of the woman and the birth of the child. Some of them had hung on the Christmas trees in the *Ozymandias*. Now, they were grains of salt and sand and ice. Zoë brushed them aside.

From under the folds of her jacket, she brandished the bundle that had been Tycho. She opened it out, spread the wings wide, laying it where the brittlestars had been. Its head lolled. The homemade beak fell askew. The claws were clenched into scaly fists. The bird sprawled on Lizzie's grave, the only black thing in the frosted whiteness of the cemetery. It steamed a little in the brilliant sunlight, as bright as jet.

Zoë said nothing, but she watched her father and smiled as he felt at the words on the headstone. Then they left the bones and the bird and returned to the boat.

20

It was summer again. The estuary began to steam and stink.

Under a white sky, the shallows lay still, scummy with brown and yellow bubbles. The movement of the tide did nothing to cleanse the mud, which sweated and staled like the flesh of something sick. Eels writhed in the pools that the sea had left. On the foreshore, the weed was baked crisp; it seethed with millions of insects. The air was loud with the droning of big, black flies. It was a sweltering summer, nine years since Lizzie had died and Zoë had been born.

Harry continued to look at the stars, although the heat haze veiled the constellations. Zoë took no more interest, now that the charts were destroyed. While he reclined in the easy chair with his eye to the lens of the telescope, or lay on deck with the old binoculars, the child seemed to watch him. She smiled faintly. She sneered. The man and the child were alone together, adrift on the *Ozymandias*, adrift on a dead calm.

The others had gone overboard: Helen, whom Harry sometimes met by chance in town, where they talked inconsequentially and glanced at one another's hands and lips as though remembering the touch and the taste of them; Dewi, whom he never saw again; Frank, who would wave from the wheel of the Morris in the streets of Caernarfon; Seamus, the kitten, who'd survived no more than a fortnight before finding poetic fulfilment in a vase of dead roses; Tycho, the jackdaw, who'd been broken and mended and broken again, thrown out like a rag, disposed of. Lizzie was long gone.

Harry and Zoë were alone together, becalmed on brackish water.

And something odd was happening, all the odder because the summer was so hot. Zoë was cooling. She grew weary and pale. For a while, Harry had associated this with the general lassitude that the weather had brought: the whole world was dazed. But her weariness was deeper than that. Her eyes, which had glittered so brightly, had gone dull. Her silvery hair had lost its lustre. In the touch of her skin there was a strange clamminess, a chill that grew colder by the day. All her boiling energy, which she'd sucked from her mother until the woman was drained to death, was leaving her. Her heat would soon be quenched.

And, in the way she turned her eyes on him and smiled, Harry could see that she knew.

21

It was Zoë's ninth birthday. "Pick me up a bit later from school, Daddy," she told her father. "Mrs. Henderson said we can have a party this afternoon."

Harry told her that they'd have their own private party in the evening, on board the *Ozymandias*.

So he had more time to spend alone on the estuary: alone, except for the hundreds of gulls and waders among which he moved so slowly, so persistently. The tide was rising, a scum of simmering bubbles. The sun was hidden by dense white clouds, but the heat was stifling. There was a smothering haze. Harry trudged along with his head down and his hands in his pockets, blind to the birds and careless of the heat.

The morning passed and the tide crept in. He returned to the boat to eat. He lay on the bed, and such an apathy came over him that he thought he would search the sands no longer, but let them be covered by the sea. He thought he might lie there and wait for the moment when the boat would be lifted, which would signify that another day was gone and his searching had been in vain. However, when he glanced at the scar on the beam above his head, when he felt under the pillow and touched the little present he'd wrapped for Zoë and hidden there, he sprang up with renewed determination. This was a special day, an anniversary. He had it in mind to find the brittlestar, that odd, antique creature which had been a kind of talisman for him.

The rising waters drove the birds more closely together. There was keen competition between the curlew in their flock, between the oystercatcher, the redshank and the godwit, as they probed the diminishing expanse of mud. The sun was filtered through a gauze of cloud. The heat was heavy on Harry's head. As he walked, shelduck shouldered their way from pool to pool. A single crow sprang among the waders, and when it opened its wings in the sunlight it was no longer black, but as bright as silver. The sea inched higher. The man and the birds moved on a shrinking island.

All of a sudden, the birds were up. They rose in one great, clamoring crowd and beat around his head. When they'd gone, separating into squadrons of different species, only the crow remained with him on the hard, flat sand. It continued to work alone, a freebooter. The beak was in soft flesh, and, for the crow, there was nothing else: no sky, no sun, no sea, no man. Beak into flesh, that was all. Harry walked within a yard before the bird noticed him and flapped away, toward the shore.

It had left him the pieces of a brittlestar. A poor thing it was, beached and broken and dead, but it was what he'd been looking for. By now, the shallow water was all around him. He was quite alone on the estuary. Bending down and pocketing what the sea and the crow had abandoned, he splashed from the sandbank, knee-deep through the channels, onto the boulders and the weed of the foreshore.

He put the brittlestar on the bookcase and cycled to town to collect Zoë.

She'd aged. Born a boiling baby, a meteoric child who'd consumed all the energy around her, she'd passed through maturity and into old age within a matter of weeks... or so it seemed to Harry. It astonished him that no one else had noticed. Her teacher didn't remark on it, and the children with whom she shared the classroom and the playground were apparently oblivious. But Harry could see it. Zoë was wan and fragile. Her prime was past. She sat behind him on the bicycle, and her arms around his waist were cold, a cold that enfolded him and penetrated his bones. She didn't say a word during the journey home; there was no accompanying clamor of gulls, no entourage. Whatever magnetism the child had had was gone. Zoë clung to her father as he rode along beside the beach, and there was no warmth in her, although the day was so hot.

In the cabin of the *Ozymandias*, her cold was more powerfully contagious. A shiver passed through Harry's body, between his shoulder blades, as soon as he and the girl stepped downstairs together... only a tingle at first, but then the hairs on his neck stood up. She stared around the cabin.

"Well, Zoë?" he asked her. "What do you think?"

He'd decorated the place for her birthday, with streamers and cards. It looked very pretty. As she negotiated her way about, to find what was different, she stumbled uncharacteristically, knocking into the corner of the bed. After exactly nine years of learning the cabin so that she was familiar with every corner, she was suddenly uncomfortable in it. Steadying herself after a bump on the bookcase, she put out her hand to the wall... and she frowned, her face puckered with puzzlement, at the feel of the blobs of glue which were all that remained of the seashell constellations. She was finding it hard to remember what they were. She caressed the tube of the telescope, as though for the first time. Watching her, Harry shivered again.

"It's lovely, Daddy," she said. "Thank you." There was a quiver of uncertainty in her voice. "This is our special place, isn't it, Daddy? Just for us two? And for Mummy, of course?"

She held up her face for him to kiss, her eyes opened wide, her lips dry. The cabin grew cold, although the world outside was steaming in a heatwave.

"Here's your present, Zoë," he announced, and he produced the parcel from under the pillow. He watched intently as she unwrapped it. It was a book in Braille, an anthology of poems for children, which she flicked open and explored with nimble fingers. She touched his hands and smiled. He had a cake for her, too. She blew out the nine candles with nine tiny breaths and then asked him to place them around the cabin and relight them.

"And close the curtains, Daddy!" she said. "Let's just have the two of us and the candles, and have the curtains shut! Our little secret place, for Zoë and her daddy!"

In this way, on a sweltering afternoon in July, the man and the child were shut inside the candlelit cabin. Zoë moved from flame to flame, cupping her hands around them to feel the heat, as though to tap as much of the energy as she could. The candles cast an orange glow on her white face. She looked exhausted.

"I think you ought to be in bed, Zoë my love," Harry said after a while. "I know it's a shame, on your birthday, but you must have picked up a bug or something in school. What do you think?"

She consented to this, too wasted to object. As Harry undressed her, helped her into her pajamas and tucked her under the blankets of her own bed, he felt the chill in her. It filled the cabin. He was shivering too. She lay with the sheet right up to her chin: that ineradicable smile, that unblinking stare.

"Poor Zoë," he whispered to her. "Poor poorly Zoë, poorly on her birthday. Sleep a bit, my little love."

She nodded. He didn't know it would be the last time he'd ever see her awake.

Yes, the cabin was cold. Harry left the curtains closed and the birthday candles lit, and he decided to light the fire in the stove; for Zoë had seemed so sickly, her breath had smelled so stale, like a draft from a damp cellar. He used the brightly colored wrapping paper from her present, crushing it into a ball inside a handful of twigs, and the flames blossomed straight away. With the hatchet, he split some driftwood and fed it to the fire, and he sat on the bed with his face to the blaze. Even so, there was a cold in his back. The candles guttered in a breath of icy air. He cuddled himself closer to the stove.

Reaching for the book he'd bought for Zoë, he leafed through its pimpled pages; it was a mystery to him, quite meaningless, just as the smooth pages of his own books would be meaningless to her. He put it on the shelf, slipping it among the others, where the child might find it in the morning and be pleased that it had a place among her daddy's poetry books. To make a space for it, he took out another book. The pages fell open, yellowed, wrinkled, where something wet had been.

So he reread the poem by Robert Frost about the star-splitter, in front of the stove where the cello had gone, beneath the telescope for which the cello had been destroyed. Nine years before, when he'd found the fragile limbs of the brittlestar impressed upon the poem, he'd thought he'd read it carefully and understood the message. But he'd got the gist, that was all. He'd made the beginner's mistake, which applied to poetry as much as it applied to the stars, which he'd explained to Lizzie so long ago: the trick was to look askew, "to look at a star by glances, to view it in a side-long way." Dazzled by the narrative, the simply told tale of a man who'd perpetrated an insurance fraud in order to buy himself a telescope, Harry had missed the nub of the poem...

"We've looked and we've looked, but after all where are we? Do we know any better where we are and how it stands, how different from the way it ever stood?"

Over and over, aloud and silently, Harry read these lines, while Zoë was asleep, oblivious of the words. The telescope had taught him nothing: it had sent him on a wild-goose chase around the heavens, culminating in nothing more imaginative than the seashell charts he'd stuck on the walls of the cabin....

"We've looked and we've looked, but after all where are we?"

He repeated this question time and time again. And the answer? He was stuck. Harry Clewe was stuck, like the winkles on the wall, as much inclined to soaring into space as a barnacle was inclined to swimming.

"Do we know any better where we are?"

No, he didn't. Although he had Zoë, in whose blindness was the gift of a limitless vision.

The telescope towered above him. The fire roared inside the stove. He held the book open a little longer, until, slipping deeply into desolation and bafflement, he leaned forward and slung it into the flames. The book was consumed in seconds. And then he was still more downcast, cursing himself for the pointlessness of the gesture. He shuddered with cold, got up and crossed the cabin, where he stood and looked at the child.

More horror, more madness... In the candlelight, it was a face he'd seen before, a cold, white, puffy, vacant face: the dead Lizzie, laid out in a hospital morgue, with the sheets up to her chin so that the terrible damage to her throat shouldn't be seen. The dead Lizzie, who'd swung from the beam with the wire cutting deep, and the sleeping Zoë, who'd burned so hot and was now cooling... Their faces were the same.

Teetering on the brink of nightmare, he flung himself onto his bed and pressed his wet eyes into the pillow. But no escape. He heard the fire fizzing, and it was the fizzing he'd heard nine years ago, on this day, each time Lizzie's dangling, blood-wet legs had touched the stove. The smell of the burnt book was a nauseating memory of what he'd seen. He pushed his face harder into the pillow.

So, in the twilight of that evening, he didn't hear the arrival of a car on the gravel track by the sea wall; he didn't see the arcing of headlamps through the curtains of the cabin. He was unaware of footsteps on deck. He didn't realize that someone had come down the steps and was standing in front of the stove. When he felt the touch of a hand on his hair, he mumbled without looking up, "You should be in bed, Zoë. I'm all right. Get back into bed now, Zoë...."

When the hand remained, he emerged from the pillow and saw Helen.

The woman touched his cheeks and his lips. Without speaking, she slipped off her jacket and sat on the edge of the bed. Her perfume filled the cabin; she smelled of drink, too. When she leaned down to him, her mouth was open and hot and he felt his bones dissolve with the softness and weight of her body on him. He wanted to push his face into her blouse, where the perfume was so strong it made his head swim, where he could feel the deep womanly warmth of her in contrast to the unnatural chill of the boat. She smothered the firelight with the swinging of her sleek, dark hair... and this was all he wanted, to stop himself from remembering, from thinking, from shivering....

"Thought I'd come and see you, Harry," she whispered. "I was all on my own in that big, empty house. I got a bit pissed, to tell the truth."

She made him look at her, lifting his face up from where he was burying it into her breast. "Hey, what's the matter, Harry Clewe?" she said. "You crying or something?"

"Nothing!" he replied. "Nothing!" His throat ached with tears. "But I'm so glad you've come, Helen! You've no idea how glad I am!"

She rocked him gently, as though he were a child who'd had a dreadful nightmare, and he sobbed uncontrollably, stifling the noise against her. She held him very close.

"Glad I've come?" she said, as Harry became calm again. "You haven't seen me for months and then you burst into tears the moment I step into the room! Funny sort of glad, that is! Well, maybe you can show me how glad you are... soon."

She slid off the bed and was back again in a swift, rustling movement, with a bottle she'd picked up from under her jacket.

"Let's get you a drink first of all," she said. "Looks as though you need one. Come on, get some of this down you!"

She promptly upended a bottle of gin in the direction of his mouth. He'd swallowed several gulps before he realized what it was, while a great deal more slopped over his face and into his clothes. As he choked it back, Helen was glancing about the cabin, at the candles and the cake.

"Looks as though I've missed a party," she said. "What was the occasion? Zoë's birthday or something?"

She slapped her hand over her mouth, too late to retract her words. "Oh shit, oh shit, oh shit..." she mumbled for a moment, and then she leaned down to Harry and kissed him very softly on his eyelids and his cheeks, over and over and over again, as though she could make amends by sipping away his tears.

"I'm sorry!" she whispered, kissing him until his eyes were dry again. Squirming with embarrassment, she hid her face from him. "Forgive me, Harry! Zoë's birthday! When your wife died! Oh God, what an awful anniversary for you!"

She sat up and slid away from him, to the edge of the bed. "Well, now that I've blundered in like a clumsy great cow," she said, "do you want me to blunder out again? Do you want me to clear off and leave you to it?"

Harry smiled at her. The heat of the gin and the warmth of the woman had revived him wonderfully. On impulse, he said, "She wasn't my wife, Helen. Lizzie wasn't my wife. We weren't—"

"Whatever she was, I'm sorry," the woman said, leaning over to silence him with her fingers on his lips. "I wouldn't have come if I'd known what day it was and how wretched you must be feeling. It's none of my business whether you and Lizzie were married or not. I'd assumed you were, like everyone else must have done. I suppose that's why Lizzie took your surname. Anyway, whatever the reason for her doing that, you loved her, she loved you, and you've got Zoë to show for it.... Now, tell me straight, Harry. Do you want me to stay, or shall I clear off and leave you alone?"

Driven to confide in her, to bring this hot, fragrant woman even closer to him, he blurted, "But Lizzie didn't take my surname, Helen! That was her name! Her real name was Lizzie Clewe! She was—"

To stop him from talking, Helen upended the bottle again, more accurately this time. Harry swallowed his words with a mouthful of gin. Indescribably grateful, he succumbed to it and to her.

The gin and the perfume went straight to his head. Indeed, they flooded his body with a sudden heat. Amid gusts of muffled giggling, the bottle held up by one for the other to drink, while they stifled their laughter by holding their faces against one another's clothing, Harry and Helen tumbled more vigorously on the bed. They drank, they giggled, they whispered, they fumbled at buttons and belts. The smothering of laughter made them mad. The candlelight, the firelight, the giddying perfume, the splashing of gin, the excitement of trying not to waken Zoë... it made their lust more wonderfully furtive. Soon, most of their clothes were on the floor. Noisier and noisier, they were past caring, too engrossed to notice that Zoë had got out of bed. Until, as Harry appraised the smoothness of Helen's naked shoulders, he saw the child's stealthy movement in the corner of the cabin.

"Helen! Sssh!" he said sharply. "Hang on a moment! It's Zoë!"

The woman rolled off him. Out of breath, they lay and watched as the child emerged from behind her curtain and moved from wall to wall, her fingers on the blobs of glue. Harry sighed with relief.

"Good," he said. "She's asleep. She's sleepwalking. She does it quite a lot." He wriggled away from the woman and stood up. "She's miles away. I'll put her back to bed."

The child froze in the middle of the cabin. She was sniffing like a rat, her nostrils twitching. With some difficulty, Harry maneuvered her, so small and soft in her cotton pajamas, through the curtain and onto her bed. Sitting her down, he swung her legs up and covered her with a blanket before she could resist. She relaxed and lay still, exhaling noisily, although she wrinkled her nose and frowned before she was settled again. And she was Lizzie, the dead-cold Lizzie, as soon as Harry pulled the sheet to her chin.... He was shivering when he rejoined Helen.

"What the hell was she doing?" the woman asked him. "And what the hell have you done to this place, with all this gloomy paint and bits of stuff stuck on the walls?"

Before he could answer, she pulled him close and shook her head so hard that her hair flicked on his face.

"No, don't tell me, Harry Clewe!" she said. "Some crazy scheme or other, I suppose! More importantly, what were we doing? Let's get out of all these things...."

They threw away the rest of their clothes. She sat astride him, spread all her body on his and dangled her breasts on his face, dancing her nipples on his mouth and his eyelids. She lowered her lips onto his lips, touched his tongue with hers. Then, stretching to the floor beside the bed, she felt for her handbag and took out a tube of lotion. She squeezed it onto the palm of his left hand and massaged it into his fingers, his palm, his knuckles, until his entire hand and wrist were lubricated.

"Will you, Harry?" she whispered. "Like you used to?"

So she rolled off him and lay back, with her head on the pillow. Harry leaned over her. Gently at first, pushing harder and harder, he eased his hand inside her. After the initial penetration of the fingers, there was a resistance until he timed his pushes to the woman's breathing, and he slid into her. She closed tightly on his wrist. He watched her face, how she grimaced, how her eyes squeezed shut, how her mouth worked fast and silently. He bunched his fist inside her. That was all he had to do. He waited. It excited him enormously, the clench of her muscles, so hot and strong and gripped, as though she must crush his hand. With the flames of the fire on his back and buttocks, he leaned over her and waited for the beginning of the contraction which would start a sudden, slippery expulsion.

At the same time, the woman gave voice. A moan broke from her lips, became a rhythmic grunting. Her breasts and her belly were beaded with sweat, and, as Harry put down his tongue to taste her, her cries grew louder and louder. "Oh yes yes yes... Oh yes oh yes oh yes...!" At last, she forced out his hand with a spasm which arched her body from the bed.

For a moment, the man and the woman were blinded by the emotion of that climax. They shuddered together. His hand lay on the inside of her thigh, steaming and sticky and quite newborn. But only for a moment, as Helen's ecstatic "Yes yes yes!" was echoed by a yell from the other corner of the *Ozymandias*.

"No no no! No!"

Zoë sprang across the cabin. She lunged with all her weight and butted her father in the back. As Helen leaped up, her breasts wet and hot on Harry's face, the child rammed her into the wall on the further side of the bed. Harry tumbled onto the floor. Zoë flew at the woman, who was winded by orgasm and stunned by the unexpectedness of the attack. There was a bedlam of shrieking and spitting.

Catlike, Zoë raked with her claws, tearing at Helen's eyes and hair. The child screamed a torrent of guttural gibberish, fragments of ugly words and harsh noises. Helen shouted, as she parried the blows and lashed out with her hands and feet, "Get her off me, Harry, for Christ's sake! What's the matter with her? She's crazy! Get her off me!"

But, befuddled by drink and the soporific aftermath of Helen's climax, Harry watched as though it were a dream he was having, a dream of flamelight and flailing limbs. He stood away from it, away from the bed, and he could feel the warmth of the stove on his legs. It was an extraordinary spectacle. In the flickering of nine birthday cake candles, there was a fight going on, on his bed: a little girl in pink pajamas was biting and punching at the full, white, shining body of a naked woman... the woman was yelping, welted with blood which smeared on the child's pajamas... a tiny, silvery head was butting and banging into the woman's face... the woman was yelling, slick with sweat; the child was spitting and snarling....

To Harry, it seemed like an hour, a long, long dream he was having, but it must have been seconds before Helen was on top of Zoë, straddling her in the same way she'd been straddling the man a few moments before. She heaved, streaked with blood. Her breasts lifted and shuddered over the pinioned girl. Woman and child remained in a panting silence, the conflict halted.

Zoë lay still, unable to move. She stared up at Helen. She laughed without making a sound.

"Christ! Is she crazy or something?" Helen spluttered. She turned to Harry. "Well, she's your fucking daughter, for Christ's sake! What are you going to do with her? Or am I going to sit like this for the rest of the night?"

The moment she eased her grip on the child, Zoë writhed a claw in the direction of the woman's face. Helen recoiled from it and then bore down with all her weight.

"See?" she shouted. "She's poison! No wonder Lizzie took one look at what she'd got and then strung herself up! Who'd want a fucking monster like this one! Don't just stand there, Harry! Come and help me!"

Another commotion broke out. As Helen released her grip so that Harry could take over, Zoë landed a blow on the side of the woman's head, drawing blood from a long scratch, tearing out a fistful of dark hair. The three of them, man and woman and child, wrestled across the cabin. Helen, sobbing with anger, returned a slap on Zoë's cheek, so that at last Harry was roused from his dreamy appraisal of the scene and was himself enflamed with anger.

"You don't bloody hit her!" he bellowed at Helen, dragging her and his daughter in the vague direction of Zoë's bed. The child screamed high and loud and stared wildly around her, her face marked red with the slap. She lashed and kicked indiscriminately. Helen wept, her body scored with scratches, her eyes smudged with tears. Harry cursed the child, who was quite hysterical, and he cursed the woman as well. In this way, two naked, sweaty adults maneuvered a screeching, writhing, blind nine-year-old girl from one corner of the cabin to another.

"Now what?" the woman shouted. "Now what, for fuck's sake?"

Having no idea what else to do, Harry blurted the first thing that came to him. "The telescope! Let's get her to the telescope! I'll hold her! Get your tights, Helen! Quickly now! Get them!"

Helen groped on the floor, while Harry restrained the child. Zoë's strength was phenomenal. The energy blazed inside her, although her skin was so cold. Unraveling the tights which he'd so tenderly peeled from the woman a few minutes before, Harry bound them as hard as he could around the little girl's wrists, knotting her to the mounting of the telescope. It was a nightmare. The man and the woman were drunk, dazed by candlelight and orgasm. Zoë was insane. They secured her to the telescope and stood back, panting.

The child fell silent. She eyed them.

"What is she?" the woman was whispering. She struggled to control her breath, to control her sobbing. "What the fuck is she? What's she trying to do? No wonder Lizzie killed herself! She must have known something was wrong, right from the moment the thing was born! What is she, Harry?"

"I was going to tell you, Helen," he was saying, although the woman, smearing the tears from her cheeks, had already bent away from him and was starting to retrieve her scattered clothing. "I was going to tell you. For Christ's sake listen to me, will you? Listen to me!"

He heaved the woman upright, gripping her arms so hard that she squealed with pain. She wriggled, she tossed her hair, she rolled her eyes, as hysterical as the child had been, until Harry fetched her a slap like a whiplash on the side of her face. She stared at him, aghast at the blow. Holding her so close to him that their foreheads and noses nearly touched, he bellowed at her through clenched teeth.

"Listen, Helen! Listen! I was trying to tell you the reason for everything! We were brother and sister, Lizzie and me! Harry and Lizzie Clewe! Brother and sister! That's why Lizzie killed herself, for the guilt she couldn't stand! And that's why the child's blind, because of the blood in her, the inbreeding! That's why Zoë's the way she is! She killed Lizzie, as good as murdered her, and now she's trying to kill me! We were brother and sister, Lizzie and me! Do you hear what I'm saying to you?"

The woman went limp. There was a long silence, broken only by the crackle of the stove. Then Zoë started chuckling, a chuckle like the noise the jackdaw used to make. At this, Helen blinked very hard. She stared around her and into Harry's face as though she were trying to work out whether the place and the man were real or just part of a particularly unpleasant dream she was having.

"Brother and sister?" she said at last. "You and Lizzie?"

She'd heard the words, but her mind was struggling to make sense of them. She glanced from Harry to the giggling girl, and to the beam above her head which was scored so deeply. She was beginning to understand. She spoke very slowly, panting.

"I thought you were man and wife," she said. "Everybody must have thought so. Your secret, your guilty secret, until, with a baby coming, Lizzie couldn't stand it any more. So that's why she did it. She couldn't live with it, so she... Oh, Christ! And Zoë, born blind... is that something that happens? Oh, Christ, I'm starting to see it now!"

Her words tailed off. Zoë had stopped giggling. She hung on the telescope, her face white, her lips blue, and the grin on her mouth was cold and hard. Still naked, Helen drifted across the cabin. Tentatively, as though daring to stroke a dangerous animal, she reached out to touch the child's head. Zoë watched the hand come closer and closer, and then she snarled like a stoat. The woman recoiled with a shiver.

"Starting to see, Aunty Helen?" the child hissed. "That's a good one! Starting to see!" She giggled again, a horrid rattling in her throat, but the effort was too great for her. Her strength, her life, was almost extinguished.

Helen grabbed her clothes. Without pausing to put them on, she bundled them under her arm and made for the cabin door. Frightened beyond words, she bolted on deck and sprang onto the sea wall. Harry followed her, too slow to try and stop her from leaving. He saw her naked figure in the summer twilight, as she fumbled with her car door, as she slung her clothes inside, as she jumped in and started the engine. She maneuvered to turn the car round, throwing up gravel as the tires spun.

Harry was helpless to prevent her. He stood naked on the deck of the *Ozymandias* and he shouted, sobbing and wringing the words out until his chest was aching and his throat burning with tears. "We loved one another! I loved Lizzie! She loved me! What was wrong with that? Why should we be punished for it? Why? We loved one another!"

He sank to his knees, weeping, as Helen drove wildly away.

22

Harry must have stayed like that for ten minutes or fifteen minutes or half an hour. At last, when he came to himself, he stared around at the darkening estuary.

It was the same summer's night as the one, nine years ago, when he'd cycled into town to telephone the hospital about Lizzie's imminent delivery. Exactly the same. It was warm and still. The tide was up, stirring softly in the weed on the foreshore, high enough to move the grass on the edge of the track. Very gently, the *Ozymandias* rose and fell. The stars were veiled in a haze of cloud. The only sounds were the cries of the curlew, somewhere in the distant dunes, and the fluting of a blackbird in the hedgerow. A lovely night. The lights of the town glowed in the northern sky. High above the ocean, a shooting star flared and faded and fell to the horizon.

The same night. As Harry knelt on the deck of the boat, he wondered whether it had all been a terrible dream. Now, if he went below, he would find that Lizzie was there, that the baby was due, and he would cycle to town to phone for help... then back to the *Ozymandias* in time for the ambulance to arrive. They could go to the hospital together, and everything would be all right. Yes, he'd imagined it all. What a dream he'd had! What a nightmare!

But two things told him he wasn't dreaming, that the nightmare had been real and he was still inside it. First of all, he was stark naked. And then, from the cabin below, he heard the sound of breaking glass....

Harry stood up. He inhaled very deeply. Steeling himself for what he might find, he tiptoed downstairs.

The cabin was in darkness. The candles were out. Peering into the shadows, he saw the dull red embers of the dying fire. A flame fluttered in the stove, enough for him to see that Zoë was no longer bound to the telescope; he made out its looming shape, the glint of it, the tights still knotted on the mounting. But no Zoë. He strained his eyes for a movement, strained his ears for a sound. There was neither.

"Zoë?" he whispered. "Zoë? Are you there?"

Silence. The flicker of the fire. The pungency of dead candles. The lingering perfume. No sound.

"Zoë? Where are you, Zoë?"

He stepped forward one pace. Something crackled under the soles of his bare feet, and he gasped with pain. Gingerly, he took another step. The floor was littered with broken glass.

He limped to the bed to avoid cutting himself more, and, at the same time, as the firelight flared and lit the room, Zoë appeared from her corner. She saw her father, naked and nursing his feet, and she smiled as she moved toward the stove. She was barefooted too, but she didn't wince as she trod on the splinters of glass. They crunched with every step, until she stopped and reached up to the barrel of the telescope.

"I broke this as well, Daddy," she hissed, the smile set hard on her face. "Like I broke the seashells. They were silly, weren't they? And this was silly too. You couldn't really see anything in it, could you, Daddy? Well? Could you?"

She tilted the tube. An avalanche of glass fragments slid out. They flashed in the light from the stove, a fusion of fire and ice.

"I used this again, Daddy!" she whispered. "Like I used it on the seashells!" She brandished the hatchet at him.

He looked away from her glittering face. Her eyes were too bright for him. He threw a glance at her most recent wreckage, the telescope which drooped its head and shed its tears of ice; at the walls too, where, with the same hatchet, she'd smashed the seashell stars. In the darkness of the cabin, the embers of the fire lit up the little girl's hair She gazed at him, this child whose eyes were so cold and whose skin was so cold. She was ice, with only a wasting core of fire.

He heard himself whisper, his voice distant and disembodied. "Who are you, Zoë? What are you? Are you awake or asleep? Are you alive or dead?"

She blinked at him.

"Why did you come here?" he whispered. "To punish us? For the wrong we did? Was it wrong?"

She blinked at him.

More loudly, he said, "Have you done enough, Zoë? Wasn't it enough for you, what you did to your mother? Are you finished now?"

The child frowned. She shivered so hard that she almost dropped the hatchet. A spasm took hold of her and rattled her bones. In a kind of fit, her lips went blue, a froth of foam appeared on her mouth, and she squeezed her eyes shut for a second or two. Zoë didn't answer any of his questions. Instead, when she opened her eyes, she was smiling again, a thin, cold smile. She beamed those eyes which were no longer blind. Licking the spittle from her lips, she hissed a plume of frosty breath. She hefted the hatchet in both hands and sprang at him.

In this final hour, awake or asleep, alive or dead, Zoë possessed a terrible strength. It was too much for Harry Clewe. She was no longer a child. Perhaps she'd never been a child. She was a mad thing, which screamed and frothed and spat. The nightmare was here, in the cabin of the *Ozymandias*.

Harry rolled from the bed and recoiled from the thing which was attacking him. He leaped from her, and his flesh was scorched on the stove. His feet were flayed. He scrambled behind the telescope, heard the clang of the hatchet on the mounting as he avoided an arcing blow, as he ducked from the hiss of the blade. Crying out, her face contorted to a mask in which the eyes blazed white, Zoë pursued him to every shadow of the room, from the darkness to the light and into darkness again. The nightmare was endless. Her mask was before him, the ice of her breath was on his naked skin, the flecks of her spittle on his mouth.

The cabin lunged. The fire flared into tumbling sparks. There was no sensation of time: this was a dream from which he couldn't wake. When he stumbled, when he fell to the floor with his arms held out to lessen the impact, Zoë was above him and the axe was raised high....

The blade came down. With a whoop of manic laughter, Zoë struck with all the dregs of her strength. The hatchet hit Harry's wrist. The blade embedded in the floor of the cabin. And his hand, his left hand, was severed from him.

No pain. But a starving cold which pounced on him and gnawed at his bones. Blood spurted from his shattered wrist, gobbets of blood which pumped with the rhythm of his pulse.

No pain. But a draining of heat and a flooding with cold. A lot of blood. His body was no longer white, but glistening red.

No pain. But a feeling of overwhelming puzzlement. He gazed about in a stupor, while the cabin swam and swayed.

He noticed how Zoë staggered from him, clutching the hatchet which she'd tugged out of the floorboards, how she looked down at her blood-spattered pajamas, how she looked around the room and frowned into the darkness. Zoë was shivering too. The cold was too much. She stooped to the floor and picked up her father's hand. She sniffed it, grimaced horribly, and tossed it into the stove, where the wetness of blood and the stickiness from inside the woman began to hiss. Harry watched, disinterested, as the hand blistered and crisped. The fingers curled into a fist. Suddenly, it crackled into flames. It blackened and charred in the embers of the fire.

Zoë moved up the steps of the cabin with enormous weariness, trailing the weight of the hatchet and bumping its bloody blade behind her. He heard her leaden footsteps on the deck. Then there was silence.

Harry Clewe slouched on the floor with his head on the bed, stark naked, drunk, ice cold in a pool of cooling blood. Perhaps he was dying. His eyes were closing. Just as they were about to shut, he made out the scar on the beam above him. It was barely visible in the fading firelight, only a hairline crack... but enough to rescue him from sleep and certain death. It was where Zoë had murdered Lizzie. Nine years before, nine years to the minute, the nightmare had started there.

And now that Zoë was cooling, now that the bright hot star was dying, Harry was startled into the realization that she would take him with her, unless... unless he could... unless he could stir himself and save himself. No one else would save him. He was on his own. He must move or be Zoë's final victim.

With a colossal effort, he heaved himself up and managed to slump on the side of the bed. Then, with his knees in the blood, where the fragments of the lenses gleamed like rubies, he dragged himself to the telescope and tugged at the tights which were knotted there. He undid them with the fingers of his right hand. Racked with a killing cold, shaking uncontrollably, pulsing rosettes of blood from his left wrist, he fumbled in the drawers of the bookcase... and, yes, they were still there, the remaining three strings he'd unwound from the cello before he'd smashed the thing to splinters and fed it to the fire. He collapsed on the bed again, with the tights and the sinuous strings.

He did it, somehow, without being conscious of how he was doing it. His instinct to survive was so strong, his instinct not to be beaten by Zoë. His instinct to escape the nightmare.

He improvised a tourniquet, padding the thickest of the cello strings by winding it inside the tights, looping it round and round his forearm and knotting it as tightly as he could by tugging with his teeth. That was the best he could do.

He tore a blanket off the bed and flung it round his shoulders. The warmth of it and the woman's lingering perfume flooded his senses. A wonderful oblivion beckoned... the oblivion of sleep. It almost overwhelmed him, the need to lie down, to fall backward and roll himself into as small and safe a ball as he could, the need to sleep... the sleep of death....

He fought it off. With a wild cry, he forced himself to stare at the beam again, at the scar on the beam. Deliberately, to fire himself with rage, he conjured a vision of the Lizzie he'd seen, dangling, gurgling, garroted, dead....

He must not sleep! He would die if he slept! Again, as it had spurred him into action with the improvised tourniquet, an instinct to survive surged through him. He wasn't dead! He need not die! Inhaling sharply, exhilarated by the icy air in his nostrils, he ground his teeth so hard that the sound was loud inside his head. He forced himself to move, in spite of the pain in all his limbs, and felt the beating of blood which might warm him and save him. His body came alive. He'd looked at death. The sleep of death had been on him. Now he shook it vigorously off and swung his legs to the floor.

Crunching on the shattered glass, clutching the blanket round his shoulders, he clambered to the deck. The movement began a terrible throbbing in his arm, an agony he could hardly bear. He jammed the stump, stanched by the binding of nylon and wire, into his right armpit. The throbbing eased and he gritted his teeth against it.

To his great surprise, the night air was much warmer than the air in the cabin. The cloud had lifted. A sliver of moon lit the sky. He squinted the length of the boat.

Zoë was there. She was standing on the edge of the deck. She was finished. She drooped, she wilted. There was no life in her. In the pale moonlight, he could make out her fragile form, silhouetted on the silver sea, and he saw how thin she was, so wasted, so worn. She was a shell of the boiling bright child she'd been.

"Zoë?" he whispered. "Little Zoë?"

She turned to him, but he couldn't see her face. She had her back to the only light in the sky, and her eyes were so dead that there was no light in them. She might have been smiling, but he couldn't see her mouth.

"Zoë? What have you done to me?"

He moved his knotted stump from under his arm. There was a pain in it like fire, as though the stump were a flaming torch he could brandish, as though his whole body were in flames.

"What did you do to me, Zoë? Look, Zoë! Look what you've done to me!" He gestured at her with the throbbing, oozing piece of arm.

And suddenly, the last thing he would have expected, he felt laughter inside him. It began in his belly, warm and good, and bubbled into his chest. Its energy coursed through him. Renewed with a triumphant, hysterical strength, he tasted the laughter in his throat. It burst from him like a shout. He cackled uncontrollably and he reeled toward Zoë. The blanket fell from his shoulders. Naked, bloody, he shook the stump above his head.

"I'm not dead!" he bellowed. "I'm not! You killed your mother but you couldn't kill me! Look at me! Look at this! I'm still alive! You can see it! You can touch it! You can feel it! You can feel how fucking hot it is!"

He jabbed the stump at the darkness where her face should have been, at the dead, cold smile that smelled of deadness. At the dead eyes, dead and empty...

She recoiled from it, retreating a step or two. He struck at her with the wrist, dangling its bracelet of wire and nylon. He aimed at the place where her eyes should be. Roaring, guffawing, shaking with laughter, he drove her backward with a series of blows, and his hot new blood was on her, with each squelching impact. She offered no resistance. She didn't cry out. She retreated, while Harry rammed at her with the weapon she'd given him. Then she stumbled. She staggered, and the only sound she made was a tiny gasp. She tottered to the very edge of the deck, and her arms windmilled for a purchase on the air.

"Zoë! Zoë!" he cried out, seeing that the child was on the brink. "Zoë! My Zoë!"

He could have reached her. He could have snatched at her, caught hold of her pajamas or her hair. But he didn't. In that long, long second, as the child leaned from the deck and into the space that yawned beneath her, the laughter died inside him. The moonlight was on her face. There was a smile on her mouth. Her eyes, as faint and as cold as dead stars, met his.

She fell into the water. There was hardly a splash. The sea folded around her, very black and very deep. For a moment, Harry saw the whiteness of her face below the surface.... Then she was gone.

Harry tumbled from the deck of the *Ozymandias*, down the stairs into the cabin. He collapsed on the bed, shivering and numb, and swam into a drowning oblivion. He would surely have died.

But Helen saved him. She came back, less than an hour after she'd left, to see how he was coping. Appalled, nauseated, she untied the cello-string tourniquet and retied it with a faded, spotted red neckerchief she snatched from under the pillow; she wrapped Harry in blankets, bundled him into her car and raced him to hospital.

23

Harry didn't return to the shore for months and months after that. Then he came back with Helen.

It was Christmas Day, a fine, cold, sunlit afternoon. She drove him to the mooring where the *Ozymandias* had been, but the boat wasn't there any more. Harry got out of the car and walked to the edge of the sea wall, looking down to the mud where the keel used to bed when the sea level dropped. The tide was right out. The sand flats gleamed, as smooth as glass, as far as the dunes on the further side of the estuary. The air was crisp and clean. With a wave at Helen, who was staying in the car, Harry signaled his intention to climb down the ladder and onto the beach. She waved back at him, smiling, and he made his way carefully down the slimy rungs, gripping with his right hand.

In the distance, where the creeks of the river drained to the sea, he saw a great commotion of birds. A flock of gulls, mingled with jackdaws and carrion crows, was shrieking wildly, falling and rising like snow in a whirlwind. Harry crossed the foreshore, over the boulders and the weed, and walked on the hard, flat sand to see what the birds were doing.

He expected to find the skeleton of the horse, a landmark on the estuary which had been there for years; indeed, as he drew closer to the hysterical flock, he thought he could see the ribcage jutting from the sand, although the size and the shape of it were blurred by the clamoring birds. The gulls and the crows gave way to him. They beat about his head and their droppings were wet on his face and his neck. He knelt to the bones, as he'd done so many times before.

But they weren't the bones of the horse. They were the bones of the *Ozymandias*.

Nothing much left. Stripped by thieves, smashed by vandals, cut loose from the mooring... and then the sea had broken the hull into pieces. All that remained was the keel, sunk in the deep mud, and the spars, which stuck out of the sand like splintered, blackened bones. The swirling tide had made a deep pool inside the skeleton of the boat. Harry knelt to it, to see what the gulls and the crows had been after. He felt with his hand, his right hand, into the cold, green water.

Brittlestars, scores of them. The pool was alive with the writhing, spidery creatures. Closing his fist, he brought a dozen of them to the surface, into the clear, bright sunlight. The gulls were wild around him; the crows beat their sooty wings. For a while, Harry stayed there, kneeling, head down, lowering his face to the brittlestars, and he saw how blindly they groped at his fingers, how blindly they sculled in the palm of his hand. He dropped them back into the water, all but one of them, and he stood up. He would slip the creature into his pocket, take it home with Helen and hang it, surreptitiously, on the Christmas tree... in memory of Lizzie.

No. As he turned away from the wreck of the boat, he changed his mind. Lizzie was gone. Zoë was gone. The *Ozymandias* was all but gone. The nightmare was over. He had a new life with Helen, in her fine, warm house: their home. So he crouched again and flicked the brittlestar into the pool. The water folded around it. It sank and disappeared.

Harry walked to the foreshore. He reached the ladder and climbed, with some difficulty, onto the sea wall. He got into the car and he kissed the soft, fragrant woman who was waiting for him.

"Let's go home, Helen," he said. "It's all finished here. It's all gone. Home's the place to be at Christmas."

She turned the car round. They drove away from the shore and the gleaming sands, where the birds were at work in the bones of the boat.

PART FOUR
ammonite

1

At last the sea came into the house.

It slithered under the door. Then it burst the door wide open. There was nothing Harry Clewe could do, as wave after wave of brown water, heavy with sand and mud, broke into the downstairs rooms.

All afternoon, the storm had driven the tide inland, over the foreshore, through the hedges, filling the ditches until the fields were flooded. Harry watched from an upstairs window as the sea came closer and closer. The day grew dark at three o'clock, a twilight of howling wind and lashing rain. He saw the waves pour into the drainage ditches and fill the dew pond. He felt the wind grow stronger and stronger, rattling the slates of the roof and making the chimneys shudder. Still the tide kept rising. At four o'clock, seeing in the whirling gloom that the fields were entirely submerged, he went down the staircase and into the hallway in time to see the tide force its way under the front door and surge toward him. The door splintered and burst open. A few minutes later, all the downstairs rooms were slopping with deepening water.

Harry was tired. His hips were hurting. But he splashed from room to room to watch what the sea was doing inside his house. The lights had gone out. He took a torch and trod through the darkened hallway and into the living room, flashing the beam around him. There was a shrieking din of wind and rain, as though, not satisfied with driving the tide this far inland for the first time in living memory, the storm was trying to shake the house to pieces. The living room shutters, which he'd closed and bolted at midday, rattled so hard at the tall windows that he thought they would shatter and fly open. The gale howled into the house, once the front door was broken by the weight of the sea, tearing pictures from the walls and books from their shelves. The water was up to his knees, a sucking current which rammed his legs with pieces of driftwood and entangled him with weed.

He waded to the fireplace and beamed the torch from wall to wall, at the chop of the waves which tugged at the grandfather clock and slopped at the legs of the piano. To balance himself, he grabbed at the mantelpiece; on it, he felt the photograph of Helen and the cold, smooth contours of an ammonite she'd found on their honeymoon, years ago. With difficulty, afraid that he might stumble and fall, he waded back to the hallway and into the dining room, where the water was rough enough to start moving the chairs around the table; then to the drawing room, where the books had been blown from his desk and scattered across the surface of the flood.

There was nothing he could do about it. He stepped onto the staircase and switched the torch off. The wind came straight off the sea, over the fields, through the front door and into his face. He was drenched and very cold, but he sat in the roaring darkness, hearing the smash of the waves on the walls of the house, enduring the sting of salt on his cheeks.

Harry sat on the stairs all night. The tide showed no sign of turning and falling. His house was in the sea. The sea was in his house. At last he went up to the landing, where his dogs were bristling like a pair of great black bears, shut himself in his room and climbed into bed.

From there, even with the blankets pulled over his head and the heavy, warm weight of the dogs beside him, he could still hear the sea downstairs: as though a huge, drunken, furious thief was ransacking the rooms, slamming doors, flinging furniture, smashing and looting and wrecking.

At dawn, when the storm abated and the noises stopped, Harry slept a little.

The flood tides had been forecast for a long time. Harry had heard all about them on his radio. However, unlike hundreds of people along the coast of Wales who'd left their homes in the towns and villages most threatened by high water, he'd decided not to move. Already, that autumn, the tide had come over the beach and into his fields, drowning the ditches, bleaching the grass, tangling the hedges with driftwood and seaweed. Day by day, he'd seen the water come closer and closer. The radio had told him that soon the biggest of all tides would be blown inland. Now the storm had driven the sea into his house.

Harry Clewe was fifty-three years old. He'd become stout and red-faced; his gingery hair had turned peppery gray, grown wild and bushy. Where his left hand had been, he had a black iron hook. He was hard of hearing, short-sighted, short of breath, and, as the pain in his hips got worse, increasingly bad-tempered. His dogs were bad-tempered as well: Gog and Magog were enormous, shaggy, coal-black mongrels, as massive-headed as Great Danes and as thick-set as Rottweilers. Harry had lived alone with them for ten years, through the 1980s and into the 1990s, since they were gluttonous puppies. Since Helen had gone.

In the meantime he'd done nothing to maintain the house. Long before the storm, there were slates off the roof and cracks in the chimneys wide enough for the jackdaws to nest in; he'd closed the living room, the drawing room and the dining room, each with their corniced ceilings, their exquisite oak paneling and marble fireplaces, leaving them chill and dark; he'd shut the biggest of the bedrooms, too. He and the dogs had retreated to the kitchen, kept warm by a wood-burning stove, and to a spare bedroom upstairs with a driftwood fire and a view across the flat, bare fields to the sea.

The house, called Ynys Elyrch, was the one that Helen had bought when she'd come to Wales after her divorce. It was a fine, big house. But the name, meaning "the island of swans," was inaccurate. It wasn't built on an island: it stood on a spit on the edge of the estuary, only a few miles from where the *Ozymandias* had been moored, isolated from the rising ground inland. There were no swans: they never came to the shore or the fields, although a flock of them roosted in the salt marsh on the other side of the estuary.

Harry had moved in with Helen as soon as he'd come out of hospital. She'd insisted on it, and he'd been glad to submit to her. Without consulting him, indeed while he was still in intensive care, she'd taken it upon herself to get all his belongings out of the boat and into her house, spending hours on her own at the *Ozymandias*, shifting his books and pictures and bedding into the boot of the Daimler and driving them to Ynys Elyrch. Once he was home with her, she'd nursed him back to health. She grew to love him; he was fond of her. Indeed, they'd married, Helen insisting on the white wedding that her first husband had denied her. For a year they'd lived together in her fine, big house.

But then, Helen was gone. Harry Clewe was alone with the dogs.

Bit by bit, year by year, he'd sold acres of land and a number of barns, until all he had left was the neglected house, a few dilapidated stables round a cobbled yard, and the rank, treeless fields which separated the property from the beach. Harry had no disposable money; Helen had spent most of her settlement on Ynys Elyrch, but the threat of flood tides had made it a poor investment. There were no other houses for miles around. For the last ten years, Harry had lived in decaying isolation... ever since Helen had gone.

Now, the morning after the storm, he came downstairs to find a state of chaotic disorder. The floors of every room were deep in silted sand and oozing brown mud. A scree of pebbles had been left behind, banked into corners, raked and swirled by the falling tide. There was seaweed everywhere, the knotted black clumps of bladderwrack and the salad leaves of kelp; dead birds, tangled and broken and sodden; the huge, translucent, rubbery remains of jellyfish; all kinds of plastic, polythene and rotten driftwood. The skirtings were buckled and the paneling had split. Some of the furniture had been turned over. Pictures and photographs lay in the pools of water which hadn't drained out of the house as the tide went down. Books were strewn about. The rain had stopped and the wind had decreased, but the shutters banged and the doors dangled on broken hinges.

Harry spent the day trying to tidy up, although he knew that the sea would come into the house again; he'd heard on his radio that, further along the coast, at Rhyl and Towyn, the storm had breached the sea walls and flooded the towns. The coastguards from Caernarfon came to see him, churning across the waterlogged fields in a Land Rover and driving into the cobbled yard; but they soon gave up trying to persuade him to leave his house and go with them to emergency accommodation inland. He was a stubborn old fool; he was rude and ungrateful. The coastguards had plenty of work elsewhere, with people who wanted to be helped. Glancing warily at his glinting iron hook, they warned him to expect worse storms, jumped back into their Land Rover as the dogs lunged toward them, and they drove away.

When the coastguards had gone, Harry stomped across the yard to the shed where the Daimler stood. The big, silver car hadn't moved for years. It was riddled with rust. The tires were punctured and perished. But when he opened the driver's door, the interior smelled dry and strangely warm. He climbed in, pulling the door shut with a gentle thud, and he sat at the wheel for a few minutes. It was a quiet, still place. He blew the dust off the clock and the speedometer; he stroked the walnut dashboard; he inhaled the scent of the soft, red leather upholstery. It reminded him of a car he'd had, long ago, when he'd first come to Wales; more than that, it reminded him of Helen and the short time they'd spent together. He thought he could smell her perfume.

At last, blinking himself out of his daydream, he remembered why he'd gone to the car: he leaned into the back seat and rummaged for the spade, the rake and the pitchfork among the other tools he kept there, and he climbed out of the car with them. That was all the Daimler was good for nowadays, as a kind of tool shed, because it was dry inside. He carried the tools back to the house.

Gog and Magog climbed the stairs to the landing and flopped down. They watched as Harry shoveled the mud and sand through the front door, as he raked out the seaweed and the litter of dead birds, as he speared the jellyfish with the pitchfork and lifted them outside. He'd adapted to his disability; indeed, he used the hook as a versatile tool. He hammered boards across the broken front door and nailed the shutters into the window frames. Resting from time to time, he splashed through the living room and leaned at the fireplace, where he stared at Helen's photograph on the mantelpiece. He'd taken the picture himself, on their honeymoon in Lyme Regis. Dark and sleek and beautiful, she was clutching an ammonite she'd found on the beach, although the fossil was so heavy she could hardly hold it for more than a few seconds. Next to the photograph was the ammonite itself. Sometimes Harry would take it from the mantelpiece, heft it in his hand and try to imagine the warmth of the woman in the dead, cold stone.

Back to work. He had an idea to make the job easier. He pulled up the carpet, which was heavy with sand, and rolled it aside, thinking to open the trap door in the floorboards and simply shovel the rest of the debris into the cellar. The cellar was very deep; it was years since he'd looked into it. Now he knelt and peered into the blackness under the living room floor. He flashed his torch. The cellar had filled with water. Holding his breath, he strained his eyes and ears at the glistening darkness. He gagged at the blast of dead, cold air which came up and slapped him in the face, a clammy, rotten smell which seemed to suck the breath from him. He shivered so hard that he almost dropped the torch. Something was moving down there... he thought he could hear it, he thought he could see it.

Suddenly so frightened that his scalp prickled and his heart began to thump, he recoiled from the hole, slammed the trap door shut, scrambled to his feet, threw down the torch, grabbed the shovel and flung sand and shingle on top of the trap door as fast as he could... to keep it closed.

At last he stopped, breathing very hard, staring wildly around at the disordered room. When the blood had stopped pounding in his ears, he listened again, cocking his head at the floor. He thought he heard something knocking down there. But it was only the slopping of deep, black water.

2

The storms continued through October and into November, driving bigger and bigger tides ashore. The waves forced over the fields; they tore up the hedges, broke down the walls and left the grass whitened by salt and the scouring of sand. All day and all night, at high or low water, the wind hurtled off the sea. It was very cold. The sky was gray, boiling with black cloud.

Harry's efforts to barricade the house proved futile. The front door burst open as soon as the sea leaned on it, and the waves poured into the hallway. Again and again, all the rooms were flooded. The water came higher and the gales grew stronger, until the shutters blew in, the windows exploded in splinters of flying glass and the storm roared into the house more fiercely than ever before. The tide slopped up to the third step on the handsome staircase; another night it slopped at the fourth; then the fifth. The cellar boomed, filling with water which forced up the floorboards so hard that the trap door would open and shut with a sudden, startling report. It was no good trying to keep the sea outside or clearing the debris once the tide had gone down. So Harry surrendered the ground floor of the house completely.

The rooms filled up with deeper sand and bigger banks of pebbles, forming pools which didn't drain when the sea receded. Soon, the living room, the drawing room and the dining room were part of the foreshore, bizarrely furnished with tables, chairs, grandfather clock and piano. Furthermore, the sea began a systematic removal job, the better to occupy the house with the things it wanted....

Coming downstairs after another night of huddling under the bedcovers, Harry found that most of the furniture had been carried outside. Tables and chairs had been lifted up, swirled about, floated through the hallway and sucked out of the front door by the falling tide. They were dumped in the fields. His books were scattered in the hedges. See-ing that the grandfather clock was missing, he waded through the mud and the debris until he found it floating in a deep ditch, a hundred yards from the house. Even the piano was shifted, a foot here, a foot there, out of the living room and into the hall, until it stuck in the front door.

Harry didn't care. Like the Daimler, these things were relics of a different life. It had been a fine grandfather clock, a longcase in oak banded with mahogany, made by James Berry in Pontefract in 1774; a solemn moon and a smiling sun rotated above the clock face; its chiming, ev-ery fifteen minutes of every hour of every day, had marked the progress of Harry's gentle convalescence once Helen had settled him into her home. For him, the sound had been part of the house, as much as the scent of polish and cut flowers. The piano was a Bechstein baby grand, which, along with the flute, Helen had been learning to play. The trompe l'oeil painting of a blazing fire, executed with such depth of perspective on the oak paneling that it cast a glow right across the living room, was by Rex Whistler, done at the same time as the artist was working at Plas Newydd for the Marquis of Anglesey. Now it was ruined. All these things were ruined.

No matter, Harry thought: let the sea smash everything, drag out the contents of the house and replace them with the sand and stones and weed it brought in. No matter, he mumbled to himself as he stared at the wreckage. Ynys Elyrch was a trompe l'oeil. From a distance it looked like a fine, handsome house: in reality, it was a piece of the beach, for the sea to requisition and rearrange as it liked. And Harry Clewe was a trompe l'oeil as well, he thought bitterly: he looked like a man, but he was a fossil, stiff and cold, with all the life crushed out of him... as dead as the ammonite on the mantelpiece.

He waded from room to room. As well as the dead birds entangled in the weed and branches, Harry found some of them still alive: a gull, its wings broken or its legs wrapped up in plastic string, sculling around the hallway like an over-wound clockwork toy; a curlew, lying in the wreckage and panting as though its waterlogged body would burst; a duck, garroting itself with a length of fishing line. He knocked them dead with the ammonite he fetched from the living room mantelpiece and slung them to the dogs, which crunched them in their heavy jaws and swallowed them whole, beaks and feet and feathers and all.

After the wildest of storms, the house was loud with hundreds of starlings which had blown inside for shelter. Carrion crows worked through the shattered rooms for all the wounded and dying things they could find.

Another morning, there was a sheep in the flooded drawing room, matted and heaving, staring with wild, yellow eyes. Its front legs were broken. Harry slugged it with the ammonite. Replacing the fossil on the mantelpiece, he floated the sheep into the hall, maneuvered it past the Bechstein jammed in the doorway, into the yard, where he gutted it with a very sharp knife. He fetched the axe from the Daimler and dismembered the carcass. The dogs watched and waited, and then they fell on the pieces, devouring them entirely. Soon, only the fleece and the head remained, which Harry dropped into the cellar.

Such was the power of the sea. Such was the ferocity of the storm. Night after night, Harry Clewe lay in his bed, buried with Gog and Magog under the blankets, and felt the house shaking.

Harry made himself comfortable upstairs. He carried sacks of potatoes up to the landing and all the tinned and dried food he could find in the kitchen. He cooked on a little gas stove. He had boxes of candles. The spare bedroom he'd used since Helen had gone, with its narrow bed and single arm-chair, had an open fireplace; now, working through the blustery hours of daylight, he gathered armfuls of driftwood,

sawed it and split it in the yard and carried it up to the bathroom, where he stacked it in the deep, rusty bath. He would
never run out of fuel, as long as the tides brought him more
and more wood to cut and store, and there was plenty of
kindling in the furniture that the sea had smashed. One
evening, giggling at the irony of it, he prised the remains of
the Whistler from the living room wall and took it upstairs,
where, for the first and only time, the trompe l'oeil was a
real fire, casting a warm glow on his face.

All day and all night, the flames flickered in the spare
bedroom. Harry and the dogs were snug up there, however
the storm might roar, however the tide might drive into the
house, however the rain might lash his window. He rescued
a few books from the drawing room. He had his radio. He
battened himself into the little room while the house
trembled around him, while the sea swelled and surged at
the foot of the stairs.

Furthermore, Harry had a double-barreled shotgun and
boxes of cartridges. Squelching across the fields, he would
pot at the wildfowl on the shore. And then the dogs, which
could still swim strongly although they were old and arthritic, would retrieve whatever he'd hit. He gutted the birds
in his ruined hallway and fed the entrails to Gog and Magog.
In the evening, as the tide rolled over the fields and filled
the house to a depth of four or five feet, Harry and the dogs
were shut in the candle-lit bedroom. A fire blazed in the
hearth; a teal turned golden brown on a spit across the
flames; a pan of vegetables bubbled on the gas stove.

Sometimes, when the tide was up in the daylight and
Harry was in his room with dogs and fire and radio, he shot
from the landing window. And then Gog and Magog would
tumble downstairs, dive headlong into the water sloshing
in the hallway and swim powerfully through the front door
to retrieve the prize. For this reason, Harry left the gun
loaded, leaning on the landing, ready for the rafts of duck
which floated around the house.

Thus he was self-sufficient. For him, the flooding wasn't so terrible. He'd been alone for years, a recluse, avoiding other people as much as possible; now the floods made it easier to avoid them. He was rude to the coastguards when they came back in their Land Rover. When the yellow rescue helicopter from Anglesey hovered overhead, churning the water and lashing the fields, he would flap his hand and gesture with his hook as though the huge, deafening machine were no more than an irritating insect, a gigantic horsefly or a hornet, until it swerved away without bothering to try and land.

Harry had everything he wanted. He didn't want people. The floods kept them away.

3

No, not everyone. Two sorts of people came onto Harry Clewe's land: beachcombers and windsurfers. He tried hard to discourage them.

After the big tides had gone down and the fields were drained, the beachcombers wandered along the foreshore. They were families from inland who wanted an exhilarating day out with their children and dogs on a blustery beach, who sifted through the wreckage to see what they could find; or else they'd come simply to see the damage to other people's property. Spotting them from the landing window, as they struggled to pull the grandfather clock out of the ditch or tugged his dining-room chairs from the mud, Harry would stumble downstairs and hurry outside, urging his dogs to go with him.

"This is still my land!" he would roar. "And this is still my house, as long as I choose to stay in it!" Waving his hook at the wreckage of spars and furniture and washed-up rubbish, he would shout, "All these things are mine, so long as they're on my land! Bugger off and don't come back! Or the dogs'll have you!"

Gog and Magog would lunge forward, bristling and huge, so that the beachcombers scurried away.

The windsurfers were harder to see off. The first time they came, Harry was so startled by the whoosh and crackle outside his window, by the flash of a brightly-colored sail, that he leaped for his gun, imagining for a moment that some great, exotic bird was swooping around the house. He stared and stared. The dogs barked excitedly. The craft passed close to the building, the blue and yellow and purple sails rippling like flags, the boards cutting through the water like sharks; muscular figures gripped and crouched and flexed, gleaming black in skin-tight rubber suits. And, seeing the man at the upstairs window of the flooded house, the windsurfers would wave and grin at him.

Harry stared from his landing. The windsurfers were trespassing on his property. But he couldn't go out and chase them off, with the water so deep and rough around the house, and there was nothing the hounds could do. Flinging open the window, he shook his hook. Feebly, he threw potatoes as the windsurfers rushed past, but the potatoes splashed into the water. The windsurfers shrieked with laughter, scudding as close as they could to draw his fire, ducking easily, taunting him with grins and shouts.

One of them, a blond youth controlling a gorgeous purple sail, caught one of the potatoes in his outstretched hand, and, in one athletic movement, without losing his balance or speed or direction, hurled it back so hard that it burst on the wall of the house, spattering Harry with juice. Then he shouted an obscenity that Harry had never heard before and hurtled away.

So the windsurfers came back again and again, to enjoy the sport and the spectacle of the bilious, wild-haired man throwing potatoes from his window. Harry tried to ignore them. He battened himself into the upstairs room with his dogs in front of the fire.

One day in the middle of November, when the tide had gone out and left the foreshore littered with weed, Harry spotted another trespasser on his land: a slim figure in a baggy jacket and jeans and black wellington boots, bending swiftly to the things that the sea had left behind.

"A job for you two!" he said, and with his foot he woke the dogs, which were snoring very noisily on the fireside rug. They went downstairs together, across the rock pools in the hallway, squeezed past the piano which was still jammed in the front door and stepped out of the house. He kept the dogs close, holding them as tightly as he could on short chains, thinking to approach quietly and give the trespasser a surprise. The land was a mess of uprooted hedges, mounds of driftwood and seaweed, flapping black plastic bags, the littered contents of the downstairs rooms he'd abandoned to the tides. Around and about, Harry saw the potatoes he'd thrown out of the windows.

Within twenty yards of the preoccupied figure, Gog and Magog caught an unfamiliar scent and broke into a shambling run. Up to their bellies in mud, they gathered speed, dragging Harry with them. He shouted, outweighed, out of control, and the dogs snarled with a high-pitched, gurgling snarl as they strained on their chains. As a flock of starlings materialised from the weed and whirled noisily into the air, the figure on the foreshore straightened up, turned and stared in horror and started to run as well.

There was a chase across the beach, the trespasser dropping handfuls of seashells and pebbles, the man and the dogs in breathless pursuit. The four of them stumbled and slipped on the wet rocks. Gog and Magog, despite their age and weight, were nimblest. When the beachcomber cried out and tripped, sprawling headlong in a deep pool, the dogs were there at once, snarling horribly, tearing at clothes and boots to make a wounding bite.

Harry tugged with all his strength to hold the dogs off. He seized their collars with hand and hook and heaved them away from the figure in the rock pool, who was huddled face down in the knee-deep water to keep away from the dogs' teeth. Gog and Magog strained to close again, foaming, wild-eyed, until Harry knocked their heads together and they stood still.

Scrambling upright, spluttering mouthfuls of water, the beachcomber turned toward him. For a second, Harry saw a pale, young, girlish face, bleary with tears; long, dripping, blond hair; bleeding, white fingers where either the dogs must have bitten or the skin had been torn by the barnacled rocks... and then, as he restrained the animals by holding their collars, while they lunged again with all their weight, the beachcomber flicked the bleeding hands at Harry's face and turned to run off, clumsy in the big black boots and waterlogged jacket, loose-limbed like a girl.

Harry hung on to the dogs. Heaving with breathlessness, he watched the figure stumble away. At last, when he could hold the animals no longer, he let them go; too late to give chase, they sniffed at the rocks where the beachcomber had fallen. Harry knelt at the pool. There was blood on the surface of the water, which was gone as soon as the dogs splashed in.

"Well done, you ugly buggers!" he whispered. "The little bitch won't come back after that!"

He returned to the house, calling the dogs with him. They were delighted with the chase; they fanned their tails in the keen afternoon air and grinned enormously. Harry was pleased too. He went upstairs and sat by the fire, brewed some tea, listened to a play on the radio and watched from his window as the tide crossed the fields and surrounded the house.

As dusk fell, he heard the waves breaking into the hallway. All evening, in the flame-lit room, he heard the sea smashing at the foot of the stairs. In the darkness of night, the storm blasted the house so hard that the walls and the chimney seemed to quiver. The gale shrieked. The flood tide crashed and sucked. But the man and the dogs were warm and dry.

The flames burned low. It was time for bed. Harry got up to fetch some wood, to fuel the fire for warmth and comfort through the night. Shielding his candle from the gale that howled up the stairs from the gutted hallway, he crossed the landing to the bathroom, where the wood was stacked.

There he paused to look at himself in the shaving mirror. His face was deeply lined, burned by the salt wind, reddened from all the years he'd spent on the *Ozymandias* with Lizzie and then Zoë, his years at Ynys Elyrch with Helen and since Helen had gone. He peered closer. He rubbed at a smear of mud on the bridge of his nose. No, not mud...

Holding the candle to the mirror, he peered closer still. His cheeks and forehead were spattered with blood. He puzzled for a moment before he remembered the trespasser that the dogs had chased, who'd flicked at him with bleeding fingers before running off. He rinsed the blood from his face, shuddering with distaste to think that it had been there all afternoon and evening. Satisfied at last that he was clean, he picked up an armful of wood from the bath, crossed the landing to the spare room, built up the fire and climbed into bed.

For a little while, as he huddled under the blankets and squeezed his eyes shut, the beachcomber's face seemed to swim before him: distressed, angry, smeared with tears.

"Bitch," he whispered. He said it again. He rubbed at his cheeks, where the blood had spattered and dried, then he pulled the dogs closer and fell asleep.

A few days later, Harry was watching the fields from his bedroom.

He moved to the landing, opened the window as quietly as he could and reached for his shotgun, which was leaning nearby. It was already loaded. To aim more steadily, he knelt on the floor and rested the barrel on the windowsill. He squinted along it at a pair of shelduck which were paddling in the wet mud: handsome and plump, gleaming white and black and rufous in the low, winter sunshine, they waddled close to the house, slapping with their broad webbed feet and feeding in the pools of water. Sometimes the drake, a bigger bird with a knob on its red beak, stood very upright, gooselike, and scanned the field for danger.

Harry concentrated hard: the drake would be a fine dinner for him. He snuggled the butt of the gun more comfortably into his shoulder. As the shelduck moved, he moved the barrel on the windowsill so that the bird was fixed at the focus of his vision. He took a slow, deep breath and squeezed his finger on the trigger.

Too late. Suddenly the ducks were up, taking to the air after a pattering run on the waterlogged field. With short, powerful wingbeats, they made for the shore and disappeared. Something had startled them into flight.

Harry remained kneeling on the landing, squinting down the barrel of the shotgun. He swore viciously with all the breath he'd been holding in his chest. The dogs, which had been sitting behind him and staring out of the window as well, stood up and started to pace about, slobbering horribly. They knew what the noise and the smell of the gun meant, that the man would send them downstairs and into the fields for some flapping, floundering, wounded thing; and they knew they must bring it back alive and drop it into the man's hands or else they'd have their heads knocked together. But this time, after so much breathless waiting, there was no deafening explosion, no cloud of acrid smoke. So the dogs paced backward and forward. Harry peered down the gun barrel, training it over his field of vision to try and see what had disturbed the ducks.

He saw a figure in a baggy jacket and jeans and black wellington boots, splashing along the foreshore.

Harry swore again. He trained the gun on the approaching figure, just as he'd trained it on the duck. Moving the barrel as the figure moved, he snuggled the butt into his shoulder, held his breath and tightened his finger on the trigger. The figure came closer, pushed through the wreckage of the hedge, stepped over the rubbled wall, and with a short run and a jump, sprang easily across the flooded ditch... paused to look at the grandfather clock, stopped to turn over a couple of dining room chairs which were stuck in the mud, and walked toward the front of the house.

Harry locked the gun on a head of flopping blond hair. His sights wavered on a small, pale face. Suddenly finding that his chest was hurting with holding his breath so hard, and that his finger was crooked on the trigger, he swore again, scrambled to his feet and leaned the gun in its usual corner. He turned to the dogs, which were waiting with an unbearable tension for the great bang.

"Don't just stand there!" he hissed at them. "Send her off, you buggers! Go on! Send her off again!"

Shoulder to shoulder, the dogs careered downstairs. They cleared the hallway in a single leap, fought for a few seconds to squeeze past the piano and then hurtled into the yard. Harry remained on the landing. He knelt at the window to keep out of sight and he watched. His heart thudded with excitement.

He smiled to see how the trespasser looked up and stared as the great, black dogs came splashing through the front door of the house. He smiled to hear their deep, grunting barks. He grinned when he saw the trespasser's face go paler still, the mouth hang open and the eyes widen as the dogs lumbered closer.

But, to his own surprise, the figure didn't run away. As the dogs charged closer and closer, the trespasser knelt in the mud, pulled something from the pockets of the baggy jacket and met the slavering animals with a pair of the biggest and meatiest bones they'd seen since Harry had butchered the sheep he'd found in his living room. Gog and Magog slithered to a halt. They paused for a second, sniffed and hesitated and leaned forward to take the bones very gently in their mouths. Then, as the dogs flopped down in the wet grass, crunching the bones so loudly that Harry could hear them splintering as he peered from the landing window, the figure knelt closer still and fondled the animals' ears. They consented to this, growling softly.

Harry was astonished. In all the time he'd had the dogs, no one had stroked them like that. He himself was increasingly wary, now that they were as short-tempered as he was, although he'd fed them every day for the past ten years. He was rough with them; he controlled them with his voice, with his boots and stick, and by knocking their massive heads together. But he sometimes felt, by the look in their eyes and the way they bared their teeth, that their tolerance of him was a fragile, finite thing. So he stared from the upstairs window, open-mouthed with amazement, as Gog and Magog lay on the field and devoured the bones they'd been given, as the trespasser knelt between them and felt at their shaggy, black ears.

At last, Harry struggled to his feet. His knees hurt him, and so did his hips. It was a sudden, lancing pain that made him very angry. He ground his teeth, squeezed his eyes shut and growled as the spasm shot through him. Then, opening his eyes, seeing the figure outside his house who'd trespassed on his land, startled the wildfowl and was now cuddling the dogs that were supposed to be keeping trespassers away, he snorted with rage and went stumping downstairs. He forced his way past the piano. By the time he emerged from the front door, he was purple in the face and foaming at the mouth.

The trespasser glanced up and saw him. Again the eyes widened and the jaw fell open, because the man looked a great deal more dangerous than the dogs; and there was nothing in the pockets of the baggy jacket to hold out as a peace offering.

As the beachcomber stood up and turned to run away, Harry started shouting, "This is my land! These are my dogs! Why do you think you can start nosing around here? What difference does it make if the sea comes onto my land? It's still private property, isn't it? Bugger off, and don't come back!"

But the beachcomber, seeing that the dogs were too preoccupied with their bones to give chase and that the wheezing, red-faced man was incapable of more than a harmless, lumbering charge, had stopped by the flooded ditch. Harry stopped too, winded so badly that he thought he might retch. He stood with his hands on his hips, glaring. He appraised the long, blond hair and the soft, white face; the slender figure in jeans and jacket and boots.

"Bugger off and don't come back!" he spluttered. "Or the dogs'll have you! Bugger off, you nosy bitch!"

He had to stop. He could hardly breathe, let alone shout. He thought the beachcomber was going to call something in reply, because the mouth opened and shut so that Harry caught a gleam of teeth and the glistening of a wet tongue. But then the figure turned to the ditch, crossed it with an easy, coltish leap and started running toward the foreshore. The brown jacket and flopping blond hair dropped behind the remains of the hedge.

"And sod the bloody dogs!" Harry managed to croak, a feeble attempt at triumphant humour now that the trespasser had been put to flight. "Don't come back unless you bring something for me to eat next time!"

Gog and Magog had finished their bones. Even the rounded nub ends were crunched and swallowed. Harry limped to the dogs and lowered his hands toward them, to touch their ears as the beachcomber had done. But they showed their teeth. They snarled very deeply, a horrid, gurgling snarl through a mouthful of bone splinters, so that, seeing the cold, black light in their eyes, he backed away and stomped to the house.

He went up to the landing, to wait at the window with his gun. The dogs had eaten well, but he hadn't. He blasted and missed when a pair of mallard flew down to his field. He waited another hour. In the failing light of a November dusk, he blasted and missed when the widgeon came to roost. The duck clattered away, whirling into the gathering darkness to find shelter in the salt marsh on the other side of the estuary. And then it was twilight, too late to wait and try again. Disconsolate, he boiled some potatoes on the flickering flames of his diminished gas stove and ate them with a tin of sardines.

That evening, downstairs, the tide was inside his house again, breaking into the hallway and onto the staircase. It boomed in the cellar. The gale blew through the front door and the shattered windows, banging the broken shutters, smashing the remains of the door and the panelling.

Upstairs, Harry heaped his fire with driftwood; he lit a candle and turned up the radio. The dogs snored on the rug. At last he went to bed and buried himself under a mound of blankets.

But, however he tried to plug his ears, nothing would deaden the din of the storm. However tightly he squeezed his eyes closed, nothing would dim the grin of the beachcomber, the gleam of teeth and the glistening of a wet tongue.

"Bitch," he whispered a few times, before he fell asleep.

4

No one came along the shore for several days, to pick at the wreckage in the fields or to stare at the big, gray, derelict house. Even the windsurfers stayed away. Harry Clewe was alone with his dogs. No, not alone. As well as the starlings which habitually roosted in the living room, as well as the gulls which blew in with the gales, the farmyard rats were driven indoors by the floods.

They came gradually at first, so that Harry, seeing from the landing that a rat was swimming in the hallway, could blast it with the shotgun before it tried to scramble onto the stairs. Or else the dogs were dispatched to deal with it, splashing up to their bellies in sea water. Then, more and more rats sought shelter in the house. And when the tide rose higher, they started to climb the stairs. They settled in the chimney and the remains of the oak paneling; on still nights, when the wind had dropped and the sea lapped gently at the walls of the house, Harry could hear them snuffling and scratching where they'd found a quiet, warm place to hide. He tried to ignore them, although they reminded him of an earlier life he'd had, long ago, and the shocks they'd caused him.

Other creatures came in too. Among the driftwood in the bath he found a pair of hedgehogs, rolled up and fast asleep. Either he'd carried them there with an armful of branches or they'd made their own way upstairs to beat the rising water. He tried not to disturb them. He covered them with twigs and dry leaves and left them snoring gently.

There were toads burrowing under the landing carpet, and he would pick them up and hold them, to recall their rubbery squirming. There were mice in the cupboards, making nests in his clothes by shredding the material with their teeth. There were spiders, up the taps and down the plugholes. There were bats in the wardrobe, folded like soft, black leather gloves...

No, Harry wasn't alone. Whenever the wind dropped and the world was a slowly lapping, breathless place, he would sit in front of the fire and hear the house whispering around him. Surrounded by sea, it was more like a great, groaning ship than the house it had once been: more like the ark, where a man, two dogs and countless other creatures took refuge from the flood.

Something was moving in the cellar.

That night, there was a dead calm. Not a sound in the house, but the scurry of a mouse or the creak of a toad...

The fire burned low. The embers, powdered to ash, fell inwards with a sigh and a golden flare brightened the room. Then the room was dark again. Harry had been dozing all evening in front of the fire, listening to his own breathing and the breathing of the dogs and the silence of the night which had folded like a thick, black blanket around the house. The tide was very high. There was a huge, silver moon. When he stared out of the window, it seemed to him that Ynys Elyrch was the island its name implied, in a lake as smooth and as still as oil.

Not a breeze, not a ripple. The cry of a curlew far away. The snoring of the dogs. The whisper of a dying fire. The scratching of mice. A gentle, rhythmic thump, thump, thump...

He listened as hard as he could. He held his breath so long that his chest began to hurt. He hoped that the thump, thump, thump was the pulse of the blood in his temples. He strained to hear. And when he glanced down and saw that the dogs were listening too, he knew he hadn't imagined the thumping. It wasn't the sound of his own heartbeat: it was a real sound, somewhere in the house, somewhere downstairs... a gentle, insistent thudding which made his scalp prickle.

He shivered very violently, so that the dogs lifted their heads from the rug and stared at him. He knew where the thumping was coming from. He'd heard it before, in his worst and sweatiest nightmares. This time it was real. It was coming from the cellar.

Gog and Magog heaved themselves stiffly to their feet, hackles up. But Harry slipped out of the room and shut the door on them. He stood on the landing and stared down at the deep water slopping in the hallway. The moonlight beamed through the front door, past the piano, where the sea rose and fell very gently, like a beast that had slithered into the house and curled asleep at the foot of the stairs. Harry listened. The hairs on his neck stood up, as the hackles of the dogs had stood up. Again he held his breath. When he squeezed his eyes shut, he could see a piece of the dream he'd had, the nightmare which haunted him, in which the thump, thump, thump was the beat of the fear in his blood. Terrified, he flicked his eyes open again. This time the haunting was real, not a dream from which he could struggle and sweat and suddenly surface.... In a kind of trance, he started to go downstairs.

He stepped into the water, although it was icy cold and knee-deep and the footing was treacherous. Lifting his face to the moonbeam which fell through the front door, he paused to listen for the thumping again... but he knew in his heart where the sound was coming from. He turned to his right, waded across the hall and into the living room.

Again he stopped, gazing from the doorway to see how the moonlight gleamed on the surface of the water, on the silvery corpses of stranded jellyfish, on the ammonite, spiraled on the mantelpiece. Then he trod heavily into the middle of the room.

His heart seemed to burst in his chest. And as the blood in his head banged louder and louder, beating in time with the beat of the thing which was thudding under the floorboards, so the trance fell away from him. A blinding panic took over. He started to shout. He kicked at the water to shatter the stillness of the reflected moonlight, to try and block out the thumping. Hysterical with fear, yet powerless to resist being drawn to the pulse beneath his feet, he threw aside the slippery dead weights of the jellyfish, he flung handfuls of tangled weed, he plunged into the water and groped for the bolt on the trap door. Finding it at last, he shot it across, caught his hook in the ring and heaved with all his strength, roaring and roaring, unable to pull the trap door open because the weight of the sea was too much for him to lift... and all the time, although he shouted so loudly and thrashed the water to a foam, he could hear the thump, thump, thump of the thing which was moving down in the cellar.

Suddenly the trap door flew open. Harry fell backward, sitting down with a great splash. Straight away, he struggled to his knees and stared into the hole in the living room floor, peering into a current of the iciest, blackest water which welled out of the hole and swirled at his legs.

Something swam out of the cellar. It floated to the surface, bobbing toward him... a thing he'd seen in his ghastliest nightmares.

A face, a woman's face, from which the skin and the flesh had been nibbled by the fish.

No nose, but two black holes in gray bone.

No eyes, but black empty sockets writhing with eels.

No lips, no gums, but long, yellow teeth which grinned as the face broke through the surface.

A mat of filthy black hair which knotted round his fingers as he tried to pull his hands away...

With a cry of disgust, as he heaved so hard that the contents of his stomach rose into his throat, Harry staggered to his feet. Instinctively, he felt for the mantelpiece and the ammonite on it. And then, kneeling into the water again, screaming with horror and retching at the same time, he crashed and crashed at the thing which had been knocking under the floorboards, which had floated toward him when he'd opened the trap door. He smashed and smashed until the skull was stove in. And still he continued to smash. He smashed with the ammonite until he was too exhausted to lift it up. Then he dropped the fossil and knelt there, sobbing, heaving, gibbering, while the water lapped and subsided around him.

At last the pool was calm again. The moonbeam fell through the windows. It glistened on the surface of the water. It gleamed on splinters of bone and teeth.

Harry knelt in the living room for a long time: all night, because when he stood up, in great distress at the cold in his body, it was dawn and the tide had gone out of the house. No moon, but gray daylight. He got to his feet very painfully and stretched himself, staring around the wreckage of the room, at the sand and the shingle and the weed and the shells, at the shattered windows and skirting and paneling. The sea had been in his house again. The sea was still in his cellar, black and deep and as cold as ice.

He saw the ammonite on the floor. He saw the skull he'd pounded flat and the hair wound round it. So it wasn't a nightmare he'd had. The knocking he'd heard was real, and so was the face which had floated toward him. But when he knelt in the sand to pick up the ammonite, when he bent to examine the remains of the skull, he cursed himself for a stupid, hysterical, short-sighted fool... because the skull he'd smashed was only the skull of the sheep he'd tossed into the cellar a few weeks before, and the hair was only the matted fleece.

Not the woman whose face was a part of his nightmares. Not Helen, whom he'd killed with the ammonite she'd found on their honeymoon. Not Helen, whose body he'd dropped into the flooded cellar. Not Helen, whose rhythmic knocking under the floorboards had haunted him ever since. Not Helen. Only a sheep.

Harry put the ammonite back on the mantelpiece. He studied the honeymoon photograph: Helen, smiling, sexy, sleek, pleased to have found such a fine specimen on the beach. He remembered her laughter, harsh and cruel, a year later, when the emptiness of their marriage had made them hate one another. Even now, he thought he could hear her taunting voice as she'd stood by the mantelpiece and shouted, "Look at this! The other fossil in my collection! Just like you, Harry Clewe, it's dead and cold and fucking useless!"

He'd gone blank with rage. That was when he'd slugged her with the fossil she'd picked up on Lyme Regis beach.

He opened his eyes again. The laughter and the voice faded. Crossing the room, he kicked the pieces of bone and the hank of fleece into the cellar and then he closed and bolted the trap door.

He was shivering with a terrible cold; he ached in all his limbs. Upstairs, he lit a fire as quickly as he could, threw off his clothes and pummeled his body with a rough, dry towel, and then he crawled into bed.

He slept soundly and warmly. The thump, thump, thump from the cellar had stopped, for the time being.

5

There were bright, dry, squally days at the end of November.

Harry built up his supply of firewood, spending hours on his fields gathering the branches and spars that the big tides left behind. Expert with the axe and the wedge and the sledgehammer, despite his disability, he worked in the yard with his sleeves rolled up and then he carried the fuel upstairs to stack it in the bathroom. He didn't care that, in every armful, there might be a thousand spiders or a hedgehog or a toad or a trembling shrew; he didn't mind the starlings that flocked in the drawing room or the rats that sneezed in his chimney. He was glad of the isolation from human beings that the floods guaranteed.

His gas bottle was empty. The batteries of his torch and his radio had run out. He had no more candles. One day he thought of walking to Caernarfon, four miles along the shore; but the prospect of meeting other people — people who would ask him how he was coping and might try to persuade him to quit his house and move to accommodation inland — was so unappealing that he decided against the expedition. He had plenty of firewood. He was warm and dry in his little spare room at the top of the stairs. He had sacks of potatoes and parsnips. He had plenty of cartridges. He didn't need people.

When the tide ebbed, he worked the harvest of flotsam and jetsam, a bounty replenished every day; when the tide flowed, he was poised with his gun at the landing window for all kinds of wildfowl that floated within range, for the waders that fed on the sodden fields.

A feast every evening, in front of a blazing fire: widgeon or teal; shoveller or shelduck; merganser, whose flesh was rank with the flavor of fish; woodcock, wonderfully meaty for a bird that felt as light as a sparrow when the dogs brought it to him; curlew, tasting of mud; oystercatcher, salty and tough. Plucked and gutted, basted on a spit hung over the flames, served with vegetables boiled in sea water, this was all the food he wanted. For days on end, Harry Clewe saw nobody and spoke not a word except to the dogs. This isolation suited him well.

Then the beachcomber came back.

Harry was kneeling at the landing window, leveling the gun at a mallard drake which was feeding on the edge of the flooded ditch. A fine picture he had, as he squinted down the barrel: a sunbeam on the gleaming green iridescence of the bird's head, on the vivid blue wing flashes, on the pearly pink-gray plumage of its back; behind the duck, the round, white face of the grandfather clock, sticking up from the ditch.

As he steadied his breath and started the gentle squeeze on the trigger, he wondered where the dogs were. He hadn't seen them for hours. Usually, they were near enough at any time to know when he was waiting to shoot, and they would wait with him, ready to react to the noise and smell of the gun. No matter: wherever they were, they would come at the sound of the shot. Harry squeezed the trigger.

The gun rocked against his shoulder. The explosion made the windows rattle and filled the air with smoke. A flock of curlew fled from the field, crying hoarsely, and dozens of jackdaws whirled into the sky, but the mallard drake was grounded. Still squinting down the barrel, Harry saw the bird thrashing in the mud, beating and beating until its wings were brown and sodden.

He looked around for Gog and Magog, exasperated that, in their absence, he'd have to go out and retrieve the injured bird. They must have heard the shot. So he waited at the window, expecting at any moment to see the big black beasts come lumbering into view, to see one of them lifting the duck from the mud and turning to bring it back to the house and up the stairs.

But for a minute, a long and puzzling minute for the man at the window, there was no sign of the dogs.

His heart jumped when a figure in jeans and a baggy brown jacket trotted across the field, followed at heel by Gog and Magog. He watched, so angry that he could almost have blasted again with the second barrel of the gun, as the figure picked up the duck and killed it with a sudden tug on its neck. Then the beachcomber, the same one that Harry had already chased twice from his fields, started walking toward the front of the house, dangling the duck by its feet, whistling the dogs to heel. Gog and Magog followed meekly with their tongues hanging out. The sunlight gleamed on the dead duck's head and the beachcomber's fine, blond hair.

Harry stood up and spun round, lurching downstairs to go and meet the trespasser outside in the yard. As he forced his way past the piano, the dogs ran toward him, barking gruffly as though *he* were a trespasser... but they fell away when he brandished the gun at them, because they knew the crash and the stink and the death it made when the man exploded it from the landing window. And there was the beachcomber, who'd stopped in the field to wait for the man to come out, who was standing fifty yards from the house. The face looked very frightened, drained of blood to an opaque whiteness. The mouth hung open; even from that distance, Harry could see the lips trembling. The duck shook as though it were still alive, but it was the beachcomber who was shaking as the red-faced, bushy-haired man came stomping closer, waving the gun and roaring like a stag.

The beachcomber didn't run away. Harry was greeted as the dogs had been greeted the last time the trespasser had come to the fields — with gifts: the mallard in one hand, and a parcel wrapped in greaseproof paper in the other. Harry stopped short, amazed that anyone should defy his bellowing. As the dogs had done before him, he leaned his face forward and sniffed.

"Sausages," the beachcomber said. "I brought sausages for you. I nicked them from the kitchen. You told me to bring something, so I did...." The voice trailed away. The parcel swayed in midair and the duck ruffled its feathers in the breeze.

Harry swung with his hook, snatching the bird with it. Horrified, the beachcomber staggered backward and sat down in the mud.

"My property!" Harry snarled, shaking the duck like a rag. "On my land! What the hell do you think you're doing on my fields, unless you want to get eaten by the dogs or blown to pieces?"

He brandished the gun at the beachcomber's face. With his hook, he shook the duck even harder, so that droplets of blood flew from it and spattered the beachcomber's cheeks.

"Yes, blood!" he shouted. "My bloody duck on my bloody land! How dare you come three times onto my property?" Then, much more softly, he said, "And my sausages as well, thank you very much, since they're now on my property."

He leaned down and hooked the parcel from the beachcomber. He lifted it to his face and sniffed. It smelled very good.

"Get up," he said gently. "I'm not going to shoot you. And it doesn't look as though the dogs are going to eat you, does it? Bloody useless animals!"

So the beachcomber stood up, sniveling noisily, slapping at the mud on jacket and jeans, smearing at the blood on cheeks and chin. Harry whirled toward the house, with the gun in his left hand, with the duck and the precious sausages dangling from his hook.

"The name's Harry Clewe, by the way!" he barked over his shoulder. "Mr. Clewe, to you! You've got a name, I suppose?" And he stomped away, hardly listening to the breathless reply.

Again he barked, without bothering to turn round. "Eh? What's that? Christine, d'you say? Well, you'd better come into the house, and get your face cleaned up! Are you hungry? It's weeks since I ate a sausage! Come on! You'll have to excuse the mess inside! The water's been getting in a little bit!"

Now, if Harry had waited another moment before stomping indoors, if he'd paused to look round at the beachcomber before heading for the house with the duck and the sausages, he would have seen that the muddy, bloodstained figure was opening and closing its mouth as though it wanted to say something very important... opening and closing its mouth without saying a word... wanting to call out, trying to call out, but still too afraid to do so as the bad-tempered man with the gun and the hook went squelching off through the mud... wanting to say that the man had misheard, had got the wrong impression, indeed that the man had had the wrong impression since the very first encounter on his fields. But Harry made for the house without turning round.

The beachcomber had said Christy, not Christine. He was a boy, a boy of fourteen with long, blond hair and a pale face, dressed in jeans and boots and a khaki jacket. But, by the time he found his voice, the moment had passed: the man, Mr. Clewe, was fifty yards away, at the entrance of the big, old house, forcing his way past what looked like a piano jammed in the doorway and disappearing inside.

The boy frowned, pursed his lips, rubbed at the blood on his cheeks and trotted after him.

6

Indeed, it was a piano. Wondering why there should be a piano fixed sideways in the front door, the boy squeezed past it and found himself in the strangest house he'd ever seen.

First of all, it was the biggest: he'd never seen such a great, high room as the hallway he stood in, such great, high rooms as the ones he could see to left and right, such a fine, wide staircase as the one which rose before him to a landing with a great tall window. Furthermore, he'd never been in a house so deep with sea-water pools, strewn with shingle and sand and barnacled boulders, scattered with clumps of seaweed, where enormous gray and pink jellyfish lay about the floors.

Speechless, he gazed at the broken windows and splintered doors, turning to look again at the capsized piano... so aghast at the size and state of the rooms and the staircase that he'd forgotten he was going to call out to the man and tell him his name was Christy, not Christine, that he was a boy and not a girl, that the man had made a mistake. Instead, he simply stared, wide-eyed, open-mouthed. It was wonderful, a house with a beach inside it: a beach like the one he'd been exploring when he'd heard the shot and come running to pick up the wounded duck. He'd returned to the foreshore to bring the sausages, lured by an irresistible curiosity for the strange man and his enormous dogs: the best and most exciting kind of curiosity that a boy can have, flavored with fear, laced with danger. And here, better than he could have hoped for, was the oddest house he'd ever been into.

Hearing the man gruffly calling, seeing that the dogs were wagging their tails on the landing, Christy crossed the hall and mounted the staircase. Near the top, he squealed loudly when a rat bolted downstairs toward him. He flattened himself against the banister as it sprang headlong past him, as the dogs thundered after it. One of the dogs caught the rat before it could reach the front door, crunched it in its jaws and flung it from side to side. The other dog snapped at the dangling body.

Harry had appeared at the top of the stairs. He bellowed with laughter at the efficiency with which his dogs dispatched the rat, at the look of horror on his visitor's face.

"Good work, Gog! Good work, Magog!" he roared. "That's your supper taken care of!" To his visitor, he shouted, "What's the matter? Afraid of a little mouse? After the way you faced up to the dogs? Come on, the sausages are cooking!"

He disappeared from the landing. The boy climbed the last few stairs, glancing uneasily from side to side in case another rat might launch itself at him, and went into the room where the man had gone.

It was more like a normal room in a normal house, smaller than the downstairs rooms. There was a bed and an armchair, a rug, a big window with a view across the fields to the sea. A fire was burning in a handsome fireplace. The mantelpiece was stuck with the stubs of molten candles, spattered with wax. On the floor there were heaps of books and yellowing newspapers; there was a radio, a gas stove; clothes bundled here and there; tins of beans and sardines and peaches and prunes stacked in one corner; sacks of potatoes and carrots in another. The sausages were sizzling on a griddle across the flames, but the smell of their cooking didn't disguise the smell of stale clothes, stale sheets, the smell of the man's unwashed body and the smell of the dogs. Christy sat on the bed.

There wasn't much talking, because Harry had lived so long in a house where the only sounds were his own: the sounds of his dogs and the gathering gulls; the sounds of the sea and the wind which were so much a constant part of the place that they seemed like a rushing inside his head, a sound he carried within him wherever he was. He had voices on the radio he could turn on when he wanted them, turn off when he was tired with them: that was all the talking he needed. So, without saying anything, Harry appraised his visitor, who sat on the bed and ate a sausage.

He looked at the fall of the soft blond hair, the long lashes, the lick of a little tongue on wet lips and the movement of a slender, white throat. He couldn't help staring. When the boy went into the bathroom to wipe the blood from his face, Harry followed and stood behind him so that their faces were framed in the bathroom mirror; as the boy rubbed at the blood on his cheeks and chin, Harry felt at his own face, where, a fortnight before, he'd smeared the blood which the beachcomber had flicked at him.

Christy smiled at Mr. Clewe's reflection. Back in the bedroom, he smiled again as he tested the heat of the sausage on his lips.

The boy was too frightened to say anything. Any confidence he'd felt as he dealt with the dogs outside had ebbed, now that he'd come into the strange house. The man glared fiercely, as though he regretted having invited the trespasser to share the sausages: and Christy, taking a deep breath to blurt out that he was a boy and not a girl, decided against it for the time being. It wasn't the right moment to correct the man's misapprehension. Mr. Clewe, pacified temporarily by the gift of food, was reverting to his previous biliousness, looking angrier and angrier in direct proportion to the steady disappearance of the sausages. So Christy said nothing, afraid that the man would think he'd deliberately made a fool of him for being cantankerous, short-sighted and hard of hearing.

The minutes went by and the sausages were gone. Christy made to leave. Perversely, that was when Harry started to ask questions, while Christy shifted from foot to foot by the bedroom door.

"Where do you live?" he said. "You've walked from Caernarfon, I suppose?"

"Yes, Mr. Clewe, I've walked from Caernarfon," the boy replied softly and politely. "I'm on my way home to Bontnewydd, just a couple of miles inland. I often come along the shore, after school."

"Bontnewydd," Harry said, rubbing at his chin. "Well, you won't get the floods there, will you? Things will have to get pretty bad before the tides reach Bontnewydd! This house would be completely submerged by then! The sea would be right over the roof! What about your father and mother? They'll be wondering where you've got to, won't they?"

"I haven't got a mother and a father," the boy said, looking at the threadbare carpet.

"Oh," Harry said. "Divorced, are they? Adopted, are you? Taken into care? Well, speak up, girl. Speak up."

"They're dead, Mr. Clewe," the boy answered. He looked up from the floor, his eyes level and cool. "They died when I was three. I can't remember them at all. They were drowned in a boating accident. I live in the orphanage in Bontnewydd. I go to school in Caernarfon, by bus in the mornings, and then I usually walk back along the shore, if the weather's not too bad. I prefer it, being on my own, looking for things on the beach. As long as I'm in time for Mrs. Bottomley's roll call, it's all right. She's the matron."

There was a long pause. The dogs fidgeted on the rug, glancing hopelessly at the scraps of sausage on the griddle. The fire fizzed when some of the fat fell into the flames.

"Drowned," Harry whispered. "Drowned... and you go moping along the beach looking for things." He chuckled. "A bit morbid, isn't it? What sort of things do you expect to find? Eh? What sort of things do you expect to find washed up on the seashore? You should be larking about on the bus with your schoolfriends on the way back to Bontnewydd in the afternoons, not moping about on your own on the seashore!"

The boy shrugged. "I suppose so, Mr. Clewe. But I like it down here, on my own. That's all."

"Well, so do I," Harry said very softly. "So do I."

He turned in his chair and stared out of the window. It was dusk. The waves were driving across the foreshore and into the fields. The wind rattled the slates on the roof. A freezing rain, blown straight off the sea, spattered on the glass, as though the tide were already up and flinging a spray at the house.

"Time for you to bugger off then," he murmured. "Bugger off for Mrs. Wigglebottom's roll call. If you don't go now, you'll have to swim. You saw the mess downstairs, didn't you? The water's five feet deep downstairs when the tide's in. That's why the rats have come upstairs. Get going while the going's good."

Harry heaved himself to his feet and together they went out of the room, onto the landing. As they looked down the stairs, they saw that the sea was just beginning to come into the house. Slowly, slick and sinuous like a long, brown, muscular snake, the water slithered past the piano. Nosing a scum of foam, rolling aside the weed it had left behind on a previous visit, it pooled in the hallway.

He remained at the top of the stairs with the dogs as the boy hurried down. The noise of the wind was so loud, whistling into the house through the open door and the broken windows, that when he shouted from the landing the boy could hardly make out a word he said. He could hardly see the man either, because the house was suddenly very dark. But Mr. Clewe was shouting, raising a hand to lob something which landed with a splash at the foot of the stairs.

"For the torch!" he was bellowing, a looming black figure silhouetted at the landing window. "That's a dead battery! Bring some new ones like that one if you're coming back! Otherwise don't bother coming! Now bugger off! Go on! You'll have to run for it!"

The boy bent to the pool, which was already deepening around his boots, picked up the torch battery and slipped past the piano out of the house. Harry remained at his landing window. He watched the slight, slim figure go splashing across the fields and through the broken hedges, disappearing in the darkening dusk. Then he went back into his room, closing the door behind him.

He sat in the flamelight, while the house boomed and quivered, while the sea was in the downstairs rooms. Sometimes, throughout the evening and into the night, he got out of his chair and stared at the white-capped waves which foamed around him.

"I expect she got back all right," he muttered to the dogs at the fireside. "Stupid bitch, coming out here! We're better off on our own, the three of us, without other people poking around."

Whenever he knelt to the fire to build it up, he would pick at the crumbs on the griddle to get a taste of the sausages he'd cooked there. He picked the griddle clean. Late into the night, he sat in the armchair, licking his lips, staring at the flames until they were dead.

7

A few days later, one of the windsurfers returned.

Crackling like a volley of pistol shots, the purple sail slackened as the board came close to the house. Then, with a sudden explosive snap of wind, the sail filled, bulging taut. The youth grinned, tossing his bright blond head, because he knew without looking up at the windows that the man was watching him. He flexed himself so that his black rubber suit glistened in the thin, cold light. He gripped tightly, leaning from the sail as the board raced away through the chop and spray of the tide.

Yes, Harry was watching. He seethed with an impotent rage as the sail crossed and recrossed his fields... or, rather, the sea where his fields had been. Time and again, it sped toward the house, so that the youth could turn the board as close to the windows as possible, so close that the snap and flap and the bulging of the sail were impossible to ignore. Sometimes the youth shouted, whooping with exhilaration or calling out to make sure his spectator was still there. At first, Harry had lunged from his fireside to the landing and thrown the window wide open, where he'd stood and shouted until he was too hoarse to shout any more. Gog and Magog had joined him, barking very loudly, and Harry, infuriated by the blatant way in which the windsurfer was trespassing on his property, had kicked them downstairs as though they might swim around the house and somehow chase the trespasser away. But the dogs only sniffed at the water, balked, turned round and limped upstairs again, to flop in front of the fire in the bedroom.

The tide was as high as it had ever been; the water was six feet deep in the hallway. Ugly brown, churned with mud and sand, it looked like coffee gone cold and scummy. All kinds of driftwood and debris were slopping about, banging on the walls and the stairs. Outside it was worse: the flood was choppy with white waves as the wind blasted from the open sea.

No, Gog and Magog weren't interested. They abandoned Harry on the landing, where, unable to shout any more, he gripped the windowsill and shuddered with anger as the sail raced toward him. For a mad split second, he groped in the corner where the shotgun was leaning, but then he left it where it was. Blinded by spray and tears, all he could see was a vivid purple shape zigzagging here and there on a background of brown and white water; as it came closer, he made out the gleam of a blond head and the flash of grinning teeth, the bending and leaning and stretching of a shining black body. Deafened by the wind, he heard the bang of the sail; he heard the youth call out some nonsense about potatoes and then a schoolboy obscenity. The windsurfer raced away. At last, exhausted by rage, Harry shut the window and joined the dogs in the bedroom.

Without thinking, he bent to the fire and picked up a knife from the mantelpiece. It was a very sharp knife, the one he'd used for the butchering of the sheep a few weeks before. He sat in his armchair, fitted the smooth wooden handle into his right palm and stroked the razor edge of the blade with his thumb. He tried to be calm. He relaxed the muscle in his shoulders. He stopped trembling and the tears in his eyes dried up. He steadied his breathing until he thought he'd controlled his anger... but, as he heard the shouting of the windsurfer close to the house, he pressed on the blade so hard that he cut his thumb quite deeply. There was blood all over his hand. Too tired to get up and go to the bathroom to wash himself, he tossed the knife onto the bed and flicked his fingers at the fire, where the blood fizzled in the flames.

He'd picked up the knife because the gleam of the windsurfer's black rubber suit had reminded him of an unusual find he'd made on the fields that morning: a porpoise, the biggest and most beautiful of all the dead things washed onto his land since the flood tides had begun. He'd flensed it with the butchering knife, so that the dogs could gorge on the rich, lean meat, and he'd cut a huge steak for himself to fry on the griddle. The gulls and the crows would have the rest of the carcass.

Now he sucked at the blood which welled on the ball of his thumb. The flex of the windsurfer's suit had reminded him of the way in which the knife had sliced cleanly through the porpoise, the way that the flesh fell away from the blade. Thinking of this, with his thumb in his mouth, Harry got up and went to the window. But the purple sail had gone.

8

Harry was still in bed the next time the beachcomber came to the house.

Waking in the darkness of early morning, he'd heard the sea downstairs and the wind moaning at his window. He'd peered from under his blankets to see nothing but the tiniest golden spark in the ashes of the fireplace. He'd turned over, huddled more deeply under the covers, and slept again until first light at eight o'clock. It was the only way he could tell that midwinter was close, by the lateness of the morning light and the earliness of dusk: the shortest, dreariest days of the year.

At dawn, he got out of bed for a few minutes, to see from his window that the tide was ebbing from his fields, and he trod down the stairs to piss into the sea in the hallway. Yes, the tide was going out, leaving a scum of foam as high as the seventh step; at the same time, as though drawn by the same forces of gravity which were draining the house, a hundred starlings whirled out of the living room, beat around the hall and funneled like a swarm of angry bees out of the front door. The water was falling fast. It eddied around the piano and swirled into the yard. In another hour, where the sea had been six feet deep in all the downstairs rooms, there would be tidal pools, boulders and weed and banks of gravel. Harry pissed into the water and then he went painfully up the stairs again, where he lay in bed and watched the sky lightening at his window.

The dogs told him that someone was coming. They'd left their rug in front of the cold grate, padded downstairs and outside to scavenge whatever the sea had dropped around the house. When he heard them barking, Harry detected the note of menace in their voices which they used whenever trespassers were on his property; but then the note softened. Without getting out of bed and looking from the window, he knew that the visitor must be someone the dogs recognized and had learned to accept. It could only be the beachcomber... Christine, she'd said her name was.

He lay still, heard the dogs fall silent, heard footsteps in the shingle of the yard and then the splash of boots in the hallway. Swearing, quite unaccustomed to anyone coming into the house, especially while he was still in bed, he struggled from under the covers. He didn't need to dress: he kept all his clothes on at night. He simply stepped into his shoes and stomped from his room onto the landing.

"Don't just bloody walk in!" he bellowed.

Through bleary, sleep-reddened eyes, he could see the figure in boots and jeans and khaki jacket at the foot of the stairs.

"Just because the door's gone and the windows have gone and the bloody sea comes in and out without bloody asking," he roared, "it doesn't mean that you or anyone else can just wander in and out as you bloody well please! Does it? Knock next time! Knock on the bloody piano and wait for me to invite you in!"

He spun round and back into his room. From there, throwing himself down in his armchair and dragging a blanket from the bed to wrap around his legs, he called out, "Well? What are you waiting for? Are you coming upstairs or not?"

It seemed to take a long time for his visitor to arrive at the landing and turn into the bedroom. Harry could hear splashing in the hallway, going in and out of the living room and the drawing room and the dining room... a good deal of splashing, as though the beachcomber were nosing around downstairs, wading from room to room with the dogs in tow. He drew an enormous breath and shouted again, "What the hell do you think you're doing down there? Get yourself up here or bugger off and don't come back! You're on *my* property!"

Suddenly the figure appeared at the doorway. Without saying anything, before Harry could say anything, Christy came into the bedroom and held out a brown paper parcel.

The boy's cheeks were flushed, his eyes were gleaming, his breath was short, his face gleamed with excitement. He'd seen writhing, silvery creatures in the cavernous downstairs rooms: in the flooded, boulder-strewn caverns where the sea had been spouting and foaming and had left all kinds of wonders behind....

"Fish!" he blurted, so thrilled at what he'd seen that he forgot the apology he was going to make for walking uninvited into the house... so thrilled that he thrust the parcel into Harry's hands and spun back onto the landing to stare down at the pools at the foot of the stairs. "Fish!" he said again, as he whirled into the bedroom. "There's fish, Mr. Clewe! Great big ones! In all the rooms! Come and have a look, Mr. Clewe! Come on!"

Without thinking, without fear, the boy seized Harry by the hand. He tugged him from the chair so that the blanket fell to the floor, stood him up, pointed him at the bedroom door and dragged him onto the landing. "Look, Mr. Clewe! Look!"

Harry was speechless: not as much at the sight of a shoal of fish surging this way and that in the diminishing pool in the hallway, although that was impressive enough in itself — as at the touch of the warm, young hands on his hand. He hadn't touched another human being for years. No one, no human being, had touched him in all that time. And now, this little blonde beachcomber, whom he'd met as a trespasser on his land just a fortnight before, was squeezing his hand very tightly, leaning against him, hopping from foot to foot beside him. He felt the heat and strength in the slim, young fingers. He felt the warm breath on his face. He felt such joy as he'd never felt for years and years and years.

"Look at them, Mr. Clewe!" the boy cried. "I've never seen them as big as that before, except in a fish shop! Look at them dashing about!"

The fish, stranded in the house as the tide went out, wriggled and flapped in the shrinking pools. They were bass, fine, fat bass, some of them over two feet long. They surged about the hallway, a dozen or twenty of them, struggling on the shingle where the water was so shallow that they bellied and writhed like great, muscular snakes. They lay on their metallic, scaly sides, heaving and gaping and staring, mustering the force to slither from the sandbanks and into the water again, and then they surged in a seething, silvery shoal across the hallway until they banged their snouts on the piano and turned back into the house.

A grand sight, not often seen in the living rooms of country houses. Hand in hand, the man and the boy stood on the landing and gazed down at the thrashing commotion. They remained like this for a long minute, until Christy prised his fingers from the man's grip and, glancing quickly upward, saw that Mr. Clewe wasn't staring at the fish but straight into his own face. There was a strange smile on the man's mouth and a curious twinkle in his eyes.

"Another fine present you've brought me!" Harry whispered. "What are you? Some kind of an angel? Or a mermaid perhaps, washed ashore with the big tides? Sausages one day, and gleaming, fat fish another!" Then he boomed with laughter. "Bass! Ever eaten bass? Well, they're here for the taking! And what else did you bring?"

Quickly, urgently, because he could hear the fish flapping downstairs as the tide drained out of the house, he inspected the contents of the parcel his visitor had given him in the bedroom.

"Good girl, good girl!" he said, examining the torch batteries. "Yes, these are the ones! And bread and cheese as well!" He pressed the food to his face, inhaling noisily with his eyes closed. "Well done!" he whispered. "You can come as often as you like if you keep on bringing wonderful gifts like these! Well? What are we waiting for?"

The boy drew a deep breath, to shout his name as clearly as he could, to put the man right. Too late again... another moment passed. Tossing the parcel onto the rumpled bed, Harry spun out of the room and onto the landing. He stomped down the stairs, chuckling with glee, bellowing, "Come on! Come on!" and the boy was left behind in the bedroom, opening and closing his mouth like the fish stranded in the hallway. When Christy turned to follow him, Harry was already at the foot of the stairs, kicking off his shoes and socks, rolling up his trouser legs, splashing into the shallow water, glancing up at the landing with such a gargoyle grin on his face that the boy forgot what he'd meant to say, grinned back and skipped down the stairs as well.

Side by side, banging and barging together, the man and the boy waded after the fish. They drove the shoal this way and that by beating the water with their hands and churning it with their feet. They laughed, the crusty, arthritic widower and the institutionalized orphan, the first time for a long time. Harry's was a hooting laugh which started in his belly and rattled hoarsely in his throat before bursting out; the boy's was tinkling and high-pitched. It was glorious sport. Treading after the gleaming fish, they flung water at one another's faces. They whooped, as though they were herding bullocks, and the bass shimmied to avoid capture. From time to time, the man or the boy would grasp a fish and, roaring triumphantly, hold it aloft in a spray of sea water and slime-slippery scales; but the fish, with an arching thrust of its muscular body, would wriggle free and fall into the pool again.

At last a fish was taken. Separated from the rest of the shoal, beached on a bank of shingle, the biggest of the bass lay panting, heaving, gaping a mucous mouth, staring a jet-black eye. The man and the boy crouched in the water beside it. Careless of the cold and wet because they'd so thoroughly splashed one another already, they knelt in silence and steadied their own breathing after the mad exertion of the chase. The fish flexed and flapped. Drowning, dying, it opened and closed its jutting lower jaw.

So that the boy blurted, once he had the breath to speak, "Do something, Mr. Clewe! Bash it with your hook or something! Or shall I put it back in the water?"

Harry snorted. "Don't be daft! We didn't go to all this trouble to catch it just so that we can put it back again. You stay there and make sure it doesn't flop away."

Harry heaved himself upright, groaning at the pain in his hips, and picked his way carefully, barefooted, across the hallway into the adjacent living room. The boy watched him. He saw the man go to the mantelpiece and lift down a big, black, strangely coiled stone, turn round and tread gingerly back again.

"Ammonite," Harry said, as he knelt beside the fish. "A fossil. Very useful for this kind of thing. In fact, the only thing it's ever been bloody useful for. Here, hold the fish still!"

Christy gripped with both his hands so that the bass was pressed onto the shingle. Only its tail twitched. Harry knocked it on the head, a single blow which made a crunching sound and left a stove-in, oozing bruise where the eye had been.

The fish didn't move any more. There was another silence as the man and the boy knelt in the pool.

"A shame to waste the rest," Harry said at last, looking around at the other fish in the hallway. "They'll all die when the tide goes out of the house. The water won't be deep enough for them, and then they'll flap and flap and the dogs will mess with them and there'll be an almighty bloody stink with what's left behind. Here's an idea! While I go and light the fire and get this beauty ready for frying, this is what I want you to do..."

Christy did as he was told, once the man had hooked the dead fish by the gills and carried it upstairs. He rinsed the ammonite and lugged it into the living room, where he heaved it up onto the mantelpiece. He paused for a moment to look at the photograph of a woman in a summer dress, who was smiling at the camera and holding the same black, spiraled rock in her hands... and then, as the man had told him to do, he used the shovel which was leaning by the fireplace to clear away the shingle and sand in the middle of the flooded room until he could see the ring and bolt of a trap door in the shallow water. It took all his strength to heave the trap door open. He stood back as a good deal of water poured into the hole with a loud sucking noise as though a big bath were being emptied, and then he stepped forward again and peered down.

The water looked very deep and very cold. It was black. It lapped and glistened as though it were breathing, a gigantic eel coiled beneath the floorboards or a whiskery catfish with a huge, gaping mouth. He leaned closer. A blast of icy air came up from the water and slapped him in the face, and he thought he could see some pale and shapeless thing come floating from the deepest, darkest place and bobbing toward the surface....

The boy fell backward and sat in the water. He shuddered with the cold from the flooded cellar and the cold in his wet clothes. His neck prickled. Eager to do what the man had said, so that he could slam the trap door and get upstairs to the fire as quickly as possible, Christy went into the hallway again, found the shoal of bass struggling in a shrinking pool, and he stampeded the fish back into the living room. It was easy, then, to flop them one by one into the cellar, where they disappeared in the black water with a powerful flick of a tail. When they'd all gone, he lifted up the trap door and let it fall shut with a great splash. He bolted it firmly. He hadn't liked what he'd seen down there.

Before he was halfway up the stairs, the sound of crackling wood and a sizzling pan came to him... and the smell of frying fish. The dogs must have heard and smelled the same things, because Gog and Magog sprang into the hall from outside, where they'd been gnawing at the bones of the porpoise, and overtook the boy before he reached the landing.

Still barefooted, with his trouser legs rolled up to his knees, Harry was kneeling in front of the fire. The fish head and tail and its tumbled innards lay on a piece of newspaper beside him. There was a blaze of driftwood, burning blue because of the salt, and Harry had put the frying pan on top of the griddle, where the flames could reach up and lick the sooted bottom. Cut into four fillets, the fish was sizzling in the dark, rich oil left in the pan from the porpoise steak. It smelled delicious. The room was wonderfully warm. The dogs flopped by the bed, claiming the blanket that the man had dropped when the boy had tugged him to the landing.

"Come to the fire," Harry said over his shoulder. "We both got bloody wet, fooling around like that. Cut some of the bread. Here, use this knife. Be careful, it's very sharp."

He handed Christy the butchering knife from the mantelpiece. The boy wiped the fish scales from it, drawing the blade across his thigh, and sliced the bread with it.

Soon the fish was ready. The man and the boy knelt on either side of the fire and ate in reverent silence. Words were unnecessary to acknowledge the flavor of freshly caught bass fried in whale oil. Harry glanced at the boy and grunted. Christy looked at the man and nodded. The dogs panted, without daring to beg for a taste, although the smell was so good and so strong; years ago, they'd been taught not to scrounge, learning from the number of times they'd had their heads cracked together. Now, they sighed very loudly and eyed the pan on the griddle. Harry and the boy ate all the fish without speaking a word; then, wedges of bread dipped in the sweetly combined juices of porpoise and bass.

A fine feast. When it was finished, Gog and Magog were allowed the head and tail and the pungent entrails. Only a scrap of the fish remained: the scales, like sequins, on Christy's jeans.

"What are you doing out here this morning?" Harry asked, breaking the silence, wiping his mouth with the palm of his hand. "Why aren't you at school? I was still in bed when you arrived."

"It's Sunday, Mr. Clewe," the boy replied. "We don't have school. We can have permission from Mrs. Bottomley to come out all day if we want to. I pinched the torch batteries from her room and the bread and cheese from the kitchens and came down here because I could see from the hillside that the tide was going out."

"Makes no difference to me what day it is," Harry said. "I can tell it's December by the shortness of the daylight, that's all. Otherwise I've lost track of time completely. The batteries in my radio went dead about the same time the torch batteries did. I used to listen to the radio quite a lot, to get the news about the floods and so on. What's the date, anyway?"

Christmas was three weeks away, the boy told him. He knelt so close to the fire that steam rose from his wet jeans. When he shook out his long blond hair, he saw that Mr. Clewe was watching and holding his breath at the same time. This made the boy uncomfortable. He knew from the previous visit that the man's patience was short, that his hospitality in the storm-wrecked house diminished once his appetite for food was satisfied. So, to keep the man sweet and to avoid the looks which lingered on his hair and his mouth and the fish scales on his thigh, Christy got up with the plates and moved to the door.

"Shall I rinse these, Mr. Clewe?" he asked. "Are the taps still working in the bathroom?" And he went onto the landing, as Harry nodded and turned his fire-reddened face to the flames.

Intrigued by the size and state of the downstairs room, the boy was eager to see what wonders he might find upstairs. He'd decided he would give up waiting for an opportunity to tell the man that his name was Christy and not Christine. What did it matter? What difference did it make if the cantankerous old fool was so hard of hearing and so short-sighted that he'd taken him for a girl? The visits to the dilapidated house would be even more exciting. The misunderstanding might add the spice of danger....

He giggled at the thought of it, surprising himself by the accidental girlishness of the giggle. As he rinsed the plates under a flow of rust-brown water in the bathroom sink, he studied his face in the pitted mirror, turning his head from side to side, tilting his chin; there was a spot coming next to his left nostril, blooming red and a bit sore. He wetted his lips with the tip of his tongue and tried a smile; he shook his hair, as he'd done in front of the fire, so that it fell loose and long and blond around his ears. Leaning to the mirror, he made to kiss his own reflection, but his nose got in the way. He giggled again at this and whispered to the face in the glass....

"Hello, Christine," he said very softly. He said it three more times for practice.

The bathroom was the biggest he'd ever seen. As well as the rustsplashed washbasin with dribbling brass taps, there was a water tank, fat and round and coppery gleaming; a throne of a toilet, horribly stained inside the bowl and lapping with brown water; and the bath itself, a monstrous affair on four brass feet, piled with driftwood chopped into small enough pieces to go on the fire in the bedroom. Some small animal was moving in there, rustling the twigs and dried grasses to make a nest to hibernate in. The walls bloomed a black, fungal damp. The floor was sweating green linoleum.

Christy tiptoed out of the bathroom and onto the landing, where the shotgun leaned in a corner by the window. A rat ran over his feet and slithered down the stairs; seeing that the tide had gone out, it plopped onto the sand, crossed the hallway and disappeared through the front door. The boy shivered so hard that he nearly dropped the plates he was holding, but he went along the corridor away from the landing window to try the door handles of the other rooms. They were all locked. He knelt at the keyhole of one of the doors and squinted through it: nothing but darkness, a musty cold darkness and a stale cold smell.

Sure enough, Harry had reverted to his original grumpiness. When the boy took the plates back into the bedroom, he saw that the man had heaved himself into his armchair and was drying his toes with a corner of a blanket. He'd taken the pan off the griddle and given it to the dogs to lick, and he'd built up the fire with more sticks.

"Before you go," he muttered, hearing Christy coming in and putting the plates down, "bring some wood from the bathroom and put it next to the grate. Then it's time for you to bugger off. Get some wood, get the fire going properly, and get me another blanket to wrap round my legs. I'm aching with cold after all that ridiculous splashing around downstairs. Stupid idea, that was, all for a bloody fish! Come on, girl, don't just stand there gaping! Get a move on!"

Christy was glad to be going. He was cold, too, although he'd had his boots on during the fish hunt, because he'd knelt and squatted in the freezing water. Since, by the look of things, he wasn't going to be allowed the benefit of the fire after the feast, he was better off leaving and running back across the fields to the orphanage. He responded meekly to the gruff commands, fetching the wood, stacking it by the grate, and then arranging Harry in the armchair with a pillow and blankets so that he was comfortably wrapped up, like a geriatric in an old-people's home. The dogs lay at the man's feet, where he could wriggle his stiff, yellow toes in their warm fur.

"And next time you come," Harry said, "—not that there has to be a next time, since I've managed perfectly well on my own for the last God-knows-how-many years — bring some batteries for the radio. What the hell am I supposed to do all day, propped up like this in front of the fire like a bloody invalid? Well, what are you waiting for? You let yourself in, didn't you? Now you can let yourself out."

So the boy left, closing the bedroom door behind him, taking one of the batteries from the radio so that he'd know which sort to thieve from matron, as the man ungratefully put it.

Harry settled to the warmth of the blaze, to the comforting crackle of firewood. He was warm and well fed, snuggling himself into the blankets, pressing his feet on the belly of an obliging dog. He chuckled as he thought of the silly, childish way he'd thrown off his shoes and socks and splashed after the fish, hooting with laughter with the giggling girl. He remembered how she'd flicked her blond hair to dry it in front of the fire. He'd seen the redness of a spot coming at the side of her left nostril. He remembered the silvery scales on her thigh. He remembered her warm hand in his hand.

"Christine," he said softly to himself. He said it again. He wondered if the beachcomber might come back quite soon, the next day perhaps. He hoped so.

9

Indeed, Christy came back every afternoon the following week.

He'd decided it was too late to correct Mr. Clewe's misapprehension about his name and sex. It didn't seem to matter. He'd asked about the dogs' names and the man had told him the legend of Gog and Magog, the only survivors of a monstrous brood of giants whose mothers had all murdered their husbands; the rest of the giants had been killed by King Brute, but Gog and Magog were taken to London and made to do duty as porters in the royal palace.

He'd asked about the house too. "It's not an island and there aren't any swans," Harry had grunted when Christy queried the origin of the name, Ynys Elyrch. "Although it's more like an island these days than it's ever been before. There are swans on the estuary, roosting in the dunes on the far side, but I've never seen a single swan on the fields or the shore near the house, not in all the years I've lived here. They don't like the look of the place. They're afraid of the gun, maybe, or the dogs. Afraid of me, I suppose."

It was a bit unfair, the boy thought, that the dogs' names and the house's name should be so thoroughly accounted for, while his own had been misconstrued. Never mind. What did it matter? He would continue to visit Ynys Elyrch, the island of swans, until his curiosity was satisfied. For the time being, the daily expeditions were a novelty. Harry Clewe was dangerously unpredictable; it added an extra shiver of excitement to the little adventure, to string him along a bit. One day, sooner or later, when the fun of the visits had worn off, the boy would drop his pants, watch the expression on the man's stupid, grumpy, red face and then run off, crowing with laughter. And that would be the end of it.

In the meantime, Harry and Christy spent the winter afternoons together. Cold days, lit by watery sunshine, as the wind came off the sea and cut across the treeless fields, but good days, as the crusty widower and the orphaned boy kindled a little warmth from each other's company. For Christy, it was a taste of all the rapscallion adventures that, fatherless, he'd never had. For Harry, it was an echo of the lightness of spirit he'd briefly enjoyed in years gone by: in pursuit of the little blonde Sarah, of whom the beachcomber sometimes reminded him; in love with his sister Lizzie; in thrall to the child Zoë; in the warm, capable hands of Helen... culminating in a moment of blinding rage, when he'd knocked Helen dead with the ammonite and dropped her into the cellar.

Dead. All of them dead. Sarah and Lizzie and Zoë and Helen... And now Christine, the beachcomber...

They caught more fish in the flooded hallway, blenny and scad and wrasse, all kinds of dabs and flatties, and they fried them over the fire. They found a conger eel, eight feet long and as strong as a boa constrictor, stranded in the living room: a coiling, thrashing, muscular monster which, after a titanic struggle, they caught in an improvised net and dragged out of the house, onto the beach, to release it triumphantly in the shallows of low tide.

Harry showed Christy the remains of a more monstrous beast, the porpoise whose bones had been scattered all over the fields, and the two of them spent a whole afternoon absorbed in trying to fit the skeleton together again.

They walked the foreshore with dogs and gun, and the boy watched, amazed at the deafening noise and the whiff of cordite, as the man bagged widgeon or snipe. The dogs splashed after the kill and retrieved it, a limply flapping thing which Christy wrung dead with impressive expertise. "That's something not many girls could do," Harry admitted. "But don't get any ideas about having a go with the gun. I'll bloody thrash you if I see you so much as touch it!"

They gathered driftwood together, and Harry instructed Christy in wielding the axe, the sledgehammer and the splitting wedge. When the boy fetched the tools from the car, he'd asked excitedly, "What sort is it, Mr. Clewe? Is it a Jag?" and he'd slithered onto the smooth red leather of the driver's seat and gripped the steering wheel, stretching to the pedals, craning to see over the long silver bonnet, blowing the dust off the big, round dials.

Grand days for the boy, for whom the ordered routine of the institution was all the world he knew; good days for the man, for whom the past was a blur. Harry felt himself unfossilizing. Some of the stiffness was gone. His body worked better, his blood was warmer, when the beachcomber came. Somehow, the house itself, which had been as cold and dead as the ammonite, was alive again.

There was a bright, blustery Sunday, when, for the first time, Christy was caught in the house by the rising tide.

It was the best of all his adventures so far, to see the waves spill into the hallway and flood the downstairs rooms. He crouched on the landing, glowing with joy and excitement, unable to tear himself from the spectacle of the sea surrounding and filling the house. It lapped to the third step on the staircase, then the fourth and fifth and sixth and seventh. While the man sat by the fire and listened to a play on the radio, Christy gazed from the landing into the deepening well of water in the hall, as the sea smacked and slapped at the walls and sent slow, rumbling rollers through the living-room windows. He thought he could feel the foundations rocking, shuddering with the beat of the swell... as though the house were no longer a house but a great ship, adrift on a steel-gray ocean. He stared from the landing window and trembled with the thrill of it.

The whoosh and flap of a purple sail made him jump with surprise as a windsurfer raced past the window. He instinctively lifted a hand to wave at the youth in the gleaming black suit, and then changed his mind, thinking it best to drop out of sight when the youth glanced up. He peered out, his eyes above the sill, and watched the top of the sail accelerating across the flooded fields, before he got up again and stood at the window. His feelings were curiously mixed when he saw the windsurfer turn and start to come back, as the board cut a foaming white slice through the waves, as the sail grew swollen and taut, as the youth bent at the helm.

A fine sight, and a crackling, ripping, white water sound... but, at the same time, a bubble of anger rose in the boy's chest, a bubble of jealousy, a jealous anger that some-one else should have come to Ynys Elyrch, where only he was allowed to come.

"Mr. Clewe!" he hissed, shuffling into the bedroom on his hands and knees to keep out of sight of the windsurfer. "Mr. Clewe! There's a—"

Harry had already heard the snap of the sail outside his bedroom window. He'd been trying to stay calm, to stop him-self from lunging out of his armchair and onto the landing. Now he snapped, "I know, I know! Get off the floor! What the hell do you think you're playing at?"

He kicked out viciously at Gog and Magog, which had hardly moved a muscle at the sound of the sail. They stumbled to the door to get out of range of the man's boots.

"Bloody dogs!" he bellowed. "Worse than useless when a trespasser comes onto my property on his stupid sailboard! And you, all you can do is crawl around on your hands and knees, as though there's a bloody air raid or something!"

He heaved himself out of the armchair and staggered to the window.

"I'll get the gun to him one of these days!" he muttered. "Let's try a few of these, next time he comes close."

He reached into one of the sacks in the corner of the room and groped at the potatoes.

"Get out of the way!" he barked at the boy. "Get off the floor! Give me some space, for fuck's sake!"

Christy slunk onto the landing, as cowed as the two dogs, but Harry followed him out there, shoving him aside with his boots as though he were just another jellyfish or bundle of weed that the sea had fetched up. With his hook, he flung open the window. He weighted a potato in the palm of his hand, winced as he loosened the muscles in his shoulder, and he waited for the purple sail to turn at the top of the field and start racing again toward the house.

"Come on, you bastard!" he muttered. "Come on! Come as close as you bloody well like!"

But the potato he threw fell hopelessly short of the target. The plop it made in the rough water was lost in the noise of waves and wind. The surfer neither saw nor heard it, although he brought his board within a few yards of the house and turned it right beneath the landing window. Very hurriedly, too angry to aim properly, grunting with frustration, Harry threw again. The potato splashed close to the board, so that the youth glanced up and guffawed at the sight of the quivering, red-faced, wild-haired man who'd thrown it. Harry threw a third time. The youth stretched out to catch the potato and hurl it back, where it burst on the side of the house with such an impact that Harry staggered away from the window, spattered with juice.

The surfer maneuvered the board into the wind. For a moment the sail flapped, baggy and loose, and the youth wobbled precariously with nothing to lean on.

Christy stood up. He stepped to the window and grabbed a couple of the potatoes that the man had dropped. Aiming carefully, sighting on the head of hair which was bright against the tightening sail, he hurled them one after the other with all his strength.

The first potato hit the sail with a loud slap and dropped into the water. The second one hit the windsurfer very hard on the back of the head... so hard that the youth rocked forward, pushed the boom away from him, and fell headlong into the sea.

Harry had seen this from the bedroom, where, to relieve his powerlessness, he'd been kicking the dogs back to the fireside. He gave a squeal of pleasure when the first potato hit the sail. He bellowed like a bull when the second potato smacked on the windsurfer's head. Lunging to the window again, shoving Christy to one side, he stood there, crowing, as the youth collapsed into the water.

So that, when the youth surfaced and turned to face the house, he only saw the man at the window. As far as he knew, there was no one else in the house. He clambered on board and sped away, scowling, tossing his head and flinging the water from his hair.

Christy found himself wrapped in a bear hug of an embrace. Harry enfolded his arms round the boy and heaved him off his feet to swirl him round and round the landing. And all the time he whooped with joy, a hoarse, hysterical whoop of triumph.

"You darling! You treasure!" he shouted, when at last he could say the words instead of simply hooting. "So the mermaid's a tomboy, after all!"

Together, hand in hand, the man and the boy turned back to the window to see that the purple sail was disappearing on the dim horizon.

That was a very good day, when the windsurfer was routed. To celebrate, they shared a fireside feast of the provisions that the boy had brought from the orphanage kitchens: crumpets, toasted in the flames and spread with butter and jam; fruitcake and oranges; the first tea that Harry had tasted for more than a month. By dusk, the tide had gone down enough for Christy to go splashing across the waterlogged fields, turning and waving to the man at his firelit window, running inland to be back at the orphanage in time for Mrs. Bottomley's roll call.

More and more good days, afternoons of clear, cold sunshine and salty winds. The man and the boy walked the shores with Gog and Magog and the thundering gun. They stalked the silvery bass in the flooded hallway. They scoured the beaches for the treasures that the storms threw up.

10

"It's me, Mr. Clewe! It's me!"

Arriving at the house, Christy squeezed past the piano, paused in the hallway and called out in a clear, high voice. Then he combed out his hair and shook it loose before going up the stairs to hand over the gifts he'd brought.

Christy kept the secret of his sex from the man: he thought it was exciting and naughty to do so. Harry Clewe had a secret too, naughtier and more exciting than the boy's. When the boy came closer to discovering it, Harry was suddenly and terribly angry.

For the past couple of weeks, the man and the boy had warmed to one another. Harry was a little less bilious and cranky than he'd been over the previous ten years. He kicked the dogs less often, no more than a dozen times a day. Unconsciously at first, without thinking of what he was doing, he washed more thoroughly and shaved more carefully when he thought the beachcomber might visit... thanks to whom he had soap and razor blades and toothpaste, batteries for the torch and the radio, candles and sometimes a newspaper. He would look forward to a bit of company, and the gifts too. He would peer at his reddened face in the bathroom mirror and smile when he heard footsteps in the shingled yard, when he heard the clear, high voice calling, "It's me, Mr. Clewe! It's me!"

But he lost his temper that day, when he found his visitor trying the door handles of the other upstairs rooms....

Thinking the man was asleep in his armchair, having propped him with pillows and wrapped him with a rug after building the fire to a crackling blaze, Christy had tiptoed from the bedroom and onto the landing. First of all, without daring to breathe at the same time, he picked up the gun from the corner. It was much heavier than he'd thought it would be; he could hardly point it anywhere for more than a few seconds, out of the landing window or even down the stairs, before the barrel drooped toward the floor. Silently, remembering the man's warning, he leaned it back in its corner. Then he crept along the corridor to the door of another room and knelt to peer through the keyhole, as he'd done once before. There was nothing but dusty darkness and a cold draught, an odd, faintly tinkling noise, like splinters of ice falling onto a pavement. He stood up and twisted the handle, but the door was locked.

And suddenly, there was Mr. Clewe on the landing.

In a split second of startled awareness, Christy could smell the man before he heard him and saw him. The whiff of stale clothes wafted down the corridor and made the boy whirl around in a moment of gasping terror. Harry lurched onto the landing, dropping the blanket he'd been holding at his belly. He'd only been going to the bathroom; but when he saw the boy turning the door handle and pressing the door and then spinning, open-mouthed, wide-eyed, to face him, he flew into a terrible rage.

It was a short and nasty scene, over in less than a minute. Harry moved faster than he'd moved for years, as though all the arthritis and cramps had fallen from him. Nimble as a bear, and just as fierce, he sprang the length of the corridor. Before Christy could duck away, he seized the boy by the hair, yanked his head backward and forward and banged his face hard on the locked door. With each word, he banged the boy's face on the door.

"My house! My doors! My rooms! Locked! Keeping... nosy... bitches... out!"

He flung the boy to the floor. Hearing the noise, the dogs had lumbered out of the bedroom, away from the fire, and now they joined in the commotion with a volley of barks which boomed in the long corridor. As Christy crawled to the top of the stairs, as blood burst from his nose and his eyes stung with tears, Harry pursued him and kicked him with his slippered feet. One of the kicks landed so heavily that the boy tumbled from the landing and cartwheeled

down the first few stairs before arresting his fall with an in-
stinctive grab at the banisters.

"A guest in my house!" Harry bellowed. "Nosing around!
Trying the doors! Peeping through keyholes! There are
things in this house you don't want to know about! For your
own good! Now bugger off, you nosy bitch! Bugger off and
don't come back!"

Christy rolled down the rest of the stairs and scrambled
to his feet in the hallway. Through bleary eyes, he could
barely see the man and the dogs on the landing; the shouting and the barking were a welter of nonsensical noise. He
caught some of the words the man was bellowing, but not
all of them, and the ones he heard were a meaningless
blather. Smearing the blood and the tears with the backs
of his hands, he felt for the piano in the doorway and fled
from the house.

For a long time, Harry remained on the landing. He
heaved with breathlessness, after the shouting and banging
and kicking. His head hurt. The pains in his chest were so
bad he thought he might retch. With all the strength he
had left, he seized the dogs by their collars with his hand
and his hook and he banged their skulls together; they slunk
back to the fire in the bedroom. Then he sat on the top
step of the staircase, stared down into the hallway and listened as a great, cold, empty silence fell on the house.

No, not quite a silence. A tiny, tinkling noise, like the
tinkling of splintered ice or the ringing of cut glass...

Harry heard it. He shook his head to clear the pounding and he held his breath to catch the sound. It was coming from the locked room, the room the beachcomber had
been trying.

He got to his feet, slowly and painfully, and tiptoed into
the bedroom. At the fireside, the dogs bared their teeth as
he reached over them and felt for something he'd hidden
behind the clock on the mantelpiece: something he'd put
there and never touched for years and years. It was a key.

He took the key and went out of the bedroom, crossed the landing and tiptoed down the corridor... hardly breathing, because he could hear the faint, cold tinkling and wanted to keep it inside his head.

Before he fitted the key to the door, to delay the moment of unlocking and opening, he did what the beachcomber had done, creaking to his knees and putting his eye to the keyhole. He felt a draught of stale air. He tasted a whiff of musty dampness. A little louder, he heard the chiming of cut glass.

Gripping the door handle, he heaved himself to his feet. He rattled the key into the keyhole. It turned stiffly, grating in the rusty lock. Then he turned the handle, pushed the door open and took a step into the room.

It was the room he'd shared with Helen. Since then, it had stood empty, its heavy curtains drawn. The darkness was dead and cold, but the smallest of draughts was stirring the chandelier on the high ceiling so that the cut glass tinkled very faintly. After a minute, as Harry blinked his eyes and sipped at the air, he could just make out the bulk of a big, wide, four-poster bed and a huge wardrobe. He crossed the room to the dressing table, whose mirror was so deeply furred with dust and blurred with cobwebs that his reflection stirred like a ghost.

No light. Harry strained his eyes. As he groped on the dressing table, he felt and fumbled before he closed his grip on a hairbrush: a woman's hairbrush, silver-backed, soft-bristled, entangled with fine, dark, silken hair. He inhaled through his mouth and he shivered. He could taste the staleness of long neglect. He threw the hairbrush down, recoiled across the room and into the corridor, where he slammed the door with a bang which made the chandelier tinkle more loudly. His breath was short and hoarse. His fingers shook so violently that when he tried to lock the door he dropped the key three times before he could fit it into the keyhole and turn it. At last, swearing horribly, spitting cobwebs, he stumped back into the spare bedroom and flung himself into the armchair.

He squeezed the key in his palm. He stared at the blazing fire. He remembered with a shudder of regret how he'd knocked the pretty blond head on the door and booted the beachcomber down the stairs. He felt the key in his cold, stiff fingers, and, as he bent forward to put it back behind the clock on the mantelpiece, he did what he customarily did to relieve his anger or frustration: he kicked the dogs as hard as he could until they got off the rug and limped out of range. Then he kicked them onto the landing and shut them out.

Dusk fell and turned to night. The fire died. Harry Clewe sat on his own. He heard the sea come into the house, the slapping and boom of breakers in the downstairs rooms.

11

He was on his own the following day, the day after that, and the day after that. And the day after that.

He waited for the crunching of wellington boots in the yard. He listened for the voice calling from the foot of the stairs. No one came. He cursed himself for a vile-tempered fool. He realized, after years of solitude, how much he missed the beachcomber's visits.

The house was alive with the noises it had always had: the whirring of a hundred starlings which roosted in the living room; the shuffle and flop of the dogs; the roar of the wind and the movement of dark, deep water; the slither of rats in the chimney, the flitter of bats in the roof, the scuttle of toads and the snoring of hedgehogs in the bathroom woodpile... but for Harry, a cold and lonely silence filled the long, long days.

Sometimes he switched on the radio, but he only half listened, because his ear was tuned to the sound of a splashing footstep across his fields, the welcoming bark of the dogs, a shout from the hallway. So he switched the radio off, tired of the news, bored by the voices.

Once, he took off his shoes and socks, rolled up his trouser legs and went splashing through the scummy pools downstairs, feeling blindly for the bass and the bream which were stranded there. But it was no fun on his own. It was silly. He got thoroughly chilled and very angry as he stampeded the fish out of the hallway, past the piano in the front door and into the yard, where the gulls and the rats could have them.

Moping in the empty house, he would wade to the mantelpiece in the living room and stare at the photograph of Helen. He would press his eyes close to it and whisper her name: no, not his wife's name, but "Christine, Christine, Christine," hissing the word over and over again. Then he would pick up the ammonite and test the familiar weight of it in his hand, the smooth, cold stone that the beachcomber's warm, strong hands had held.

Sometimes he went shooting on the foreshore, but he banged and banged and often missed; even when he hit, Gog and Magog were uselessly apathetic. They yawned and sniffed instead of lumbering after the wounded bird. Indoors, they fidgeted on the landing or wriggled by the fire, unable to settle, because they were listening too, as Harry was listening, pricking their ears in case they might hear approaching footsteps.

In this way, the house was wrung to a higher state of tension. Harry and the dogs held their breath for the spark of laughter and life they craved.

But it didn't come. If, for a short time, the house had seemed like a great ship riding a steel-gray ocean, now the ship was a hulk whose crew drifted hopelessly on a dead calm.

As for Christy, he'd staggered across the fields with blood and tears streaming from his face. Reaching the road, he'd washed himself in a rain-filled gutter before walking back to the home. Shocked but unhurt, he'd made an excuse to Mrs. Bottomley about his wet and muddy state and why he was late for roll call, and he'd resolved never to go back to Ynys Elyrch. Never.

For the next few days he attended his lessons, went in and out of school on the bus, settled to the ordered routine of the orphanage.

But he thought about Mr. Clewe. He thought about Gog and Magog. He thought of the dilapidated house with the piano wedged in the front door, where the sea rolled through the downstairs rooms and left tidal pools, banks of shingle, barnacled boulders, mattresses of weed and all kinds of leaping, flapping, silvery fish.

At night, lying awake in his dormitory bed, he remembered the conger eel they'd found coiled in the living room, the struggle to net it and drag it to the shore; he remembered the sea monster's skeleton, the biggest bones he'd ever seen in all his life; the bang of the gun that made his ears ring, the stink of smoke that made his nostrils sting, the plummeting duck that splashed in the flooded fields....

So much to remember! Such strange and secret things! The joyous dance on the landing, the smell of the man's embrace and the triumphant whooping, once the windsurfer had been knocked into the water with a well-aimed potato! The gleam of the hook where the hand should have been! The fireside feasts! The jellyfish and dogfish and thornback rays, the crabs and urchins and squids, all the washed-up treasures that he and the man had found! The silver Jag, or whatever it was, lined with walnut and leather and used as a sort of tool shed!

With a shudder of fear as he lay in the softly snoring, moonlit dormitory, he remembered a thing he thought he'd seen in the cellar, floating in the black water....

He remembered the tiny tinkling noise through the key-hole of the locked room....

He brooded on the extraordinary way in which Mr. Clewe had lost his temper. What was the man hiding, to react with such violence? What had he been shouting from the landing? Christy, confused by the bellowing and bark-ing and the fall downstairs, had caught a few words, that was all. What sort of nonsense was it? What was floating in the cellar? What was the man hiding upstairs? What was the big secret?

Christy pondered for a week. Fourteen years old, he'd been institutionalized since he was three. His curiosity for the eccentric, the bizarre and, above all, the forbidden, was highly developed. The more he thought about the house on the seashore and the man who lived in it, the more he was intrigued. Until he realized that, however he'd been abused and terrorized on his last visit, he must go back. He had to. How could he not go back?

Of course he was frightened. He would have to appease Mr. Clewe. The day he determined to visit again, he sneaked into Mrs. Bottomley's bedroom and took something, as he'd done on previous occasions: this time, a tiny thing that the matron would never miss. He went to her dressing table, unscrewed and upended a bottle of perfume and dabbed the stuff behind his ears.

So he arrived at the house, trembling with nervousness. He paused in the hallway to catch his breath. He combed his long, blond, silken hair and shook it loose around his ears.

Then he knocked on the piano and called out, "It's me, Mr. Clewe! It's me! Christine!" before he went up the stairs, giggling softly to himself.

12

There was a happy reunion.

The dogs, which had been sleeping so heavily in front of the fire that they hadn't heard the visitor splashing across the fields and crunching in the yard, hurtled onto the landing and flew down the stairs to meet Christy halfway. They lolloped around him, slobbering at his hands with their soft, wet mouths, lunging as high as their arthritic haunches would allow to try and lick at his face. Harry sprang from his armchair and crossed the bedroom as though he were on fire, stopping short to compose himself at the doorway, before emerging onto the landing and greeting the visitor as off-handedly as he could. In reality, his heart had leaped as he'd leaped from his seat, and still it lunged in his chest.

"So it's you," he said flatly. "You came back. You must be stupid. Well, since you're here, you might as well come to the fire. There's tea but no biscuits, unless you bothered to bring some."

Neither of them said much as they sat at the hearth. They were both nervous. The boy occupied his hands by patting the dogs' heads; Harry was busy with mugs and teabags, powdered milk and boiling water. They eyed one another, stealing surreptitious glances. Harry frowned and sniffed and glared at Christy, sniffed again as he caught a whiff of the perfume. Christy blushed, looking away, pushing his hair behind his ears and folding his hands in his lap, and the next time he glanced up, he saw that Mr. Clewe was smiling, his face glistening because he'd been kneeling at the flames to attend to the kettle.

"Your head's all right then?" Harry said, hedging as closely to an apology as he could manage. "I can be a bad-tempered old goat, sometimes. It's nearly got me into trouble once or twice, in years gone by, but I've just about got away with it... so far, anyway. Well, it'll teach you to mind your own business. I don't mind you coming out here as long as you keep your nose out of things that don't concern you. That's a rule of the house. I suppose you have rules at the orphanage? Of course you do. And doesn't Mrs. Wigglebottom, or whatever she's called, punish you if you're naughty? Of course she does."

Christy smiled and said yes, of course she did, stopping himself from adding that Mrs. Bottomley had never slammed his face against a door until his nose was bleeding. As he nodded his head in polite acknowledgment of what the man was saying, as his hair swung around his ears, he could smell the perfume he'd put on. He could smell it on his fingers, too.

Harry leaned closely and sniffed when he passed the tea he'd poured out. "That's nice!" he said, smiling softly. "That's nice!"

So the relationship resumed, guarded, wary, precarious: precarious because its foundations were built on the secrets that the man and the boy kept from each other. Harry was as crusty as ever, although a vein of schoolboyish good humor seemed to open in the presence of his young companion. Christy was coy, unsuspecting so far that the man found this coyness provocative. The boy liked the perfume, because it masked the smells of the stale, unwashed bedding and the rancid, unwashed man, and because it made him feel nice to be wearing it: as simple as that. It made him feel different. Slightly, minutely, it altered the way he moved: the way he angled his head and swung his hair, the way he smiled, the way he moistened his lips with his tongue. He noticed these differences in himself, each time he came to the house. And Harry Clewe noticed too.

They relished their isolation, as though the house were a desert island and they were delighted to be marooned on it. Gloriously alone, the man and the boy and the dogs hunted and fished and feasted, walking the shore, wading the fields, sifting the infinite treasure that the sea brought up. No one disturbed them.

Then the windsurfer came back, and everything changed.

13

It happened like this. The boy had been caught in the house again as the tide rose. It was a Sunday; he was allowed out of the orphanage all day, as long as he reported back by late afternoon. When he'd crossed the fields to the house, he'd seen that the sea was already very high and still rising, and he'd known that, by mid-morning, he would be marooned at Ynys Elyrch. Really he was looking forward to it, that he and Mr. Clewe and the two dogs should be cut off by the swirling sea. Harry was glad, too. In the same way, he was excited by the prospect of being marooned with his young visitor.

So, that Sunday morning, once the two of them were cozily established by the fire, with tea and crumpets, with their feet warming on the backs of the great, snoring hounds, they would glance out of the bedroom window and pretend they hadn't noticed how the sea came closer and closer, how it crossed the fields, filled the ditches, poured through the hedges and the tumbledown walls, how at last it reached the house. They pretended they hadn't heard it slither through the front door and flood the hallway. From time to time, they looked at one another over the rims of their tea mugs, and they smiled. After a while, going to the bathroom to fetch an armful of wood from the bath, Christy saw that the water was slapping at the staircase. It was grand to gaze from the landing window and see nothing but chopping, white waves lit by a clear, cold sun... a swollen brown ocean. The house was in the sea! The sea was in the house! Grand!

"Looks as though you're here for the day," Harry muttered, as he stumped out of the bedroom and joined Christy on the landing. "You stupid girl! Didn't you see the tide coming in? What if I decide to throw you out? Can you swim? Eh? Didn't you say you were a bloody mermaid or something? Looks as though I'm stuck with you all bloody day...."

But his grumpiness slipped, for once, and his face split into a wide grin. Christy grinned too. They stood together on the landing and surveyed their watery isolation.

Then, hundreds of yards away on the flooded horizon, a vivid purple shape appeared... unmistakable, a splash of gorgeous color against a gray sky. Christy saw it straight away: Harry saw it a few seconds later, where it danced and fluttered like a brilliant spark. But neither of them said anything. They stiffened and stared as the sail raced toward the house.

Sensing a tension in the atmosphere, the dogs came out of the bedroom too. They peered out of the window, forcing their heads between the man and the boy, and when they caught the zigzag and flutter of the purple thing, and heard the snapping and the slapping of it, they started to bark. There was pandemonium. Harry bellowed at the animals and booted them off the landing; they skidded down the stairs, slithered to a halt when they met the sea in the hallway, turned round and clambered back up again, still barking as loudly as they could. Hooking the window open, Harry reached for the sack of potatoes which was leaning at the top of the stairs and prepared to hurl his missiles as soon as the target came in range. He shouted and shouted, a blather of meaningless threats which echoed up and down the landing with the booming noise of the dogs. The louder he shouted, the louder the dogs barked; the louder the dogs barked, the more noise the man made. And when the windsurfer veered within a few yards of the house, grinning a dazzling grin and tossing his golden hair, Harry lobbed the potatoes feebly out of the window.

Christy had kept out of the way while the dogs took the brunt of the man's frustration. Now he felt a wonderful, surging thrill inside him. This was the kind of adventure he was looking for, after the ordered routine of the orphanage: a house surrounded by foaming sea, a mad man and two booming mad hounds, defending the territory from anyone foolish enough to venture within range of whatever weapons came to hand.... With a squeal of excitement, he lunged for the potatoes and braced himself to hurl the missiles from the window.

"Let me do it, Mr. Clewe!" he yelled. "I'll get him! I got him last time, didn't I?"

He leaned from the landing. The windsurfer was turning his craft just below the window. The sail flapped, a glistening, struggling thing, and for a moment the youth fought to control it, too busy to glance up at the house although he'd come so close deliberately to draw the fire of the man who lived there. As Harry stood back and watched, his chest heaving, his mouth opening and closing, Christy took aim and threw.

He threw twice, three times. The potatoes missed by yards. They splashed into the water, nowhere near the youth or his purple sail. Before Christy could reach for more ammunition, the sail bulged with a bang as the wind filled it and the board sped away. The man and the boy could hear the windsurfer laughing.

"Useless bitch!" Harry shouted.

There was more and greater pandemonium. Harry exploded all his anger and frustration. He lunged at Christy, seized him by the hair and shook him so hard that the boy could feel the teeth rattling in his head. He jutted his face to the boy's face and shouted hoarsely, spitting crumbs of crumpet, "Bloody fluke the last time, was it? Beginner's bloody luck, was it? Now all you can do is stand there and throw like a bloody useless feeble girl! Why the hell do you come here?"

He shoved so hard that Christy staggered, fell backward and only saved himself from rolling down the stairs by grabbing at the banister. With an expression of terrible disgust, Harry wheeled away and turned his anger on the dogs, which had been barking wildly all this time. Lashing out with his feet, he drove them into the bedroom. The bellowing and barking continued, louder and louder, a scuffling of snarls and grunts as the man pursued the dogs round and round the fireside furniture.

Christy struggled to his feet. All the strength was wrung from him. Sobbing with anger and humiliation, blinded by tears, he crossed the landing to the window again. As he leaned on the sill, the house itself seemed to tremble with the slap of the waves, the gusting wind and the dreadful commotion of the hysterical man and the hysterical dogs. A hundred yards away, he saw the flash of the purple sail, slowing and stopping and turning, no more than a blur through the welling tears.

The noise increased. The house rang with a futile, impotent rage. The man's words clanged in Christy's head, and every word was a wound, which sent a lancing pain through him. Trying to blot out the roaring sounds which still came from the bedroom, he knelt at the window. As the sail grew bigger and bigger, he steadied his breathing, but the blood was pounding in his head and his chest. He felt for the gun which was leaning in the corner and he pointed it out of the window, resting the weight of the barrel on the sill.

The noise from the bedroom reached a howling crescendo. Either the man was beating the dogs to death or the dogs were dismembering and devouring the man. Christy didn't care which. He sighted down the barrel. The purple sail filled his vision. It raced closer and closer until he could see the flying, golden hair and the shining, black, muscular body.

He held his breath. He felt for the trigger. He heard the flap of the sail as it came within yards of the house. And the last thing he saw before he shut his eyes was the windsurfer's face below him, how it looked up at the window and changed from a broad, bright grin to a look of disbelieving horror...

Christy squeezed the trigger.

14

The bang was deafening. The recoil slammed Christy so hard in the shoulder that he tumbled backward, fell away from the window and sat down with a thump at the top of the stairs. He let go of the gun, which clattered to the floor. Dazed almost to unconsciousness, he lolled against the banister. His head was ringing. His ears buzzed. His eyes stung as the cordite smoke whirled around him. The whole house seemed to rock with the force of the explosion.

Gradually, as the noise subsided to a muffled echo, as the pealing in his ears faded and was replaced by a high-pitched whine which suddenly stopped when he shook his head, there was a profound stillness. The bang had erased all the sounds of the sea and the wind, all the sounds of the house, and left a silent emptiness. The dogs stopped barking. The man stopped bellowing. As Christy sat on the landing and smeared the gunpowder tears from his cheeks, Harry came slowly out of the bedroom and stared around him, gaping, blinking, opening and closing his mouth like a big, bleary-eyed fish. When his gaze fell on Christy, he frowned as though he couldn't quite place the befuddled figure who was sprawled on the floor, as though they might have met before, a long time ago, but he couldn't remember when or where it had been. Christy stared back. Neither of them spoke. When the dogs cocked their heads out of the bedroom to sniff the swirling gunsmoke, Harry turned and pushed them gently back again, closing the door with the tiniest of clicks.

No more shouting. The pandemonium was over. A great calm had settled.

Harry moved to the landing window and looked out, standing there with his back to Christy. He looked for a long time. Then, with an enormous sigh, he knelt to the gun, picked it up and leaned it in its usual corner. When at last he turned to the boy, the frown had gone, replaced by the flicker of a smile.

"Oh, dear," he whispered, breathing the words so quietly that Christy could hardly hear them. "What have you done? More of your beginner's luck? What's my little mermaid done now?"

He crossed the landing with his hand outstretched, and squatted very close.

"Don't be frightened," he whispered. "We can't be frightened. We're going to be too busy. Come on, up you get."

He took hold of Christy's hand and pulled him to his feet. Still deafened, his ears popping, the boy staggered a little, grabbed at the man's arm to stop himself from falling over, and then allowed himself to be led across the landing. They stood together at the open window and looked out.

The purple sail was floating in the water. It rippled and flexed on the surface, like a gigantic Portuguese man-o'war. The board bobbed about, tangled in the bright nylon cords. The youth was moving too, feeling into the waves with his hands and splashing his long, black, shiny legs.

But he wasn't swimming. Face down, his body jerking uncontrollably, he struggled to keep afloat. As Harry and Christy watched from the window, they heard a horrid gurgling noise from under the water, and then the youth lifted his head above the surface long enough to let out a bubbling cry before he went under again. He was drowning. With every spasm, as he kicked and beat at the water, the sea around him changed color from sandy brown to a deeper, darker red. He was drowning in a swirling stain of his own blood.

"Oh dear, oh dear, oh dear," Harry was whispering, and then he simply mouthed to himself without making a sound.

Christy stood beside him, too numb to say or do anything. He saw the stain grow bigger and bigger and blur the outline of the purple sail, and he saw how the redness colored the bright blond hair on the head which lifted and plunged, which gurgled and squealed in the bloodied water.

When Harry said, "Well, come on, we've got things to do," in a perfectly matter-of-fact voice, the boy followed him meekly downstairs. There, without a moment's hesitation, they both lowered themselves into the waves, waist-deep in the hallway; then, hand in hand for support on the treacherous footing, they waded to the front door, squeezed past the piano and into the open sea outside the house.

The water was icy. The gale whipped a spray off the waves which spattered in their faces like hail. Fighting against the suck of the tide, they trod their way around the side of the house, struggled to the next corner and turned into the field which the landing window overlooked. It was difficult going for the boy, who was wiry and strong; the man was heaving with breathlessness, cold and exertion as the water beat on his chest and splashed into his face. But it was Harry who fought on and on, tugging Christy with him. It was Harry who breasted the waves in front of the boy, taking the brunt of the spray. It was Harry who kept up a stream of encouragement, urging Christy to wade strongly onward, to feel for obstacles underfoot, to brace his body to the flood. As a slick of blood coiled round the house and welled against their chests, it was Harry who turned the corner, waded the last few paces to the stricken windsurfer and reached him first, who grabbed a handful of hair and lifted the face out of the water.

"Help me, Christine!" he shouted. "We can float him back to the front door and get him inside! Come on! Help me!"

But the boy recoiled from the glistening black body. Staring with disgust at the crimson scum which the youth had churned into froth, Christy lunged away, as though he might wade back into the house and hide in the bedroom until the nightmare was over.

Harry reacted with surprising agility, despite the weight of the water around him. Holding the windsurfer with his right hand, towing him so roughly by the hair that the youth let out a horrible, high-pitched, gargling shout, Harry surged after the boy and grabbed him to a halt, expertly hooking the belt of his jeans.

"You did this!" he bellowed. "Look what you've done! Look! And then help me to fix it!"

He summoned another burst of strength and rattled the windsurfer's head so hard that flecks of spittle flew onto Christy's face. "You did this!" he shouted again. "Not me! Think of the trouble you're in if you don't help!"

So the boy helped. As the windsurfer squealed like a piglet and writhed his slippery body, the man and the boy took hold of his arms and towed him back the way they'd come. They struggled to the front door, and there, with an immense effort of pushing and pulling and bending, they maneuvered him past the obstructive piano; until at last, after a more strenuous battle than they'd had with the conger eel, they slid the youth into the calmer waters of the hallway and beached him on the stairs.

There they all lay, spent: Harry, retching and spitting; Christy, staring aghast at the thing they'd brought in; the windsurfer, mewing very softly, his eyes closed, his mouth opening and closing, his hair plastered about his forehead, his face and fingers terribly blanched.

The lull lasted less than a minute. Christy tore his eyes from the windsurfer and glanced at Harry Clewe. There was a curious blurring of expressions on the man's face: a flickering smile and a tic, a shadow behind the eyes which warned of another outburst of violence. The windsurfer had stopped mewing. He was moaning, louder and louder, thrashing his limbs as though an electric current was passing through him. Christy stood up and started to yell, "Do something, Mr. Clewe! Please do something!" which made the windsurfer open his eyes, roll his head from side to side and groan more and more loudly still.

So the lull was over. Harry struggled to his feet. He took Christy by the hair, as he'd done before in a fit of blinding anger, and he shook him until all the teeth in his head were rattled loose. Then, leaving him blubbering like the girl he pretended to be, Harry knelt to the windsurfer. Roaring, he shook him too, and the youth squealed shrilly, the blond head lolling as though the neck were broken.

Again it was pandemonium. A fourteen-year-old boy hysterical with panic; a youth who might or might not have been dying from a gunshot wound; a man unmanned by uncontrollable fury... Certainly, the little lull was over.

"Shut up!" Harry roared at the windsurfer. Then, "Help me!" he roared at Christy.

Christy started moving, in a kind of trance. He obeyed the man, blubbering noisily, responding to the bellowed instructions like an automaton. Together they floated the windsurfer across the hall and into the living room, oblivious of the youth's gurgle of pain as he bumped on shingle and jagged rocks. And all the time, Harry shouted so wildly that his face was swollen and his mouth was frothed with spittle, "Shut up! For fuck's sake, shut up!" while he shook the youth as hard as he could; then at Christy, "For fuck's sake, help me! You did this! Not me!"

They dumped the windsurfer in the shallower water near the fireplace, and squatted beside him. All three of them were delirious with panic and pain and exertion. Harry reached to the windsurfer's throat, took hold of the zip and tugged it down. The youth screamed more loudly and more horribly than he'd ever screamed before. The suit split open as though the body were slit from throat to navel, and a pile of steaming, slithering guts fell out.

The noise reached another crescendo.

The windsurfer, seeing the wound, feeling his hot young life spill out, started to chatter like a chimpanzee.

Christy threw back his head and howled, amazed at the heat and smell and the sheer quantity of the stuff that slopped from the windsurfer's belly.

And Harry, with a mooing cry that was almost like laughter, surged out of the water. He waded to the mantelpiece, reached for the ammonite and waded back again. As Christy stared and howled, the man smashed the stone onto the youth's head. He smashed with the ammonite four times, accompanying each blow with a gritted shout.

"*Shut!… Up! Shut!… Up!*"

The windsurfer shut up. His face was stove in. Teeth and tongue and bones were mashed in a scarlet pulp.

Christy shut up, too. So did Harry, although his breathing was very loud. The blows with the ammonite had the same effect as the shotgun blast had had. As the water subsided, a great stillness fell.

For a long time, the man and the boy said nothing. They knelt in the pool, on either side of the dead youth: Christy, with his eyes and mouth wide open, his hands to his head, clutching his hair in his fingers; Harry, cuddling the coiled, black fossil to his stomach. After what had seemed like hours of nightmare, but had lasted no more than a few minutes, the house was profoundly silent.

15

It was silent for a long time. So long that, when the sea had drained out, the man and the boy were still kneeling in the pools it left behind. The room was twilit, although it was only midday; the cobwebbed cornices of the high ceiling were lost in shadow and the walls were cast in a submarine gloom. For more than an hour, without moving a muscle, the boy stared at the hole in the windsurfer's stomach and all the stuff that had come out of it; while the man, his head bowed as though he were praying, stared at the blooded ammonite.

Christy moved first. He lowered his hands from his hair, dropped them into his lap and knitted his fingers together. Harry glanced up. His own fingers started to move, caressing the sticky, dark clots on the fossil. Still, for another ten or fifteen minutes, neither of them spoke. The room grew darker. The shadows, which had formed on the ceiling like thunder clouds, seemed to fall until they cloaked the huddled figures and the body of the windsurfer which lay between them. Soon, the bright blond head had gone dull, and the guts were as black as the rubber suit they'd spilled out of. The man and the boy looked at one another until their faces were lost in darkness. Harry let go of the ammonite, so that it rolled into the puddles with a splash and a thud... and this, the first sound in the house since the ammonite itself had caused such a deadening silence, signaled that the silence was over.

The boy blinked very hard, as though he'd been asleep and had had a nightmare. When he saw that the nightmare was real, he gasped, peering again at the dead body. He looked at the pulp where the face had been, trying, in his mind's eye, to rearrange the teeth and the splintered cheek-bones to resemble the face that the youth had had. He pointed to it, lifting a trembling hand.

"You did this, Mr. Clewe," he whispered. "Not me. He was alive until you did this."

There was another silence. In the darkness, Harry shrugged and nodded. "Yes," he whispered. "I did that."

Then, with his hook, he pointed to the wound in the youth's belly that the shotgun blast had made. "And you did this, Christine," he whispered. "Not me. He was alive until you did this."

The boy shuddered so violently that his teeth rattled. "Yes, Mr. Clewe," he whispered. "I did that."

So they stared at the wounds they'd made. When Harry said, "We both did it, we did it together," the two of them nodded their heads. Harry reached over the mass of the windsurfer's body. Christy reached out as well. And they joined their icy hands, gripping until they could feel the warmth of a bond between them: a bond forged in blood, sealed in silence.

At last Harry stood up. He heaved himself to his feet, aching with a terrible cold in all his bones, and stretched his arms and legs to get the circulation going. Treading across the room, he gently put the ammonite beside the photograph of Helen. Then he leaned his forehead on the mantelpiece and closed his eyes. He remained there, without moving. He tried to think what he was going to do next, but his mind went stubbornly blank. After a while, he heard footsteps go squelching out of the room, but he didn't lift his head or open his eyes to look. He listened as the footsteps crossed the hallway and tramped upstairs, as the bedroom door was opened and then closed a few seconds later. The footsteps came downstairs, crossed the hallway and went outside, through the front door. Harry didn't know why the beachcomber had gone upstairs and then outside. He didn't care. He rested his forehead on the mantelpiece and squeezed his eyes shut.

After another minute, the boy came into the house again and stood at the living-room door.

"Look, Mr. Clewe," he said very softly, so that Harry opened his eyes and turned round. "I've been upstairs for these." He was holding up the butchering knife in one hand and the torch in the other. "And I've been to the car for these." He'd brought the axe, the sledgehammer and the splitting wedge.

Straight away, he knelt to the body of the windsurfer.

This is what he did.

He peeled off the windsurfer's suit. It came away without any cutting, folding like a blubbery skin, and the coiled entrails slithered into the water and quivered like the jellyfish that the tide sometimes left in the house. The windsurfer was wearing a pair of red briefs. Christy made to pull them off as well, but then, changing his mind in deference to Mr. Clewe, he left them on. At a nod from the boy, Harry took hold of the torch and switched it on, because an early dusk had made the room almost as dark as night. He aimed the beam exactly where the boy told him to. Harry's mind was blank and empty. His veins were ice. His heart beat faintly, the softest of thumps in the cave of his chest. But his hand was steady, so that the pool of light was as still as the rock pools where the sea had been. Quite numb, he watched without blinking, without wincing or flinching, as the boy set to.

Christy had had a good teacher. Harry Clewe had taught him, out in the yard, to use the axe, the wedge and the sledgehammer on the driftwood they'd brought from the shore. The axe was heavy and very sharp. When the boy brought it down on the windsurfer's left shin, it cut straight through and embedded itself in the floorboards. The foot was severed entirely. The boy took aim, and the right foot was off as well.

Breathing hard, he panted, "Help me to turn him over, Mr. Clewe," and together they rolled the youth onto his belly. With the rhythm and accuracy of an experienced woodsman, the boy swung the axe again. It shone in the torchlight and hit the target behind the windsurfer's right knee, so hard and so swift that the blade was through, splitting the gristle and cartilage and thudding into the floor-boards in one blow. The left leg, too, cut cleanly at the knee.

At this, Harry dropped the torch. It landed with a splash. Suddenly overcome, as though all the nightmares he'd ever had were welling inside him like an unbearable migraine, he clapped his hand to his mouth and staggered for the door. It was too much for him. Retching so hard that he thought his chest might burst, he stumbled out of the room and collapsed on the stairs.

The boy shrugged. He picked up the torch and stood it upright on the floor, so that a creamy moon quivered on the ceiling. He rested for a minute. Out in the hallway, Harry sat on the stairs with his head in his hands, and he listened as work resumed.

The crunch of the axe.

The ringing of the sledgehammer on the splitting wedge.

The crunch of the axe.

The squelch of footsteps across the room.

The crunch of the axe.

The thud of heavy, lifeless objects dropped here and there. The boy worked until the body was no longer human, until it was only the bits of a dead thing, like the other dead things that the tide had fetched up and dropped and left behind on the waterlogged fields. It held no horrors for Christy. Peeled out of the glistening black suit, the flamboyant athleticism all gone now that the arms and the legs were stacked up like stiff, hard pieces of wood in different corners of the room, it was no more human than a drowned sheep or a beached porpoise or a stranded jellyfish. But it still had the red underpants on, maintaining an absurd decency, despite everything that had happened to it.

Harry listened, unable to move, paralyzed with horror. He listened as the boy continued, unflagging, unhurried, and he matched the sounds to the technique he'd taught him. Notch with the knife; fit the wedge and slam it home with an easy swing of the sledgehammer; chop with the axe. Let the weight of the tool do the work. So Christy notched and wedged and chopped and didn't stop until the windsurfer was butchered meat.

Mid-afternoon. Outside, dusk was turning to twilight. Inside, the torch seemed very bright in the dark room.

"So it's done," the boy said at last. He was exhausted. All the panic, all the splashing and thrashing and squealing commotion and then the strenuous business of the abattoir, had overwhelmed him with weariness. He'd been up to his neck in icy water and then working hard all afternoon. He dropped the axe where he'd dropped the wedge, the sledgehammer and the knife, and he dropped himself to his knees on a bed of weed.

"It's done," he whispered, meaning to call out to the man but too tired to raise his voice. He squeezed his eyes shut and stayed still, blank with shock. He didn't hear Harry come into the room.

Harry stooped for the torch, which, having toppled over, was spilling its light in a yellow pool. He found it, straightened up and slowly pointed the beam around the room. It was as though he was seeing it for the first time — a strange room, so tall and wide that the corners were a blur of cobwebs where the torchlight fell; whose floor was a rubble of shingle and boulders, puddled with sea water, strewn with green and black weed; where a figure knelt as though praying, head bowed, breathing very loudly; where pieces of meat lay scattered about, gleaming white and red as the torchlight touched them.... A very strange room.

The boy started to tremble. His teeth were chattering very loudly. Zigzagging the torch, Harry lumbered across the room, sank to his knees and enfolded him in a huge, pungent embrace; and Christy, responding instinctively, lifted his own arms, wrapped them around the man's thick, baggy waist and linked his fingers on the other side. They squeezed with all their might, widower and orphan, bonded by the murderous nightmare they were sharing.

"Don't worry, little Christine! You'll be all right! I promise you'll be all right!" Harry was whispering, pressing his mouth in the long, fine hair, where, despite the wading in the sea, despite the gory work, the perfume was still strong. "But you've got to go back straight away, or else you'll be in trouble with matron. You've done enough. I'll do the clearing-up. There'll be nothing left for anyone to find. Go back to the home now! It's getting late!"

They hugged one another, holding their bodies as close and as hard as they could. Christy was trembling with cold, or sobbing, because Harry could feel the shoulders heave as he pressed his hands on them. But when he lifted the soft, pale face with his fingers and stared down into the bleary gray eyes, he was amazed to find that the beachcomber was laughing...

Christy was laughing so much, silently, uncontrollably, that tears ran down his cheeks and into the corners of his mouth. He tried to speak, throwing his head back and spluttering incoherently, but it was simply too funny for words...

As last he succeeded. He struggled out of the man's arms and bent to pick up the torch again. He flashed the light around, playing it on the bits of the carcass he'd dismembered.

"Trouble, Mr. Clewe? Trouble with matron?" he hooted. "We've shot a man with a gun! We've bashed his head in with a rock! We've chopped him up into little pieces! But worst of all, I'm going to be late for Mrs. Bottomley's roll call! Big trouble, that is!"

Shrieking with laughter, he dropped the torch again and bolted from the living room. He leaped across the hallway, slithered past the piano and was gone. No good-bye, no thank-you-for-having-me. Harry heard a few more hysterical squeals, receding as the splashes of wellington boots faded away, and then there was silence. The torchlight shone from the seaweedy floor and smothered the walls in gray-green cobwebs. It was the only light in the world. He was alone in the living room.

Living room! He giggled at the inappropriateness of the word. Dying room, death room, slaughterhouse, abattoir... more like it. He picked up the torch and beamed it at the hands and arms and feet and legs which, an hour before, had been expertly maneuvering a windsurfing board around the houses; at the head which had grinned with so much youthful arrogance; at the flayed flesh and exposed muscle which had bent the sail to the wind. Living room! He giggled again.

The laughter was infectious. Whatever it was, hysteria brought on by exhaustion or a release of tension once the killing and the butchery were done, Harry succumbed to it. The giggle grew bigger and bigger until it overwhelmed him and he felt his body shaking. He welcomed it. He warmed to it. He stood in the middle of the room, where the sand was soaked in blood, threw back his head and roared with such hectic madness that his body coursed with heat. As he did so, the weariness fell from him. He steamed with life and strength. The whole house seemed to tremble, as his guffaws rang to the ceiling.

And through the noise he heard an answering cry: two voices from upstairs, muffled behind a closed door, but also hot and keenly baying. The dogs...

He'd forgotten them. He stopped laughing and he listened. He wiped the tears from his face, he tasted the salt in his mouth, and he heard that the dogs were scrabbling too, as they howled and belled. Driven wild by a scent that had drifted up the stairs and into the bedroom, Gog and Magog were tearing at the door with their blunt claws, banging with their heads, clashing their teeth together. They were mad with hunger.

Harry worked quickly, fired by a new strength. With his hook, he scrabbled in the shingle and found the ring of the trap door; he heaved the door upward. For a moment he pointed the torch at the deep, black water, as though he could see something moving down there. The cold rose from the flooded cellar, dank and stale like the

air from a grave, so that he recoiled and let the trap door
bang wide open. He crossed the room and hooked the black
rubber suit, bundled it up and tossed it into the water; an
invisible current sucked it away, out of sight beneath the
floorboards. He moved to the fireplace. There, he seized
the windsurfer's head, swung it back to the middle of the
room and splashed it into the cellar. It sank, the blond hair
fanning like the tendrils of a jellyfish, and disappeared
dimly into darkness. Harry slammed the trap door shut and
bolted it carefully.

So the room was ready for the dogs.

16

He slung the tools into the hallway and went slowly up the stairs. Pausing for a moment on the landing, he looked out of the window. He could hear Gog and Magog flinging themselves about, barging into the furniture, knocking over books and newspapers, upsetting plates, scattering cutlery. Snarling horribly, they battered at the door with all their weight. But Harry ignored them. He stood at the landing window and looked out.

There was more light left in the day than he'd thought, after the flickering shadows in the living room. He could see across the foreshore to the distant beach. The tide had gone out. The fields were a mess of mud and puddles, driftwood tangled with weed, a debris of plastic bags and bottles and rags, oddments of clothing and discarded shoes. The ditches were flooded. The walls were rubble. The hedges were broken and dead, now that the tide had torn up their roots. A heron was stabbing for eels that the sea had left behind. The crows had come to the foreshore, where there were plenty of dying and drowned things to be picked at. In this world of drenching and darkness, the windsurfer's sail shone like a pool of purple water, and the board itself was bright and white. They would have to be moved.

Taking a deep breath, he flung the door open and flattened himself against the wall. The dogs fought to get out, jammed for a second until they burst through, and then hurtled downstairs. They skidded in the shingled hallway, turned right and disappeared into the living room.

"Get on with it, you monsters!" he whispered. "Eat yourselves sick! Don't ever say I don't feed you properly!"

He went into the bedroom, moving fast because night was falling and there were things to be done while there was still some light. He built up the fire; the room was in chaos, where the dogs had been brawling, but the fire was the most important thing. He waited and watched to make sure that the flames had caught, then he came out of the room, closed the door and went downstairs.

Gog and Magog were doing their part of the business. Harry glanced into the living room, as he barricaded the dogs inside by dragging the shattered doors together and winding the handles together with twine; he didn't want the animals to carry pieces of the windsurfer out of the house. Gog was in one corner, crunching bones, chewing splinters. Magog had dragged something to another part of the room and was standing over it, rasping with a long, pink tongue. Already, in the time he'd taken to go in and out of the bedroom and mend the fire, the dogs had eaten the sweetest morsels: now they were settling to the main course. They would be busy all night, unhurried, insatiable; they would chew and swallow the nub ends of the toughest bones. The few remaining shreds would be scoured out by the next tide. Whatever the dogs left, the sea could have. By noon the following day, the house would be scrubbed as clean as a slab in a butcher's shop.

He squeezed out of the front door, promising himself that sooner or later he'd try and shift the piano, and he trod around the yard. It was a still, mild twilight. The last time he'd followed this route, he'd been up to his chest in water and the spray had been lashing his face. Now the sea and the wind had dropped. He bent in the slime where the board and the sail were lying, wound a tangle of nylon cords around his hook, gripped a corner of the sail and started to pull. It was a clumsy contraption, bigger and heavier on the water-logged ground than it had looked when it was afloat. With great difficulty, he dragged the board across the fields. At the same time, as though it were a conspiracy to make the job as tiresome as possible, the last of the daylight disappeared. In the darkness, Harry struggled with all the weight and the infuriating confusion. He swore, he spat, he gritted his teeth. He hated the purple sail with a terrible hatred, more than he'd ever hated it before, even when the blond youth had flaunted it close to the house; he loathed the board, which caught in every root and rut and rubbled stone wall. It took an hour, with the dregs of his strength, to man-handle it onto the beach.

At last he could float it. Up to his waist in the water, he slid the board out to sea. He pushed it away, heard it slap on the waves, saw the sail spread like an oil slick, a black stain on the gray surface, and he waited until he could no longer hear it or see it. Then he waded to the shore. He didn't know where the windsurfer's board would go in the night, as the tide continued to fall; he didn't know where it might be beached, the following day or the day after that. Miles away, wherever the currents took it... He didn't know and he didn't care. Drained of strength, drained of feeling, he stumbled across the fields and back into the house.

Upstairs, stripped and dried and snuggled in bed, he stared at the firelit ceiling. He could barely remember how the day had started; the events of it were such a nightmar-ish jumble. Too tired to unravel them, to make any sense of them, he shut his eyes on the dancing flames and fell into a dreamless sleep.

17

There was a thin, blustery sunlight the following morning, when Harry Clewe came downstairs and undid the twine from the living room door handles. He shivered, with a blanket wrapped round his shoulders. His fingers trembled on the troublesome knots. But when he managed to push the doors open and they banged on their loosened hinges, he found that Gog and Magog had done a thorough job. They'd left nothing but a few scraps.

He shuffled through the shingle, scuffing with his boots at tag ends which the dogs had chewed and rejected. Gog and Magog hardly stirred as he walked slowly about the room. They stared balefully, yawning, panting, lolling their tongues, and when he clapped his hands at them to move, they lurched to their feet. They were stiff from lying all night on the wet weed; they were thirsty from swallowing salt water; they'd eaten until they were almost immobilized by the weight of the meat in their bellies. Gorged full, they could hardly walk. When Harry swung a boot as they waddled across the room, they growled very deeply, showing bloodied mouths; they hadn't the energy to snarl or snap, although, in their old age, they'd become as ill-tempered as their master. Their breath was vile. Their coats stank of the blood and guts that had spilled into the shingle.

Wrinkling his nose in disgust, Harry kicked the dogs out of the house; they went out of the front door, in search of fresh water. He collected his tools from the hallway and followed the dogs outside, where he rinsed the knife, the sledge-hammer and the axe in a flooded ditch. Returning to the yard, he put the clean tools inside the Daimler.

And then, that morning, the tide came in. It slid across the fields, encircled the house and slithered into the hallway. Slowly, nosing a scummy foam, forcing clusters of bubbles from the compacted sand, it flooded the downstairs rooms. For a while, it was still and calm. It didn't seem to deepen. It lapped at the skirting boards in an idle, desultory way, like a guest unsure of whether to stay or leave. But all the time, the swell was driving from the ocean, across the shore, over the fields and through the front door. By noon, the water had reached the sixth step on the staircase. Gradually the wind increased. It bore the sea inland. Bigger and bigger, heavier and heavier, foam-capped waves rolled through the windows. Soon there was a churning commotion throughout the house.

Harry watched from the landing. He sat on the top step, hugging his knees to his chest and chuckling like a boy. The dogs crouched on either side of him. He flinched from their fetid breath, shoved them away when he saw something like a toenail caught in their fur, but still he grinned and chuckled. He heard the thump and suck of the waves downstairs, felt the house shudder at the weight. He thought of the scouring of sand and shingle, the scrubbing of barnacled boulders, the cleansing, the rinsing, the sting of salt. Good! What better way to remove the remains of a murder? To have a pair of great gluttonous hounds crunch and swallow the body, and then to have the sea come in, thousands of tons of endlessly recycled water, to flush out every speck of the evidence!

He remained on the landing with Gog and Magog throughout the afternoon. He saw how the tide reached its height at the tenth step, how it paused as the wind subsided and the house seemed to sigh with a gentle throbbing swell, and then he watched as the level began to drop. It was deeply satisfying, as good as the sex he could dimly remember: a gentle penetration, a thrusting rhythm, a fine crescendo, a crashing climax, a period of profound fullness... a sucking withdrawal.

It was dusk by the time the tide had gone out again. The downstairs rooms were a foot deep in pristine sand, salty shingle and the rubbery salad leaves of fresh seaweed. The house was scrubbed clean.

Harry walked the shore with the gun and the dogs. There was no sign of the board or the purple sail, although he peered to the horizon in every direction. There was no sign of the beachcomber either; he didn't expect a visit, after the nightmarish events of the previous day. The tide dropped until the twilit estuary was exposed as acres of sand flats, muddy creeks and a trickling river. Harry spent the evening upstairs in front of the fire, turning a teal on the spit. No, he hadn't expected a visit, but still he felt a niggle of disappointment that he was on his own.

"Looks like it's just you and me," he whispered to the dogs.

Gog and Magog lay on the rug, so close to the flames that steam rose from their coats. They'd lost the stink of the night before, after a walk on the beach, a splash and a tumble in sea water as they raced to reach the teal he'd shot. Like the house, they were clean again. They smelled of salt and the cold, green ocean. Without lifting their heads, they opened their eyes and blinked at Harry.

"Just me and you," he whispered. "Gog and Magog and Harry Clewe. She isn't coming today. Bloody rude, after all the hospitality we've shown her..."

He rumpled their ears, snatching his hand away when the dogs wrinkled their snouts at him.

"And the same to you, too!" he added. "Ungrateful buggers, after all the nice dinners I get for you!"

He ate the teal, once the skin was golden brown and the juices were spitting into the fire. He wiped his mouth on a corner of his shirt, split the carcass into two pieces and dropped it for the dogs. At midnight he performed his bedtime ritual — trudging downstairs to piss into the hallway, trudging back up again to gather an armful of wood from the bath and build the fire — before closing the bedroom door and snuggling, fully clothed, beneath the blankets. He caught a whiff of perfume where the beachcomber had sat on the bed, and he snuffled at it with his flame-reddened face until he fell asleep.

He had a disturbed night. He dreamed of women, whose faces swam before him.

At first it was Sarah, blonde and pretty, the hitchhiker, the rockclimber, the toad-handler....

Then it was Lizzie, flame-haired and pale-faced, his sister, his lover, the mother of his child....

Then Zoë, his blind and brilliant daughter, the shooting star, the star-splitter, the burnt-out star...

Then Helen, warm and fragrant, who'd tried to rekindle some warmth in Harry Clewe before finding, too late, that he was already fossilized.

The faces came to him and drifted away. He heard their voices, their laughter, distant and faint, echoing through all the years since they'd been gone. And at last it was Christine, slim and blonde and pert in the baggy jeans and jacket she always wore. He could hear her childish giggle.

The dream grew hotter and louder and the faces blurred, looming close, so close that he could see their teeth shining, their tongues pink and wet... and he woke with a jump, as though he'd been lifted right off the bed and dropped again.

Sweating, breathing hard, he lay still, so that the pounding in his head might slow down and stop. And when he fingered his body, he found he was sticky between his legs, for the first time in all his years of solitude and celibacy. He'd had a dream of dimly remembered sex, evoked by the perfume on his pillow.

Troubled by this, he turned over and stared at the fire. It looked dead, no more than a heap of cooling ashes. And yet, as he squeezed his eyes shut and blinked them open again, he saw a spark, glowing red at the deep, hot core of the embers. Nearly dead, but not quite. A little fuel, a gentle fanning, and soon there would be a blaze again....

And so he thought of his dream. A spark in him, dead for a long time, was now rekindled. He sniffed at the perfume on his pillow and he tried not to think what he was thinking.

The pulse in his head was loud, a rhythmic thud-thud-thudding that didn't stop although his breathing was calm again. It was a noise he'd heard before, in his worst and sweatiest nightmares. When he struggled to sit up, swinging his legs over the side of the bed, when he heard the dogs moving as though they'd heard the noise too, he knew that the thud-thud-thudding was not a part of the dream he'd had. The noise was real. It was coming from downstairs.

Without stepping into his boots, he fumbled for the torch, crossed the room and let himself onto the landing, leaving Gog and Magog shut inside. His hair bristled, his heart pounded in his chest. A black night, moonless and still... the sea like a great, glistening creature curled up at the foot of the stairs, breathing deeply, softly asleep. The thud-thud-thudding was inside the house, inside his head. He peered into the well of darkness. He clicked the torch on. In the grip of a waking dream, he started to go downstairs.

The water was icy. The footing was treacherous. The torch beam swam on the surface like a jellyfish. Following it, he waded across the hallway and into the living room, and there, as he zigzagged the light around him to pinpoint the spot where the noise was coming from, he could feel the pounding beneath his feet. The whole house rang with the pulse. He cried out and, careless of the boulders underfoot, surged to the mantelpiece, put the torch beside the ammonite so that the ceiling was brightly lit, and stumbled to the middle of the room to grope and grapple for the trap door.

Up to his waist in the swirling tide, he scrabbled on his knees at the sand and shingle where he knew the trap door must be. He thrashed the water to foam. He bellowed hysterically. All the time, the thudding grew louder and louder. At last he felt for the bolt, shot it across, hooked the ring and stood up to try and heave the trap door open. For a moment, the weight of the sea in the room was too much for him to lift. He leaned with every ounce of his strength... and then, when the door flew up with a suck of mud and tangled weed, he sprawled backward and fell headlong in the water.

Straight away he was on his feet, blowing like a walrus. He seized the torch from the mantelpiece and beamed it into the hole in the living-room floor, the focus of a nightmare he'd had for years....

A body swam toward him. It rose to the torchlight, from the coldest depths of the cellar. Alive and kicking, it pulled through the water with long, strong arms and thrust with limber legs.

Harry recoiled with a gasp of horror. The body groped through the water and broke the surface with an explosion of air bubbles. No head. No hands. But the stumps reached out, to wind their arms round Harry's throat and pull him into the cellar.... He beat and beat at them with his hook until they fell away. Then he leaned to the hole, shone the torch where the body was swimming, and he shrieked with terror as his nightmare came to a climax....

All of a sudden, his fear was gone. When he saw what it was that had floated from under the floorboards, the relief was overwhelming, like another, more breathtaking orgasm. Sobbing, whimpering, he continued to churn the water in the great black hole... for several minutes, slower and slower, more and more feebly, until the dregs of horror dissolved and disappeared.

At last he was exhausted. The fear had drained him, as much as the exertion of heaving the trap door open and thrashing the water. He barely had the strength, once the surface was still again, to reach into the cellar and hook out the windsurfer's rubber suit. It was a limp, lifeless thing. Ballooned with bubbles trapped inside it, lit by the zigzagging torchbeam, it had seemed to swim, as though it were alive and waiting to lure him to the brink of the hole. But it was only a length of rubber, a boneless, bloodless skin. Harry cursed himself for dropping the suit into the cellar in the first place. He slung it across the room. He would destroy it the following morning, somehow.

Indeed, a disturbed night. He was spent, after the sex dream and then the recurrence of his waking nightmare. Returning to the bedroom, he searched in the embers for the spark he'd seen, teased it with paper, built a scaffold of twigs for the fire to climb, and he fed the blaze with driftwood. He kicked the dogs out of the way. Stripped, he dried himself with a blanket, and, in the firelight, he appraised his body.

Thick-waisted, slabby, but not flabby. Not bad for a man in his late middle age, he thought. As the heat of the flames fell on him, he felt strong enough to get into bed still naked. There, under the blankets, he explored with his fingers, teasing his nipples, stroking his thighs, touching himself in a way he hadn't been touched since Helen was alive. It was good. And it frightened him too.

He stopped straight away. He turned over, pressing his belly to the hollow of the bed, and he tried not to think what he was thinking. But, as he snuffled into the pillow, he couldn't help breathing the perfume on it.

18

Days passed and the beachcomber didn't come back to the house. Harry was worried that the matron knew everything. He imagined the scene: the girl in shock, distraught and blubbering, garbling an extraordinary, unbelievable tale of a mad man and a pair of mad dogs in a big old house which the sea had wrecked... a tale of shotguns and shootings, of screaming and fighting in flooded fields, of tumbled guts and a sudden slugging with a great black stone... of a youth beaten dead and then chopped into pieces. He imagined the matron holding the girl and trying to calm her; how the woman's expression changed from disbelief to amazement and horror; how, once she'd sedated the hysterical young-ster and put her to bed, the matron returned to her office and reached for the phone....

Appalled by this, struggling to control his panic, Harry spent a whole day trying to dispose of the windsurfer's wet-suit. Without thinking what he was doing, he cut the black rubber into strips, and then, gibbering with frustration, he stumped around the house and backward and forward across the fields to find a place to hide them. He tried to burn them, building a fire on the foreshore, but the driftwood was wet and he had no fuel, no oil or paraffin, to throw on it. As he kicked at the smoldering rubber, which, refusing to burn, looked like burnt and blackened flesh, the yellow rescue he-licopter beat across the strait from Anglesey, came closer and closer and actually hovered overhead for a minute... while Harry flailed at the fire he'd failed to light and scattered the spars with his boots. The helicopter whirled away. He sank to his knees and wept, loudly and shrilly, quite hysterical. At last he calmed himself, seeing that the helicopter had moved to the dunes a miles off, and he gathered up the bits of rub-ber and carried them into the house.

Upstairs, he burned them one by one on his fire. It took hours. His eyes stung as the room filled with fumes; the dogs slunk into the fields; and Harry spent an exhausting, frantic afternoon going in and out of the house to see how the plume of thick, black, incriminating smoke was gusting all over the foreshore, as though it couldn't wait to spread the news of a bloody murder and the desperate attempt at concealment.

A wearying, worrying day, but at last it was done. The suit was gone, even the zips, which were made of plastic. That evening Harry heaped the fire with the dry wood he'd stored in his bath, so that a sweet, bright, crackling blaze could clear the smell in the house and over the estuary. The dogs came back inside. He relaxed, with his slippered feet resting on the hearth, and he listened to the sea coming into the hallway and flooding the downstairs rooms. As the waves washed the house, the sound seemed to wash the worries from his head. He dozed in front of the fire and then he went to bed.

He awoke refreshed the following morning. It was a simple matter to clear the grate with a shovel, to carry the clinker of ash and rubber and plastic out of the house and scatter it in the deepest ditch, where the tide would scour it away. Later in the day, he was confident enough to be customarily rude when the coastguards came churning across the fields in their Land Rover, pulled into the yard and asked him whether he'd seen any windsurfers recently; a youth had gone missing, they said, who'd set off from Caernarfon on a board with a purple sail, and they'd found the board on Llandwyn Island, miles across the strait, but no sign of the youth himself.

Harry shrugged. Savoring the words as though they were crisp, cool grapes in his mouth, he told the coastguards to fuck off. Then he shouted for Gog and Magog, and the dogs came out of the front door so fast and furiously that the piano rang with a discordant thrumming as they blundered their heavy bodies against it. The coastguards jumped into their Land Rover and drove away, axle-deep in mud.

But still Harry was uneasy. He slept badly. He dreamed of the thudding from the cellar and the things that were floating in it. He would sleepwalk down the stairs and into the living room and wake with a terrible shout, knee-deep in weed and water, holding the dead weight of the ammonite in his hand.

And, as he put the fossil back on the mantelpiece and saw Helen's sweet, sexy smile in the honeymoon photograph, he would think of Christine and wish she would come and visit him again. He ached with wanting her.

19

Coming back at last, Christy was changed. The boy knew it. He was different, after what he'd seen and done in the man's house. His childhood had gone from him in the course of that long, dark, unforgettable afternoon when he and Harry Clewe had killed and dismembered the windsurfer.

And for Harry, the girl was different. Christine had grown up. She was more like a woman. She looked at him levelly, with cool, still eyes. Once, he'd exerted the bullying dominance of a rude man over a frightened child. But now, Christine began to exert a kind of authority over him: the authority that a desirable woman can wield over the man who desires her. Harry saw in her eyes that she knew what he'd dreamed, that she knew what he wanted....

For the boy, it was still a game. He could feel the power he had over the man. But it was a dangerous game he was playing.

Again he heard the tinkling from the locked bedroom. That afternoon, he and Harry had walked along the foreshore with the dogs, and the man had bagged a mallard. They'd eaten the duck in front of the fire, sharing the meat with Gog and Magog, and, all that time, even when the gun had barked with the same explosive bark it had made when the boy had shot the windsurfer from the landing window, neither the man nor the boy had said anything about what had happened. The subject was out of bounds.

After the meal, Christy took the greasy plates to the bathroom, leaving Harry and the dogs by the fire. Along the corridor, he could hear the tinkling, like ice or glass, from the bedroom whose door he'd tried once before; so he left the plates in the bathroom, tiptoed down the corridor, knelt at the door, turned the handle to confirm that it was still locked, and he peeped through the keyhole. Nothing... only the tinkling and a draught of stale, cold air.

Suddenly, Harry was there behind him. Christy whirled round and stood up, but by then the man had grabbed him by the hair and raised his hook as though he would hit him with it. But Harry didn't hit the boy. He didn't bang Christy's head on the door. He didn't shout, although his face was swollen with anger. Because Christy simply smiled at him.

"Don't hit me, Mr. Clewe," the boy said. He looked levelly at the man's bulging, bloodshot eyes. He licked his lips and smiled, until slowly, very slowly, Harry lowered his hook and let go of the hair he'd been holding. And then it was Christy who raised a hand and stroked the swollen, panting, purple face which loomed above him.

"Don't hit me, Mr. Clewe," he said, so softly that Harry could barely hear the words. "You don't want me to go and tell anyone you've hit me, do you? You don't want me to tell anyone anything, do you?"

He stroked Harry's face until the swelling and the redness were gone.

In such a way, the boy exerted his influence, although he still hadn't seen the room that the man guarded so fiercely. It was a week before Christmas. Every day they walked and shot and cooked and ate together. They shared the childlike fun they'd had before, fishing in the flooded hallway, scavenging the beach, feasting on crumpets and fruitcake at the fireside. One afternoon, in a bout of glorious silliness, they sat in the Daimler, the man at the wheel, the boy affecting to fix his face in the mirror inside the glove compartment, and they pretended to go driving. The car didn't move, it hadn't moved for years; but they whooped and squealed, lurching and swaying as Harry swung the splendid machine through imaginary bends; they shook their fists at imaginary road hogs; they gestured grandly as though the world had paused to watch them go by.... Harry would glance at the figure beside him, the latest in a succession of mystifying females who'd complicated the adult years of his life.

Yes, for Harry, the girl Christine had become a young woman. So that, urgently, uncontrollably, he felt a rising of desire for her.

Sensing the man's eyes on him, Christy looked back. The look lengthened. They reappraised one another. There was a sense of anticipation, as though they knew that, sooner or later, their relationship would alter again, reach a critical point and change completely. But neither of them knew when or how it might happen.

For the time being, bonded by their murderous secret, the man and the boy maintained a fragile, wary union, each afraid of what the other might do or say. In the shortest days and the darkest nights of a wild winter, when the house was filled with wrecking waves and a booming gale, Harry crouched in front of his fire. He stared at the flames. He remembered the touch of Christine's fingers on his face. And he started to plan something special for Christmas.

20

Harry had shot a swan on the foreshore.

The day was raw and damp. A dense, white mist lay on the estuary, obscuring the horizon. Early that morning, Christmas morning, there'd been a flock of forty swans slapping their wide black feet on the wet black mud, dipping their beaks in the shallow pools that the tide had left behind. Harry, having walked across the fields, across the weed and the rubbled boulders until he was also on the mud, had been amazed to see them there: the first he'd ever seen at Ynys Elyrch, the island of swans. He chose his target as the birds ignored him and continued to feed.

There was a tremendous commotion when he fired. As the explosion of the shotgun reverberated over the estuary, the flock reacted by stampeding madly in all directions, beating into the air with a thrashing of huge white wings. And when the birds had fled to the dunes on the horizon, when the rhythmic whistling of their flight had faded to silence, one of them was left on the foreshore. It lashed and lashed in the mud; it had churned itself into a deep pool before Harry and the dogs could reach it, and by then it was black all over, slick and black as though it had been fouled in oil. It scrabbled with its great leathery feet. It seemed to claw with the bones of its wings. It snaked its neck and croaked horribly, gagging and gasping, blowing mucus bubbles from its nostrils.

The dogs got there first and fell on the bird with their heavy heads and wide mouths. Harry, arriving a few seconds later, banged them away with his hook before he seized the swan by the throat. He turned back toward the beach, dragging the bird behind him as though it were a sheet of filthy, flapping tarpaulin he'd pulled out of the mud. When he snapped its neck, with a sound like the cracking of a walnut, it stopped flapping straight away.

He'd carried the swan across the fields, dunked it in a flooded ditch until it was clean again, and plucked it at the front door of the house, leaving a drift of scattered white feathers all around the capsized piano. He'd cut off the wings, which were huge and waterlogged, and dropped them in the yard. Gog and Magog ate the head and neck, crunching the knobby beak, but they balked at the rubbery webbed feet. At last, having gutted the bird and fed the entrails to the dogs, Harry trudged across the field again to rinse the carcass in the ditch and nip out a few stubbled quills he'd missed in the plucking. It was a job well done: less than thirty minutes after he'd banged the gun into the flock, less than half an hour since the flock was feeding peacefully in the shallow pools of the estuary, he cradled the warm, pink, naked body in his arms and took it into the house.

The mist clung to the sodden fields and the skeletons of the broken hedges. Harry worked all morning to prepare the house for his visitor. When he was satisfied that everything was ready, he worked on himself. Then he sat and waited.

Christy came at three o'clock in the afternoon.

There'd been a Christmas dinner in the orphanage, but he hadn't eaten anything at all. Instead, he'd stuffed his pockets with cake and fruit and mince pies, and afterwards, when Mrs. Bottomley gathered the boys in front of the television to hear the Queen's message before settling down for the Christmas-afternoon feature film, it had been easy for him to slip away. He'd gone to the matron's room to pick up a box of liqueur chocolates he'd spotted there, and he'd used her perfume too, dabbing it so liberally around his ears and on his throat that a splash of the stuff ran down the collar of his shirt; he'd felt it trickling over his belly, into the waistband of his trousers. Then he'd inspected himself in her dressing-table mirror, with a toss of his soft, shining, especially washed blond hair, a pout and a giggle, before tiptoeing out of the home unnoticed.

The lanes were choked with mist. The world was still and cold and silent. No, not quite silent. He could hear the snorting of invisible cattle in the fields, the croaking of invisible crows which wafted out of the trees as he padded between the high hedgerows. The mist grew thicker and thicker the closer he came to the shore; he seemed to swim through it, pulling it aside with his arms, burrowing into it with his head, and it was clammy like wet cotton wool. When at last he heard the sea, the rhythmic movement of the waves on the shingle, he knew that the tide was coming in, that the mudflats were covered and soon the water would fill the fields and surround Ynys Elyrch.

But he couldn't see the house at all until he was a stone's throw from it — a girl's stone's throw, at that. Then it loomed before him, huge and blank with tall black chimneys, with gaping black holes where the windows should have been. He sniffed the smell of wood smoke. Pausing, he peered ahead of him and frowned, because, in the monochrome of a dank, gray Christmas, it looked as though a fall of snow had drifted to the front door. Very puzzled, he peered again and saw a pair of enormous, pure white wings... as if a Christmas angel had misjudged its flight path and crashlanded in the yard. Blinking, rubbing his eyes to try and make out what these strange apparitions might be, Christy squeezed past the piano and into the house.

It was very dark. As the boy splashed through the shingled pools to the foot of the stairs, the man appeared on the landing and beamed his torch into the hallway.

"It's me, Mr. Clewe! It's me! Christine!" the boy called out, shielding his eyes from the dazzling beam, and the dogs tumbled downstairs to leap around him and try to slap his face with their slobbery tongues. The torch clicked off.

"Come up!" Harry shouted as he withdrew from the landing into the little bedroom. "What time do you call this? I thought you weren't bloody coming! Christmas Day's almost over by now! Come upstairs!"

But Harry was quivering with excitement, however bad-tempered he might have sounded. He grinned so hard that his face ached. His stomach churned as he heard the footsteps on the stairs and then the swish of clothes at the bedroom door.

"Come in, come in!" he cried. "Come in and see how hard I've been working to get it all ready for you!"

The room was transformed. It was lit by a blazing fire and a row of fifteen or twenty candles, too many to count at a glance, arranged along the mantelpiece. In all this glorious flamelight, the boy could see that the stale bedding and the unwashed clothes were tidied away, the books and newspapers stacked in the corners. The bedside table had been moved in front of the hearth, spread with a clean-looking cloth and set with knives, forks, spoons and glasses. There were heaps of driftwood drying in front of the fire, so that the room was sweet with the scent of salt and seaweed. There were bottles gleaming, red and green and pink. A Christmas tree, rooted in a bucket full of pebbles, so tall that it touched the darkly shadowed ceiling, bristled by the window; it exhaled a perfume of sappy resin. And, spitted over the flames of the fire, dripping its juices into a tray of roasted potatoes and roasted parsnips, the biggest fowl that Christy had ever seen, as big as a goose, as big as a....

"Sit down, sit down!" Harry was saying, flapping his hook in the vague direction of an armchair. "Bugger off, you bloody great brutes!" he was bellowing, as Gog and Magog, uncontrollably excited by Christy's arrival and the smell of cooking meat, blundered round and round in the confined space. For a few moments, there was confusion. Christy struggled to take his coat off and put it down; Harry dithered between welcoming his guest and kicking the dogs; Gog and Magog veered from the fragrant fireside to the gentle hands of the young visitor.

But at last there was calm. Christy sat down. So did the dogs. Harry knelt to the stack of fuel and laid a spar among the flames. The spar burned blue, crusted with salt, and the man and the boy stared at it without speaking. Then, when the fowl spat a jet of fat which sizzled gold and black, Harry turned from the fire, appraised the room with a smile of indescribable joy and beamed at Christy. He leaned closer and sniffed. His nostrils flared, his face glowed with excitement, his eyes shone with tears of pleasure.

"That perfume again!" he whispered. "How lovely! And how pretty you're looking! I'm so glad you've come! Do you like the tree? I went up the lane last night and pinched it from the plantation. There was a guard dog prowling about to try and deter rogues like me, but it was only a piddling Alsatian.... It took one sniff at Gog and Magog and disappeared. And what do you think of the bird? A swan at the island of swans! I shot it this morning. Did you know that all the swans in Britain belong to Her Majesty the Queen? Did you know that? Well, we'd better make sure it all gets eaten and the evidence is gone for ever, or else we'll be in trouble, won't we? Eh?"

Christy winced at this. And then Harry winced, realizing what he'd said and what it must have meant to his young visitor. He began to bluster about his own appearance, because, as well as working hard to make the house comfortable and warm for Christmas Day, he'd made a special effort with himself.

"Well, how do I look?" he asked, standing up in front of the fire and twirling himself like a mannequin. "Not bad for a decrepit old goat, eh? Will I do for a pretty girl like you, if only for a few hours while we have our Christmas feast? Well, will I?"

He'd combed his wild gray hair and plastered it down with pomade; he'd shaved very closely, so that his face was ruddy and raw in the dancing candlelight; his shirt, although frayed at the collar, looked quite clean, and he'd put a tie on, tucked into an ancient, baggy, cricket pullover. Instead of his boots, he was wearing a pair of highly polished brogues, and a pair of cavalry-twill trousers instead of the mud-spattered corduroy bags he usually wore. He grinned, bashful as a sixteen-year-old boy with the girl he was trying to impress.

Christy grinned back at him. "You'll do, Mr. Clewe! And all this is great! The tree! The fire! And that bird! All these candles! But you won't have any left if you burn all of them at the same time. You won't have any for tomorrow, will you?"

Harry threw back his head and roared with pleasure, so that Gog and Magog heaved themselves to their feet again and shook their jowls; their dangled saliva fizzed on the hearth. Charged with excitement, the boy stood up and clapped his hands. The room was sweet with the scents of pine resin, wood smoke and roasting fowl, and when Christy reached for his coat to pull out the pies and the chocolates he'd brought with him, his fine, long hair swung around his face and wafted the perfume which he'd dabbed on his throat, which he'd spilled down his chest and his belly.

Harry shuddered. He flared his nostrils, inhaling deeply. He reached for one of the bottles which were warming by the fire, gripped it between his thighs and pulled the cork with a triumphant flourish; he filled the glasses so full that some of the rich red wine slopped onto the table. He and Christy toasted one another, swallowing greedily. They licked their lips and swallowed again. So the feast began.

21

Harry carved the carcass of the swan, using the butchering knife that had proved so useful before. He laid the slices of moist, gray meat on the plates that had been warming on the hearth and spooned out the potatoes and parsnips which had cooked in the bubbling juices.

"Skin?" he asked, and the boy nodded, licking his lips as Harry lifted a crisp, golden wafer and added it to the plate. "A leg?" The boy nodded again. The limb was huge, a glistening knob of meat on a knob of bone.

The dogs watched every move as they lay on a rug by the door. Their eyes shone with a lust for the sizzling carcass, and spools of saliva dripped from their tongues; but they didn't get up or try to worm themselves closer, because they feared their master's sudden shouts and the kicks he might aim at them. Harry filled the glasses again, already the third time, and nodded at the table to indicate that Christy should sit down. Then he sat down too.

For a minute they waited without speaking, relishing the long pause, a deliberate hesitation to heighten the pleasure of eating. Smiling shyly at one another, they reached for their glasses, chinked them together and whispered a Christmas toast. The fire blazed, heaped with driftwood. The candles fluttered in a draught from the chimney. The room was bathed in a soft, golden, glorious light, trembling with dark shadows. The tree shook a fall of needles.

Harry and Christy drank their toast and licked their lips, tasting the wine which was warm in their bellies, feeling the heat of the flames on their faces. At last, they started to eat.

Outside, the mist was thicker than ever. Dusk blurred into a pitchy night. The little light there'd been that gray Christmas Day was gone. If anyone was out there, picking a way through the lanes which wound down to the shore, he might have seen the faintest orange glow from the upstairs window of Ynys Elyrch... the only light in all that clammy, fog-bound world. But there was no one. It was very still. The gulls and the geese had gone to roost; their muttered conversation carried from the distant dunes to the fields around the house. A curlew cried, a fox yelped. These voices rang and echoed and faded in the enshrouding mist.

Christmas night. Ynys Elyrch was deep in darkness. And, as the tide rose, filling the ditches, forcing through hedges and tumbledown walls, it was deep in water. Once more, the house was in the sea, and the sea was in the house. The man and the boy were quite cut off.

They ate with enormous appetite. They watched one another eating. Bending to their plates, spearing potatoes, gnawing at bones, they would glance up and their eyes would meet across the littered table. They didn't talk much, except to confirm again and again that the feast was splendid, mumbling the words through mouthfuls of crackled skin and strongly flavored meat. Harry would lean to the fire and reach for the carcass, to strip more flesh from the sharp keel of the breastbone. Christy would feel for another potato in the congealing fat. They ate as though this was the last meal they would ever eat, and they washed down the food with wine.

"There was more of this stuff downstairs than I thought I'd got," Harry said. "I knew there were a couple of bottles knocking around somewhere in the kitchen cupboards, but I hadn't realized I'd got as much as this. Come on now, drink up! Finish off the last few drops of this one, and I'll open another. And look what else I found!"

He swung a bottle of brandy onto the table. Christy giggled, licked his fingers and reached out to touch it; then he squealed and reeled away, throwing himself backward in his chair, because the bottle was very hot from the flames of the fire. The sudden movement made his head swim. He squeezed his eyes shut for a moment, and when he opened them again he saw that the man was staring at him in a curious way, at his mouth and his hair and his throat...

The boy gulped and blinked hard. He heard himself call out, his voice louder and shriller than he'd meant it to be, "Hot bottle, Mr. Clewe! Hot toddy! Hot toddy bottle, Mr. Clewe!" The words were very silly and very hard to say, so he took a deep breath and returned to the gnawing of the great gleaming knuckle of the swan's leg.

Christy was enjoying himself immensely. He'd forgotten all about the orphanage. He'd never had a meal like this one, so much meat and so much wine, in such a twinkling, flamelit room with such a gaping, gormless, red-faced man. He'd forgotten about the tide. He grinned and giggled and he swilled another glass of wine. He tore at the meat with his teeth, felt the juice run down his chin. Then, sticking his tongue out as far as it would go and running it round his mouth, he glanced across the table to see how Mr. Clewe was staring and staring, how the old goat's face grew redder and shinier in the glow of the fire.

Harry hadn't forgotten about the tide. He'd heard it come in. He'd known, an hour ago, that the hallway was flooding, that wave after wave was driving through the front door to the foot of the stairs and into the downstairs rooms. He'd heard the stirring of the water in the wreckage of paneling and furniture, a knock and a bump as though someone was going from room to room, shifting this and moving that to see if there was anything left worth taking. Yes, he'd heard the noises, familiar to him after all the weeks of autumn and winter when the house had been flooded and drained, flooded and drained, every day and every night as regular and as predictable as the waxing and waning of the moon itself... and he knew that the house was cut off. The thought of it, as he looked at the beachcomber's wet mouth and long white throat, made his stomach flip.

So they continued to eat. They didn't talk much, although the boy heard himself squealing, his voice high and distant like someone else's voice; between mouthfuls, Harry bellowed the odd snatch of a few Christmas carols. When they'd gorged themselves so full of meat that they could hardly bear to glance in the direction of the carcass, Harry suddenly reached into the hearth for it. He spiked it on his hook, bellowed crazily, "Watch out, girl! The swan's last flight!" and swung the whole thing across the table, across the room, so that it flew through the air and thudded into the corner where the dogs were lying.

Gog and Magog had been asleep. They'd given up hope of a windfall from the hilarious feast. But when the swan belly-flopped beside them, they awoke with a terrible snarling. They brawled so furiously to rip the carcass into pieces that they blundered against the Christmas tree and almost knocked it over. With a sharp cry, the boy lurched to his feet and caught the tree as it toppled. He leaned into the branches, the needles prickly and pungent on his face, while Harry lunged forward to rummage about on the floor and try to secure the stump in the bucket of pebbles. The dogs roared, splintering bones, bolting the meat, slapping their tongues to get every last drop of grease that had spattered on the carpet and the skirting boards. Harry was singing very loudly... he fumbled on the floor with his arms between Christy's legs to get at the precarious tree trunk, while the boy swooned into the needles which stung his eyelids and his lips.... There was riotous confusion, until the tree was righted and the dogs had devoured the remains of the swan.

At last, when the man and the boy sat down again, they were heaving with exertion. Their faces shone red. They slumped in their seats, their elbows in the wreckage of food that was strewn about the table, and they struggled to regain their breath despite wave after wave of uncontrollable giggling which surged through them. It took a quarter of an hour for them to stop laughing, and even then, from time to time, a bubble of laughter would burst out of Christy like a hiccough, or from Harry, or from both of them at the same time.

Exhausted, bloated, dizzy with drink, they rested like this until they were calm. There was hardly a sound from outside, nothing but a whisper of wind and the cry of a gull in the enveloping mist. Gog and Magog snored, temporarily satisfied by the carcass they'd demolished. The fire burned very hot, smelling of seaweed, and the candle flames were straight and tall now that the room was still again. Christy, rousing himself suddenly, got up, reached for one of the candles and carried it to the door. He staggered a little when he stumbled on the dogs, which were sprawled in their corner like huge, black, matted rugs, but he caught himself by grabbing the door handle with his free hand.

"Going for a wee..." he mumbled. "Bursting..." He stepped from the room and onto the landing.

Harry remained at the table until he heard the beachcomber fumbling for the bathroom door and then shutting it. He heard footsteps on the dank linoleum, the creak of the floorboards, and then there was silence. Very quickly, agile and limber despite the wine he'd drunk, he crossed the room, sprang over the dogs and onto the pitch-dark landing. His feet were silent in the supple brogues. He reached the bathroom door just in time to hear the rustle of jeans and pants, to hear the trickle and hiss of piss in the bowl. He closed his eyes. He conjured a picture to go with the sounds, a picture so vivid that he could see how the candlelight played on the beachcomber's thin, white, shivery thighs. The trickling stopped. He listened a bit longer, to the readjustment of clothing and the clank and rattle of the chain. Then, his heart thudding, his breath short, he tiptoed from the landing and back to his seat at the dinner table before Christy had crossed the bathroom and opened the door.

"No, it doesn't flush!" Harry said without looking up.

Christy came into the room, put the candle back on the mantelpiece and resumed his seat at the table.

"It's no good yanking on the chain like that," Harry went on. "It hasn't flushed for weeks. The floods must have busted the pipes, busted the plumbing, busted the drains or something."

He glanced up and grinned, seeing how shy the beachcomber was after the visit to the dark, cold bathroom. Christy flicked his hair behind his ears and stared into the fire, abashed that the man had heard his futile efforts to flush the toilet.

"Who needs plumbing, anyway?" Harry said, as he himself stood up and carried a candle to the door. "Who needs plumbing when the whole bloody house is flushed out by the sea every day? Of course, I appreciate it's a bit different for a female, but as far as I'm concerned the bathroom's completely redundant now. Who needs it? You stay where you are! No peeping! It's my turn now! I'm bloody bursting, too!"

He went onto the landing and stood there for a few moments to let his eyes become accustomed to the darkness. The shadows were huge on the high ceiling and along the corridor as he waved the candle this way and that. The flamelight gleamed on the bathroom door handle and the door handle of the bedroom which had been locked for so many years. It gleamed on the barrel of the shotgun, leaned in its usual place by the landing window. It gleamed on the water which had flooded the hallway.

Yes, the sea was in the house. A glistening, sinewy, muscular thing, it slapped at the foot of the stairs. The swell was driving through the front door, a steady, relentless current which had crossed the foreshore and the fields to nose itself past the piano and into the hall. Harry stepped from the landing. Running his hook along the banister, he felt his way carefully downstairs until he was two or three steps above the rising tide. Then he set the candle on the staircase. Tugging at the unfamiliar buttons of his cavalry-twill trousers, pissing powerfully into the water, he shivered so hard that he almost lost his balance and staggered backward, but he righted himself and sprayed a foam of bubbles onto the silken surface. The jet of urine, steaming in the candlelight, stuttered and stopped. He shook out the final drops; they were warm on the back of his hand. But it was very cold in the hallway. Although the night was so still, the mist had blown into the house, through all the shattered windows, through the broken door, and the air was ghastly chill. One-handed, he struggled with the fly buttons; his fingers were stiff and clumsy He bent for the candle, trudged up the stairs again, and he didn't realize that his visitor had been watching all the time from the landing, watching and sniggering to see how the man fumbled and stumbled and splashed his shoes as he pissed into the flooded hallway....

Christy skipped back to the fireside before Harry had reached the top of the stairs. He slopped more wine into the glasses, ready for the man's return to the room. He'd seen the sea in the hallway. So what? He didn't care that he couldn't get back to the home. There would be trouble with Mrs. Bottomley. So what? It was Christmas, the best Christmas he'd ever had! He guzzled his glass of wine and refilled it by the time the man stepped into the room and resumed his place at the table.

"For this relief much thanks," Harry said. "That's Shakespeare, by the way. I don't suppose you know any Shakespeare, do you? You don't do bloody Shakespeare at school these days. Spend all your time tinkering about with computers instead of learning to read and write.... Well, have a look at this."

The boy was going to say that they did a good deal of Shakespeare at school. He recognized the quotation. But the man was holding out a tattered tome he'd rummaged from a pile of books under the bed, thrusting it into Christy's hands. The boy took it from him.

"The complete works," Harry said. "I got it as a form prize at Wrekin, my public school, when I was about thirteen. It's practically a bloody antique by now. I've got lots of books, scattered around the house... poetry books, bird books, books about the stars. I never look at them nowadays. Might as well let the sea drag them all outside and feed them to the fish!"

Christy flipped the book open, ran a finger through the index and found the very line in a matter of seconds. "'For this relief much thanks,'" he said, smiling smugly. "It's from *Hamlet*, Mr. Clewe. Act One, Scene One. We acted it at school. I was in it! I was —"

He stopped short. Despite the quantity of wine he'd drunk, or because if it, he had the wit to embroider the truth he was about to tell. In fact, chosen for his fine hair, his willowy figure and his unbroken voice, he'd had a small part as Osric, a foppish courtier in an extravagant bonnet; but he hesitated, racking his bleary brain for another name.

"I was Ophelia!" he said. "That's who I was, Mr. Clewe! The fair Ophelia, Hamlet's sweetheart! I ended up drowned! That's why they picked me for the part, I think, because of what happened to my mum and dad when I was little!"

Then, seeing that the man was surprised, even shocked, by the silliness of his prattling, the boy slammed the book shut. His head was whirling, his mouth was veering out of control. He took an enormous breath and ducked his head, because the man was staring at him in an owlish, pop-eyed way. Balancing the book on his knees, he reopened it at the flyleaf. He blinked hard and read the inscription: Wrekin School, a coat of arms and a motto he couldn't understand, *"Aut vincere aut mori."* Below that, the ink was faded, the handwriting was loopy, but at last he could make it out. He read it again. Snorting with laughter, he slapped his hand to his mouth.

"Harold Vivian Clewe!" he spluttered. "Is that you? Vivian? But Vivian's a girl's name, isn't it? I've never heard of that before! A boy called Vivian!"

Struggling to control himself, he smeared the tears of disbelief from his face. He thrust the book at the man, who slid it back under the bed.

"It can be a girl's name and a boy's name, you ignorant child," Harry said, with a sniff and a shrug. "It can be both, or either. Anyway, names don't matter. It's what we are that really counts." He grinned. "There we are! That was my profound thought for Christmas! Now it's over and done with, let's have another drink!"

They toasted one another, for the umpteenth time since the feast had begun.

"To you, the fair Ophelia!" Harry said, raising his glass. "Or rather, the fair Christine!"

"To you, Mr. Clewe!" the boy said, raising his glass. "Or rather, Harold Vivian!"

They fell silent. They drank. It was eight o'clock. The firelight caught the color of the wine and cast a flicker of red on their faces, like smudges of blood on their cheeks and foreheads. All of a sudden, Harry leaned forward and brushed at Christy's hair with his hand, and the pine needles that had caught there during the struggle with the tree dropped onto the table. Christy giggled, recoiling from the hand by throwing his head back and tossing his hair from side to side to get all the needles out. In his turn, still giggling, he reached out to Harry, where the needles were caught in the baggy white cricket pullover, and he picked them out with minute care.

Then the giggling stopped. Strangely serious, breathlessly hushed, as though there was some kind of ancient significance in the ritual they were performing, they gathered all the needles they'd collected from one another's hair and clothing, and they leaned very close to the hearth to scatter them into the fire. There was a sizzle and a spit as the sappy green stuff burst into flames, a fume of resin, and the two of them stared so hard that their eyes watered and their brows were all but singed; so that, when they straightened up again, although the exchange had been nothing but tomfoolery and it was only the proximity of the fire that had reddened their cheeks and stung their eyes, a curious awkwardness fell on Harry and Christy, leaving them tongue-tied and bashful... like a couple whose flirting had shifted from playfulness to the brink of something more serious.

To fill the uncomfortable silence, to find something to do with their hands and faces, they reached for their glasses and swilled them empty. There was a flurry of business with bottle and corkscrew as Harry brought more wine to the table, and the boy crossed the room to his coat, which he'd hung on the back of the door, to fetch the fruit from the pocket. In doing so, he stepped heavily on the sleeping dogs, and Gog or Magog — impossible to tell which, because they'd snuggled together into a single, hairy, black monster — let out a roar and reared up, snapping its teeth on thin air with a clang like the jaws of a trap.

Christy squealed. He sprang away, dropping the fruit on the floor. An orange bounced across the room until Harry, appropriately dressed in the cricket pullover, fielded it with his outstretched hand. The dogs subsided, grunting like a pair of sows.

So the silence was broken, the awkwardness was over. Harry and Christy shifted the dining table away from the hearth. Sunk into armchairs on either side of the fire, they settled to another bottle of wine and a box of liqueur chocolates.

The night deepened and darkened. The mist grew thicker. The tide was filling the house. It shifted the piano in the hallway, it sucked at the trap door in the living room, and the weight of the water in the cellar made the floorboards bulge. Something was knocking down there, as though it was trying to get out. But Harry and Christy didn't hear, although the night was so still. They heaped up the fire. Their faces were reddened by the heat and the wine. For the time being, all the world they wanted was in that little room.

22

For the time being.

Gorged with meat and swilled with wine, stunned by the blaze, they fell into a kind of stupor. Gog and Magog snored by the door. Harry started to snore as well; his head fell forward onto his chest and a dribble of chocolate dripped from his mouth onto his white pullover. Christy watched him and continued to sip at the wine in his glass, but his eyes grew heavy. Whenever he closed them for a while and then snapped them open again, his head swam; the flickering candles were blurred, and so were the enormous shadows they cast on the ceiling. So he gave up trying to stay awake. He dropped his glass onto the floor, let his head loll back and he was soon asleep too.

Nine o'clock. Ten o'clock. The man and the boy and the dogs dozed in the hot, airless room.

They all woke at the same time. Christy jerked into consciousness, so fast and so violently that he suddenly found himself perched on the edge of his armchair. Blinking, rubbing his face and staring around him, he tried to bring the room into focus, to try and establish where he was and how he'd got there. His head was buzzing. His mouth was dry. He was cold. When he'd smeared the sleep from his eyes, he looked across the hearth to see that Harry Clewe was awake too and staring at him in a vacant, stupefied way. By the door, Gog and Magog pricked their ears and held their breath, listening very hard.

Eleven o'clock. The fire had burned down to a pile of embers; the candles were no more than stubs guttering in puddles of molten wax. So the room was quite dark. Harry and Christy sat still and they listened. Something in the night was different, something had changed since they'd fallen asleep. The wind had picked up: so that, instead of the silence which had fallen since the hilarious feast was over, broken only by the skittering of rats on the stairs and

the flutter of flames in the grate, now the house was full of
moaning. Something banged, something creaked, something
groaned as the wind drove the sea into the hallway and
slapped the waves on the staircase.

And yet, through all this noise, the boy could hear a very
faint tinkling, like icicles breaking on a pavement or the
chiming of cut glass. He'd heard it before and wondered what
it was. Like the dogs, he pricked his ears and held his
breath... and Harry, tousled and bleary from a drunken sleep,
saw that his visitor was listening. Too befuddled to distinguish the tinkling from the dull droning of the wind, he
guessed what the sound must be from the beachcomber's
angled head and frown of puzzlement.

So he smiled. He bent to the hearth, put some more
wood on the embers and leaned back again in his armchair.

"A storm's blowing up," he said very quietly. "There'll
be a big tide, almost to the top of the stairs, I should think.
You're here for the night, my girl, that's for sure."

Christy smiled, a thin smile because his cheek ached
from sleeping with the side of his face pressed into the armchair. Instinctively, he ran his fingers through his hair and
licked his lips; it was all coming back to him, not just where
he was and what he'd been doing, but the realization of what
the man thought he was: that he was Christine, a teenage
girl with long, soft, blond hair and a trickle of perfume on
her throat. The idea still excited him. The roar of the wind
and the boom of the waves excited him too, and so did the
prospect of being marooned all night in the derelict house.
The buzz in his head had gone, now that he was properly
awake. He reached to the floor for his wine glass and raised
it to his lips to drain the last few drops.

"Is there any more of this, please, Mr. Clewe?" he asked
sweetly, knowing that the answer would be yes "I'm terribly thirsty. And cold, too. Let's get the fire going."

He poked at the embers until they erupted in flames
around the driftwood that the man had put there, and soon

the room was warmly lit again. Christy added more wood, some of it entangled with dried, black seaweed which crackled and flared like gunpowder. He threw on the empty chocolate box; it exploded in a golden blaze and swarmed up the chimney like a live thing. All the time, despite the noise of the storm, he could hear the tinkling, and he knew where it was coming from, but he didn't know what it was. He thought he might screw up the courage to ask, although he remembered how furious Mr. Clewe had been to find him trying the door handle of the locked bedroom down the corridor. But just then Harry stretched out to the mantelpiece, felt behind the clock and brandished a key.

"I've got something to show you," he said. "I'll bend the rules, since it's Christmas and you're here to share it with me, and I'll take you to a bit of the house you haven't seen yet... although it's not for want of trying on your part!" Baring his teeth in a wolfish smile, he added, "Come on! Grab the brandy! That'll keep us warm! Bring a candle and I'll bring the torch and we'll satisfy your curiosity once and for all."

They left the dogs inside and shut the door tightly. It was very cold and very dark on the landing. The wind howled up the stairs, flinging spray in their faces. Somewhere down there, the sea was churning in the hallway, dragging boulders and weed from room to room, but the only light was the gleam of foam. Harry went first, along the tunnel of the corridor. He waved the torch in his hand, throwing a feeble yellow beam at the walls and the ceiling, catching the gleaming eyes of the rats which ran over his shoes and nipped at his trouser legs. Christy followed him, with the brandy bottle under his arm, with his glass in his right hand, trying to shield the flame of the candle which he held in his left hand. He kicked at the rats, whose bodies were heavy and soft as they thumped on the skirting. He shuddered with cold and apprehension as Harry set down the torch, fumbled in his trouser pocket for the key and inserted it into the lock of the forbidden bedroom.

The key turned, the door opened. Harry picked up the torch again and stepped into the room. Christy followed him.

Harry closed the door. The wind was shut outside, where it moaned in the hallway, up the stairs and on the landing. But it was very still in the room. The torch beam flicked here and there and the candle flame was tall and straight. Neither the man nor the boy spoke. They held their breath and stared at the shadows.

It was a big room, much bigger and higher than the spare room that Harry had been using. As his eyes grew accustomed to the gloom, the boy made out the shape of an enormous four-poster bed, whose pillars of carved black wood rose to a great black canopy draped with curtains. In a distant corner there was a wardrobe so tall that it almost reached the ceiling, and a dressing table whose mirrors glowed when the torchlight hit them. The air was thick with dust. The boy could taste it in his mouth and smell it in his nostrils; when he moved his face he felt the caress of cobwebs on his cheeks and lashes. An icy draught blew through the room, and the tinkling was suddenly loud again. Harry aimed the torch at the ceiling, where the beam was reflected by the dangling glass jewels of a huge chandelier. Christy shivered, almost dropping the candle he was holding and the bottle wedged under his arm. It was a dead room, like a tomb. A deep dust lay on everything, in the carpet and the drapes and the curtains. The ceiling billowed with cobwebs. It was a room of dust and deadness: dead cold.

Harry shuddered. The torch beam zigzagged between the bed and the wardrobe and settled on the dressing table. Despite the dirt on them, the mirrors shone the beam back again, so that Christy could see the man's face.

Harry seemed to be smiling. His eyes and teeth were bright in the feeble light, but his skin was white, like the skin of a corpse. He whispered, "So, Christine, now you know what the noise is. Only the wind in the chandelier. Are you satisfied now? To tell the truth, I've hardly been in here myself over the last ten years or so. Well, don't just stand there quivering! Put the bottle and the candle down on here."

He trod across the room, every footstep raising a cloud of dust which hung in the air like smoke. He balanced the torch upright on the dressing table, and Christy followed him, putting down his candle and the bottle of brandy. As the man grunted and gestured, the boy sat on the chair in front of the mirrors. Harry sat down on the bed, which groaned very loudly. The room seemed warmer, because the candlelight shone in the tarnished glass, on the bottles and combs on the dressing table; it gleamed on the brandy and the wine glasses and Harry's hook. The torchlight was soft on the cobwebby ceiling, like a full moon in shifting cloud. The chandelier was a twinkling constellation. Straight away, a little life and warmth had been breathed into the room, and some of the deadness was gone. Harry leaned forward, took the brandy bottle and poured a generous measure into the two glasses.

"Drink up!" he said. "A toast to you this Christmas! To you and to all the other darling girls who've bewildered and confused me over the years! To you, my dear Christine, and all the angels who still haunt me! Cheers!"

Then, all he would say, as they drank the fiery stuff down, as they refilled the glasses and drank again, was that he and his wife, Helen, had shared the room and the four-poster bed, before Helen had gone and left him alone at Ynys Elyrch, in the big house by the sea, the house which the sea had claimed, and he'd hardly been in the room since her death.

"That's all you need to know," he whispered, his voice hoarse with the heat of the brandy in his throat. "All the women I've known, all the ones I've loved and longed for, have picked me up and put me down again, dropped me and disappeared, gone and left me. Helen was the last one. You've seen the photograph on the mantelpiece downstairs? Well, that's her. She'd sit where you're sitting, on that chair, and I'd sit where I'm sitting, on this bed, and I'd watch as she brushed her hair and made up her face in those mirrors. Just like this, just like we're sitting at the moment..."

Christy stared at him, astonished to see the man break down; Harry's voice began to crack and his eyes grew dim with tears. He smeared at them with the back of his hand. He snorted into a handkerchief which he tugged out of his trouser pocket, and then he tossed back another mouthful of brandy. Taking a deep breath, he added at last, as though to make the beachcomber look at something other than the smudge of the tears on his face, "That's my wife's brush on the dressing table. It's still got her hair in it."

Christy picked up the silver-backed brush. Yes, as he held it close to the candle, he could see that the bristles were tangled with strands of fine, long hair, hair as fine and long as his own. His belly was warm with the brandy he'd drunk. His eyes were bright in the dusty mirror. He looked at his reflection and he tilted his head to one side so that his hair fell almost to his shoulder. When he parted his lips and licked them, they shone in the tarnished glass. He smiled softly at himself. He smiled at the man, who was sitting behind him and gazing into the mirror, who was holding his breath and staring with tear-filled eyes. Christy tossed his hair. He began to brush it, with rhythmic strokes of the silver-backed brush.

The air in the candlelit room seemed to crackle with static. Harry leaned forward, now that the tears had dried on his cheeks, until his face was so close to the boy's neck that he could smell the perfume on it. He smiled into the mirror. Then he stood up from the bed. Gently, he took the brush from Christy's hand and continued the brushing himself, drawing the bristles through the long, blond hair. The boy consented to this. he dropped his hands into his lap, moving his head from side to side and tilting his chin up or down so that the man could brush and brush until the hair gleamed in the flickering light.

Harry glowed with warmth. His body was flooded with joy at the touch of the hair on his hands, at the sweet, shy smile in the mirror. The perfume rose, stronger and stronger the more vigorously he brushed, and he inhaled it, closing his eyes tightly. When he opened them again and looked into the mirror, Christy was still smiling at him. The boy had picked up a lipstick from the dressing table. Parting his lips, moistening them with the tip of his little pink tongue, he started to apply it to his mouth.

And the room, which had been locked like a tomb for so many years, was hot and alive, in spite of the dusty darkness. For Harry Clewe, it was the bedroom he'd shared with Helen, lit with desire, scented with sex; for Christy, it buzzed with a delicious, dangerous excitement he'd only found in books, only imagined in his turbulent teenage dreams. Even the lipstick tasted good. He put it on and pursed his lips, in the way he'd seen ladies do it in films, and then he giggled to see how lovely he looked, how bright his hair and his eyes, how white his teeth now that his mouth was scarlet. Without asking the man, he poured more brandy into both the glasses; and, as he and the man drank together, staring at one another in the mirror, the boy felt his belly flaming, as though a blaze were lit inside him.

Eventually Harry stopped brushing. He put down his glass and turned away from the dressing table. Taking the silver-backed hairbrush with him, he moved across the room to the shadowy corner where the wardrobe stood. He pulled the door open and stepped aside, to let the candlelight fall inside it. Christy had watched all this in the mirror, but when he saw the man reach into the wardrobe and rustle the row of dresses hanging there, he swiveled on his chair to see what Harry might bring out. Neither of them spoke. They were too full of brandy to speak, tongue-tied, tingling and breathless. There was nothing they needed to say.

Christy stood up and crossed the room, away from the candlelit dressing table, as Harry lifted a dress from the wardrobe. Christy took the dress from him. With a nod and a little frown, intimating that the man should turn away and face the other direction, the boy made for the darkest corner of the room, on the farther side of the four-poster. There, his chest thudding with the thrill of it, he tugged his baggy pullover over his head and dropped it onto the floor; he unbuttoned his shirt and flung it off; he squirmed out of his vest; he undid his jeans, slipped them down and stepped out of them; he tore off his shoes and socks; then, coursing with heat although he was naked except for his underpants, he lifted the dress and struggled into it, head first, so that the heavy silken material slithered on his shoulders and chest. He wriggled it down his hips. The hem fell smoothly to the floor and rustled on the carpet as he swung to face the man.

Harry spun round. He peered across the room, his heart pounding with the most delicious anticipation. His whole being was tuned to what he'd heard behind him, as the beachcomber slipped into the dress. Now, his mouth fell open. His hair stood up. His body jolted as a surge of electricity passed through him. He gasped as though a ghost had appeared before him, a vision in a purple gown which gleamed and crackled as the boy walked round the bed and came toward him. The blond hair shone; the cool, gray eyes caught the flicker of the flame. The boy's shoulders were silvery white as he turned round so that Harry could tighten the fastenings at waist and back....

Unable to stop himself, his mind reeling, Harry ducked his head and planted a kiss where a little knob of vertebra stood up, below the fall of hair. Christy froze at the touch of lips on his bare skin. But when he whirled around to face the man again, he was smiling a radiant smile: the smile of a bride who knows she is beautiful for her husband.

It was the first of several dresses that Christy put on. Harry went to and from the wardrobe, the boy went to and from the dark corner on the other side of the bed, and their pleasure was greater and greater with each different dress. There must have been a dozen of them, in silk and satin and velvet, in scarlet and pink, in midnight blue and purple black. Harry appraised and reappraised his laughing, limber young bride, who swirled and swished before him, who filled the room with life and warmth and perfume. Christy tossed his head and his throat gleamed in the candlelight, so that Harry was ready with a pearl necklace he'd taken from the dressing table, to clasp it round the warm, white neck. Harry laughed too, shaking the chandelier with the booming he made.

For hours, long after midnight, Harry and Christy lost themselves in the wonderful game they'd improvised for Christmas. More than a game: it consumed them so much that the rest of the real world was forgotten.

23

Outside, the storm had got up.

The tide drove into the house. It surged and sucked in all the downstairs rooms. Great white waves broke through the front door, hurled the piano across the hallway and started to smash it on the staircase. The wind screamed at the holes where the windows had been, flinging spray up the stairs to the landing and along the corridors. The sea foamed around the house and inside the house, which was no longer a part of the land but a piece of wreckage that the waves could tumble and toss as they liked. The storm had come in, huge and black and icy.

It opened the trap door in the living room, snapping off the bolt and the hinges, and all the water in the cellar forced up and out into the churning tide. Things that had been hidden down there, hidden but never forgotten, swirled to the surface and bumped around the house in the same way that the remaining sticks of furniture were floated from room to room.

The sheep's head banged at the paneling. It bounced across the hallway in the undertow of the rollers which crashed through the front door, and at last it jammed in the kitchen, the gray fleece waving like the tendrils of a jellyfish.

The windsurfer's head was round as a ball. It spun out of the living room as the current sucked a load of shingle to the staircase and banked it around the capsized piano. The head lodged inside the piano and knocked the remains of its face on the mute strings.

A body bobbed into the hallway, its flesh rubbery-soft and riddled with wormholes after years in the water. Borne up by the waves, it climbed the stairs, as the storm drove higher and higher. Sometimes it snagged in the banisters and remained there, beached for a few moments, as the sea fell back. Then the skull seemed to grin, as though it could hear the laughter which rang from one of the bedrooms. The swell crashed up the stairs again, lifted the body and dropped it a few steps higher....

The sea lifted these things from the cellar and danced them from room to room. The waves were deep and cold. The storm was very loud. But upstairs in the scented candle-light, the man and the boy hardly heard it.

Dizzy with laughter, they poured more brandy and drank it down.

The candle had almost burned out; the wick had collapsed into the molten wax and the dying flame sent a fume of smoke into the air. The torchlight was fading; the yellow moon on the ceiling was all but lost in a cloud of cobwebs. Still the chandelier gleamed like clustered stars. Harry and Christy, pausing for breath, sitting side by side on the enormous bed and raising their glasses in yet another toast, had lost all sense of time and place. The world outside their room, beyond their game, was as distant from them as another planet. The storm, which howled at their window and rattled their door, was the dimmest of background noises; like city dwellers inured to the roar of traffic, they hardly heard it.

There was one more dress to try on. Harry had been saving it till last. He'd pushed it into the corner of the wardrobe, to be invisible until he brought it out. Taking the empty glasses and setting them down on the dressing table, he left Christy sitting on the bed in a gorgeous creation of crushed black silk, and he returned to the wardrobe. All of a sudden, the exhilaration drained from him. A terrible, debilitating nervousness swept through him at the thought that the beachcomber might not try on the dress he'd been saving until now... might not, or might try it on and something would be wrong with it. In a few seconds, all the joy was sapped from him. Instead, he was filled with the horror of an impending impotence. It loomed in his mind like a chill, pale ghost as he reached into the wardrobe for the last time.

Indeed, in the flickering candlelight, the dress he took out of the wardrobe was like a ghost. It was a vision of white satin, spangled with a thousand sequins, embroidered with a thousand pearls; it shimmered in the silvery points of light reflected from the chandelier. It was Helen's wedding dress.

There were white lace gloves too, and white shoes. Harry laid them all on the bed and then he stood back. He gazed at the dress as though it were the body of his wife, warm and alive, as though she were lying on the honeymoon bed. He turned his face from Christy's. He dreaded the reaction, a wounding or sneering or poking fun, that the rest of the game would be off. Utterly exposed, he hid his face and waited for Christy to say or do something.

A hush fell on the room, which, a minute before, had been hectic with laughter. For the first time, as the two of them held their breath, they were aware of the storm outside. The gale lashed at the window; the sea roared on the stairs and shook the house to its foundations; the door rattled as though someone very big and very angry was trying to get into the bedroom... but Harry and Christy were silent. Neither of them spoke or breathed or moved a muscle.

Then they both moved at once. The game, it seemed, was still on. With a hoot of excitement, the boy seized the dress and the gloves and whisked them away to the furthest corner. And Harry, limp with relief, turned back to the wardrobe.

Christy wriggled out of the black silk evening dress, tore it over his head and hurled it into the darkness; it vanished completely, but he could hear it settling on the floor, rearranging itself like an animal curling up to sleep. He stood there in his underpants, holding the wedding dress over his right arm, and, although he couldn't see Harry on the other side of the bed, he could hear him rummaging at the wardrobe, perhaps hanging up and putting away the other dresses. For a moment, Christy waited. The wedding dress was heavy; the sequins and pearls were cold on his bare skin, but when he touched his belly with the fingertips of his left hand he felt how very hot he was. He tugged his underpants down and stepped out of them, so that he could find a way, naked, into the dress.

It was difficult. At first it seemed to be impossible. In the dim light that came to him from the distant dressing table, he burrowed into layer after layer of material. There were yards of it, dense and soft and stubbornly unyielding, and he tore at it with his hands, butted with his face, snuffled in the infuriating stuff, to aim a headlong dive into the body of the dress. At last, at long last, he discovered that it might have been easier all the time to have stepped into the dress from the top... so now he trod into the frothing, voluminous mass of the skirt, tugged it up to his waist and wormed himself into the bodice. He shook his hair loose. Panting with exertion, tingling with the silken, cold touch of the dress all over his naked body, he reached behind him to try and close as many of the tiny press-studs as he could. He felt for the gloves and put them on, long white lacy gloves that came right up to his elbows. Then he stepped around the bed toward the dressing table.

At the same time, Harry stepped to the foot of the four-poster. He'd changed too. While Christy had been struggling into the intricate folds of the wedding dress, Harry had found his own suit in the wardrobe. He'd thrown off the cricket pullover and the cavalry-twill trousers and kicked off the brogues. He'd pulled on a dark suit and stepped into a pair of gleaming black leather shoes — his wedding outfit — ready to greet Christine.

There was no light left. The storm was shaking the house so violently that the chandelier jangled, blurring into a haze of stars. The candle was drowning in a pool of wax. The torch wobbled and fell over, rolled off the dressing table and landed on the floor with a thud. The beam died. The candle snuffed out.

Without moving, without breathing, Harry and Christy

stood in the pitch blackness. Then they reached out to feel blindly for one another. Their fingers met and locked. They didn't need to see, any more than they needed to speak. They'd had time, a matter of seconds before the lights went out, to capture the image and imprint it on their minds: of a man, upright and stout in a fine dark suit; of a young woman, breathless and beautiful in a shimmering dress... a bride and a groom, alone together in their honeymoon bedroom.

They lay down side by side, hand in hand, on the vast, groaning bed. That was all they did. It was enough for Harry Clewe that the girl was with him, that he could feel the warmth of her fingers on his. Sometimes, despite the blast of the gale, he could hear the crackling of the wedding dress. Then, once his eyes had grown used to the darkness and the room was suffused with the faintest light from the sea outside, he could make out the froth and foam of white satin, the sparkle of sequins, the gleam of pearls. It wasn't a dream. She wasn't a ghost. She was real, lying beside him, warm and alive in the fantastic dress. It was a wonder to him.

As for the boy, he fell asleep immediately. He was knocked out, after a gluttonous feast, after a dozen glasses of red wine and half a dozen glasses of brandy, after the hilarious game they'd played in the forbidden bedroom. The moment he lay down, he shut his eyes and sank into unconsciousness.

Harry wept. Tears of joy, salty and hot, ran down his face and into the corners of his mouth. He was alive again. He was unfossilized. He squeezed his eyes shut, and soon he was asleep as well.

24

Christy had no idea where he was when he woke up.

It was dark. It was cold. It was noisy. There was a tremendous storm. The wind and the waves were very close. The sea was crashing at the foot of a great cliff, and he was on top of the cliff, with the sea below him.

No, he was in a house. He could sense the walls and the ceiling and the floor, although it was too dark to see them. The house was shuddering and groaning as the storm swept through it, and he could hear thudding somewhere below him, downstairs. He shuddered too, and when he brought up his knees and wrapped his arms around his body to try and keep himself warm, he found that he was encased in layers of crackling, cold, rustling stuff.... He didn't know what it was, but he was naked inside it, in a cloying, crinkling tangle.

Frightened, he sat up. His head hurt. His tongue was furry and dry, stuck to the roof of his mouth. When he unstuck it and ran it over his teeth, they tasted sour, a row of dirty, dead things he should have spat out a long time ago. He rubbed at his face with his hands. He stared about him and made out the shape and size of an enormous bed with pillars like tree trunks rising from each corner and a great black canopy above it; and then the shadows of a room, the gleam of a mirror, the bulk of a wardrobe, the glimmer of glass in the darkness of the ceiling, the outline of a door....

Door. He had to get out. He rolled off the bed and groped his way across the room. All he knew, for the time being, was that he had to reach the door and go through it, whatever he might find on the other side, wherever he was, whether the place was real or only a dream, however great the pain in his head. He had to. There was one overpowering need to take care of, and only when he'd done it could he think about anything else. He was bursting to piss.

He was going to tug the door open, but he didn't need to. As he fumbled for the handle and turned it, the door flew open so hard that it struck him on the forehead and almost knocked him over. A hurricane hurtled through it. The wind flung the door wide open with a tremendous crack, the storm howled into the bedroom and the boy bent into it, to try and force his way out. He could see nothing in the screaming darkness. He felt layers of material wrapping around him, clinging to his legs like weed in a rock pool; his hair whipped round his face and his neck. He squeezed his eyes shut, leaned into the wind and held onto the door jambs to stop himself from being blown back into the room where he'd woken up.

At last he could wrench himself through. There, at the brink of a yawning staircase, he paused and peered down, blinking and blinking to try and understand what he thought he was seeing. At first it was black, a blackness without light or movement. Then the blackness broke in a crashing white wave which churned at his feet and spattered his face with spray.

The sea was inside the house! Icy cold! Roaring waves! A howling wind!

A silvery light, the light of moonlit foam, suffused the landing. Gradually, slowly, the boy began to see where he was and to remember what he'd been doing there. At last he could see what he was wearing, a great white dress which clung to his chest and his waist, which fell to the floor in yards of sequined, spangled silk. He saw the gloves he'd got on, held them in front of his face, saw his fingers and hands and his arms agleam in the gleam of the sea. Then the waves withdrew. They sucked at the shingle in the hallway, rumbled the boulders in the living room, and the water was black again, a gathering swell which glistened like oil. A moment later, the swell heaved toward the landing and broke in tons of churning white water at the top of the stairs. The whole house shook at the weight of the impact.

Christy wiped the spray from his face with his gloves. He fumbled at the dress, bending to the floor to try and pick up the hem, but there was so much of the flimsy stuff that he couldn't get a proper hold on it. He gathered it in his arms, straightened up, bent to gather some more... and all the time he was bursting to piss, bursting so hard that he thought he must piss down his legs, piss on his feet, piss anywhere to relieve the pain in his belly. At last, as another wave came boiling to the staircase and lit the landing with a swirl of fluorescent bubbles, he managed to hitch the dress up to his waist. The spray was like ice on his nakedness. The water gleamed on him. Jutting his hips forward, he pissed long and hot and powerfully into the sea.

The relief was wonderful. Even when he'd finished, he remained like that for a blissful moment, his eyes closed, his lips parted in a smile of satisfaction.

Then he opened his eyes. He caught a movement on the landing beside him. A gray-haired man in a dark suit and a shirt and tie was watching him from the bedroom door.

Harry Clewe had woken up when the wind howled into the room. He felt terrible. His head hurt, as though he'd been slugged with something very hard and very heavy. Now, staggering onto the landing, he gaped and gaped and tried to understand.

An angel had come for him.

She was standing at the top of the stairs, an angel with long blond hair, an angel in a glittering, spangled dress. She was more beautiful than all the angels that had visited him in all his life. As Harry's head blazed with sparks, the angel shimmered in the silvery light. She was feeling into the material of her dress with her white gloves, feeling and feeling for something in the sequined folds. Transfixed, agog, Harry stood in his bedroom doorway and he stared. It was a glorious vision. A shimmering angel, ablaze with sparks...

But then the vision went wrong. It turned ugly. The angel lifted her dress. She thrust her hips forward and started to piss. Harry goggled and gasped. The angel had a penis. A penis, aiming a jet of piss from under the folds of an angel's dress... When the angel shook it, the last amber droplets fell into the foam. Then there was darkness, as the wave withdrew.

Harry sprang forward, shrieking murder. And Christy fled for his life.

25

The boy leaped from the landing.

He felt the wind of the man's hand, then the grasp of the man's fingers in his hair, as he flung himself from the landing and into the booming, black well of the staircase. For a split second Christy smelled the man's breath and heard the bellowing beside his ear, before he hurled himself into the next wave that drove into the house. Careless of where he might fall, reacting instinctively to the gleam of pure murder he'd seen in the man's eyes, the boy dived into the crashing water.

He surfaced as the wave was withdrawing. It dragged him with it, bumping him and rolling him over and over until he felt himself land in the banked-up shingle in the hall-way. His head struck something very hard and very sharp, a corner of the piano which was being smashed to pieces at the foot of the stairs, and then he had a moment to gulp at the air, with the water boiling around him, before the next wave crashed on top of him. It lifted him right off the shingle, as though he were a piece of the storm wreckage, and he was flung up the stairs again, head over heels, lost in the foam. Opening his eyes, staring about him, he saw his legs, white and thin and bare, banging at the banister. He saw his hands and arms in the white gloves, like strange sea creatures which swayed with the swirl of the flood. He saw the great white dress billowing around him, the sequins gleaming in the gleam of a million bubbles which burst from its folds, the pearls like a shoal of tiny fish trapped in the frothing, gauzy stuff. He saw a woman, whose face was horribly bloated, who swam toward him and brushed her mouth on his in the softest of submarine kisses.... The woman swam away. His ears roared with the roar of surf; they started to whine. Once more, his head came clear of the surface, he gulped at the air, and, as the wave fell back, he was pitched down the stairs, bouncing, bumping, tumbling, until he banged so hard on the edge of the piano that all the wind was knocked out of him.

This time, finding himself the right way up for a second, the boy kicked with all his strength. He forced himself to his feet. The water raced around his waist, around his chest, but he lunged for the piano and clung to it, to anchor himself while another wave crashed up the stairs and fell back again. As he sucked at the air and filled his lungs with it, as he swept the hair from his eyes, he glanced up to the landing. There was the man, Harry Clewe, silhouetted against the moonlit window... the gleam of his wiry gray hair, the gleam of a wild eye, the gleam of his hook, and another metallic gleam which made the boy gasp and then fling himself to his left and scrabble for shelter behind the piano...

It was the gleam of the gun barrel. Harry had picked up the gun from its customary position on the landing and was pointing it downstairs into the hallway. The boy moved just in time, because the dress was a fine target, fluorescent in the silvery surf like a huge jellyfish that the storm had fetched up. There was a colossal explosion as the gun went off. For a moment, the sea was lit by a belch of white flame. The boy felt the spatter of shot in the water, splinters of wood on his face as the corner of the piano was blown into pieces... and, riding a roller which broke through the front door, he kicked toward the living room.

The wedding dress ballooned with water. It buoyed him up and bore him along. The sea hurled him out of the hallway, just as a second deafening, blinding explosion shook all the air around him. The boy plunged into the wave and let the force of it tumble him to relative safety.

In the living room, he found something of a lull in the storm. Although the water was waist-deep, it didn't churn and roar as it did in the hallway. The swell drove in; the gale came straight off the ocean, across the fields and through the shattered windows, flinging a spray from the chopping waves... but Christy could stand up. He could breathe. The sea lifted him, filling the dress so that the material frothed and shimmered on the surface. It carried him about the room, banging his feet and legs on boulders, and then it put him down again until the next swell came surging through the doorway. But at least he could breathe. His chest was thudding with the fear of what the man would do to him. The water was icy, and the storm howled around him, but the boy found his breath and his footing, and he strained his ears to hear.

He didn't have to wait long to find out what the man was up to. He thought he heard a voice above the booming of the storm, a shout and the slam of a door; for some reason, Harry Clewe had gone into the little bedroom, cursing and kicking at the dogs, and had come out again. The boy held his breath and tried to hear. Surely the man wouldn't come down the stairs for him, wouldn't plunge into the freezing waves and wade through the water to look for him....

But, as Christy cocked his head and listened, he heard the creak of the banister, a heavy footfall, a splutter and a gasp and a walrus-snorting as the man trod from the landing and breasted the next great wave that drove into the house. Harry Clewe was coming downstairs.

Before he had time to think where he might hide himself, Christy saw the bulk of the man forcing into the living room doorway, a big, black bulk borne up on a big, black wave. The sea pitched Harry forward into the room, and put him down again; it lumped him from the door to the middle of the room in a single step. The same swell that had lifted him broke in the boy's face with an icy slap. Automatically, Christy wiped at his eyes with his hands, and then he saw that the man had turned his head straight away toward him. Harry had caught the flash of the long white gloves, and was spitting and roaring and leveling the gun, which he'd been carrying over his head to keep it dry. Christy, without taking the time to gulp a breath, plunged beneath the surface.

The water folded around his head. He heard the muffled explosion, saw the blaze of light through the swirl of foam, felt a shudder in the sea itself as the gun went off. He groped at the boulder-strewn floorboards, scrabbling with his fingers for something to hold on to, something to anchor him down there, because the force of the swell in the dress was trying to lift him to the surface again. He caught at the trap door, which the waves had sprung open, and closed his fingers on the hinge. But his head was splitting as the surf thundered around him, his chest was bursting as he held his breath to the limit of his endurance... so he let go of the trap door and bobbed to the surface, buoyed up by the dress. He broke into the spray and the howling storm in time to inhale a mouthful of the next wave that rode over his face, in time to glimpse the gleam of the gun that was pointing straight at him. He drove himself downward again.

Another explosion, another flaring of flame. He thought he must drown as the sea rolled him over and over. His chest seemed to fill with water, which swelled inside him and drove every precious bubble of air from his body. Down there, the world was a booming, pounding, turbulent place, streaming with foam and tangled with weed, where he tumbled this way and that and banged on boulders, where his long, white, naked legs were rasped on razor-sharp barnacles, where he was dumped like a doll against the slab of a cold, black wall. Instinctively, knowing that he must fight his way upward and upward where the air must be, where his life must be, the boy felt at the wall and forced himself up it. At last his head burst clear of the surface. Choking, retching, his chest hurting so much that he thought his ribs must be broken, he spewed a gallon of sea water. He filled his lungs with air.

Harry was waiting for him. Hysterical with rage, bellowing murder, he flung the gun across the room. The butt caught Christy very hard behind his left ear. As the boy clutched at his head with both hands, Harry surged toward him, brandishing the dismembering knife which he'd fetched from the little bedroom before he came downstairs. The boy tried to writhe away, but Harry had him. They grappled chest to chest in the deep water. The hook came up, ripped into the material at the back of the dress and yanked so hard that the boy's neck seemed to snap. Harry thrust his face forward. His spittle hot on Christy's cheek, he screamed the words with all his strength.

"See this knife? Know how sharp it is? Course you do, you little butcher! D'you think I'm going to cut your lovely white throat with it? D'you think so? Well, you're wrong! It's not your throat I'm after!"

He drove the knife under the water. He thrust it into the folds of the wedding dress, fumbled and tore at the layers and layers of silken stuff. Christy squealed, the blade keen on his thighs, on his belly. He arched away. He squirmed his hips as the blade sawed at him, at the piece of him that had enraged Harry Clewe so much.

"That's what I'm after!" Harry roared. "You can wriggle as much as you like, but I'll get it! It shouldn't be there, should it? So it's got to come off? Yes, right off, and fed to the dogs!"

He lunged with the knife. Christy felt it on the soft bare skin on the inside of his thigh, burning him terribly. He felt his skin opening, felt the hotness of his blood come welling out. Forced back to the wall, he cracked his head again, where the mantelpiece jutted and caught him on the wound that the gun butt had made. His hands, which he'd been flailing at his groin in a futile attempt to protect himself, shot to the surface and flew into the air, the gloves long and white and dripping like a pair of leaping fish... so that Harry recoiled, freeing the hook from the wedding dress, hesitating for a second before aiming the dismembering knife at the defenseless member.

A critical hesitation...

Christy groped at the mantelpiece, knowing in an instant what he must find and how he must use it. He reached with both hands. Yes, the ammonite was there, just behind his head. The wedding gloves felt at the smooth cold stone. His hands closed around it.

Suddenly paralyzed, Harry watched. He froze with the knife under water. But, as the fingers gripped the ammonite, he smiled, because he knew that the fossil was heavy. So heavy that a girl, young and lovely in a gorgeous wedding dress, could hardly lift it...

Christy wasn't a girl. He heaved the ammonite off the mantelpiece. With every ounce of his strength, he crashed the fossil on Harry's head. He crashed it again. He crashed it a third time, aiming the blow at the flickering smile. Until the face was stove in, the teeth in splinters and bloodied spittle.

Harry sank into the sea. With the next wave that drove through the hallway and into the living room, Harry Clewe was gone.

postmortem

For a long time the boy stood in the deep water and held the ammonite to his chest. The waves lifted him gently, the swell ballooning in the wedding dress. They carried him from one part of the room to another, setting him down, lifting him up and carrying him, setting him down again. He didn't try to anchor himself; he moved with the rhythm of the sea, going wherever the waves would take him. His feet knocked on hard, sharp things, on the bulk of a big, soft thing which had sunk to the bottom of the flooded room, but he didn't know where he was or what he was doing. He was numb. His mind was blank. He didn't feel the spray on his face or hear the wind which came straight off the sea and into the derelict house. He clutched the fossil to him and he floated on the spreading folds of the wedding dress.

As the tide began to turn, the moon fell through the empty windows and lit on him, on his face and throat which were drained so white, on the bodice of the dress so trim and neat on his marbled skin, on the yards of sequined stuff which swirled around him like foam. The boy turned his eyes to the moon. But they were dead eyes. He didn't know what the moon was, any more than he knew what the sea was doing, what the wind was doing, what he was doing. It was only a light, beaming on him, and he was adrift on a deep, cold sea.

Gradually, he knew that the thing he was holding was heavy, so he let go of it. The ammonite fell through the surface of the water and disappeared. He knew that he was cold, so he waded across the room to the doorway and started to drag himself up the stairs. He only managed the first three steps before he collapsed, face down. The weight of the waterlogged wedding dress was too much for him. He was too weak, too exhausted, too traumatized to move any more.

The tide receded; the storm was over. For a few more hours, the waves in the hallway broke on the lowest steps of the staircase and rearranged the boulders around the remains of the piano; at last, with a powerful sucking of shingle and weed, they withdrew through the front door, fell back, drained across the fields and the foreshore and into the estuary. The sea dropped and the wind dropped. The boy lay unconscious on the stairs until dawn.

It was a still, soft dawn. The sky was a wash of silvery cloud, pale and luminous. There was no wind at all, not a breath. The tide had gone a long way out. The sand flats were exposed, gray and glassy smooth; a trickle of creeks zigzagged through them to the distant sea. The world was lit by a watery sun. After the violence of the storm in the night, the morning was so mild that a haze of mist shimmered like steam on the foreshore and the air was quick with midges. Hundreds of waders and wildfowl were feeding on the marsh. A heron stalked in the drains, where a feast of fish had been stranded by the falling tide.

This was the world the boy found when he woke up.

No. He didn't wake up, not really, although he opened his eyes and groaned. His body hurt, so that he tried to gaze around without moving too much. Maneuvering himself upright, he sat on the staircase, hugged his knees to his chest and stared at the wreckage in the hallway; and then he stood up painfully, for he'd been lying on the stairs for hours, wearing nothing but the wet wedding dress, while the storm had been howling around him. The dress was very dirty, with great rips in it; as he limped across the hallway to the front door, his legs were white in the angled sunlight. He stood there for a while, because the sun was good on his face and his bare shoulders. He smoothed back his hair with his hands and saw that the gloves were soiled too.

The morning was lovely. It made the blood stir inside him, as though he'd been dead and was alive again, had been dead asleep and was wide awake again. But no, he wasn't awake. His mind was blank, his eyes were blank. He saw the world as a gull would see it, through cold gull's eyes, where all that remained after the storm was bleached and broken, to be picked at and turned over. The boy was in shock. Perhaps he would be in shock for ever. So he went from room to room, turning things over with his feet, picking at things with his hands, and he did things that a waking, conscious person could not have done.

This is what he did.

He trod through the wreckage of the living room. A flock of starlings rose from the seaweed and whirred about his head before aiming for the windows and disappearing across the fields. He looked around him, but he didn't see the woman's body: it was floating face down in a rock pool, tangled in fronds of kelp and bladderwrack. He didn't see the windsurfer's head: it had rolled into a mat of grasses and driftwood. He didn't see the sheep's head, where the starlings had been picking at it.

He bent down and picked up the ammonite. Something in the shape and the heft of it made him frown, as though it stirred the dimmest of memories... but he couldn't remember what the stone was for. Turning to the fireplace, he looked at the photograph on the mantelpiece. He looked for a long time and he wondered if it was a photograph of himself, a woman holding a big stone in her slim, white hands. He didn't know who it was, and there was no one to ask. He put the ammonite on the mantelpiece, beside the photograph, where it seemed to belong.

There was a man on the floor, lying on his back in all the boulders and weeds. He was middle-aged, rather stout, with quite a lot of wiry, peppery-gray hair, and he was wearing a dark suit over a shirt and tie. Hard to describe the face... one side of it was an ordinary man's face, with a bushy eyebrow and a carefully shaved cheek; the other side was pressed in, buckled, but pink and clean because the sea and the sand had scoured it. The boy bent down to have a closer look. He studied the face and he even picked up the heavy,

cold iron hook to see if it might help him to remember who
the man was. The face was familiar. He'd seen it before,
somewhere, some time. But, though he knelt at the man's
side and felt at the hook with his fingertips, the boy couldn't
quite place him.

Hard to tell what sort of a man he'd been: good or bad,
kind or cruel, funny or sad. Perhaps he'd been all of these
things, at different times, in different places, with different
people.

Hard to tell how long he'd been dead, because he was so
cold, as cold as the coiled black stone which had been lying on the weed beside him... as though he'd been dead for
ever, as long as the stone had been dead.

An ordinary-looking man, who'd had an ordinary life.
Whoever he was, he was smiling very faintly, as though he'd
just got the point of a silly little joke that had been eluding
him for a long time.

Christy couldn't place the man. Neither could he remember how he himself had come to this extraordinary house
with the birds and the beach inside it.

Straightening up, he smoothed out the dress he was wearing and the gloves, which came to his elbows. He touched
the pearls around his neck. These things were a mystery to
him as well. But he liked the feel of the silk on his skin and
the weight of the pearls on his throat; he liked the toss of
his hair, and when he stepped across the room to the window to feel the sun on him, he liked the way his body moved
inside the long white dress. For a while he remained at the
window, looking out at the fields which were strewn with
wreckage and seaweed, and he listened to the cries of the
wildfowl on the distant estuary. He puzzled at the house,
where, by the look of it, the sea had come in during the
night and left a man lying in the living room; he puzzled at
the clothes he was wearing and the way he felt in them.

He tried to remember what he was doing there. He tried
to remember who he was, but no name came to him. He tried

to make sense of it all, to decide what he should do next. But he was numb. The calm of a lovely morning settled on him, and there was no sound or movement to nudge him awake.

Until at last another sound came to him, from somewhere inside the house. He cocked his head and listened. It was a sound from upstairs....

Something was moving up there, stirring slowly, blundering from wall to wall and nuzzling a door, trying to get out. Scratching. The scratching grew louder and louder, more and more frantic, as though there was more than one thing trying to get out. A bark, more of a yap, high-pitched and hopeful... another bark, more powerful, more urgent... and then, deep-throated, bellowing barking that sounded as if a pair of the hugest and hungriest of hounds were desperate to break free and come hurtling downstairs in search of food....

The noise was a trigger in the boy's head. Suddenly, as clear and as calm as the Boxing Day morning, he knew what he was going to do. And he knew how to do it, because he'd done it before. Quite unhurried, moving here and there with a small, thin smile on his face, the boy got busy.

There was a knife lying in the seaweed, close to where the man was lying. It was as sharp as a razor. As the boy ran it up and down the seams of the man's trousers and jacket, the material fell open. He stripped the man completely, using the blade on the shirt and tie and underclothes and tugging the remains of the clothes from under the dead weight of the body. The shoes and the socks came off. When the man was entirely naked, the boy trod out of the living room, across the hallway and stepped through the front door; the piano had gone, smashed to pieces by the storm in the night. He crossed the yard, struggled to open the big, rusty, silvery car because there were banks of weed and rubble heaped around it, leaned inside to pull out the tools he wanted: the axe, the wedge and the sledgehammer. He carried them back to the house.

No preliminaries. No wavering. No thinking to be done. The boy got busy.

The body was slabby and white, less than lifeless, simply a poundage of meat. It was cold and very stiff, the fossil of something that had lived a long time ago and been buried under the weight of the sea. The boy jointed it at the wrists and ankles, at the elbows and knees, swinging the axe with power and rhythm and accuracy. He breathed easily. The axe was heavy and beautifully balanced. The blade was keen. Let the tool do the work, someone had once told him....

He stacked the hook and hand and feet, as well as the forearms and lower legs, in a corner by the doorway. Then he took the knife to the thick throat, parted the skin, made an incision big enough for the wedge to balance in, and he swung the sledgehammer. Let the tool do the work....

With a crunch, the wedge was through. A single, effortless swing of the axe, and the head was off. The boy picked it up by the hair, which was coarse and thick like wire wool, and he put it on the mantelpiece. It seemed to belong there, beside the ammonite and the photograph.

Ignoring the hysterical noises from upstairs, he worked for another hour. It was clean work, because the body had been tumbled by the surf all night; opened up, it evacuated into the sand and seaweed which the storm had left in the room. In any case, the wedding dress was already soiled, because the boy had slept on the staircase and there were traces of blood where his thighs had been cut. So it didn't matter if the satin was spattered when he jointed the ribcage, when something squirted from a ruptured organ, when he smeared his hands on the sequined bodice. The dress dried on him. The dogs were maddened by the sounds and the scent that came to them, up the stairs, but the boy shut out their furious barking. He worked steadily, methodically... flaying, flensing, dismembering.

Until there was no body. Only meat, skillfully butchered.

And then he was tired. He dropped the tools and crossed the room to the doorway. He paused there for a moment, looking back to the man's head on the mantelpiece. Now he could place it. The name came to him.

Mr. Clewe! Harry Clewe, the strange, solitary man who lived in the strange old house on the seashore, where the waves came in and out as though the downstairs rooms were part of the beach. Harold Vivian Clewe!

What a Christmas they'd had together! But always, after Christmas, such a lot of clearing-up to be done...

The boy went out of the room, across the hallway and up the stairs. The door of the little bedroom banged and bulged as the dogs hurled all their weight at it, and the sound they made was no longer barking but a horrible, keening howl of uncontrollable hunger. He turned the door handle and dodged to one side. Gog and Magog came out like a pair of locomotives. They ignored the boy, or didn't see him. Huge and slavering, they launched themselves from the landing, crashed down the stairs, skidded as far as the front door before they could stop themselves and scrabble for traction in the banked-up shingle, and then they swerved into the living room. Immediately, there was quiet. The dogs stopped howling. From the landing, all the boy could hear was the subdued gurgle of big snouts into soft meat, big teeth on moist gristle.

He didn't stay long in the little bedroom. The fire was out. The dogs had overturned the table and chairs to get at the remains of the feast. They'd licked the plates and the pots clean, and broken some of them in their frenzied brawling. The carpet sparkled with splintered glass from all the wine bottles they'd knocked over. The bedding was strewn everywhere. The Christmas tree was felled. The curtains were down, wrenched from the windows. It looked as though the storm had been in the room, but Gog and Magog had wrecked it, hearing the shouts and the gunshots in the night, lusting for meat in the morning. The boy closed the door. He went down the corridor and into the honeymoon bedroom, shutting the door behind him.

When he drew the curtains, the morning light fell into the room. The dust swirled in the air as he opened and closed the door and crossed to the window. The chandelier tinkled. He saw the wardrobe wide open, the gorgeous dresses flung on the floor, his own clothes dropped in the corner; the burned-out candles; the glasses and the brandy bottle; the imprint of two bodies, side by side on the four-poster bed. He sat at the dressing table and looked at himself in the pitted, tarnished mirror.

"Oh dear," he said. He turned his head this way and that, tilted his chin, licked his lips and pursed them. "Oh dear, oh dear. What a mess! Now, do something with yourself."

The silver comb and the silver-backed brush were close at hand. He reached for them, the gloves no longer white but soiled red and brown and black, and he worked at his long, blond hair until it shone like gold. Taking the same lipstick he'd used the night before, he applied it to his mouth so that his lips gleamed and his teeth seemed to glisten by contrast. When he angled his head at the mirror, his hair swung soft and loose around his ears, brushing his bare shoulders. The pearl necklace slithered on his skin.

At last he was satisfied. He smiled at himself. There was some brandy left in the bottle, so he drained it into one of the glasses and drank it down in a single gulp. His body was flooded with warmth. His cheeks reddened and his eyes sparkled.

"That's better!" he whispered, his throat hoarse because of the heat of the brandy. And at that moment, the name came to him. He remembered who he was.

"Christine!" he said to the girl in the mirror. "That's better, Christine! Now you're lovely again!"

At the first sound of the helicopter, she tugged her eyes from the mirror, looked out of the window and saw the big yellow machine beating along the foreshore.

With a dazzling smile at her own reflection, she stood up. She adjusted the straps of the dress and swirled the sequined folds around her. Hurrying to the landing, down to the hallway, careful not to trip on the mass of material, she burst from the front door and into the sunshine of a glorious winter's morning, just as the helicopter was hovering over the field at the front of the house.

She forced her face up into the blast. She shouted and waved and saw a man wave back at her. She clutched the dress with both hands, gripped with her gloved fingers to control the shimmering, frothing stuff in the wind from the helicopter's blades. The machine landed, the blades slowed down and the buffeting decreased.

A man in a yellow suit and a black helmet dropped from the helicopter. Bent double, he ran across the waterlogged field. He paused there and he stared, his mouth open, his eyes wide... not expecting to be met by a girl in a wedding dress, a pretty, smiling young bride whose lips were red, whose eyes were bright, whose hair was fine and shining as though it had just been brushed. He gaped at her. The dress was torn, her legs were bare and white as the blast from the helicopter lifted the gauzy material. There was blood on the bodice, smeared and dry, and there was blood on the gloves as well. She had blood on her thighs, a virginal bride so urgently deflowered that she'd bled into her wedding dress.... He glanced past the girl's shoulder at the derelict house, and tried to shout something at her, but his words were lost in the whirling noise.

Christine guessed what the man had said. Glancing round to see the dogs coming through the front door, she giggled and called out as loudly as she could, "Don't worry about them! They've been fed this morning! All the Christmas leftovers!"

The blades of the big yellow machine had slowed down. The ugly, buffeting noise had stopped. The morning was still and quiet again. Another figure in a helmet and a yellow suit jumped out of the helicopter. The two men walked toward the house, warily skirting the dogs, which were too bloated to do more than raise their hackles and snarl. One of the dogs had been holding something in its mouth, but it dropped whatever it was into the mud, the better to show its teeth... and the men, who'd stared so curiously at the bloodstained, bright-eyed, Boxing Day bride, stared at the thing that the dog had dropped before they disappeared through the front door of the house.

Christine followed them. She leaned at the living-room window and looked in.

One of the men had crossed to the middle of the room. He was nudging the seaweed with the toe of his boot, turning something over, and then he knelt and picked at the weed with his hands. Crying out, he recoiled so suddenly that he fell backward into a rock pool. He leaped to his feet and stood gaping at the mantelpiece.

The other man, who'd gone into the room for no more than a few seconds, had stumbled straight back into the hallway. He was sitting on the stairs, with his head between his knees, retching very loudly, retching and spitting and retching again.

Christine turned away from the window. It was another ugly noise that the men had brought with them, to spoil the stillness of a beautiful Boxing Day morning. She hoped they wouldn't stay long. Now that she'd tidied the downstairs of the house, clearing the mess of a hectic Christmas, the sea would come in and rinse everything clean. She had a lot to do upstairs. The little bedroom was upside down, but she'd soon have it right again, and a good fire burning. In the meantime, waiting for the men to finish whatever they were doing and leave her in peace, she crossed the fields away from the house.

She walked with a swing of her hips. She liked the way she felt, the way she moved in the long white dress and the way it touched her all over. Lifting the hem to try and keep it out of the mud, she wandered to the beach, arranged herself on a boulder and tilted her face to the winter sunshine. She sat there, swanlike. She smiled to see that the swans, unafraid, had come to feed on the foreshore.

She sat and she smiled and she thought about Harry Clewe. She wondered what sort of a man he'd been: good or bad, kind or cruel, funny or sad. No doubt he'd been all of these things, at different times, in different places, with different people.

BIOgraphy

Born in Derby, England, in 1952, Stephen Gregory spent his schooldays in North Wales. He took a degree in Law at London University but never practiced, working instead as a teacher in Britain, Algeria, and Sudan. He quit teaching in 1984 and rented a cottage in Snowdonia, where he wrote his first novel, *The Cormorant*. The book won the Somerset Maugham Award (a prize previously given to such authors as Doris Lessing, Kingsley Amis, VS Naipaul, Ted Hughes, Martin Amis, William Boyd and Ian McEwan), which enabled him to travel for nearly a year through some of the remotest parts of Ecuador, Peru, Bolivia, and Argentina. *The Cormorant* was adapted for television by the BBC, in a feature film starring Ralph Fiennes. Stephen Gregory's second novel, *The Woodwitch*, written during a drizzly autumn and winter in another Snowdonian cottage, was published in 1988. Moving from the mountains to the seashore, he wrote *The Blood of Angels* on the wild and lovely estuary known as Foryd Bay. He now lives in Caernarfon, within the medieval walled town, and continues to give tours of the castle.

available June 1996...

THE CORMORANT
STEPHEN GREGORY

The small cottage tucked away in a quiet village in the mountains of north Wales, a legacy from a distant, estranged uncle, is a dream come true for a young couple and their infant son. The one condition of the inheritance, that the family keep Uncle Ian's beloved pet cormorant, seems a small price to pay for the luxury of a rustic country life — or so they believe.

They soon discover that the cormorant left in their care is no mere bird, but a foul and malignant creature — and it may exact a greater price than they are willing to pay.

Gradually, the bird's dark presence begins to subsume the lives of its keepers, wreaking havoc and planting the seeds of evil. And as it becomes less clear whether man or pet is master of the household, the family is slowly torn apart by turmoil, fear, grief... and ultimate tragedy.

The Cormorant, winner of the Somerset Maugham Award, is artfully written by British author Stephen Gregory.

BOREALIS

Horror
Paperback Novel
ISBN 1-56504- 918-7
WW 12027

WHITE WOLF
PUBLISHING